BLOOD OF THE BETRAYED

The Blooded Bayou Trilogy – Book II

Anaiis D. Roet

Published by Blackvault Books

ISBN: 9781968115609 ebook

ISBN: 978-1-968115-61-6 paperback

Cover Design By: Tirado Designs

For Nia...my fast bestie, my anchor, my unexpected gift.

You walked into my life right when I needed you most, and without even knowing it, you saved me. With every moment of light you brought, you reminded me that friendship can heal in ways nothing else can. I will carry that with me, always.

CONTENT NOTE

Alright, babes, new book, same deal. This series isn't all sunshine and cinnamon rolls. Inside them you'll find:

- Blood. Lots of it.

- Creeps who don't understand the word *no*.

- Power games that blur way past polite.

- Trauma, grief, and some heavy emotional shit.

- Sex that's hot, messy, and sometimes rough enough to leave marks.

If any of that makes you squirm in the *wrong* way, maybe grab something fluffier. If not? Buckle up.

PLAYLIST

1. "Wicked Game" — James Vincent
2. "Adorn" — Miguel
3. "Untitled (How Does It Feel)" — D'Angelo
4. "Roses" — Musiq Soulchild
5. "Any Time, Any Place" — Janet Jackson
6. "You're Makin' Me High" — Toni Braxton
7. "All the Things (Your Man Won't Do)" — Joe
8. "Risk It All" — Ella Mai
9. "Take You Down" — Chris Brown
10. "Pretty Wings" — Maxwell
11. "Bed" — J. Holiday
12. "Gonna Love Me" — Teyana Taylor
13. "Ordinary People" — John Legend
14. "Pony" — Ginuwine
15. "Prototype" — OutKast
16. "Adore" — Prince
17. "Sure Thing" — Miguel
18. "Earned It" — The Weeknd
19. "Slow Motion" — Trey Songz
20. "Redbone" — Childish Gambino

Contents

PROLOGUE 5

ONE 17

TWO 30

THREE 40

FOUR 50

FIVE 60

SIX 74

SEVEN 88

EIGHT 95

NINE 100

TEN 108

ELEVEN 113

TWELVE 119

THIRTEEN 132

FOURTEEN 143

FIFTEEN 157

SIXTEEN 164

SEVENTEEN 174

EIGHTEEN 183

NINETEEN 199

TWENTY 205

TWENTY ONE 215

TWENTY TWO 226

TWENTY THREE 232

TWENTY FOUR 239

TWENTY FIVE 253

TWENTY SIX 265

TWENTY SEVEN 280

TWENTY EIGHT 287

TWENTY NINE 297

THIRTY 308

THIRTY ONE 319

THIRTY TWO 326

THIRTY THREE 336

THIRTY FOUR 345

THIRTY FIVE 355

THIRTY SIX 361

THIRTY SEVEN 373

EPILOGUE 380

PROLOGUE

"We're always with you," Mary-Ange chimed, her voice carrying like a hymn through the meadow. Behind her, the circle of women, my ancestors, blurred; their outlines dissolving into smoke, into light, into memory. My chest ached with the loss even as the bond to Rafe pulsed hard, dragging me back toward the world I had left, toward the pain waiting for me there.

"Go on home," she said again, softer this time, like a lullaby wrapped in farewell.

The meadow tilted. Darkness spilled across the sky, and the ground vanished beneath me. I fell through the forest floor, gravity a vengeful beast clawing me down; and when I hit, the force rattled through my bones, crushing the air from my chest. Pain lit every nerve. I curled in on myself, clutching my head, breath sawing ragged through my lungs.

"Zaria, dinner!" Mama's voice rose sweet and sharp, as though carried on the air itself.

"Ok, Mommy." A smaller voice answered her. *My voice*, though higher, unformed. My voice...*but not mine.*

The pounding in my skull eased just enough for me to look around. It was my house, but earlier. I was in my childhood bedroom, perfectly preserved in the way memory gilds everything; pink bedspread smoothed across a tiny mattress, toys scattered in lazy abandon, sunlight pouring through lace curtains.

I pushed myself to standing, the floor both steady and unsteady beneath my feet, and wandered toward the dresser. The top was cluttered with picture frames: photographs of me with my parents, but also others; women I had only just seen in the meadow. Ancestors whose faces were strangers until moments ago, captured here as if they had always belonged. My fingers trembled as I placed the frame back, and with that motion came the low hum of voices, beckoning me forward.

Down the hall, I caught sight of her...of myself. I was no more than five or six years old, wrapped in a silver dress dotted with polka spots, the ruffles at the hem swaying as she moved. She lingered in the doorway, curly hair and wide eyes flicking toward me as though she sensed the intrusion, though I knew she couldn't see me. Still, the way she closed the door — slowly, almost tenderly — sent a shiver through me, as though I were being shut out of my skin.

Then came the pull. Gravity again, fierce and unrelenting, drawing me into the room with her. I stumbled forward without weight, without will, until I was inside the room with her, like a passenger pressed tight against the glass of my memory.

She moved — *I* moved — dragging a chair across the floor; the scrape echoed too loud in the quiet. The chair was small, but the bookshelf loomed high above it, lined with volumes that pulsed faintly in the haze, as though the books themselves breathed. I remembered this room. I remembered the shelves being empty. Yet here they were, filled and waiting.

My small hands braced against the wood as I climbed. A tiny foot pressed onto the lower shelf for leverage, a stretch of her fragile arms reaching higher, higher, until fingers brushed a book bound in cracked leather. Ancient, heavy, humming with something alive.

She dragged the book down with a grunt, the weight of it nearly toppling her, and dropped onto the floor with it clutched to her chest. Settling cross-legged, dress spilling around her in a fan of silver and ruffles, she laid her palm across the cover. The sigil etched into the leather shimmered faintly, shifting like ink stirred through water.

Her fingers drifted over it, lingering. Solemn. Captive. Mesmerized. She couldn't look away.

And neither could I.

When she opened the book, her head snapped back as though struck, arms falling wide to her sides. Energy burst outward in waves, crashing against the walls, rattling the air until the light became too much to bear. I flinched, raising my arm to shield my eyes.

But a hand clamped down it, forcing it away.

Mary-Ange stood beside me, her grip tight, eyes fixed on the *child me* writhing in the flood of power. *"Watch."*

My heart hammered against my ribs. Zaria's eyes—my eyes—blazed white, burning with a light that wasn't human, wasn't mine.

The door slammed open. Mama burst into the room, her scream curdling the air. *"Nooo!"* Her voice cracked with terror. *"Bernard, git' yo things! Now!"*

She plunged forward, but it was like the light itself resisted her; every step slow and straining, her body wading through waves of power that shoved her back. Still, she fought through, reaching me at last. Her hands slammed the book shut with a force that shook the floor.

I was thrown onto my back just as Daddy rushed in.

Mama looked younger than I remembered; thinner, fragile

in a way that made my chest ache. Her face was pale with fear, hair clinging damp to her temples.

Mama clutched me to her chest, voice raw and breaking. *"Bernard, bind her! Do it now!"*

He staggered forward, shaking his head, grief carved deep in his face. *"Claudine... we cain't. Non, baby, not like this. You know what it gon' do to her. You know da kinda life she gon' have if I lay dat bind on her."*

"Bind me?" I whispered to Mary-Ange, heart pounding. *"What does that mean?"*

She only tipped her chin toward the scene, silent, commanding me to keep watching.

"I ain't gon' have my baby end up like Mama did," Mama snapped, clutchin' me tighter. *"She done lost her mind, Bernard. You do it now—bind her fo' it too late."*

Daddy's hands shook as he dropped to his knees beside me. His eyes darted over my small body, the glow leaking from my eyes; the light pulsing beneath my skin like it wanted to tear free. He looked at Mama, then back down at me, and his face crumpled.

"I cain't do dis, Claudine," he whispered, voice thick. *"Dis our bébé. Our bébé. You askin' me to cut her soul in half."*

"You do it!" Mama's cry cracked the air. *"I ain't gon' watch her burn up like Mama did,"* Mama spat, clutching me tighter, her words breaking rough in her throat. *"I ain't puttin' my own baby in the ground 'cause you too damn weak to act, Bernard!"*

Daddy pressed a hand to his mouth, shoulders trembling. Then slowly, he reached for me.

From where I stood with Mary-Ange, my breath caught in my throat. *"Daddy, no. Please, don't."* The words tore through me, but they couldn't hear me. My child-self lay limp, eyes burning white, chest rising and falling too fast.

Mary-Ange's grip tightened on my arm. *"Watch,"* she said. *"You need to see, child."*

Daddy's hands hovered above my chest, then pressed lightly to my sternum. He bowed his head, whispering words that vibrated through the floor, through the marrow of my bones. I felt it, an ache like hooks dragging something out of me. The magic that had bloomed seconds before twisted, recoiled, fought to stay, and then... began to still.

"Nooo," I whispered, tears burning my eyes as I reached for him, though there was nothing for me to touch. *"Don't take it from me."*

Daddy's voice cracked as he worked. *"Forgive me, cher. Forgive yo papa. I do dis to save ya."*

The glow in my child-self's eyes flickered. Dimmed. The air grew quieter, the pressure in the room releasing like a held breath. My body went slack in his arms, small and too still.

Daddy clutched me to his chest, sobbing into my hair. *"I sorry, bébé. I so damn sorry."*

Mary-Ange's voice whispered at my side, softer than the light. *"Now you know. Now you remember."*

The vision shifted.

Mama stood in the study, her arms full of books, snatching them from the shelves one by one and tossing them into bins with sharp, angry motions. The spines cracked as they hit, a hollow sound that made the floor hum beneath my feet.

In the corner, the child me sat cross-legged with toys scattered around, humming softly to herself, untouched by the storm unraveling in her mother's hands.

Daddy leaned against the doorway, his shoulders slumped, tears streaking his face. *"Claudine, don't do dis. Cher, please...keep 'em safe. She gon' need dem one day."* His voice broke, ragged with the kind of grief that leaves no air behind it.

Mama said nothing. Her jaw was tight, her eyes set forward, and still she threw book after book into the bin, never once looking back.

When the shelves stood empty, she rolled the bin out the back door into the yard. The air outside shifted, heavy, as though it knew what she was about to do. She poured lighter fluid over the heap, the acrid scent rising bright in the night air. Then came the powder that shimmered faintly as it rained down, clinging to the old pages.

With a single strike of a match, she set them alight.

"What is that?" I asked Mary-Ange. *"That powder? What is it?"*

"Elden Ash." Her expression darkened, grief and fury flickering across her face. *"It's taken from the funeral pyres of witch elders; stolen, sold, traded on black markets. To humans, it looks like powder. To us, it's control. Elden Ash bends the Blooded. Wolves, witches, vampires—it makes them obey. It can silence, subdue, command. A handful blown in your face, and even the strongest can be forced to heel."*

It took a minute for her words to sink in. And when they did, they sank me. Her mouth tightened, trembling just once before she spat out the last words. *"It's the worst kind of desecration."*

The fire caught fast, devouring the books with a hiss that almost sounded like voices, like the words themselves crying out as they turned to smoke. Purple sparks flared and snapped, rising high into the dark, scattering like dying stars.

Daddy fell to his knees in the doorway, his sobs carrying across the yard. Mama only watched the flames, her face hard, implacable, lit by the glow of everything she'd chosen to erase.

Another shift.

I was a teenager again, rifling through the shadows of my parents' closet. My hands found the chest wedged behind old coats; heavy, iron-latched, its wood dark with age and scarred like it had survived fire and flood. The metal fittings were etched with faint runes, dulled by time but still humming faintly beneath my fingertips.

I dragged it out across the floorboards. The lock clicked loose under my touch, almost eager, and when I lifted the lid, the scent of dust and sage poured over me. Inside were books. Stacked in neat rows, their spines cracked, their pages pulsed like they were waiting for me.

I didn't know what I was looking for, only that I had to find it. They called to me. Whispered to me. And once I started reading, I couldn't stop. I devoured every line, every hidden word until my head spun with a weight I didn't yet understand.

When I slid them back into the chest and tucked it where I found it, I caught my reflection in the mirror across the room. There was a glow coming from me now. Faint, but there. A light that hadn't been there before I'd opened the chest.

Shift.

The grocery store. Fluorescent lights buzzing overhead, linoleum floors squeaking under the cart wheels. The glow that had been a flicker before was a beacon now, blaring from under my skin. No one else seemed to notice.

I was wandering the canned goods aisle when he appeared; a boy about my age, maybe a little older. Hands in his pockets, smile lazy. He came close, close enough that I smelled cool earth and copper. His smile widened slowly, and when the light hit just right, one pointed canine flashed.

A vampire. I hadn't seen it then.

He reached out, the back of his hand grazing my cheek like he had every right. At his touch, the glow around me pulsed harder, blooming. His eyes darkened with hunger.

"Mmm, chère..." His voice was low, honeyed, rolling with an accent thick as molasses. *"Ain't you a succulent lil' somethin'. All dat power hummin' under ya skin... and you out here walkin' round a grocery store like you ain't meant to be commandin' legions."*

I laughed nervously, brushing it off like I always did when I didn't know where else to put my hands. *"Well, I don't know about all that,"* I said, flirt tugging at the edges of my voice. *"But thank you. That's a kind thing to say."*

His smile widened, running his tongue along the tip of one of his fangs, head tilting with curiosity. *"Mais non... you don't even know what you are, do ya, chère?"*

How did I not remember the fangs?

Before I could answer, Daddy came around the corner. A six-pack of bottled water tucked under one arm, a mesh bag of garlic bulbs dangling from the other. He stopped cold when he saw us, his whole body locking up tight. His eyes narrowed, pointed right at him.

The boy faltered. His smile slipped.

"You go on now," Daddy said, voice slow and smooth. Steel wrapped in Southern charm. *"Go on, leave us be now, boy."*

The vampire's grin twitched, then faded altogether. He slid past me without another word, but the hunger in his eyes clung long after he was gone.

Shift.

Mama's voice, tight with panic. *"It's back, Bernard. You saw dat thing lookin' at her in the grocery store—he was drawn to de light. We gotta bind her again, harder dis time."*

Daddy's voice cracked with fury. *"I ain't doin' dat again, Claudine. Not again. You know what it cost her the first time. We shielding her put her in danger, she didn't see the fangs, she cain't see Bloodeds, Claudine."*

"You don't do it," Mama hissed, stepping in close, *"and I'll put her down myself, Bernard. I swear fo God, I will. She not gon' end up like Mama."*

The words burned, seared into me even as the memory shifted again.

Shift.

A kitchen table. A steaming mug was pressed into my hands. *"Drink dis tea, now, bébé,"* Mama said, her voice low, coaxing, her eyes hard with something unspoken. The liquid shimmered faintly, bitter steam curling under my nose. I drank because she told me to.

Another shift.

Darkness. A bed. My teen-self lying limp, breath soft and shallow.

"She out, Bernard." Mama's voice trembled, but her tone stayed resolute. *"Do it now."*

Daddy's shadow loomed over me, his hands shaking as he reached. His voice cracked, a broken prayer spilling through the room. *"Forgive me, bébé. I so damn sorry."*

Shift.

The world buckled, and suddenly I was back in the alley with Deveraux. But not the Deveraux I remembered. This version of him wasn't a man—he was a vampire. Fangs bared, eyes burning. My leg was hooked around his waist, his body pressed tight to mine.

"Tell me you want me to claim you, Zaria," he demanded, his gaze locked into mine, predatory and sure.

The words came from my lips before I even understood them. Not English. Not any tongue I'd ever spoken before. *"You have no power over me."*

His eyes widened. His fangs retracted. His grip loosened.

In that moment, he was about to turn me—but the words had stopped him cold.

Shift.

Darkness again; but now a door burst open in the void, light spilling out like a flood. The sound of it was deafening, like a cannon firing at close range. I staggered back, shielding my face as another door swung wide, then another, each one slamming open with a violence that rattled my bones.

With every door, a torrent of memory poured into me; not mine, but theirs. My ancestors. Wave after wave of agony and ecstasy, anguish and triumph, heartbreak and desire, anger and love; striking me so hard I was left crawling on hands and knees, gasping, clawing at the ground as the weight of generations pressed down.

And then—the final door.

It opened slowly, creaking, but no light poured out. Only shadow.

I dragged myself to my feet and stepped forward. Through the threshold, the vision crystallized; Mama, standing over Mary-Ange. My grandmother. A knife clutched in her hands, its black blade buried deep in Mary-Ange's chest.

Her voice was quiet but clear, as though the echo carried centuries. *"I was three hundred an' six years old when Claudine took my life,"* she said, eyes fixed on the memory. *"I had only worn the mantle of High Matron a short while, only three months, before that blade found my heart. But the power... the power lingered in my blood long before it woke. It kept me alive, stretched my years far past what should've been."*

I watched in horror as Mama pulled the knife free. Her movements were cold, deliberate. She sprinkled the same violet powder she'd poured over the books, and when it touched the wound, flames caught; purple fire curling around Mary-Ange's body, devouring her until nothing but ash remained.

Mary-Ange turned her gaze to me, composed and unflinching. *"That knife, the one Claudine use, it's the only thing in this world that could end you, child. But you have the strength inside you now to fight it. Fight that poison."*

Tears streaked my face, hot and endless. *"Why?"* My voice cracked. *"Why did she do this?"*

Her voice carried the timber of her unshed tears. *"To protect you. To keep you from inheritin' what runs in our veins. Claudine thought bein' High Matron made me lose my mind, made me dangerous and unstable. But she never understood."*

Mary-Ange's eyes flickered toward the vision of Mama watching the body burn, her expression unreadable. *"I wasn't crazy. I was powerful. There's a difference. It takes strength, more than Claudine ever dreamed, to hold that kind of power and not let it spill into everyone around you. What she saw as madness was restraint. Every whisper I swallowed, every vision I locked down, every spell I refused to cast — that was me keepin' the world safe from what lived inside me."*

She turned back to me, gaze pointed. *"But fear don't see nuance, bébé. Fear sees only threat. To Claudine, I was unravelin'. To her, killin' me was mercy. She thought she was savin' you from a legacy of madness. But in truth, she robbed you of the tools, the teachins', the years you would need to bear the weight. And now it's yours, anyway. It's untamed and hungry, bébé. Claudine weren't Blooded. She weren't coven. And because it skips generations, that meant you, child, could be. She was pregnant with you when she struck me down. She believed if the line was cut before you drew breath, it would wither. She thought you'd be born clean. Free."*

I shook my head, choking on the sob tearing out of me. *"But I wasn't free."*

Mary-Ange's eyes softened with sorrow, but her tone never wavered. *"Non, bébé. You bein' so close to the Bloodeds, it called to you. Called to your bloodline. When you were in danger in that alley, it woke. Every bind they laid on you, every tea they fed you, it was only a bandage. The truth has been stirrin' in you all along. And now?"*

She leaned close, her presence pressing through me like fire through my veins. *"Now you know. Now you carry all of us."*

She touched my cheek, her palm warm against my skin, eyes brimming with a love that ached down into my bones. *"They waitin' on you now, child,"* she whispered. *"But listen, your own body gon' turn traitor. The haze, the hunger, it'll fight to keep you still. You push through it. You hear me? Push hard, now."*

Her thumb brushed a tear from my cheek. *"Your alpha is in danger. You get to him quick, before your fanged one tears him apart."*

ONE

Rafe

Bernard's arms slipped around Claudine, soothing her trembling body as the brilliance in the room finally began to dim. The wild wind that had rattled the walls softened, fading into nothing, until the curtains stilled and the house seemed to exhale with us.

The glow around Zaria clung stubbornly, inch by inch receding, reluctant to let go. Then the last trace winked out, leaving the room looking almost ordinary again; it looked like none of it had ever happened, like we hadn't just witnessed the impossible.

We stepped further inside cautiously, each footfall careful, as though even the creak of a floorboard might shatter the fragile spell still heavy in the air.

Zaria sat upright on the bed, her small arms reaching high above her head, a soft sigh slipping past her lips as though she'd only drifted awake from the gentlest nap.

But the truth was anything but gentle. For three days, her body had burned like a forge. Heat rolled off her in waves so fierce, the very air shimmered. Fabrics didn't stand a chance; clothes seared against her skin; sheets smoldered beneath her.

We'd learned quickly to keep her bare, shrouding her instead in wards and cooling charms, laying only a thin veil of linen across her when modesty demanded it. Even then, the fabric blackened at the edges if left too long, curling like paper near flame.

The bite marks Deveraux had carved into her flesh were gone. The faint scars life had once left scattered across her skin, gone. In their place, perfection. Her body gleamed as though polished by unseen hands, hair sleek as satin, nails gleaming like they'd just been lacquered. The vampire blood hadn't created her beauty; it had heightened it, until it was something near unbearable to look at.

Then her eyes opened; white, gleaming and endless.

"D'ere she is now," Bernard whispered, awe and dread tangling in his throat. "The Matron reborn."

The sight rooted me where I stood, my chest pounding, caught between terror and reverence.

She looked... *ethereal.* Her hair tumbled over her shoulders, strands humming faintly like they carried the charge of lightning still. Her skin glowed with a soft light that hadn't fully dimmed, and her breathing was slow and deep. Measured.

Her gaze found Claudine first. The voice that left her lips was sweet, lilting, innocent and ancient all at once. "Hi, Mama. Hi, Daddy."

Bernard's eyes shone. Claudine's lips parted, but no sound came.

Movement flickered in the corner. Simône and Markus leaned into the doorway, their eyes wide, faces pale. I lifted a hand sharply, barring them with nothing more than the command in my gesture. I didn't know if the storm had passed... or if it was only gathering strength. Better they stay out. Better they not test whatever fragile spell hung in this room.

They obeyed, slipping back into the shadows without a word.

Her gaze shifted to me.

Those impossible pearly eyes locked to mine. Her lips curved into a smile so radiant it ached to look at, warmth and light braided into a face I thought I knew but suddenly didn't.

"Hi, my Alpha."

Then, in true Zaria fashion, she cut through the silence with two words. "I'm starving."

But before anyone could move, her head tilted, gaze drifting past me; back to Bernard, to Claudine. The smile stayed, but it sharpened, becoming something else entirely.

"You tried to *bind* me."

Claudine's gasp cracked the air. Her hand flew to her mouth as though to cage the sound, but it was too late. Bernard's arm clamped around her shoulders, holding her in place as his own voice broke into a whisper heavy with awe, with dread.

"But I'm free now."

And then she blinked, and her eyes were simply Zaria's again. The echo of that radiant glow clung to the air around us, heavy and inescapable.

Bernard let out a strangled laugh; the sound of a man balanced between relief and madness. Claudine's hand trembled against her chest, but she forced a smile anyway, nodding too quickly.

Zaria's eyes slipped closed, her lashes trembling like she was caught between prayer and hunger. She tipped her head back, throat bared, nostrils flaring wide as if she could drink the whole house, the whole world, into her lungs.

And then it bloomed.

The veins came first, branching slowly beneath her skin, black lightning crawling outward, each pulse searing and alive. They branched across her chest, her throat, down her arms, fractal and endless, until she looked lit from within by something dark and divine.

She writhed, back arching, breath breaking on a sound that was half moan, half snarl. The shift gripped her, and it was *too much*...too sharp, too consuming, too close to pleasure. Her hands dragged up her body like they didn't belong to her, fingers tracing the curve of her ribs, the swell of her breasts, lingering as her body shuddered under the power flooding her veins. Naked, unashamed, she touched herself like a predator testing the shape of its own hunger.

Her fangs slid down slowly, purposely, gleaming in the dim light.

The girl they knew was gone.

In her place sat a devastating contradiction, the devil to her own angel, the predator to her own priestess. Sacred duality torn raw, yin and yang bleeding into one another before our eyes.

Silence thickened the room into something suffocating, a substance of awe and horror that clung to the walls. They weren't witnessing their daughter anymore. They were witnessing a desecration.

"Fuck." The word ripped out of me, unbidden, shattering the quiet.

Her head quickly snapped toward me. A smile curved her lips. It was fucking terrifying.

"There you are. Hmmm. So sexy." Her tone was taunting

and dangerous.

One hand closed over her breast, claws sinking deep enough to score the flesh, crimson welling in delicate lines that glistened down her skin. The other drifted lower, leisurely, boldly parting her folds as though the room were hers alone. A grotesque parody of intimacy, raw and so fucking obscene.

Her tongue traced slowly over the tip of her fang, savoring the sharp gleam.

Claudine buried her shaking face against Bernard's chest like a child warding off nightmares. Bernard turned his away, staring at the wall, eyes brimming with tears. This wasn't their daughter. This was every parent's worst fear made flesh; beautiful but monstrous.

"You'll feed me, won't you, Alpha?" The title coiled around my throat, a chain I'd worn before and knew too well.

Claudine choked on a sob, muffled into Bernard's jacket. "Take me home."

"Chérie—" Bernard's voice was thick with helpless grief.

"No." Claudine lifted her head, her voice sharp, brittle as shattering glass. Terror had drowned all maternal love from her eyes. "Dis—whatever dis ting is—it is not my fille. Take me home, Bernard. Now."

The command hung in the air. And for a heartbeat, the predator's mask slipped. Zaria's head tilted, that eerie, carnal calm fracturing into something heartbreakingly, devastatingly childlike.

"Mama—?"

Her hand lifted, palm open, fingers trembling, reaching for comfort the way any daughter would. But the fangs glinted, the veins so dark across her caramel kissed skin. The gesture, even the longing, was monstrous now.

Claudine jerks back, a strangled sob tearing free. "Don't. Don't you call me dat."

The words hit harder than any curse. Zaria's hand hangs in the air a moment longer, frozen between hope and shame, before curling slowly into a fist. She lowers it to her lap with a composure that wasn't hers. Not fully.

Bernard's face was wrecked; eyes wide, mouth working soundlessly as he looked from his wife to his daughter, torn straight down the middle. Claudine didn't wait for him to choose. She gripped his arm hard, nails biting through his shirt.

"Take me home, Bernard. Now."

He faltered, gaze flicking once more to Zaria; who stared at the space where her mother had stood like there is a war between who was and who her mother now feared. Bernard swallowed hard, nodded, and gathered Claudine close, ushering her toward the hall with murmured words that sounded more like prayers than comfort.

With one last glance in my direction, the door clicked shut behind them.

Zaria's eyes lifted to mine, the black in them threaded fully, nothing human left.

"She doesn't understand." Her voice wavers between the girl I know and something much colder. "But you do... *don't you, Alpha?*"

I can feel her hunger through our bond, searing hot, like it's burning me alive from the inside out. But beneath it, threaded through the fire, there's something else. Softer. Almost singing.

She rises from the bed, what was left of the sheet slipping from her and pooling at her feet. She doesn't bother to hide herself. Every step toward me is deliberate, a saunter that makes my vampire pace restlessly inside my chest, ready to tear and defend.

"I missed you while I was away, Alpha."

Her arms loop around my neck, pulling me in, and all I can do is hold her. There aren't words for this; what she is now, what I am to her. If she means to kill me, she'd better do it quick. Because the truth scorches worse than her hunger ever could. I can't imagine life with her sired to another man. And the vampire blood humming in her veins makes that an actual possibility.

I press my lips to her temple, adjusting my voice before it betrays me.

"Let's get you dressed," I murmur. "We'll go downstairs. Talk this through."

"Please, Alpha..." Her voice drops to a velvet plea, thick with hunger.

Her fangs graze the crook of my neck, a featherlight scrape that makes my whole body lock tight. She moans when she tastes the heat of my pulse beneath her mouth, a low and sultry sound that slides straight into my bones. If it weren't for the circumstances, that sound alone would've made my cock twitch.

Instead, it terrifies me. Because her hunger is real. And if I give her what she's asking for, I'm not sure I'll survive it, at least not as the man I was before.

"Just a small taste, Alpha." Her voice drips with wickedness.

I shift, pulling back, my hands wrapping around her wrists, pinning them between us. I hold her gently, trying not to turn this into a battle. Her skin burning into my flesh.

"Let's get you downstairs, baby."

The words were barely passed my lips before the world flipped. In a blur, I was flat on my back, the table beside us shattering under the force. Wood splintered; glass skittered across the boards.

And she was on me. Grinding. Writhing. Her hands roamed her own body like she was aflame, and I was the only thing in this world that could put her out.

"Zaria." My voice cut sharper now, firm, desperate. "I don't want to hurt you, baby. Please."

Her movements slowed. Her gaze lowered. Those glowing eyes gleamed down at me, a wicked smile curling her lips like sin carved in flesh.

"As if you could stop me." The whisper ghosted in my ear.

Her free hand slid down, pushing my sweats down, freeing my cock as it betrayed me instantly, swelling against her intrusion, no hesitation, no sense of the goddamn danger. Just pure animal desire.

With one roll of her hips, I was inside her.

Heat. Fire. A fucking inferno. Pain and pleasure twisted together, searing me open, hollowing me out, undoing me from the inside out.

"Fuck, Zaria. Not like this."

But I couldn't even pretend I meant those words. My vampire was euphoric, howling inside me.

"Hmmmm. Fuck, Alpha." Her voice dripped with hunger as her pussy clenched tight around me, so viciously snug my eyes rolled back in my skull. She rocked once, twice, slowly and barbarous, wringing sounds from me I didn't even recognize.

Her hips ground down with a rhythm that was both feral

and calculated, like she knew exactly how to tear me apart. Every roll dragged fire through me.

One hand held my wrists captive above my head, claws digging just enough to remind me she could snap me in half with a flick if she wanted. Her other hand pressed to my chest, pinning me harder into the floor as she rode me like I was hers to break.

And Gods help me, I was.

More black veins started to branch out along her collarbones, over her breasts, down her stomach, glowing faintly beneath the cascade of movement. She was sin made flesh, a predator dressed in ecstasy.

She slammed down harder, the sound of our bodies colliding echoing like thunder. "God yes, Alpha," she moaned, drawn out, decadent. Her other hand left my wrists, now planting both on my chest as she rolled her hips in circles that made my cock throb violently inside her.

I gripped her hips and started bucking up, meeting her grind with brutal force, driving deeper. Her cry was savage, her nails raking across my chest and carving red welts that burned in the best possible way.

"It's going to be such a shame when I rip you apart. What a waste." She moaned.

Get a fucking grip, Rafe. She's about to kill you.

"Gods," my head tipped back, every muscle straining. I *knew* the danger I was in. But my vampire was ravenous for her. For this. With her, I didn't have to hold back. I could let him off the leash.

In a blink, I flipped her. She gave a breathless groan as I shoved her down onto her hands and knees. She weighed nothing in my grip, not fragile... unbreakable, and I slammed into her from behind with a groan so guttural, it scared me. One hand fisted in her hair, yanking her head back, the other clamped down on her neck, pressing her cheek hard into the rug.

Her ass was high, back arched, and she moaned into the floor while I fucked her with savage, ruthless thrusts. My fist twisted deeper in her curls, my arm like iron. She rocked back against me, desperate, meeting me stroke for stroke.

"Fuck," I rasped, my voice torn open, gritted teeth bared. My knot swelled, the beast in me clawing to the surface. "Yes. Like that." I growled, my fangs extending.

"Harder, Alpha. Let him out!" Her voice was muffled by the rug, shredded by the sound of her own pleasure.

"You fucking love this, don't you?" I snarled into her ear as I dragged her upright, forcing her back against my chest, pinning her on my lap. I let him out—fangs snapping down, black veins spidering across my skin, my wolf and the vampire clawing to the surface together.

My hand closed around her throat, claws biting just enough to make her choke on a moan.

"There he is." Her voice broke, trembling but triumphant. "I've been waiting for you."

I slammed into her harder, the shift in angle driving me so deep it wrenched a sob straight from her lungs. "Such a greedy little fucking cunt."

"Yes," she cried, The monster in me had risen to meet hers, and the two of us were nothing but teeth and hunger and ruin. Her nails raked at my thighs, slipping, catching, leaving burning trails as my thrusts shoved her across the rug, her knees raw and streaked where the fabric tore at her skin.

Her strength surged again; unnatural, terrifying and

fucking intoxicating. In a blur, I was on my back again, the rug where her body had just laid burning against my shoulders, my body still buried deep inside her.

She braced her hands on my chest, grinding down with a predator's unforgiving rhythm. Her nails raked across my skin, reopening welts, painting me in heat.

"Fuck, Zaria," I groaned, my hips jerking up against hers, but she was in control. She had been this whole time. Completely. Her pace quickened, every roll of her drawing gasping moans from her lips. My cock throbbed, swelling harder inside her with every clench of her slick cunt.

Her head tipped back, throat bared, hair clinging wet to her shoulders. "Fuck... yes..." she screamed, voice breaking on the edge of a sob. Her walls clamped tight, spasming around me as her orgasm ripped through her, her cry echoing off the walls like a hymn to hunger.

Her shudders dragged me under with her. I growled, claws gripping her hips as my body bowed, my release slamming into me so hard my vision blurred. The monster in me roared, and I spilled into her in hot, violent pulses that felt like I was giving her everything I was.

"Yes..." she purred, her hips rolling slower, milking me until my body shook. "Yes... come, Alpha. Hmmm." Her tongue dragged up the curve of my jaw, fangs grazing the vein thrumming wild beneath my skin. Her wicked smile curved.

"You're going to be *so* fucking delicious now, Alpha."

Fuck.

The aftershocks still owned me, every nerve bitter and trembling, as her mouth opened wider. Her breath scorched my neck. Fangs lowered. My body braced for it; I was caught between the high of my release and the certainty of my death.

And then...she *froze.*

Her eyes flashed wide, a flicker of something not hers, and her body jerked violently, ripped clean off me. She flew backward, slamming into the wall so hard the drywall splintered.

Something had torn her away.

I scrambled to my feet, shoving softening cock back into my pants, chest heaving, horror crawling through every vein.

She was suspended midair against the wall, feet dangling, her head jerking side to side. The scream that tore from her chest was inhuman, like a steam engine venting rage.

The door bursts open. The pack stormed back inside, their eyes sweeping over the scene in the room before locking on Zaria on the wall.

My pulse hammers, instinct screaming to go to her, but I freeze, powerless. What the hell could I even do?

Then slowly her black veins receded. Her fangs slide back up into her gums. The scream dwindles to ragged breaths until her head falls forward, curls spilling across her face. Her feet finally touched the floor, settling her.

The room stills. No one moves. We're all statues, eyes flickering between each other and Zaria like a single wrong breath might set her off again.

"Fuck," she whispers, voice shattered, her hands dragging over her face like she's trying to rub the last of it away. Whatever *that* was.

Then she lifts her head. And for the first time since she woke, her gaze finds me; not as the Matron reborn, not as a predator. Just Zaria.

"Rafe!"

Her voice cracks, coarse with fear and need, and then she's

running, trembling, pressing herself against my chest like she's trying to burrow inside me.

I snatch up a sheet with one hand, dragging it around her shoulders, wrapping her bare body before the others can see more than they already have. She doesn't care. She's clinging to my neck, fingers tangled in my shirt, her whole body shaking.

"Easy, baby." My arms cinch around her, holding her tight, shielding her from eyes that don't matter right now. My heart is still slamming from the chaos, but I center my voice for her. "I got you. I got you."

She buries her face against my throat, her breath hot, uneven, desperate. Her words are muffled, but I hear them like they're carved into my bones.

"I'm so sorry she almost hurt you. I'm so sorry. I was almost too late."

The room is silent. I can feel the pack watching. Waiting to see what happens next. But none of them exist to me right now.

Just her. Just Zaria.

And the brutal, terrifying truth pressing into my chest: I didn't know if I could save her from what she was becoming. And worse; I didn't know if I could save myself from what I had just let myself become.

TWO

Zaria

It was like clawing my way through fog just to get back into my body. It's hard to explain. How do you put words to watching yourself from the outside? Watching *her*...my vampire...fucking him like I wasn't even there.

And the worst part? He enjoyed it. Every ragged breath, every thrust. It was like standing helpless in the corner while the man I—*while Rafe*—was with another woman. My skin, my hands, but not *me*. The jealousy was so painful it made me sick.

For a heartbeat, I thought I'd be too late. That I'd have to watch her use me to tear him apart. I wouldn't have survived that. Not his blood on my lips. Not his body breaking under my hands.

By the time I shoved her back and caged her, I was shaking; every nerve was screaming. The pain of forcing her down was like barbed wire pulled through my veins.

Rafe's hands framed my face then, warm palms cradling my jaw. He pressed soft, frantic kisses over my lips, my cheeks, anywhere his mouth could reach; like he could tether me back here, hold me together with nothing but touch.

"Fuck, baby," he whispered, the words cracking in his throat, maybe more for himself than for me. "What *was* that?"

It was strange, feeling the tremors of an orgasm that I hadn't actually lived. I was slick between my thighs, my skin buzzing like it had been lit from inside. My pussy ached, tender from his knot. But it wasn't *me* he came with. It was her. My vampire. The thought still lodged like glass in my chest, and I swallowed it down before it could cut deeper.

"I feel like I need an exorcist," I breathed, forcing a smile that didn't quite land. "But maybe we can start with some bacon?"

I feel the way his chest loosens against mine, the way his heart slows to something steadier. Our bond hums like a wire between us, alive and so strong, but his fear is bleeding through into me, seeping into my veins. *Fear of me.* Though he didn't seem to be afraid of *her*. And that single truth makes my throat burn with the urge to cry.

"Bacon it is." He managed to smile for me, but it was thin and strained. "I'm not leaving your side, so we'll get you dressed and head down together."

I nodded, though my gaze snagged on the doorway where the others still stood, frozen. Simône. Elodie. Markus. Marek. All of them watching me like I might snap, like one wrong move could shatter the fragile calm.

Their emotions bled into the air, thick enough I could drown in them.

Simône's worry carried first, intense but grounding. Earthy, like sage bruised fresh under fingers, with a curl of mint at its edges. Concern, not fear.

Elodie and Markus were different. Their fear was fresh, untempered, and it reeked of sweetness; like dark chocolate melted down until it was almost bitter. My vampire stirred at the scent, prowling beneath my skin, drawn to it like a lover.

And then there was Marek. His scent was the strongest of them all. It rolled over me heavy and complex, subtle but obvious. Not sweet like fear. Not nearly as bright. It was something wilder, like smoke curling through amber, or iron kissed with heat. It rooted itself in me, but I just couldn't place exactly what it was.

"Fuck... we are... uh." Simône clears her throat, shifting her weight from one foot to the other. "We'll let you two get downstairs. Sorry. We were just worried."

The others are silent. Eyes flickering.

"We'll be down in a minute," Rafe says, his voice clipped as he pulls a t-shirt and sweats from his drawer for me.

But my eyes find Marek again.

And in that instant, the fragments of Deveraux's memories burn in my blood. The truth is there now. Marek is the one. He's been working with Deveraux all along. He's the one who wanted me dead. The knowledge is carved into me like I lived it myself.

Marek knows I know. I see it in the tight flicker of his jaw, the way his gaze falters for a fraction of a second before he turns with the others and slips out the door.

The scent was clear now. *Hatred.*

My head spins under the weight of everything at once; Mama and Daddy recoiling from me, Rafe unable to look me in the eye, the monster that nearly tore into him, the monster that still claws at my insides now. I don't even know how I stopped it. My last clear memory before all of this is Deveraux's mouth on me, draining me until the world bled away.

"Zaria?" Rafe's voice cuts through the spiral. He holds out

the clothes. "Some clothes, baby?"

I lift my chin to him, but his eyes slide away. He looks at my hair, my cheek, anywhere but into me. Into the truth staring back.

"Thanks," I murmur, taking the bundle from his hands. "I just need a minute."

I brush his arm in passing, a small touch meant to reassure, but the spike of fear and guilt that jolts through him hits me like a hammer through the bond. I let my hand fall away and closed the bathroom door behind me.

The clothes land on the counter with a dull slap. I grip the sink, force myself to look up, to face the reflection staring back.

There wasn't a scar left on me. Not one. Not the faint white line on my forehead from a childhood fall, not the burns on my arm from years ago, not even the smallest mark life had carved into me. My skin was flawless now, gleaming in a way that felt wrong. Beautiful, yes, but not mine. A beauty enhanced until it cut, unnatural in its perfection.

Vampire.

I braced myself for the sight of his bite marks as I let the sheet fall, expecting to see them crowned across my breasts in bruised rings; a grotesque necklace of memory I never asked to wear. But there was nothing. No trace. No visible reminder of what he turned me into.

Just the hunger; excruciating and hollowing, burning raw in my throat.

The flash of him surged back; Deveraux's hand striking, his fangs tearing into me before I could stop it. The pain, the helplessness, the horror of being consumed against my will. It hit me all over again, leaving me gasping in the wake of its shadow.

And all I can think is that I don't know which is worse; what he did to me, or what I almost did to Rafe. Even though I managed to fight the monster back, the hunger was still there, clawing, insistent. I can't quiet it. I can't control it. And I'm terrified of what happens if I break again, if I can't control her.

I don't want to be near Rafe when I do. I don't want to be near anyone.

I pull on the clothes he gave me with trembling hands, then move to the window. I lift it carefully, easing it open so the frame doesn't creak, so no one will hear. The night air brushes my face, cool and damp, and I climb through.

I land as soft as a cat, soundless, crouched in the dark. The grounds are guarded, so I slip along the edges, keeping to the shadows, hugging the line of the fence until I find a gap I can scale.

And then I ran.

My feet strike the earth faster than they ever have, carrying me into the dark, away from the house, away from Rafe, away from all of them. I don't know where I'm going. I just know I can't stay.

Because if I do...if that monster gets loose again, she'll destroy them all.

When I'm far enough, I finally let myself slow down. I've been running for nearly forty-five minutes, but my lungs aren't burning, my chest isn't tight. Not a bead of sweat. It would thrill me if it didn't seal the truth I've been avoiding: I'm Blooded now. The very thing Mama hates. The very thing people fear.

By the time I lift my head, I realize I've ended up five minutes from Sophie's place. My feet brought me here before I even knew it. What I need is simple: clothes, shoes, and a phone. Something to anchor me while I figure out what the hell to do next.

It's late. Definitely too late to be knocking. But I do anyway. The sound echoes against the quiet street, and almost instantly, I hear the rustle of movement inside. My hearing sharpens, sonar precise.

"Are you expecting someone?" a man's voice asks. *Joey.*

"No," Sophie's voice answers.

"I'll get it. You stay put. I'm not done with you yet."

Gross.

The door creaks open and Joey freezes, mouth falling open when he sees me.

"Hey, Joey."

"Zee?" Joey steps out the door and yanks me into a hug so fast I barely register it, his voice cracking with relief. As quickly as he wrapped his arms around me, he let go. "Where the fuck have you been?" He twists his head back toward the apartment. "Soph! Baby, get in here!" he shouts.

He walks in, and I go to follow...but I hit a wall.

Hard.

My body can't pass it. I'm not invited in.

For a second, I just stand here, disbelief clawing at my chest. Then realization clicks. Guess that little urban legend is true. Vampires really do have to be invited in.

Fuck. I want to cry.

"Come in, come in." Joey says as he steps inside.

Thank fuck. The words are plain, ordinary; but they're everything. His invitation loosens the knot in my chest, the shield melting away.

Joey looks back, his eyes sweeping down to my bare feet. His brow furrows. "Zee, you're barefoot."

"It's a really long story," I murmur, stepping past the threshold like it's a lifeline, like I might crumble if I don't move fast enough.

Sophie stops mid-step when she sees me. Her hands fly to her mouth, tears spilling before she can stop them, and then she's running. She collides with me hard enough to knock the breath from my chest, arms tight around my shoulders. "Zee, we've been calling, texting. I went to your job. It's been days; where have you been?"

"I was sick for a few days. I'm better now." The words are muffled against her shoulder, my voice smothered in her warmth.

And... oh fuck, does she smell good. The scent of her skin, the pulse in her throat, the blood thrumming underneath. It hits me like a drug, like the only thing in the world that matters.

No.

I clamp down hard, forcing air out through my nose, burying the hunger that claws against my ribs.

I tighten my arms around her, but it isn't comfort...it's control. If I let go, if I lean in even a fraction, I'll tear into her.

Sophie pulls back just enough to look at me, her face blotchy from tears, hands gripping my arms like she's afraid I'll vanish if she lets go. "What's going on? Why are you barefoot? Why are your clothes so big? How did you get here? And *these*...these tiny black lines on your face, what are they?"

Her questions tumbled out in a rush, one after the other, her voice thin with panic.

I swallow hard, forcing a smile I don't feel. "It's... a *really* long story, Soph."

Her gaze flicks down to my borrowed clothes, then back

up to my face, worry etched into every line. But all I can feel is the constant drum of her pulse beneath her skin, the warm, living scent of her curling around me until my stomach twists with hunger.

"Can I, uh..." My eyes shut tight, like I can willpower it away. I swallow hard, forcing my voice to balance out. "Can I borrow your key to my place?"

Sophie's nod is immediate. "Yes, of course." She glances over her shoulder. "Joey, grab Zee's key from the bowl."

He shuffles off toward the kitchen, and Sophie turns back to me, eyes glossy, arms still holding tight.

"So..." she says softly, "you're not going to tell me what's going on, are you?"

The question lands heavier than it should. Because part of me wants to; wants to spill everything, to confess the monster gnawing under my skin, the way Rafe's fear bled into me like poison, the betrayal burning behind Marek's eyes. But the words wedge in my throat, jagged and sharp.

All I can manage is a weak smile. "Not tonight."

Her expression folds, but she nods anyway, choosing not to push. And that hurts worse than if she had.

"How did you get here, Zee?" Joey asks as he comes back, jangling a set of keys in his hand before pressing them into mine. His gaze lingers too long, pointed and suspicious.

"I walked."

Both of them just... *stare* at me.

Sophie's brow furrows, confusion flashing before she schools her face back into something softer, but her grip on my arm tightens.

Joey isn't so careful. His eyes narrow, sweeping down me again—barefoot, oversized clothes clinging to me, hair tangled from the night air. He doesn't say anything at first, but uncertainty is written all over him.

"You *walked* here," he says finally, like he's testing the story. "From where? At this time of night, barefoot?"

Sophie shoots him a stern look. "Joey, stop." She turns back to me, her eyes shining wet again. "She's here. That's all that matters."

Her voice breaks, and she tugs me into her arms again, pressing her cheek against mine. I force myself to hold still, to breathe through the wave of hunger her warmth stirs in me.

Joey lingers in the doorway, arms crossed, watching. Not letting it go.

"Wait here," Sophie says, pulling back with a last squeeze before rounding the corner.

Joey's eyes stay on me the whole time, unwavering.

"What's going on with you, Zee? It's *us*. Soph and me. If you can trust anyone, you can trust us. Did Rafe hurt you?" His voice drops low, the edge of anger creeping in. "Because you look like you're escaping a domestic violence situation right now."

If only you knew.

"No." I shake my head, quick and firm. "He would never."

Joey's frown deepens, suspicion still burning in his gaze, but I push the words out anyway, calm as I can manage.

"I'm fine. I promise."

It tastes like betrayal, but it's all I have.

Sophie comes back and presses a phone and credit card into my hands.

"This is Joey's phone; the code is 1213. And my dad's credit card if you need *anything*. He'll live." Her mouth twists into something meant to be a smile, but her eyes are still brimming. "Please don't disappear. Just... let me know when you're wherever you're going."

Then she hugged me again, tighter than before, her tears soaking through my borrowed shirt. Her voice trembles against my ear. "Whatever's going on, I'll always be here. You come to me. Promise?"

Gods, this is gutting me. Because I want to give her that promise. I want to mean it. But with a vampire scratching at my ribs and Deveraux's memories crawling through my veins, I don't know if I'll ever be able to keep it.

By the time I'm outside, the door clicking shut behind me, their voices bleed through the wood.

Joey's tone is full with suspicion. "She's a fucking *Blooded*, Soph. I know it."

"No, Joey." Sophie's voice frays like she's begging him as much as herself. "She would tell me. She wouldn't keep that a secret."

"Did you see the black veins, Sophia? She wouldn't come in until I invited her. She *walked* here barefoot? Come *on*, and didn't you say she suspected Rafe? He fucking turned her."

That was all I could take. The words pressed into me like nails, pinning me to the dark. My chest caved in, and before I could stop it, I bent double on the sidewalk, choking back a sob that still clawed its way out.

THREE

Marek

"You're so fucking gorgeous with my cock in your mouth. Take it deeper, baby."

The words are half out of habit, half to hear him moan around me. Stupid sweet talk, but it works. Lionel groans low, the sound vibrating down my length, and it's enough to push me over. I spill down his throat, my hand tight in his hair, holding him there until I feel the swallow.

Lionel. One of the grounds security guards. Kid follows me around like a stray dog waiting for scraps. Thanks me every time I let him on his knees, like I'm doing *him* a favor.

Means to an end. Nothing more. I tuck my cock back into my pants, already done with it while he's still catching his breath.

Because the truth is, I needed the release. These past few days? Stress doesn't even fucking cover it. Zaria was catatonic one minute, fucking Rafe senseless the next, then trying to rip his throat out. The whole pack pacing the floors. And me, caught in the goddamn middle with my dick in someone else's mouth just to quiet the noise in my head for five fucking minutes.

"Same time tomorrow?" Lionel asked, wiping his mouth

with the back of his hand, thumb grazing his lip before it wandered up my chest.

I caught his wrist and shoved it down. "I'll let you know. Get back to work."

He slipped out the door, and almost instantly Rafe's voice split the air wide open.

"It's been six fucking hours, do your goddamn job!" His roar rattled through the walls, chasing Lionel down the hall, before he stormed off toward his study.

He came barreling down the stairs hours ago, wild-eyed, when he realized Zaria had vanished. Slipped out of the bathroom window like mist. And he hasn't stopped raging since.

I stand in the corner, silently watching.

The great Alpha Rouxel...*shattered*. His precious mate gone, his bond hummed with panic so loud, the entire house could feel it. He tries to hide it, but his wolf is fraying at the edges. And gods, it's almost pathetic.

She's made him weak since the first day she walked into that meeting late. We all felt it then, the shift in him. What kind of Alpha runs after a human like a lost pup? She was always going to be the death of us if we let her. And now...Simône, Elodie, even Markus—the hardest of us all—they're all tangled in her spell too. The strong-willed human who supposedly brought our *beloved* Rafe back to life.

It's bullshit. She's a fucking rot in our foundation.

Deveraux was supposed to handle her. But here we are, left to choke on Rafe's tantrums and rage because his pet slipped through his fingers.

I made my move the night our investigators identified him after Rafe's office attack. Deveraux's family had been ravaged, and he wanted blood for blood. Fine. It was a win-win. He got his vengeance, and we got rid of her. The pack would survive.

The night Rafe claimed her; I let Deveraux into the house. The plan was simple: wait until the bond was made, then end her. It would look like the claiming failed, just like with their father. Rafe would be crushed, yes, but he'd recover. The pack would endure.

But Deveraux couldn't help himself. The greedy bastard had to go and try to turn her.

When we came back from the office, his fangs littered the floor, pools of blood soaked into the boards, sprayed across the walls. And now here we are.

"He doesn't have any idea where she might have gone? Any place we can help look?" Simône's voice breaks through as she steps into the kitchen.

I don't turn. I'm gripping my mug too tight, staring into the black swirl of coffee like it can drown out the chaos in this house. I came here to get away from it; Rafe's shouting, the endless pacing of guards, the stench of fear hanging in every corner.

"Fuck if I know, Simône. If she wanted to be found, she wouldn't be hiding."

Dammit. I was agitated, and it's showing, my irritation bleeding through.

Simône leans against the counter, watching me with that calm, patient stare that's always made me want to break something. "I just mean... maybe she needed space. The claiming might've been too much for her to process right now."

I huff out a humorless laugh, bitter. *Space.* As if that girl hasn't had enough *space* to dismantle Rafe from the inside out since the day she walked into our lives.

"You're being a dick, Marek." Simône's eyes narrow, voice sharp enough to cut.

"I'm being *realistic*, Simône." My tone stays level, but the bitterness coils tight in every word.

Simône and I don't usually clash. It's always been her and me against the noise, even though Rafe's the one who shares her blood. Elodie and Markus...well, they've always been a pair orbiting each other, circling in ways that made everyone else uneasy. I once walked in on him finger-fucking her, confirming what I'd already suspected. They were embarrassed, sure, but what else do you expect when you live stacked like sardines, no walls thick enough to muffle secrets?

There were times I wanted Simône, when tension burned too hot to smother. And once, we did cross that line. One reckless night about five years ago, drunk on exhaustion and the ache of needing someone, anyone. We didn't even talk about it after. We just woke up, split off to our rooms, and carried the weight like it never happened.

So, she's more than pack; she's my friend, my person. I wouldn't ruin that.

But today, aggravation bled over all of it. My patience was stretched thin, and Simône saw it in my eyes. She opened her mouth, ready to bite back, but then the door slammed.

Rafe stormed in, dragging the storm with him. Elodie and Markus flanked him like shadows. His presence hit the room like thunder cracking overhead. The bond thrummed through me, rattling my teeth, panic pouring off him in jagged waves I couldn't block if I tried.

"I'm headed back to her apartment." He didn't even look at Simône or me at first; just carved through the room like the decision had been carved in stone long before he spoke it.

"Elodie, Markus; you stay here. Simône, check in with Vanessa. Anyone she might've known from the office. Marek—" His eyes cut to me. "You go and check in with security."

I nod once, the picture of obedience. The loyal beta. The good soldier.

But inside, I'm laughing. With any luck, she's already gone halfway across the world, putting oceans between herself and this mess.

Yeah, I know. This all makes me sound like a complete dick. But the truth? Zaria just doesn't belong here. She never did. I'll do whatever I have to do to protect this pack, even if our Alpha's too blind to see the damage she'll bring.

Rafe's bond is still screaming in my vein; his anger, his panic, that constant drone of *'where is she, where is she'* rattling my bones. Six hours of it, and I'm done. I pull back, close the door in his face, and wall him out. The hush drops like a stone into deep water, and for the first time tonight I can fucking breathe.

He'll throw a fit when he realizes. *We're stronger when we're connected. You don't shield unless I tell you. I'm the Alpha.*

Blah, fucking blah.

I make my way to the security lodge, doing my due diligence, because that's what a loyal second would do.

Chaos hits me the second I push the door open. Screens flashing, radios buzzing, men talking over each other like they're the ones who lost her. Reeling, scrambling, useless.

The lodge is more than a checkpoint; it's a whole damn house inside the perimeter, five bedrooms, built like a bunker. The permanent security team lives here, with its own maid service, its own cook, the whole setup. One crew runs the access gate on a rotation; the rest manage the grounds. Everything tidy, orderly.

Except right now.

Right now, it's all panic and noise, like the scent of Rafe's desperation has infected them too.

"Any news?" I ask, snagging an apple from the bowl on the counter. I bite into it, leaning back against the edge. "Where did the apples come from? I should have these added to the main house." No one answers as I chew, savoring the tart sweetness, letting it sit heavy on my tongue while I watch them flail.

"I'm waiting to hear from Edwards," Tony blurts, voice high with panic. He's the lead officer, supposed to be calm under fire, but he looks like a man unraveling. "He thinks he may have spotted her on the west side, near the Marigny."

The room shifts. Radios crackle. A few of the younger guards stiffen like they're already bracing for orders.

I take another bite, the crunch loud in the sudden quiet. It's a really fucking good apple.

"Then why the hell are you waiting?" I ask, voice calm, almost bored. "If he's got eyes on her, you don't sit around reporting—you move. Do your fucking jobs or we'll find a fresh set of assholes to do it for you."

Tony flinches. Scrambles for the radio. Starts barking into it like he should've been doing all along. And I lean back against the counter, chewing, watching them spin their wheels, and thinking about how close I am to getting what I want.

While they scramble, trying to get the ground crew moving, I slip out and make my way to one of the SUVs and take off.

Marigny isn't far. Right across from the Quarter, caught between neon Bourbon and the worn bones of the Bywater. There's a hotel there that takes cash, no questions, no ID. Cheap and quiet enough. If she's running without shoes and carrying nothing of her own, that's the kind of place she'd hole up in.

All of her things are still at the manor. Clothes, purse, ID. Hell, even her phone. She's out there with nothing but the clothes on her back. Which means my guess is right; she is headed for the Marigny. Unless of course she's smartened up and decided to get the hell out of dodge, altogether.

But Zaria never struck me as the running type. She'll stay close, at least for now. And if I'm the one who finds her first, maybe I'll finally get the chance to clean up the mess Deveraux couldn't.

I get Rafe's obsession, I really do. Under different circumstances—if she wasn't a walking detonation wired under everything I care about, I could even like her. Hell, more than like her. She's sharp-tongued, quicker on the draw than most men I know, and gorgeous in that infuriating way that gets under your skin and stays there.

Those freckles scattered across her nose, the soft dusting beneath her eyes. And her body, *fuck...* yeah, I've noticed. I've thought about it more than once, especially when she strolls into the office wearing something that makes it impossible *not* to.

One morning she showed up in this sheer shirt, the outline of her bra like a deliberate weapon, abs cut tight and unforgiving under the fabric. A skirt that skimmed her thighs just enough to make my throat go dry. Completely fucking inappropriate for the office, but try telling that to my cock. I lasted all of five minutes before I ducked into the bathroom and jerked myself raw, her image burned into my skull.

So yeah, I can understand it. Being near her, tasting her, fucking her...I imagine it could drive a man to obsession. It's not weakness, not entirely. It's chemistry. It's the kind of hunger you can't reason your way out of.

But here's the truth—and it doesn't care how she looks, or how many times I've imagined her mouth wrapped around my cock. She's a risk we can't afford. A liability wrapped in pretty skin and pointed edges; and she's no good for us. No good for Rafe. She's a fucking *human*.

My thoughts get re-centered as I pull into the cracked lot of the hotel. The drive into the Marigny didn't take long, not even at this hour. The streets were mostly empty, neon still bleeding onto the wet pavement from bars that never really close. Perfect place to disappear.

I kill the engine and sit there for a moment. Pull out my phone. Scroll through her socials until I find a photo I can show the front desk. It's all just pictures of her smiling, soft and alive in ways that make me want to crush the screen in my hand.

They'll stonewall me, no doubt. Try to play righteous about "privacy" and "policy." Which means I'll have to get rough with them. And I'm dying to crack open a skull today.

The lobby reeks of stale cigarettes and cheap disinfectant, the kind of place people crawl to when they want to disappear. The clerk behind the counter glances up as I walk in. His shoulders stiffen, eyes flicking quick, like he's deciding whether to breathe or run.

I don't waste time. I pull up the photo on my phone and lay it on the counter. "This girl. Seen her?"

He stares at the screen too long, then back at me. There's no recognition of her, why would there be? She's just another guest to him. But he recognizes me. The weight of who I work for, who my Alpha is. His throat works as he nods.

"Yeah. She paid cash. Checked in a few hours ago." His voice dips. He slides a keycard across the counter, eyes skittering away like he doesn't want to watch where this goes. "Room 214. We don't want any trouble."

I pluck the card from the laminate, tuck it into my jacket. "Then you won't get any."

That's all it takes. The clerk drops his gaze like he's already erased me from his memory, eager to go back to pretending none of this ever happened.

The carpeted stairs groan under my boots as I take them up, the key heavy in my pocket, heavier still in my thoughts. The hallway smells of mildew and smoke; the wallpaper is peeling. This is the kind of place where anonymity is worth more than comfort.

Room 214 waits at the far end, the brass numbers crooked, like everything here.

Inside, the air still clings with damp heat. The mirror fogged, a towel left twisted on the bed, edges dark with water. She's not here, but she hasn't been gone long.

I ease the door shut behind me and drop into the chair by the window. No rush. She'll be back. People always circle back to the places that feel safe, even if it's nothing but a cracked lock and mildew.

My phone buzzes when I type out the update.

Marek: Following up on a lead in Marigny, so far a dead end. I'll keep everyone updated if I hear anything else.

Rafe answers first, fast.

Rafe: Thanks, brother.

Then Simône.

Simône: Do you need me to come that way? Just left the office seeing Vanessa.

I sigh, thumb quick.

Marek: No.

Marek: I got it, I'll let you know if it leads anywhere.

The replies stop after that.

I slip the phone back into my pocket, letting my gaze drag over the room.

I'm not here to play hero. I'm not here to carry Rafe's heartbreak back to him. I'm here because somebody has to put a fucking end to this cancer.

Rafe's been alone for centuries. His routine's never changed. He heads to the city or the Bayou, find a woman, bring her home, fuck her, send her on her way. No strings, no questions. That was him. Reliable and controlled.

So, this fixation on Zaria is both surprising and infuriating. Not only that, but it's also dangerous. An Alpha can't afford that kind of distraction. This pack is the only family I've got. That's the only thing that matters.

Yeah, I had feelings for him once—but that has nothing to do with this. That was a stupid time when I still believed in love and happy fucking endings. Then something shifted in him. Hardened him. He became the man we could trust to lead. Until her.

What makes *her* the one who gets to break down his walls? Isn't that the million-dollar fucking question. But she won't be around long enough to answer it.

Now that she's a vampire, I'll take particular pleasure in watching her die at my hands.

FOUR

Zaria

My skin feels like it's on fire. I tried to take a cold shower, but the bathroom steamed up, anyway. Steam rising off me, not the water.

So, I filled the bathtub with cold water and filled it with ice. This is my eighth trip to the ice machine, lugging buckets like some addict chasing a fix, dumping them in until my hands are red from the chill. The water doesn't even stay cold, so these trips don't matter. My body turns it into vapor, into heat, like I'm boiling alive from the inside out.

There's something else humming under my skin; something beyond the vampire clawing at me. A vibration I can't scratch out, can't smother, can't breathe past. It makes me feel like I'm unraveling thread by thread.

At this rate, I'll call the white-jacket people on myself. Let them lock me up, throw away the key. At least that comes with free meals and television. Give me a padded room and all three seasons of *The Summer I Turned Pretty,* and I'd call it a vacation.

Instead, I'm here.

This is by far the seediest hotel I've ever set foot in, and I've seen some shit. The carpet is sticky with things I don't want to even guess at, the wallpaper peeling in strips like old scabs. The air hums with low voices, subtle laughter, and the copper tang of blood so thick it coats my tongue. Sweat, sex and iron; the cocktail of predators.

It's crawling with Bloodeds of every kind; fangs flashing in the shadows, claws catching dim light, eyes burning with hunger. None of them look twice at me, but every part of me feels *seen.*

I'd heard rumors about this place. That it was where Bloodeds went when they didn't want to be found. Where they fed, fucked, and killed in equal measure. Close to the river.

The "Blood Bayou" isn't a bayou at all. It's just a squat building hunched on the river's edge, its doors yawning wide like a warning no one listens to. Inside, the floors stay slick with what's spilled there. Blood runs thick enough to seep into the pavement, washing into the river until the current drags it downstream.

About sixty years back, one night turned the river red for miles. They still talk about it. The name stuck...Blooded Bayou.

The hotel sits close enough that when the wind shifts, you can taste the rot in the air. That's why the Bloodeds hole up here. Close to the source. Close to whatever the hell still calls to them from that place.

All of it courtesy of Deveraux. His memories don't fight me anymore. They've settled in, like squatters who know they're not getting evicted. The killing parties. The orgies. The bloodletting. Nights where he fed and fed, reveling in it like the whole place was his goddamn church.

And the rest comes with it whether I want it or not; his family screaming while Rafe tore them apart, his dealings with Marek, the shit he thought he'd buried. Now it just runs on a loop in my head, grainy and endless, like some bootleg horror film I can't switch off.

My stomach twists at the memories. I shove them aside and slide the keycard through the lock. The light flashes green, the latch clicks, and I push the door open, and there I see Marek sitting in the corner as if he were invited.

This motherfucker.

"Zaria."

He sits in the chair by the window, leaning forward with his elbows on his knees. Just there, patient, his gaze locked on me.

I step inside without hesitation, the bag of ice crinkling in my grip. The door shuts behind me, and I drop the ice onto the dresser with a careless thud.

"Wow. This. Is. *Ballsy*, Marek. Even for you," I say, keeping my tone deadpan and unimpressed. My eyes never leave him. "To what do I owe the honor? Come to finish what you set Deveraux in motion to do?"

His breath snags for a split second, but I catch the scent of his fear.

"I haven't decided yet." His voice is even, almost casual.

He rises from the chair and crosses the space between us with the quiet certainty of someone who feels like he doesn't need to rush.

"Why'd you run?"

"That's not your concern." The words snap out easily enough, but then he moves closer.

That's when I smell him.

Not like Sophie, who was soft and warm, skin and salt and everything human.

No. Marek's scent hits me like something I used to crave before everything changed. Sweet. Familiar. Like warm cinnamon rolls pulled from an oven, like whiskey on ice, like melted chocolate I would've killed for on a bad day.

Only now, all I want to do is tear his throat open and stick a straw in.

The thought slams into me so fast, so vivid, that I stumble inside my own head. *What the fuck?*

I clench my fists, fighting it back, but it's there humming under my skin, crawling down my throat; a hunger I can't laugh off this time.

He just stares at me, still as stone, like he's weighing it. Whether he wants to strike.

And I almost want him to. To give me the excuse, just one reason to tear him apart for what he's turned me into. He's the one who set Deveraux on my path, the reason my veins burn with this hunger, the reason I'm caught between what I was and what I can't escape becoming.

I want to kill him for it.

I want to feel his bones break under my hands, his throat split open under my teeth.

But I don't.

Because if I did, if I tore him apart here and now, it wouldn't just be his blood staining me. It would be Rafe collapsing under the grief of it, a weight so heavy it would hollow him out until nothing of him was left.

And I can't. Even when every muscle in me is screaming that I should.

"You have something to say, Marek? Or are you just trying to stare me into being intimidated?" My lips curl. "News flash, it's not working."

His hand snaps to my throat in a blur, claws sinking into my skin as he squeezes. And I mean he squeezes *hard*.

But the pain doesn't come. Neither does the panic. There's just a strange calm blooming in my chest, almost soothing. My lungs *should* be burning, my body should be fighting; but instead I just look at him. And man, does he notice...

I smirk.

His grip tightens.

I drag my hand slowly down the length of his free arm, unhurried and utterly calm, until I reach his wrist. Then I guide his hand up to my throat, pressing it there myself, a dare written in the lines of my smile.

"Try two hands this time."

The flicker in his eyes tells me he knows this power is beyond his reach. But being the stubborn bastard he is, he doubles down. Both hands at my throat now, claws biting deep. I feel my windpipe crush under his grip; hear the wet snap inside me.

My body just knits it back together as fast as he breaks it.

He lifts me clean off my feet, claws ripping through my skin like he's trying to carve his way in. And still, I wonder why he doesn't shift. If he really wanted me in pieces, he would've by now. Not that he would make it that far, but the question still remains.

No, this isn't about killing me.

This is about watching. About trying to see life die out of my eyes.

Jealousy? Vengeance? Maybe both.

Ugh. I'm bored now.

I tilt my head and tap him on the hand.

"Are you done with this yet?" My voice is smooth, unbroken, like he hasn't crushed me half a dozen times already. "Because I have some questions."

"Fuck youuuuu." He grits it out, jaw tight, and squeezes harder.

I flick my wrist.

He slams into the wall like a rag doll, plaster cracking under the impact. His body slides down in a heap, dazed but still conscious, still glaring.

"Goddamn it, Marek." I groan, stretching the fabric of my shirt away from my neck where his claws had torn through. The cotton is damp, sticky with blood. "I just bought this shirt."

I glanced down at my grey V-neck with white lettering that says *I Speak Fluent Sarcasm* that I'd just bought not a couple hours ago. Now it's stained, shredded at the collar and ruined.

"Mother. Fucker." I say under my breath, letting the collar go.

When I look back up, Marek's rage spikes, dialed so high it practically hums in the air. He shifts mid-step, teeth flashing, claws extended, and launches at me *again*.

This time his strike lands across my chest, claws raking deep, blood spilling hot down my skin. For a second, the room swims red; then the wounds knit shut as fast as they're opened.

He just stares at me, wide-eyed, chest heaving, while I look down at the shirt. My fingers pinch the hem, lifting it away from the sticky mess.

"Not everyone has millions of dollars to replace clothes, Marek." My voice stays hollow, bored, like we're talking about laundry instead of the blood dripping onto the carpet. I glanced up, matching his wild eyes with calm steel. "Ugh...Sit down, Marek. You're pissing me off now."

He's still in wolf form, chest heaving, a low growl rumbling from deep inside him. Massive. Tall even crouched, thick through the shoulders, fur bristling in dark shades that catch the weak light. And God help me, it's beautiful. Of course it is.

But it tracks. Rafe's always had that reckless, too-pretty look; like Ezra Miller in their long-hair era, if you shoved it into a six-foot-five, two-hundred-thirty-pound Balkan frame built for war. He's a fucking ten in human skin. So of course, his wolf would carry that same brutal, dangerous kind of beauty.

I flick my finger.

His body jerks, the shift pulling at him fast, snapping him back toward human before he can fight it. Bones pop, fur retracts, claws split away.

I don't even watch the total transformation. I turn instead, grab the sweats and shirt Rafe left me last night, toss them over my shoulder toward the floor.

"Cover yourself," I say, annoyed, already tugging off the ruined shirt. His tantrum was nothing more than a nuisance, but aggravating non-the-less. "I'm sure you have questions. I'm just not in the mood to answer them. Go home, Marek. Once I'm finished with what I'm doing here, I'll go back, and we can all have a nice little chat."

"You're not coming back to the fucking manor," he spits. His chest is still heaving, sweat gleaming on his skin. "Zaria — or whoever, whatever the hell you are. It's done. It's over. Just *leave.*"

I take a step toward him until I'm close enough for him to feel the heat rolling off my skin, close enough to see that his threat lands nowhere.

"I'm not *leaving*, Marek. I'm bonded to Rafe now. This is it.

Like it or not."

The scent of his fear coils off him, intense and sweet, cutting through the air between us until it's lodged in the back of my throat.

"You're afraid," I murmur, tilting my head as I study him. "Afraid I'm going to tell him what you've done. That once I do, you'll lose him forever."

His jaw locks, but the flicker in his eyes is enough. I don't need him to answer; I already know.

"I won't tell him."

That gets him. His gaze snapped to mine, the first real crack in his control. "I don't believe you."

"I won't," I say again. "I give you my word. But..." I lean forward. "You'll need to do something for me in return."

His eyes narrow, suspicion sparking. "What?"

"Let me feed from you."

The look on his face is priceless, like I've spit in it. His mouth pulls tight, eyes sparking with outrage. "Are you out of your *goddamn* mind?"

"It's the only way this works," I crack back. "I need to be near Rafe. Be *with* him. But this hunger—" my hand presses to my chest, the burn crawling under my skin "—it's a fuse I can't control. If I don't feed it, I'll hurt him. I'll hurt one of you. I won't risk that."

"Then don't fucking come back!" he snarls.

"If I don't go back, neither do you!" I yell. "That's the fucking deal here, Marek. All or nothing."

His head shakes back and forth, his knee bounces. Underneath the rising rage, that sweet note of fear keeps curling through the air.

"Goddamn it." His voice cracks under the weight of it all. "He'll find out. Someone is going to find out."

"I'm not going to say anything," I tell him. "And I know the last thing you want is for it to come out that—*one*, you tried to have me killed. And *two*, that you're feeding a vampire."

That lands. His whole body goes rigid, the fight still in him but chained now, cornered by the truth.

"Just..." His jaw works, teeth gritted, like the words are knives in his throat. "Just fucking get it over with."

He yanks the shirt off and flops it onto the floor, still glaring, still seething, sweatpants hanging low on his hips as if dignity could be stitched back together with cotton.

I hover, now suddenly unsure, my hands trembling. "What do I do? Bite your wrist, or your neck, or something. You're not a human, so...?"

"I don't fucking *know*, Zaria." The bass in his voice makes my bones ache. "I'm a wolf, not a goddamn nightcrawler."

The words hit, and the weight of it all crashes down. My throat tightens, my chest aches. "I didn't ask for this, Marek. I would've rather let him kill me."

Ugh, I don't fucking need this.

I turned, shaking my head. "Put your shirt on. Just... forget I asked."

For a second, I think maybe he'll soften, maybe he'll say something that isn't edged in fury. Instead, he snatches the shirt from where it hangs and jerks it back over his head like armor. The anger pours off him, thick enough to choke, but underneath it I feel the flicker of something else. Something he'd rather burn out of himself than admit.

"Fine," he spits. "Let's go then. A deal's a deal. You keep your fucking mouth shut." His jaw tightens, his glare is brutally intense. "Not my fault you got cold feet."

I watch as he stalks out the door, slamming it behind him.

Everything in me wants to ask him why he hates me this much. What I ever did to earn it. I've only ever tried with them. Rafe's pack. Tried to belong. Tried to be kind. But Marek has worn disdain toward me like a second skin since the day we met, and now it's carved between us, worse than ever.

My emotions are everywhere, frayed and clawing. I've been fighting the itch under my skin all night. The front desk had blood bags, their version of room service, I guess. I even considered one of the desperate humans who lined up in the lobby, waiting to offer their veins as tribute.

But I forced half of the bag down, enough to blunt the edge. But hunger didn't stay quiet. The burn came back, hotter and deeper. The blood only whetted my appetite and left me restless and starving.

And now Marek of all people is the only thing standing between me and losing control.

FIVE

Rafe

It had been nearly an hour since Marek's text: *Located her. Heading back to the manor.*

I called him the second it came through, but he didn't pick up.

Now the pack was gathered in the living room, all of us waiting and watching the door, and I couldn't sit the fuck down. My boots kept dragging grooves into the floorboards, back and forth, until Simône finally muttered something about me pacing straight through to the cellar. No one laughed. Not even her.

I hadn't said a word since that text.

The bond was still there. Faint and all but muted. Like someone had thrown a blanket over it, muffling everything but the barest hum. I knew she was alive. I knew she was breathing. But either the venom in her veins dulled everything between us, or she's muting us. And what I *couldn't* feel was eating me alive.

Wherever she'd gone, whatever she'd done, I was just thankful Marek had found her. Thankful he'd gotten to her before the worst of the poison did.

So much had happened in too short a time; disasters stacked on disasters, a storm that never gave me a moment to fucking breathe. Not her waking, not the hunger gnawing at her, not the way she'd looked at me before locking herself in the bathroom and slipping out that window like a ghost.

And underneath it all, guilt chewed me raw. The way I'd touched her. The way I'd fucked her while she was shifted. She wasn't herself then. Hell, she was something else entirely — and I'd still taken her. When she came back to herself, it was like looking into the eyes of a stranger I'd already betrayed.

I didn't know what the fuck she was now.

All I knew was I needed her back in front of me. Alive. Breathing. So I could stop pacing, stop replaying every mistake. So I could look at her and know I hadn't already lost her for good.

When the front door opened, I was there within a second. My chest finally unclenched, breath tearing out of me as I grabbed her, pulling her into my arms like I can fuse her to me if I just held tight enough.

Marek slips in behind her, silent, and heads straight upstairs without a word. I don't miss the way his shoulders are tight, the way he doesn't so much as glance at us. He's been a dick to her about leaving, I can feel it.

I tip her chin, searching her face, desperate for answers. "Why, Zaria?" My voice breaks harsher than I intend. "Why'd you run?"

Her eyes flick to mine, wide, shining with exhaustion I can feel down to my bones.

"You're afraid of me," she whispers. Then her gaze sweeps the room, catching the others watching from the edges,

Simône, Elodie, Markus, all frozen, all too quiet. Her throat works as she swallows.

"You all are." Her voice drops to something smaller, rawer, and it slices through me. "I'm afraid of me too."

"It's only because we don't know what's happening, Zaria," I say, softer now, willing her to believe me. "We were supposed to talk as a pack last night. As a family. Then you left."

Her mouth trembles, eyes dipping away. "I'm sorry. I shouldn't have left."

"Then come talk to us," I urge, my thumb brushing over her knuckles. "Tell us what's going on."

She nods with a tinge of hesitance, and I take her hand, leading her toward the sofa where the others are waiting. The pack shifts, making space, every eye fixed on her as though she might splinter in their hands.

"Simône," I say, trying to keep my voice even. "Can you drag Marek back down here? We need to do this together."

Simône flicks a look toward the stairs, her jaw tight, and for a moment I think she'll argue. But then she rises, squaring her shoulders, and heads for the steps.

"Are you okay, Zaria?" Markus asks, his brow furrowed.

Before she can answer, Elodie crosses the room and pulls her into a hug. But she jolts, her arms tightening for a second before easing back just enough to look at her. "You're vibrating."

Zaria's smile blooms, warm and almost tender, as if this were the most ordinary thing in the world. "I know. And thanks, Markus. Yes, I'm okay."

Simône and Marek made their way back down the stairs, voices low, eyes heavy with things they weren't saying. I barely noticed. My focus was locked on Zaria; her fingers were fragile in mine. I traced slow circles over her knuckles, trying to find her through the muted bond, trying to feel anything more than that faint thrum dulled by either the venom or choice.

Her gaze lingered on our joined hands, and for a long moment I thought she might stay silent. Then she drew in a breath that sounded too heavy for her chest and finally spoke.

"Deveraux turned me," she said softly, her eyes fixed on our joined hands.

The room went still.

"He paralyzed me with Elden Ash. Bit me. Taunted me. Put his venom into my blood."

My chest clenched. I had to shut my eyes, because the picture of her body limp on the floor hit me like it had just happened.

"But that's not... it wasn't just that." Her voice steadied, like she was bracing herself. "Something was already happening before he touched me. I didn't know what it was, but it was there—like heat under my skin, humming low. Waking up."

Her chin lifted, and this time her gaze found mine.

"When he bit me, when the venom hit... it fused with what was already there. My grandmother—" she swallowed, her lips pressing tight, then forcing the words out. "She was the High Matron of her generation."

She paused, allowing us to sit with that information for a beat.

"I didn't know it, not really. My mom tried to bury it, and kept it hidden. They bound my gift over and over again. But it didn't just disappear. It's like it waited. And when the venom mixed with it..." She gave a bitter little laugh. "It was like pouring gasoline on a fire I didn't even know was burning."

Her gaze swept past me now, over Simône, Marek, all of us.

"So yeah," she finished, her voice softening, losing some of its edge. "I'm vampire. And I'm the new High Matron. And I don't know what the hell that makes me. That's the humming you felt, Elodie. The vibration under my skin."

"Holy shit," Markus breathed, barely more than a whisper.

The words hung there, heavy, the kind of silence that could either collapse or combust. Zaria let it stretch, her eyes moving from face to face, taking in the way they stared at her like she was something fragile and dangerous all at once.

"Other than the magical powers, the bloodlust, the fangs, and the new skin..." She wiggled her fingers in the air, giving her best over-the-top spirit fingers and flashing a bright grin. "It's still me, guys. Still the same goofball Zaria you've all grown to love...or hate."

The joke landed in the thick silence like a spark in a storm — half the room didn't know whether to laugh or flinch, and the other half tried to do both at once.

Her eyes had flicked toward Marek when she said hate, the edge in her tone unmistakable. He doesn't rise to it. He just looks at me for half a second, then drops his gaze to his lap, fists clenching tight.

"I've heard about the High Matrons," Elodie says, her voice soft. "They are the ultimate power when it comes to witches, Zaria. Mixing that bloodline with vampirism—" she swallows, her eyes wide, "—you're stronger than all of us."

The words ripple through the room like a crack in the floorboards, something they can all feel but none of them know how to brace against. We were all eerily quiet until

Zaria's voice cut through the lull.

"That's why I left," she says, her tone firm but her gaze fixed on her hands as though she can't bear to see their faces. "I didn't want you all to look at me like I was a bomb about to go off. Like I was something dangerous none of you could control. I felt it in your eyes. In Mama's. In Daddy's. Even in yours, Rafe. You wouldn't say it, but I could feel it bleeding through the bond—your fear. And, gods, I don't blame you."

She lifts her head then, her gaze sweeping the room, daring them to deny it. Simône's lips part but no words come. Markus shifts uncomfortably in his chair. Elodie's arms tighten protectively around herself, as if she isn't sure whether to lean closer or pull away.

Only Marek doesn't move, his fists still clenched in his lap, his jaw hard, eyes fixed on her.

She took a deep breath and stood. "I just wanted to come and explain things; let you all know that I'm okay. I need to grab my things, and then I'll head back to my place. I'll see you all at the office tomorrow."

"No," I cut in immediately, raising my hands as I stood. "No. That's not happening."

"You don't have to leave, Zaria," Simône adds quickly, her tone gentler, pleading where mine is command. She leans forward, hands out like she could anchor Zaria in place if she tried.

"Please don't go," Elodie whispers, looping her arms around Zaria's shoulders, clinging to her as though letting go would mean losing her for good.

But Zaria just smiles faintly, untangling herself from the embrace with careful hands. "Deveraux isn't a threat anymore. And even if he were, I can take care of myself."

She starts walking slowly towards the door. "It's best if I get back to... whatever *normal* is going to look like for me now." Her gaze sweeps the room, lingering on each of them before finally locking onto me. "For all of us."

She turns and heads for the stairs.

I'm moving before I even realize it, the weight of her words settling heavy on my chest. "Zaria, just wait...*Zaria*!"

She stops halfway up, her hand tightening on the banister. Her back is to me, shoulders squared but trembling.

"Rafe..." Her voice cracks, low and pained. "I can't stay here. *I can't*. I need to go home. Things are too... complicated now."

She starts upward again, leaving me rooted at the bottom of the stairs.

The words tear out of me before I can stop them. "Can I still see you? What does this mean for us? Our bond?"

She hesitates on the landing, and for a breath I think she might turn, might answer, might ease the ache clawing through my chest.

But when she feels me behind her, she moves again, step by step toward the bedroom.

"I *have* to leave, Rafe," she breathes, the words almost breaking. "Please don't stop me."

"Are you muting it?" The question came out sharper than I meant, slicing through the quiet as the bedroom door clicked shut behind us. The question echoed like an accusation. "Our bond? Or is it the venom?"

"I'm muting it."

Her answer was immediate. No hesitation. She turned her head, eyes locking on mine, and for a second, I forgot to breathe.

"Rafe..." My name shuddered off her lips, soft and wrecked. "It's like—" she swallowed hard, her body trembling, "—every instinct, every truth, every shard of knowledge I shouldn't know is inside me now. Like it's been poured straight into my veins. I feel everything from them. Every ancestor. Every memory. And everything in me is amplified at a volume so high it's unbearable. If I don't mute the bond, it'll spill into you. It'll drown you. I know it will."

Her voice broke, trembling with a kind of grief that hurt to hear. "If I stay here—if I slip, even for a second—I could hurt one of you. Because your blood..." Her throat closed, the words fighting their way out, jagged. "Your blood smells like it's the only thing I've ever craved."

Her hand presses hard against her temple, like she could physically hold the storm back if she just pressed hard enough. Her shoulders shake with the effort.

"I *know* I'm powerful," she whispers, tears shining in her eyes. "More powerful than anything any of you have ever faced, and I'm only getting stronger. It's like his venom supercharged my bloodline. And I never asked for it. I don't even fucking want it. But it's here now, rattling in my skull like a thousand lives screaming at once. My ancestors. Their memories. Their pain. And Deveraux's—his rage, his murders, his hunger—they're all inside me, clawing at me."

Her chest heaves. "I can't stay here when I unravel. I *am* unraveling. I'm barely holding it together now."

The words hit me like fists, shoving the air from my lungs. Fury and fear knotted tight in my chest until I couldn't tell them apart.

"Then let me feel it, Zaria. Don't shut me out. Let me in. You're underestimating what I can handle."

She takes a step towards me. "I'm not underestimating

you. I *know* how strong you are. I can feel it in my bones. But I also know you can't manage this." She swallows, her voice breaking sharper now. "I know you're afraid of me. Not just of me, of what my vampire does to yours. I watched you with her. With...me. How unchained you were. How you lost yourself."

My cock twitched at the memory before I could stop it. My vampire stirred, hungry, restless, clawing at the edges of my control. I squeezed my eyes shut, forcing it down, choking on the shame that came with it.

Her eyes narrowed. "That spike of guilt and arousal just now?" Her voice cracked higher. "I feel it. I feel *all of it*."

Fuck.

I dragged a hand down my face, shaking my head, trying to ground myself, trying to claw back some semblance of control. "Zaria..." My voice broke low, rough, half-growl, half-plea. "I..."

She cut me off, her words soft but jagged. "It's fine. I get it. It's not like you cheated or anything." Her gaze dropped, then lifted again, her mouth curving into a bitter half-smile that didn't reach her eyes. "It was still me, technically."

The way she said it, like it was a joke she wanted to believe, like it was supposed to make it hurt less; it made my chest cave in. Because she was wrong. It wasn't fine. It was anything but.

"Please show me," I begged, my pulse hammering like it might rip straight out of my chest. "Please. I need to feel you. You don't understand what this silence is like for me."

She shook her head, exhaling like the fight had bled out of her. Then, softly: "Okay, Rafe. Sit on the bed."

I nodded, moving on instinct. Dropped onto the edge of the mattress, palms braced on my knees. My throat was dry, my body strung tight as a bowstring, waiting for the arrow to snap.

She stood over me, trembling but resolute. "I'm going to open everything first... just about halfway." Her voice cracked like a whisper meant for confession. "It's going to hit you pretty hard, okay?"

"Do it." My voice was raw, broken, already shaking.

Then the world detonated.

It slammed into me like fire under my skin, a thousand voices screaming through my marrow. Rage that wasn't mine clawed down my spine. Betrayal split my chest open like a blade twisting deep. Lust surged, fierce and drowning, tangling with grief so thick I could hardly breathe. Death. Murders. Blood. Screams so loud I couldn't tell if they were in my head or ripping raw from my throat.

I was burning alive. Unraveling. Every ancestor of hers pouring into me through the bond—every memory, every desire, every atrocity. It was endless, unbearable.

And still—threaded through the chaos, shimmering like a vein of light—was her. Love, desperate and aching. Fear that she'd break me. Hope that I'd hold on.

I doubled over, clutching my skull, my teeth bared in a feral snarl. "*Fuck*...Zaria."

"Breathe, Rafe." Her palm pressed to my chest, and it tethered me by a thread. "This is what I'm carrying. This is why I mute it."

I dragged in a ragged breath, vision swimming in fire. "It's...gods, it's too much."

"This," she said, her own voice fraying, "is me opening halfway. Not even all the way."

The bond thrummed between us, splitting me open and

hollowing me out in the same breath. And I knew with absolute certainty; if she ever *did* let it all loose, if she ever showed me everything, it would burn me down to ash.

"Now," she whispers, her palm still pressed against my chest, "just the hunger."

And everything else drops away.

The voices vanish. The grief, the rage, the betrayal; it all slams shut like a door, and what's left is sharper. Honed. A single blade.

Hunger.

It coils through me like fog, thick and copper-rich, seeping hot into my lungs until I taste it. My mouth waters against my will. The air is laced with it; iron, heat, something primal and metallic. Not mine. Theirs.

Simône. Elodie. Marek. Markus.

I can almost see them; dark tendrils twisting through the room, curling like living things, every thread leading me straight to the source. To them.

My pulse spikes, hammering in my throat like it wants to tear itself free. My skin burns, fire licking under every inch of me. The bond hums, alive, vibrating like it has teeth, and the only thought left in my skull is feed.

"Fuck..." The word rips out of me, ragged and strangled. My nails dug deep into the mattress, claws threatening to break through. "Zaria—"

The hunger grips tighter, clawing through my veins until I can't tell if it's hers bleeding into me or mine being born from her. It doesn't matter. All that matters is the ache, the gnawing desperation under my skin screaming for release.

How the fuck has she not ripped us all apart?

"Gods," I rasp, my chest heaving, body shuddering with

restraint. "This—this is what you live with?"

Her nod is small, controlled. But her eyes—*fuck, her eyes*—they hold something that cuts deeper than the hunger itself.

Pity.

"Last one, Rafe. Then we'll stop."

Her voice was quiet but threaded with warning. She took a step back, putting distance between us like she already knew what was about to break loose. Her chest rose and fell, steadying. "This, Rafe..." She drew in a breath. "...is my rage."

The bond flared open like a vein split wide.

And it hit me.

Not just emotions this time...*visions*. I didn't even know the bond could do this. Didn't know if it even *was* the bond or Zaria forcing it through.

Deveraux's smirk seared behind my eyes, his voice taunting as his hands moved over her paralyzed body. Her voice calling for me, desperate. His fangs sinking into her flesh. His hatred for me flooding into her veins as he bit down. The way she fought it with love for me—and how it twisted, warped, clashed inside her chest until it curdled into something raw and poisonous.

Then it widened.

Her parents recoiling, their eyes laced with fear. Claudine jerking her hand away. The sting of rejection. The loneliness. Rage at what she'd become, what she never asked for. Rage at what was stolen. Rage that the world would only ever see her as a monster, never a daughter, never a friend, never a mate. And then—Marek.

The fury sharpened, shifted, bent toward him. I tried to hold on, tried to make sense of why, but it blurred, slipped through my grasp like water. Before I could pin it down, the vision swerved again.

Shifted to me.

Me with her. My body tangled with hers, fucking her while she shifted. While I was shifted. The ravenous way we tore each other apart. It scorched through me like acid in my veins, searing me open, devouring everything I thought I knew about restraint.

I wanted to tear the fucking walls down, rip flesh from bone, drag the city into the streets and set it all on fire until nothing remained but ash.

I couldn't breathe. Couldn't think. The bond was choking me, drowning me, flooding me with red until all that existed was...

Burn. Destroy.Kill.

The bed flipped with a single swing, wood splintering as it crashed into the wall. My claws ripped the lamp off the nightstand, sparks scattering across the floor. My throat tore open with a scream that wasn't fully human. I carved grooves into the drywall, chunks of plaster raining down, a table smashing to pieces against the far wall.

Tears cut hot tracks through the dust and blood on my face as I clawed at my own skull, desperate to rip the fire out, to silence the scream rattling inside me.

"Please!" My voice shredded itself, hoarse, broken. "Fuck!"

Her rage. Her torment. Her everything...it was killing me.

And gods, I knew this was just a fraction of what she lived with every second.

"STOP!"

And then—just as quickly as it came—it was gone.

Silence sat where the storm had been. The absence was so abrupt it consumed me, and I collapsed, knees cracking against the floor. A sound ripped out of me so broken that it took a second to realize it was my own wail.

I clutched my chest, curling in on myself, and for a moment I wasn't Alpha, wasn't wolf, wasn't anything but a boy again. Small, powerless and lost.

The door burst open. The pack flooded in, voices crashing over me in waves. Panic, fear—they'd felt it, the surge through the bond, the violence bleeding into the house. Questions flew fast and frantic, but I couldn't answer them. Couldn't even hear half of what they were saying.

Zaria knelt beside me, her hand landing light on my forearm. Her eyes were unshaken and unbearably calm.

"That's what I'm walking around with, Rafe," she said softly. "Full volume. Every second."

Her voice didn't even shake. But I guarantee that if I'd tried to speak, mine would have.

Her gaze flicked to the others, then back to me. "What if I let it slip in my sleep? What if I wake up craving wolf stew at three a.m.? I can't stay here. Not until I get a handle on this."

Her hand slipped away from my arm, and the loss was instant, a cold that cut deeper than the fire ever had.

"That's why I have to leave." The words landed like stones, heavy and irreversible. "Because I can turn it on, and I can turn it off—but if I stay here, I don't trust myself to keep it sharp. Not with you this close."

Her eyes locked on mine, soft but unflinching.

"I won't risk you," she whispered. Her voice cracked just enough to twist the knife. "I won't risk any of you."

SIX

Marek

"How are we on the Murdock merger, Mason?" Rafe asked as we filed into the conference room, the scrape of chairs and shuffle of papers filling the silence until we all settled.

He looked like hell. Wrinkled suit. Tie loose, like it hadn't been straightened since yesterday. His beard was just long enough to suggest neglect, shadowing the cut of his jaw. Braids down and unkempt. Still the picture of command; but thinner around the edges, like the foundation underneath him was beginning to crack.

It had taken hours to pull him out of the wreckage Zaria had left him in yesterday. Literally hours. He'd torn his quarters apart; shredded furniture, splintered wood, bloodied hands—all from being inside her emotions for minutes. Just minutes. And the pack still wonders why I think she's a threat.

"Good," Mason replied, flipping open his binder with hands just a little too quick. "Legal is finalizing a couple of liability clauses to ensure we aren't held responsible for any negative DOW impacts for the first two years."

Rafe nodded once, ran a hand over his mouth. "Well done."

The words hung in the air.

Mason's head jerked up, startled, eyes wide like he thought he misheard. "Uh...thanks...thank you, sir."

This was no small thing. Rafe Rouxel didn't hand out praise. His philosophy was simple: *do your job, you get to keep it.* That's your reward. A paycheck and continued breathing. But to hear him say *well done* out loud? That was currency. Rare as hell.

And it only underscored the tension winding through the room; because if Rafe was offering compliments, then something was already off balance. And the pack could smell it.

And cue said imbalance as Zaria walks in.

Let me be clear...I'm not "hot for teacher." I've seen beautiful women before. Hell, I've bedded enough of them not to trip over myself now.

Listen...Zaria was beautiful before the change. No doubt about that.

But now? *Holy. Fuck.*

She shifted the gravity of the room when she entered. A skintight white pencil skirt hugged her hips, falling just above her calves. A black sleeveless turtleneck tucked neatly at her waist drew every eye to the curve of her body—slim in the middle, all lush power at her thighs. Her hair was down today, dark curls spilling over her shoulders, catching the light as though it existed just to follow her around.

Otherworldly. That was the word. A creature in mortal skin.

And everyone knew it. The whole room paused. Mason's pen stopped mid-scratch, ink blotting the corner of his notes. Brian blinked too slow, his gaze catching on her and dragging like he'd forgotten how to look away.

And Markus. *Fucking Markus.* The one who always pretended nothing rattled him, straightened in his chair like his spine had just remembered it had bones, then slid a hand low to adjust himself under the table.

The scent gave him away. Thick arousal spiked through the air so fast I almost gagged on it. No way Rafe didn't catch it. Hell, I don't see how he didn't rip Markus's throat out for it right then. Elodie's face said the same thing; her eyes snapped to him, mouth curling, like she was half a second from drawing blood herself. She quickly played it off, considering I'm the only one in the room that knows they fuck around.

I guarantee every woman in the room felt smaller the second she walked in, and every cock twitched whether they wanted it to or not.

She slipped into her usual seat beside Rafe, and that was when the air shifted from thick to unbearable. Their eyes met for a second. And then came the same damn dance it always did; that silent exchange, that exchange of glances that belonged only to them. Not words, but close enough to vows. Like the rest of us were just props in the room they'd built for two.

And right there, in the middle of a conference call about Corporate America bullshit, the reminder sat heavy in my chest: she was the storm, and he was the fool still pretending he could stand in it without being torn apart.

Rafe cleared his throat, trying to officially kick off the meeting, like the world hadn't just shifted around Zaria's silhouette. He straightened, forced command back into his spine, then froze. His gaze snagged on something at the far end of the room.

I leaned forward and followed his line of sight.

Juliette, our mergers and acquisitions manager, was standing stiffly at the back of the room. Her hands trembling at her sides, her eyes locked—not on Rafe, not on the rest of us—but on *Zaria*.

"Juliette?" Rafe's voice cut fast, flicking between her and Zaria. "What is it?"

She swallowed hard, then bowed her head. "I'm so sorry, High Matron."

The words landed like a bomb.

Her hand lifted, trembling but firm, gesturing to two others at the table. "*Stand up*." She whispered.

They rose without hesitation.

Zaria jerks back in her chair, eyes wide. "I'm sorry, what are you... why are you—please, I don't know what's happening." The words tumbled out, broken, almost panicked.

The women moved toward her, one after another, bowing low. The gestures they made were unfamiliar, but there was weight in them. It seemed old, almost ritualistic. Definitely something handed down through bloodlines, not memos.

"Ladies, take your seats," Rafe snapped, voice crisp with authority.

Normally, that Alpha tone would've been enough to slice the air in half, drop every head, and snap every spine into line.

But this time? Nothing.

Juliette stayed bowed. Megan and Delilah waited silent and motionless. His authority cracked against whatever Zaria held inside of her and shattered on impact.

Zaria's eyes flicked up, darting from Rafe to the rest of us, panic threading through each shaky breath. Her chest rose too fast, trembling like she was caught between bolting and breaking.

Finally, hesitant and trembling, she gave the smallest nod.

Only then did the women return to their seats. Like puppets cut loose, they sank back into their seats, stiff but obedient.

Yeah. That wasn't fucking awkward at all. The silence that followed was stifling. A chorus of soft throat clears, a shuffle of papers, every damn one of us pretending we hadn't just watched Rafe's command bounce off them like a blunt knife. No one wanted to meet his eyes. No one wanted to be the unlucky bastard who caught the edge of his temper when it was already bleeding in the room.

And here it was, the part no one else wanted to say out loud: Zaria hadn't asked for this. She looked like prey trapped in the wrong ritual when they bowed to her, like she wanted to crawl out of her own skin. But they bowed anyway. They chose her anyway.

Let me explain the significance of what just happened. These meetings are Rafe's *kingdom.* We don't start until *he* says. We don't interrupt when he speaks. His word is law, his authority absolute. He is the Alpha, the deadly CEO whose reputation alone has kept this empire intact.

And yet—these women didn't just interrupt. They didn't just break protocol. They refused to even sit until *she* gave them permission.

Not Rafe. Not the Alpha.

Zaria.

Like I said... *cue the imbalance.*

Rafe launches back into the agenda, his voice clipped, intense, as if sheer force of will could hammer the meeting back into shape. Pages shuffle, pens scratch, the illusion of order trying to reassert itself.

But my eyes don't leave her.

I'll admit...I gained a lot of respect for her after what went down with Rafe yesterday. The way she blocks the tidal wave of chaos from crushing him. She's carrying it all herself, when the easier thing would be to let it bleed out, drown him, let the rest of us suffer with him. But she doesn't. She holds it. Alone. Never letting it reach him.

Now she sits stiff in her chair, shoulders drawn so tight you'd think she was bracing for a bullet. Nerves sparking so loud I swear I can taste them at the back of my tongue. She reaches for a pen in front of her, hand trembling—then the thing slides off the table and drops clean into her palm, like she reeled it in on an invisible string.

Her mouth falls open. Eyes wide. The whole room freezes with her, every breath caught for a beat too long. Then she slams her jaw shut, curls her fingers tight around the pen, and pulls in one slow, careful breath—like maybe if she just pretends hard enough, she can convince herself it didn't happen.

But then—later, while Rafe drones on about the London properties we're supposedly acquiring next month—her fingers twitch again. And one of his braids slips forward over his shoulder.

He doesn't notice. But the rest of us do.

Her eyes flick around the table—not panicked this time. No. She's goading. There's a smirk cutting across her face as she bites her lip, eyes bright with mischief.

"Brian," Rafe says, flipping open another folder, all business as usual. "Do you have an update on the orals for the RFP with DeLuca & Sons? It's been months since we've touched on that."

Brian opens his mouth to speak. "Yes..."

But then another braid shifts, this time standing straight up like a flagpole. Zaria's grin breaks wide, all teeth.

"Oh, holy hell." Brian coughs hard into his hand, trying to smother the laugh. A couple of others join in, hacking out fake coughs, covering smiles that are splitting their faces open. I drag my hand over my mouth, hiding my own.

She's bouncing her gaze from person to person, practically glowing, that massive ass smile daring us not to laugh while Rafe stays oblivious.

Brian clears his throat again, eyes watering from holding it in. "We have an oral presentation in two weeks. Excuse me." He swallows, takes a quick sip of water. "I'll send you the updates as soon as we have them."

Good save, Brian. Good save.

The corner of my mouth twitches. I shouldn't enjoy this, but gods help me, I do. Watching her stumble in her own power is... *something*. The girl is unraveling in real time, and still so fucking playful. It's dangerous. She has no idea what she is yet, no idea how much she terrifies them, or how much she intrigues me.

And then I feel it...eyes on me.

I shift, slow, and find Simône across the table. Her gaze is fixed on me like she knows exactly what I was thinking, exactly how long I let myself look.

The smirk dies in my throat.

I straighten, sit back in my chair, and drop my gaze to the notepad in front of me. My hand moves, scrawling across the page, words without meaning. Numbers, shapes, fragments of sentences. Anything to make it look like I'm focused anywhere but on Zaria.

Because if Simône saw, who else did? I'm just curious,

because that much fucking power walking around unchecked is not ideal.

The rest of the meeting passes in a blur. None of it sticks. When Rafe finally calls it, he asks Juliette, Megan, and Delilah to stay behind, and for a flicker of a second, I wonder if I'm about to watch him rip their throats out.

Zaria slips out quickly, headed for the kitchen. I drop my things on my desk and follow, coffee cup in hand, not even thinking about it.

She's pacing in front of the machine while it drips, back and forth like a caged animal, too wrapped in her head to notice me. My gut knots. She's gonna tell him...I know it.

"What's wrong with you?"

She jolts like she's been shot, her hands flying up defensively, making my coffee cup explode in my grip, porcelain splitting clean down the middle. A shard drives deep into my palm.

"Goddamn it."

"Fuck. Fuck, I'm sorry, Marek."

Before I can even react, she's on me, snatching the cup out of my hand, setting it hard on the counter. Her fingers wrap around mine, pulling the shard free in one quick motion. Her touch burns like fire, worse than the glass itself, but then—just like that—the wound seals over, smooth, untouched, like it never existed.

She traces the crack in the cup with one trembling finger, and I watch the porcelain knit back together, whole again. She held it out to me, her eyes finally lifting to mine, glassy and uncertain.

"Sorry about that."

The words are too light, too nothing, for what just

happened. I took the cup, but my gaze doesn't leave her. "What's wrong with you, Zaria? You pacing around in here because you're about to run to him?"

Her whole body stiffens, like I just struck her.

"*No*...my friend Sophie just texted and asked if..."

She stops mid-sentence when she glances down and sees my blood smeared across her hand. Her breath catches in a gasp, and she whirls to the sink, scrubbing under the running water like she can scour it away.

My chest tightens, my jaw grinding. "We had an agreement, Zaria." My voice low. "And now you're walking around here like you're ten seconds from spilling every goddamn secret to big Alpha."

Maybe I was off base. *Maybe*. But that little circus act in the conference room had me rattled, left my nerves exposed. I couldn't afford to wonder where her loyalty lined up. I needed to remind her what the stakes were.

I step closer, close enough that she can feel the heat of my anger radiating off me. "You even think about telling him what happened with Deveraux, and you don't just sink me, you sink yourself. Because you knew. You let me live. And I promise you, Leighton, he'll never forgive either of us."

Her shoulders stiffen, jaw tight, and then she spits it out like venom. "Just fuck off, why don't you, Marek."

She turns to go, but instinct overrides reason as I catch her wrist. "I mean it, Zaria." My grip hardens, desperate. "Keep your fucking mouth shut."

She whirls on me. And that's when I see it.

Black veins branching down from her eyes, crawling along her cheeks and throat like cracks in glass. Her irises glow molten gold, lit from within. The air around her hums, bright and electric.

"I already fucking told you," she snarls, her voice laced with something not entirely human. "I won't say anything. *Leave. Me. Alone.*"

My breath catches. "Zaria. Your... your eyes and skin."

For a second she doesn't seem to understand, but then her fingers lift to her face, brushing across the dark veins crawling down her jaw, her throat. Her gaze flicks toward the glass panel of the coffee machine, and she sees what I see.

She gasps, stumbling a step back, and the hum in the air flares, violent and unstable. "Shit."

I take a half-step forward without thinking, but she throws up her hand, warning me off. The power rippling off her is enough to raise the hair on my arms.

"Don't," she hisses, voice shaking now, her earlier fury cutting into panic. "Don't come near me."

I should stop. I should walk away. But I can't tear my eyes off her, can't shake the way my gut knots at the sight—equal parts fear and something else I won't even give voice to.

"Zaria," I say again, lowering my timber. "You're losing control."

Her laugh is bitter, cracked. "You think I don't know that?"

The black veins deepen, crawling further. Her body trembles like she's fighting something that wants to tear its way out from under her skin.

And for the first time since this all started, it hits me; this isn't just fucking dangerous. It's unsustainable.

She yanks her hair forward, curls tumbling over like a curtain to shield her face, chin dropping as if she can hide the veins already spidering under her skin. Then she bolts out of the kitchen and down the hall.

I'm right behind her.

She snatches her purse off her desk, fumbles the strap over her shoulder, moving too fast, too frantic. Rafe's still locked in the conference room, oblivious. Which leaves only me, shadow dogging her all the way to the elevator.

She whirls on me, eyes sharp, feral. "What the fuck do you *want*, Marek? Why are you following me?"

"Why are you losing control?" My pulse is hammering.

"You think this is the safest choice for yourself right now?" she snaps back.

Well, fuck. That's a threat if I ever heard one.

"Just answer the goddamn question, Zaria."

Her breath shudders, breaking on the word when it finally comes: "I'm thirsty." Her tone was laced with panic and fear. "I just need to leave, okay?"

"How far away do you live?"

She blinks, startled. "Ten minutes. Why?"

"Take me to your place," I say evenly. "Then we'll come back after."

Her whole body goes rigid, the fight flaring in her eyes. "No. I'm fine. You can go back to hating my existence and staying the fuck away from me. That works best for both of us."

The elevator dings. The doors slide open. I step in beside her before she can argue.

"What's the alternative here, Leighton? You walk out hungry, half-shifted? Fangs—" I motion to her mouth, where they're already showing. "—fangs flashing, and tear into the first human stupid enough to get in your way? Or you feed safe and controlled. With me. Like you planned to do, anyway."

I ran my hand through my hair, frustrated with the situation.

"Look, I see it now, okay? You're going to hurt someone. Just let's fucking go and get it over with."

Her hands ball into fists at her sides, trembling so hard I can feel the vibration. I can feel her unraveling through the air itself.

"Fine."

"*Jesus.* Thank you." The words grind out of me like gravel. Infuriating, every inch of it.

The drive is short, but it feels endless. The longer it takes, the worse she gets. Her caramel-kissed complexion flushes to a fevered crimson, sweat slick on her throat, her skin shimmering with heat that makes the air inside the car feel too small, too close. She fans herself with her hand, which proves useless. Her breaths coming out shallow and ragged.

By the time we reach her building, she's trembling so violently she can't even get the key into the lock. The metal scrapes, misses, and clatters against the frame. Twice.

"Move," I mutter, closing my hand around hers just long enough to take the keys from her. Her skin scorches against mine.

I unlock the door, and push us inside.

She staggers inside, heading straight for the kitchen. Grabs a glass, fills it, drains it in three gulps like it might douse whatever's burning her alive. Even her skirt has singed from the heat radiating from her skin.

I peel off my shirt, leaving just the black tank clinging to me, and toss it across the back of her couch. My voice is rougher than I want when I speak. "Where do you want me?"

Her eyes flick to mine, wide and frantic, then dart to the

couch.

"Right there's fine." She walks over and stands in front of me. "In Deveraux's memories..." She swallows hard, voice tight. "I just...I need to straddle you. Okay? It's easier that way."

My brow furrows. "Easier?"

"I need control over your wolf. In case he tries to fight back during the feeding."

I let out a humorless huff. "Yeah, because that worked out so well for me the last time I tried to fight you."

She hides her trembling hands behind her back, but I catch it anyway. She doesn't realize how obvious she is, how close she is to shattering.

"Fine," I grit, the word dragged out of me. My body already knows I've lost this argument.

Her relief is almost invisible, just a flicker in her shoulders; but then she steps forward. She places one knee on the couch beside my thigh, lifting her skirt, then the other, then fully climbs onto my lap. The heat coming off her is near unbearable. She keeps her distance at first, thighs bracketing me without letting her weight fall, her trembling hands braced against my shoulders.

It's already too much. Her skin is like touching fire.

Her fingertips graze the side of my neck, light as a test. "Here, okay?"

"Yes." My jaw tightens. "Just fucking do it, Zaria."

She leans in, her curls brushing my face, her breath hot against my skin. I tip my head, exposing my neck further, and then her fangs break through.

Fucking *fuck.*

It's instant. Like a electricity jammed straight into my

veins. The closest thing I can compare it to is that split second before an orgasm—the coil snapping, the rush flooding everything all at once. My toes curl hard inside my boots, my head snapping back against the cushion. My hands claw into the couch, grip so tight the leather creaks under me.

It's not just my neck. I feel it *everywhere.* A surge that races down my spine, sets every nerve alight, thrums through my chest like I've been cracked open and poured full of fire.

SEVEN

Zaria

The moment his blood hits my tongue, the world detonates.

Oh, fuck.

It's hot and sweet and so goddamn potent I almost jerk back in shock. This is wolf's blood. Not the stale metallic sludge I choked down from a seedy hotel bag. This is alive. Like lightning in my veins.

The taste floods me with fire and sugar, molten and wild, tearing me apart and stitching me together in the same breath. Nothing I've ever tasted as a human or this, nothing could ever come close.

I release him with a gasp, lips slick with red, breath ghosting across his throat.

"Fuckkk, that's good," I breathe, words spilling unfiltered into the heat between us.

My eyes drag up instinctively; his fair skin, kissed with scars and shadow, the strong line of his jaw bristled in stubble. His chest heaves under the snug black tank, fabric stretched taut over shoulders built like stone. And those eyes—gods, those green eyes—staring down at me like he's split between fury and surrender.

Then, I sink back in.

The rush hits harder, doubling me over. Every nerve sings, buzzing like I've been wired into a storm. The itch under my skin? Gone. The burn in my chest? Snuffed. For the first time since this curse began, I feel whole.

Marek growls low, the sound rumbling out of his chest and vibrating straight into my pussy that's growing wetter by the second. His back is iron beneath my hand, stable even as he shudders.

Memories slam into me; Deveraux feeding, victims writhing in his lap, his orgasm tangled with theirs before their deaths, and my stomach twists.

Fuck. His blood isn't just feeding me; it's drugging me. Desire, spiked and brutal, coils low.

And then the veil drops.

His thoughts bleed into mine, so jagged and desperate.

What's happening?

The panic isn't mine. It's his.

Fuck, I feel like I'm gonna come.

A moan tears free against his throat, my hips grinding down before I can stop them. His head snaps back, baring his neck further, and the scent of him—iron, cedar, a hint of sweat—hits me like a second intoxication.

How is this happening?

His voice snarls through my skull, fractured, hungry, and it ruptures something inside me.

His arousal slams through me, molten, igniting every nerve. My hunger warps, mutates, until I can't tell where the need for blood ends and the need for him begins. And it loops—my arousal flooding back into him, amplifying, doubling—until we're both drowning in it.

This isn't supposed to feel like this. Feeding is supposed to be about survival. Transactional.

But my fangs stay buried, locked deep, and my body betrays me. My hand fists in his hair, yanking his head back as I suck harder, grinding into his lap like the two hungers can't be separated anymore.

His moans grow heavier, chest rising like he's fighting the tide, but every roll of my hips drags another sound out of him. He hisses through clenched teeth, the vibration shuddering against my lips. A moan rips out of me into his skin, crude and shameless.

I can feel her. Fuck, I can feel her everywhere. I've never felt anything like this. I'm gonna come. I can't—

The harder he fights it, the sharper his pulse crashes against my tongue, dragging me deeper, burning me whole.

And then it shifts.

His hips start to thrust up into me, desperation breaking through his control. The movement collides with mine until it feels like sex, like torment, like we're locked in a rhythm that shouldn't exist but does.

Yes—fuck, grind harder, Zaria. Don't stop. Goddamn, you feel amazing.

That thought rips through me like a climax, detonating low in my belly, and I tear myself off him with a choked gasp. My fangs retract, blood dripping down my chin as I stumble back, pulse thrumming like I've just been torn out of a fever dream.

My breaths come in ragged gasps. His eyes are heavy-lidded, glazed, his chest rising and falling too fast. For a moment, our gazes lock, and it feels like a confession neither of us asked to share.

"Uh... thanks. Thank you." The words come fractured, nonsense, but they're all I have.

I bolt for the bathroom, slam the door, and catch my reflection in the mirror. Blood streaks my mouth, smearing across my chin. My curls cling damp to my temples, my skin flushed, my pupils blown wide and predatory, hunger still glittering in my eyes like something that doesn't belong to me.

I scrub my face, strip off my shirt, fling it into the hamper like I can throw the shame away with it. But it doesn't matter.

The connection's still there. His thoughts are still pouring into me, like waves crashing against the shore.

What the fuck was that? I'm so hard. Why did that make me hard? Fucking repulsive.

And gods help me—my stomach twists—because I feel the same.

I soak a towel with warm water, wring it out, and force my legs to carry me back into the room. He's still sitting where I left him, broad shoulders slumped, chest heaving, his green eyes unfocused like he's come back from war and isn't sure which side he was on. The scent of his arousal pours off of him in waves, thick and heady, impossible to ignore.

I kneel in front of him, close enough to feel the heat radiating off his body. His hands rest on his knees, fists clenched tight, and when I lean forward with the towel, he tips his head without a word, giving me his throat. The trust—or maybe the surrender—nearly undoes me.

I clean carefully, wiping the blood from his skin in slow strokes until the red is gone, replaced with the pale, unmarked curve of his neck. His pulse thrums strong beneath my fingers, but the air is deafening. Louder than any growl. He keeps his eyes on me, unblinking, and the weight of it is worse than the silence itself.

"Are you okay?" I whisper once there's no more trace of blood left to distract me.

"I'm fine." His voice is clipped and angry. He doesn't move, doesn't soften. "You got what you needed. You don't need to ask me that."

The words cut harsher than the venom ever could.

I swallow hard, lowering the towel to my lap. My voice shrinks against the weight of him. "Can I get you anything? Water? Anything?"

"No." He spat. "How often do you need to do this? I have a fucking life, you know."

The sting makes me flinch, but I force myself to answer. "I can do bags. This was just... a delicate situation today, I guess."

"Do you have bags?"

"No."

"Do you know where to get them?"

I shake my head, frustration pinching at my chest. "No. I only got one from that hotel. I was going to go back, maybe ask one of the Bloodeds there for help. It's not like I know what I'm doing with any of this."

He shakes his head, running his hand through his hair; fury laced in his tone. "Don't fucking go back to that place. I'm surprised you didn't get yourself killed the first time." His jaw locks tight, muscles flexing. Then, softer but no less commanding: "I'll just meet you here. In the mornings. Before work. Does that work for you?"

I blink, caught between his scolding and the offer beneath it. He's so fucking mercurial; burning me one second, binding me the next.

"Why would you even offer?" I whisper, voice cracking at the edges.

He just stares at me, green eyes even, unreadable; like maybe he's asking himself the same damn question.

Finally, his jaw ticks. "We had a deal. I'm a man of my goddamn word, Zaria."

He snatches his shirt from the back of the chair, shoving his arms through the sleeves like he can bury himself in the fabric, hide whatever just happened between us under black cotton. The movement is quick, efficient, soldier-clean, but I see the tremor in his hands.

"Can we fucking go now?" His voice slices through the air. "The veins are gone and you look better, so there's no reason to still be here."

Better. As if that's all this was. A fix. A patch job. Nothing more.

I clutch the towel in my lap until my knuckles ache, swallowing back the retort burning on my tongue.

Then it hits me; I'm still only in my cami, the thin straps falling off my shoulders after I tossed my blouse into the hamper. Barely anything between me and the chill of the room, barely anything between me and him. My nipples are tight, hard peaks straining against the fabric, not just from the air but from the goddamn aftershock still sparking through my body.

"I need to grab another shirt," I murmur, my voice thinner than I want it to be.

His gaze flicks down, fast as a strike. But I catch it—the flash of green darkening, the intense flare of hunger before he jerks it back under control.

His jaw locks, his shoulders tense, and when he finally

speaks, his voice is raspy. "I'll meet you in the car. Just fucking hurry up, I got shit to do."

And then he's gone, storming toward the door, leaving the air colder in his wake.

EIGHT

Rafe

"So, I hear our Zaria is officially a Blooded. That didn't take long. How is she holding up?"

Vanessa doesn't wait for an invitation. She just slips into the chair across from me, laying a manilla folder on my desk.

I lean back, rubbing a hand over my jaw. "I don't really know, to be honest. She seems... *okay*. But she's just getting her footing." It's the best answer I've got, and even that feels like a stretch.

Vanessa nods once, then flips the folder open. "I had a discussion with Juliette, Delilah, and Megan." Her eyes cut to mine, pointed. "You can't *fire* them for what happened in the boardroom. Not for interrupting you, not for disobeying an order. That's grounds for a lawsuit."

My mouth tightens. "They disrespected me. In front of the entire room."

"They acknowledged the High Matron," she corrects smoothly. "That's not the same as disobedience. Legally, they'll argue religious freedom, cultural recognition, whatever they have to. And they'll win, Rafe. Publicly."

Publicly.

Vanessa leans in, her nails tapping once against the folder. "I'm not telling you to let it slide. I'm telling you to be strategic. You've built LeRoux on discipline and fear. If you start swinging at this the wrong way, it won't be Zaria that topples you; it'll be your own people."

"Fuck." I run a hand through my braids. "Then what now?"

"Nothing for you to do. I've already let them know their jobs are safe. You *have* to run terminations by me, Rafe. They need to be legit, not because your ego's bruised when someone outshines you."

"The hell?" My eyes narrow. "That's bold."

Vanessa doesn't flinch. She leans back in the chair like she's settling in for a sparring match. "It's not bold, Rafe. It's my job. You pay me to keep this company bulletproof, not to stroke your ego. And right now, your ego is the liability."

The words grate like gravel down my spine. Nobody talks to me like this. Nobody *gets to.*

"You forget yourself," I say, lowering my timber to Alpha.

"Look, Rafe. Yes, you're Mr. Big Bad. And yes, typically I am afraid of you—*as we all are.* But you brought me here for a reason. If you want me to do my job, then let me *do* it. Intimidation doesn't scare me into incompetence." She folds her hands neatly over the folder, eyes unwavering. "I remember exactly who I am. And I remember who you are, too—the ruthless Alpha who built LeRoux brick by bloody brick. But tell me, Rafe—" she tilts her chin toward the conference room doors, "—what does it say when your own people kneel to someone else in front of you? If you fire them, you look weak. If you lash out, you look threatened. The only way to win this game is to lean into it. Use it. Spin it until it looks like it was always your play."

I hate her.

Vanessa smooths her hand down her skirt and rises from the chair. "I'll handle them. You focus on keeping the High Matron from unraveling in public. That's where the real danger lies. And Rafe?"

I lift my eyes to hers, the weight of her words coiling tighter in my chest.

"You should start asking yourself if you're more afraid of her power, or of how much of it she has now."

Then she leaves me with that truth sitting on my desk, heavier than the folder she carried in, and for a long moment I just sit there, staring at nothing, Vanessa's words echoing in my head.

I sink back into my chair, rub both hands over my face, and reach for my phone when a notification pings.

Pack Chat

Marek: Headed home for the day.

Simône: Why?

Marek: I don't need a fucking reason. I'm going home.

Rafe: You've been so damn pissy lately. What's up with you?

Markus: I second that.

Elodie: Yup. Moody Man Marek.

Markus: Good one, Elle.

Marek has left the group chat

Simône added Marek to the group chat

Marek: Fuck right off, Simône.

I snort despite myself, the sound subtle in the empty office. The group chat always bleeds chaos, but today the edge is different. Marek's fuse is shorter than I've ever seen it, and the rest of them are circling like wolves that smell blood.

Vanessa's words roll back through me like gravel: *Afraid of her power, or of how much of it she has now?*

And, gods help me, I still couldn't decide which terrified me more—that Zaria was unraveling, or that Marek was unraveling right alongside her.

When she walked back into the office, I felt it like a pull in my chest. The instinct to go to her, to close the space between us, was immediate. But I didn't move. We hadn't spoken since she left yesterday, and the quiet between us had grown jagged. Knowing what she carried now—knowing she could have me on my knees with a whisper—scared the fuck out of me.

What if one day she decided I was her enemy? What if it was Simône, or Markus, or anyone in my pack?

I still didn't know what this rage was she held for Marek. I'd asked him last night, but he gave me some evasive, half-assed answer about her not liking how mean he was. I knew it was a lie. But I didn't press. Truth was, he'd been a dick to her since day one, so she had every right to hate him.

I just didn't know where to go from here.

She passed by my office window, offering the smallest smile—soft, careful, like she wasn't sure I'd take it. She didn't step inside, and I didn't go after her.

And in that moment, it hit me how far apart we'd drifted. Same building. Same bond. Same storm tying us together. But gods, it felt like we were worlds apart.

I picked up my phone and reached out to the only person who might have answers.

Rafe: *Elowen. Sorry to contact you here, but it's urgent. What do you know about High Matrons?*

Elowen: *Plenty, Alpha. What's your real question?*

Rafe: Can you bind one, if the need arose?

Elowen: ...I would need to meet her. There have been rumblings.

My jaw tightened, thumb hesitating before I typed again.

Rafe: She's here. With us. The amount of power she's carrying, Elowen — it's... concerning. It may be best you come to the manor as soon as you're able. To witness it for yourself.

The pause stretched long enough that I felt the weight of her deliberation on the other end.

Elowen: There are risks. Binding a High Matron should be done before her power manifests. Doing so after... could kill her.

The words burned cold in my chest.

Kill her.

A smarter man would have stopped there. Closed the conversation. Pretended I never sent the message in the first place.

But the truth was a rot already spreading under my skin. I was afraid of her. Afraid of what she was becoming, of how much power over me she already held in her hands. Afraid that one day she'd decide I wasn't worth saving. That the bond between us wouldn't be love, but a leash.

And fear, I'd learned, was poison to an Alpha. It made you weak. It made you reckless. I closed my eyes, jaw grinding until it ached, and typed the word anyway.

Rafe: Yes. Come.

NINE

Marek

I wish I could tell you what the fuck happened in Zaria's apartment. Truth is, I don't know.

I don't want to fuck her. It's not like that. Not even a little. It's not that she isn't beautiful; she is, painfully so. But that's not it. She's... human. Or she *was*. Fuck if I know anymore. Either way, that isn't what this is.

Her feeding from me was a means to an end. Transactional. A quid pro quo to keep me from losing the only friendship, the only brotherhood, that's ever mattered. I let my anger run hot, tried to scare her off, and now I'm left knee-deep in the wreckage that came after.

The bite stung, sure; but not like I expected. What I didn't see coming was her climbing onto my lap. At the time, I told myself it was better than the bed. Because the bed would've been too much. Too intimate.

And then the shit shifted. She moaned. Fucking moaned, like my blood was getting her off, and I swear it lit up every dark corner of me. I didn't need that. Didn't need to know what she sounds like when she's turned on. Because now it's all I fucking hear. Every time I close my eyes, every time I try to think straight, it's her. That sound.

Her hands clutched at me. She ground down against me, slow at first, then sharper, snapping her hips over my cock with nothing between us but her panties and the thin barrier of my clothes. And yeah, I got hard. Of course I did. Any man would've. That's biology, not desire. It didn't mean a goddamn thing.

But gods—she's so fucking powerful. More powerful than any of us. At the hotel she laughed at my anger, mocked it. Tossed me aside like I was nothing. One flick of her wrist and I was airborne. One snap of her fingers and I was stripped bare, human again.

She's a force I never saw coming. And part of me...hell, most of me was impressed. Not terrified in the way that makes you run. Terrified in the way that drags you closer, just to see if you survive the fire.

That doesn't mean anything either.

And it sure as hell doesn't mean anything that I took the rest of the day off, came home, to stand under the shower with my forehead against the tile, fist around my cock, replaying every second like it was branded into me.

The way her hips rolled at first, smooth, fluid, like water. Then snapped hard, piston-quick, grinding down until I was one second from losing it in my fucking pants. The way her body shook the instant her teeth sank in. The way she smelled—sweet and salty, nothing but pure arousal.

The exact moment my cock dragged against her through our clothes, friction so hot it nearly broke me right there. And then she ground again. And again. And again. Until—

"Fuckkkkk."

The sound tears out of me as I come in white-hot spurts

across my fist, scalding in its honesty.

I grit my teeth, chest heaving, water pounding down, washing away the mess even as the shame clings to my skin like it belongs there. I squeezed my eyes shut, jaw tight, the same words echoing in my skull like a curse.

It didn't mean anything.

It doesn't mean anything.

I barely remember crawling into bed. Didn't even bother pulling on clothes after the shower; just collapsed, damp and cold, the sheets sticking to my skin.

When my phone buzzed, the red glow of the clock read 7 p.m. I blinked blearily at the screen, and my chest went tight.

Zaria: *Sorry to bother you, Marek. Can you come by?*

The next message stopped my breath cold. It was a photo snapped in the bathroom mirror. Her half-shifted, veins crawling black under caramel skin, eyes golden, black already threading through.

My thumbs moved before my brain caught up.

Marek: *Yeah. Be there in 20.*

I typed out another — *Are you ok? Do you need me to bring you anything?*

The fuck?

I stared at the text until my throat ached, then backspaced every word.

Marek: *Also, you can't fucking text me in the middle of the evening and expect me to drop everything and run to you. I'll do it this time, but figure out a fucking plan on your own when I'm not there.*

The three dots blinked once, then disappeared. No reply.

I tossed the phone on the nightstand and dragged a hand down my face, but the image of her—half-shifted, trembling, *asking for me*—burned behind my eyes.

I was already on my feet, grabbing the first pair of shorts I could find, pulling a black tank over my head. Keys. Wallet. Sandals. Door slamming shut behind me before I could talk myself down.

Luckily, her place wasn't far. A ten-minute drive, maybe fifteen if traffic hit wrong. *Not lucky,* I corrected myself, jaw tight as I slid behind the wheel. Just... *convenient.* Convenient that I didn't have to drive all goddamn night to get to her. That was all.

By the time I hit her building and started up the stairwell, I could already hear soft and rhythmic knocking. Not frantic, but insistent.

"Miss Leighton, I won't tell a soul. I swear it. Are you okay?" *Knock knock.* "Miss Leighton?"

I rounded the corner, teeth bared before my brain caught up. Some middle-aged man stood at her door, knocking like a goddamn metronome. His posture was nervous, shoulders hunched, and there was a fresh bandage around his hand. The guy looked like he'd just crawled out of a grave.

The growl tore out of me before I decided on it. "Who the *fuck* are you, and why are you knocking on her door?"

He flinched back instantly, pressing himself against the stairwell railing when he got a good look at me. Smaller frame, streaks of gray in his hair, eyes wide as a spooked rabbit. He jabbed a shaky finger toward Zaria's door.

"She...uh...Miss Leighton helped me. I'm security here, and I cut my hand—some little punk tried to mug me outside, pulled a knife. She bandaged me up. But the blood—" he swallowed, throat working, "—I think it made her sick. I'm just checking on her."

I dragged a hand through my hair, muttering a curse under my breath. "Fuck."

His bandaged hand trembled against his chest, and I saw the way his eyes kept darting back to the door. Whatever he'd seen in her when she smelled that blood...it rattled him.

"Did they catch the fucker?" I asked, softer now, but still clipped.

"No, he ran off. Miss Leighton heard me yelling, came down, and—" his brows pinched, confusion tugging at his voice, "—I don't know how she heard me from four floors up."

I bit back another curse. Yeah. I knew exactly how.

"I've got her," I said firmly, stepping closer, putting my body between him and the door. "You need anything? Otherwise, head on home. If management gives you grief for leaving early, let Miss Leighton know and I'll deal with them."

He nodded too quickly, relief washing over his face like I'd just pardoned him.

"What's your name?" I asked.

"Art. Arthur. I'd offer a hand but..." He lifted his bandaged palm, sheepish.

"Listen, Art." I let the weight settle into my tone. "Whatever you saw, *or didn't see*, tonight? It stays in this stairwell. You feel me?"

"Not a word," he promised quickly. "All I know is Miss Leighton wasn't feeling good. That's all I know."

"Good man. Go on home."

He muttered a quiet thank you and disappeared down the stairwell, footsteps echoing quick, eager to be gone.

Now it was just me. The hallway. And the weight of her

behind that door.

I set my palm flat against the wood. "He's gone, Zaria," I said low, knowing she was right there on the other side.

The lock clicked. The door eased open.

And she stood there trembling, tears carving hot streaks down her face. Fully shifted and ghostly.

Fuck me, even like this, she was gorgeous. It pissed me off just looking at her.

She had on this thin little slip of a near sheer dress, nothing but straps holding it up, hanging loose past her knees. The kind of thing you wear when you're home alone, when you don't think anyone's gonna see you. No bra either—because of course not—and her nipples were right there, tight against the fabric. Perfect. Distracting. Infuriating.

Does she not fucking realize her effect on the male species? Goddamn it.

I clenched my jaw, forced my eyes higher, but the damage was done. Burned into me. Now I had to live with it.

"He won't say anything," I muttered, stepping inside, letting the door shut heavy behind me.

"Thanks." Her voice broke on the word, a sob riding through it. "I'll get the bags in the morning. I... I found a guy to help."

For fuck's sake. My jaw tightened. We'll circle back to that disaster waiting to happen.

"We'll talk about that after you've fed." I moved toward the couch, dropping onto it with the expectation she'd climb into my lap like before. But this time she sat beside me instead. Close. Her hand wrapped around my wrist.

"We can do it this way."

Her grip was trembling. I studied her, pulse drumming,

every instinct telling me not to question when she was this close to the edge. "Will you get what you need that way?"

"Yes."

A beat stretched between us.

"Okay."

Her grip tightened, and then she bit down.

Pain ripped through my wrist, white-hot and jagged. I can handle pain; hell, I've lived in it. But this? This was different. It wasn't the sharp sting from before—it was deeper, rougher, like her teeth were cutting into more than flesh.

I hissed between clenched teeth, biting back the curse on my tongue. There was no connection this time. No rush of arousal, or pull straight to my cock, thank every goddamn star in the sky. Just pain. And a strange...*emptiness.*

Her pulls were tentative, shallow, like she was afraid to take. Barely sipping. Barely trusting herself.

"Zaria?"

Her eyes flicked up, wide and uncertain.

"What is this?"

Her brows pulled tight, confusion flashing across her face. "What do you mean?" She wiped her mouth with the back of her trembling hand, smearing blood across her skin.

"Your veins are barely fading," I growled. "Why the fuck are you doing it this way? You're not getting what you need."

"It's fine," she whispered. "This way is better."

"Better?" I barked out a humorless laugh. "You're starving yourself."

"I said it's fine."

"Fucking hell..." My patience snapped. I grabbed her waist and hauled her onto my lap.

Her petite, perfect little body pressed against me.

Goddamn it. Get a grip.

"Just drink, Zaria. I don't have all goddamn night to play this timid bullshit."

"Why do you have to be this way about it, Marek? I didn't ask for..."

Her voice cracked on the last word, and she sagged, the fight bleeding out of her shoulders. She sighed, tears threatening again, and shook her head. She started to push off my lap, already retreating. "Never mind—"

"Don't." The word tore out of me harsher than I planned, my hand tightening at her hip, keeping her anchored in place. My chest burned, my pulse hammering where her body pressed flush to mine.

She froze, her glare cutting into me, molten hazel daring me to let her go. But then, something inside her cracked.

The sound she made wasn't just anger. It was grief, fury, wreckage all tangled together. And before I could shape another word—

Her fangs sank into my neck.

Searing pain lit me up, stealing the air from my lungs. My hiss ripped out of me raw, my fists knotting hard at her waist.

"Fuck..."

My head snapped back, breath tearing in gasps, every nerve alive with the fire she poured into me.

TEN

Zaria

I don't know why I didn't fight him off. When he yanked me onto his lap, when his hand clamped my waist and he snarled at me to drink; I should've shoved him away, walked him out the door, slammed it in his face. But I didn't.

Because the truth is, taking his blood this way feeds something deeper than hunger. Something filthier than thirst. I should've gone for his wrist again and been fine, bought myself a few hours of quiet. I was afraid—terrified—because the last time, I barely managed to stop. There was this gnawing urge to drain him dry, to drink until his heartbeat faltered beneath me, until the fight left his body.

And the worst part? The arousal of it. The way his body had bucked beneath mine, the edge of his climax threading into me through his veins. It was intoxicating. Better than any high I'd chased in my reckless college years. The most addicting fucking feeling I've ever known. And he pissed me off. So, I did what he said.

Now I'm too far gone. My hips grind harder, rougher, matching the rhythm of his pulse. My moans break ragged against his skin as his blood floods my tongue—hot, sweet, thick, laced with his arousal until it's all I can taste, all I can breathe.

His thoughts batter me, erratic and wild since the veil dropped. He's holding back physically, fists planted at his sides, but in my head he's unchained.

Fuck, you're perfect. Just like that. This fucking body. Gods, it's fucking addicting.

The words ignite every nerve. I sink deeper, grinding harder, chasing the edge with no thought left for control.

No...no, I'm gonna come. Fuck. This is sick. So fucking sick.

His head snaps back, a husky growl ripping from his chest, and then he breaks—his orgasm tearing through him, and through me with it. The taste shifts instantly, intense and magnetic, his release flooding me like fire, dragging me under.

I cry out against his neck, the sound half moan, half sob, as my own climax crashes—violent, shredding. Every muscle locks, pleasure ripping me open until I'm trembling in his lap, lost in the feedback loop where I can't tell if I'm feeding on him or if he's consuming me. Both. Everything.

When the last wave finally ebbs, I tear my mouth free, gasping, blood slick on my lips. He's drenched in sweat, chest heaving, eyes squeezed shut like refusing to look at me might erase what just happened.

The silence is deafening.

"Get the fuck off me."

What?

His tone was so cold, nothing like the thoughts that had just snared through me. My body goes rigid. Shame crawls under my skin as I slide off his lap, wiping at my mouth.

He doesn't move right away. His fists are still clenched, his cock straining, the damp spot on his grey shorts undeniable proof of what we'd both just torn out of each other. Heat twists in my gut, humiliation burning hotter than hunger ever could.

Finally, he sucks in a jagged breath and stands, still not looking at me. "I don't know what kind of fucking vampire-matron bullshit you just pulled," he grits out, voice thick with fury—or fear; they smell too much alike. "But the deal is off."

He shoulders past me toward the door. "That will *never* fucking happen again."

"I didn't—" My head shakes, desperate. "I didn't do anything. I didn't cause it."

"Bullshit." He whirls, nose-to-nose with me, snarling. "Bullshit."

His eyes rake mine, then drop to my mouth, then my breasts, his chest heaving. "You're a fucking vulture, you know that? A pathetic, sick nightcrawler getting your pussy wet off wolf blood. Stay out of my head, Zaria. And stay the *fuck* away from my pack."

Then he rips the door open, slamming it so hard the windowpane behind me shatters.

I stand there in the aftermath for what feels like an hour. My body won't move. Tears streak hot and endless, shoulders slumping under the weight of it.

I'll always be this monster. No matter how much I hold back, no matter how much I try to be the same Zaria—they'll never see me that way again. I should've stopped. But, gods help me, I don't think I could have.

***

It didn't even register that I'd gotten into my car, let alone driven the three-plus hours, until the tires crunched onto the familiar gravel drive of my parents' house. My hands were stiff on the steering wheel, my face sticky with dried tears, but my body moved on autopilot. Before I could think better of it, I was out of the car, bare feet pounding across the path, fists slamming against the front door like a child begging to be let in from the storm.

I needed someone. *Anyone.* Someone who could still see me...just me. Not the monster. Not the Matron. Not the mistake.

The door cracked open, and Mama's face appeared in the sliver of light.

That was all it took. My chest caved, the sob tearing loose like something that had been waiting days to escape.

"Mama."

For a heartbeat, I swore she might pull me into her arms. Her hand flexed on the frame; her lips parted like a prayer was about to fall. But then her eyes changed, darkening, shuttering. And whatever fragile hope I had collapsed right there on the porch.

You ain't s'pose to be here," she whispered, her tone was more cold than angry. "Go on, bébé. Go on back now. Dis house ain't yours no more'."

The words hit harder than claws. Harder than Deveraux's teeth. My knees buckled, gravel grinding under them as if the earth itself wanted to remind me I wasn't welcome anywhere.

"What? No...Mama, it's me. *It's still me—*" The words stumbled out, wrecked and useless.

Her chin trembled, but she shook her head, curls shifting across her cheek. Still, her eyes wouldn't meet mine. "Non, bébé. Whatever dat is... it ain't you. Not no more."

"Mama, *please*." My hand lifted before I could stop it, reaching for hers like a child, desperate for that old safety. But when my fingertips brushed the air between us, the seal around the house vibrated like struck glass; and the realization split through me like lightning.

I wasn't invited in.

I couldn't cross the barrier. Not even my hand.

My home.

The sound I made wasn't human.

From deeper in the house, I heard Daddy's voice, muffled. "Claudine? Who is it?"

She didn't answer. Didn't dare. Her hand clamped tighter on the doorframe, her jaw steeling as her eyes finally found mine. And gods, I wished she hadn't looked at me at all. Because what I saw there wasn't anger. It was pure fear.

"You got your Alpha now," she whispered. "You got your pack. Das where you belong. Not here. Not wit' us."

And with that, she closed the door. Just a slow, measured closing, like she was laying me in a grave. Maybe she was.

The latch clicked. And I broke.

The porch boards caught my weight as I crumpled, gravel biting through my knees, tears spilling down so fast I couldn't even wipe them away. My fists hit the wood, once, twice, the sound swallowed by the stillness of a house that would never be mine again.

ELEVEN

Rafe

The floor slammed against my spine, or maybe I was the one slamming against it; I couldn't tell. My body convulsed, jerking so violently I couldn't control where I ended, and the ground began.

"Hold him down!" someone barked.

Hands clamped onto my arms, my shoulders, but it was like trying to chain lightning. My muscles tore against them, snapping, thrashing.

"We're fucking trying!" another voice grunted.

The air cracked with the sound of bone against bone. A piercing cry. "Shit, he kicked me in the nose! Motherfucker!"

I tried to speak, tried to force words through the roar in my chest, but all that came was a feral growl, dragging itself out of me like it belonged to something else.

"What's happening to him?" A woman's voice—Simône? Trembling, panicked.

"I don't fucking know, Simône!"

It burned. Gods, it burned. Every vein in my body felt like

it had been filled with fire, every nerve ending open and screaming. I could feel my claws itching beneath my skin, my teeth aching, my body tearing itself apart from the inside out.

"He's shifting!" someone shouted.

The words rang true. Too true. My body wasn't listening to me anymore; it was choosing for me. Splitting me open, remaking me.

"Grab his legs, get him to the corridor!"

And then the dark came rushing in. A tide so thick and absolute it swallowed every sound, every voice, every hand that tried to hold me.

Darkness.

But not empty.

I can see her. *Zaria.*

She's caught in the heart of a storm; wind screaming, dirt and debris spiraling around her in a violent funnel. She's on her knees in front of a house, her hair whipping wildly across her face. The ground cracks under her palms like the earth itself is afraid of her.

"Zaria!" My voice rips out of me, coarse, carried into the squall. I try to run, but my feet keep sliding back, like the storm itself is pushing me away. "Zaria!"

She doesn't look up at first. She's crumpled, shaking, and the sound of her sobbing cuts harder than the wind.

"Zaria, look at me!" I fight forward, every step a battle, claws scraping against invisible ground. The air tastes like blood and fire, copper and ash. My lungs burn, but I don't stop.

Finally, her head lifts. Her eyes are wide and glowing.

Behind her, the house looms. Old wood, a porch sagging under years of memory. And in the doorway—two figures.

Claudine. Bernard.

Her parents.

And they're turning their backs on her.

"No!" The word tears from me like claws across glass. "No, Zaria. Don't you fucking let them leave you!"

The funnel tightens. Her scream tears out, and it's not just sound, it's a blade. It slices through me, drives me to my knees. My skull feels like it's splitting open, my claws tearing at nothing just to hold myself together.

The voices bleed in; distant but inside me, the pack shouting over the storm.

"He's breaking through!"

"It won't hold!"

"He's gonna kill someone if he gets out!"

"Zaria!" My own roar drowns theirs. I fight forward, every muscle straining, until she looks at me. Finally, her gaze meets mine.

But it isn't her.

It's something else staring out through her face. Golden, endless, furious.

And then her mouth opens, wider than sound, and the word slams through me, not spoken but commanded.

"LEEEEAAAAVVVVEEEE"

It explodes inside me. Fire, force, violence ripping through every nerve. I'm hurled back, out of the storm, out of her, out of the dark.

The world reassembles in a crash.

I hit the manor wall so hard the stone cracked, claws dug into the floor, hybrid form had ripped through my skin. My chest heaves, my vision is white with bloodlust, and beyond the bars of the corridor I see the pack. Their faces pale, eyes wide, fear written across every line.

"Alpha—"

"Rafe, control it—"

"Rafe, it's us!"

I drag air into my lungs, forcing it past the beast clawing at the cage. Every breath is fire, every muscle screams to tear, to burn, to kill. Slowly and painfully, I force it down, skin peeling back into human.

But her voice doesn't leave.

Her scream, her rage, her command; it's still there, echoing in my skull like shrapnel that won't stop tearing.

"Zaria." Her name rips from me on a ragged breath as my knees hit the floor. My skin feels like it's on fire, like every vein is blistered open. The bond had been wide; fully fucking open, and it shredded me from the inside out. And then, just as fast, it was gone. Shut tight. Locked me out completely.

"She's at her parents," I rasp, dragging air into my lungs like I've been drowning. "Something's wrong. She's in pain."

"You can't go anywhere right now, Rafe," Simône's voice snaps fast from the other side of the bars. "We're not opening this until we know you're settled."

"No." My head jerks up, sweat dripping into my eyes. "Don't open it. Not tonight. Someone else, go. Now."

"I'll go," Marek cuts in without hesitation. He's already moving, boots pounding the corridor. "Somebody text me the address!" Then he was gone before anyone could say more.

"What the hell just happened?" Simône's voice cracks, panic threading through it as she presses closer to the barrier.

"Rafe, what's going on?"

"The bond," I grit out, clutching my chest, feeling the phantom tear of her emotions still clawing at me. "It was open. Wide open. She's in pain, and she doesn't even realize it opened."

The words taste like blood and truth, and the hush that follows is laced with the weight of all the things I'm not saying: if she's unraveling this bad, if the bond can pull me under like that, none of us are ready for what's coming.

Markus hasn't moved, just standing there with Elodie curled into his shoulder, her quiet sobs muffled against him. Neither of them has spoken since it started. Since I came apart.

My breath finally starts to center, each inhale less jagged than the last. I shift back against the wall, muscles still twitching with the phantom aftershocks, and drag a scrap of clothing over my body; some semblance of dignity against their eyes, even if it's pointless now.

The stone at my back is cold, grounding, but my head tips against it all the same, heavy with exhaustion.

"I felt like I was dying." The words scrape out of me bitter, torn. "She's so fucking powerful. She's three and a half hours away, and she just pulled my Lycavor straight out of my skin."

Elodie's sobs taper into shuddered breaths, Markus' jaw tightening as he presses his lips to the top of her head. Neither argues. Neither denies it.

Because they felt it too.

The weight of it hangs in the air, pressing down on all of us until it feels unbearable.

"We need Elowen."

"I was just thinking the same thing." Markus exhales through his nose, a slow, weary sigh that says more than words—about how deep this goes, how far out of our depth we already are.

Elodie lifts her head from his shoulder, eyes reddened and wet. She doesn't say it, doesn't need to. We're all on the same page: Zaria's storm is bigger than any of us. Bigger than me. And if Elowen can't help...

Then there may not be anyone who can.

TWELVE

Marek

I don't know what I thought I'd find when I drove out here. Maybe Zaria pacing trenches in the dirt, maybe the porch torn apart under her rage. Hell, maybe nothing at all. But not this.

Zaria's crumpled on the porch like she belongs to the earth itself, curled in on herself like a child who's been left out in the cold. Fetal position. Shaking. Gravel jittering around her with every sob, vibrating harder each time her chest heaves. Her fingers trace frantic little circles into the dirt, over and over, manic, aimless.

And me? Fuck if I know why I volunteered to come. My mouth got ahead of my brain, like something shoved me forward before I could stop it. And now here I am, staring at the most terrifying thing I've ever seen: her broken.

I kill the engine and step out. Boots crunch against gravel, loud in the quiet night. I move slow, hands raised like I'm approaching a wild animal that could rip me apart. Which—let's be honest—she damn well could.

The cold bites hard, my breath fogging in the air. She's curled on the ground, still in that flimsy excuse for a dress from earlier, the thin fabric clinging, riding up so far I can practically see her bare ass. It's forty degrees, and she's damn near naked, trembling in the dirt.

I shrug off my jacket, ready to drape it over her shoulders, ready to give her something, anything. Another step. Then another.

The circles she's been scratching into the dirt slow, then stop. Dead still.

Her head lifts, eyes cutting straight into mine.

A flick of her hand, casual as brushing away lint.

And I'm airborne.

My back slams into the oak at the edge of the yard hard enough that the trunk splinters, the crack racing up the bark like lightning. My breath is ripped from me, stars dancing behind my eyes.

"Ahh, *fuck*—" The groan claws its way out, pain buzzing through my ribs.

She doesn't move. She doesn't say anything to me. Just stares. And the longer I hold her gaze, the less sure I am she even sees me. Like I'm not Marek standing here, but another ghost in whatever storm that's tearing her apart.

Great. Real fun night this is turning into.

I push forward again, slower this time; not by choice, but because my ribs scream every time I breathe. Hands up, palms open. Surrender.

The gravel that had been vibrating across the yard now goes still. *Not* a good fucking sign.

Then she sits up. Her eyes are wild, fever bright, as they pin me where I stand. Oh, I'm fucked.

Her hand lifts.

And with it—so do I.

"Mother. *Fucker.*"

I'm airborne again. The world blurs. My spine smashes into the oak, higher this time, the crack of wood splitting echoing like a gunshot. Then gravity takes over, meaner on the way down. Shoulder. Ribs. Skull. Every branch I clip explodes in pain.

I hit the ground in a heap and decide maybe I'll take a second to just... admire the view from here. Sky's real nice. Stars and all.

I'm gonna die here tonight. All because I couldn't keep my mouth shut and play it smart. *'I'll go.'* Might as well have jumped up and down, waved my hands, and begged for a turn. *Fucking idiot.*

My insides are bleeding; I can feel it sloshing wrong. Did anyone try to stop me? Did I hear a *No, Marek, don't do it. It's too dangerous*? Nope. Not a damn word. They let me stroll right to my deathbed in bumfuck Louisiana. Goddamn it.

After a few... let's call them *moments of self-pity,* I stagger back to my feet. Vision white with stars, head ringing, bending forward with my palms braced on my knees just to drag in a breath.

My laugh comes out ragged, humorless.

"Whew. *Goddamn* Leighton. You are *really* trying to kill me tonight, huh?"

The ground still thrums under me—either that, or it's just my bones rattling from round two against the fucking oak. Doesn't matter. I sag back against the bark, coughing copper, tasting blood, and force a grin even though my lungs feel like someone's grinding glass inside them.

"Gotta say, Leighton...if this is your way of saying you

missed me, I've had warmer welcomes."

Yeah. Jokes. Brilliant. Definitely what she wants to hear while she's half feral and I'm bleeding out my mouth. Real smooth, Marek.

Third time's the charm, they say, right? Except this charm's about to snap my goddamn spine in half. Every step I take rattles, my ribs scream mutiny, but I lift my hands, anyway. *Surrender.*

Her gaze doesn't waver. Her hand rises again.

No. Please Gods, no. Here we fucking go again. Yep...this is definitely where I die.

My feet leave the ground, my body jerking like a marionette on strings, lungs crushed by the invisible fist around me. Fuck, she's got me higher this time; high enough it looks like a dollhouse below.

"You hurt Rafe!" The snarl rips out of me cold, more instinct than thought.

And that—*finally*—makes her pause.

The grip doesn't vanish, but it stills, tight as a noose waiting for a verdict. I can barely suck air through it, but I force the words through the crack.

"The bond opened. All the way. It ripped through him, Zaria."

That's when she drops me.

Yep. *Drops me.*

Not an *oh no, let me set you gently back on your feet there, Marek* kind of drop. No mercy in it. Not even a slow ease-down. Just cut. Like she snipped the string and let gravity do all the dirty work.

Fifty goddamn feet.

I hit the ground hard enough, my vision whites out, pain detonating through my body until I can't tell if I'm breathing or choking.

By the time I manage to drag air back into my lungs, she's already storming toward her car, slamming the door as the engine coughs to life.

And I'm left sprawled in the dirt, staring up at the branches of that ruined oak, wondering when the hell I became the guy she practices executions on.

When you called her a vulture.

When you called her pathetic

When you called her a nightcrawler.

Ugh. *Fuck.*

"No, Zaria. Wait." My voice scrapes out like gravel, and I roll, groaning, half crawling, half stumbling upright. Every bone in my body screams, but I force myself forward, one staggering step at a time. "I'll take you."

Her door flies back open, her fury hitting me like heat off a furnace.

"Fuck you, Marek!"

She's coming at me now, and every instinct in me screams stop, drop and shift, roll belly-up, let my wolf beg forgiveness with his paws up and his tail between his legs. But I grit my teeth and stay standing, my tail between my legs only in spirit.

"I can fucking drive myself!"

And because the universe clearly fucking hates her as much as she hates me, the tree she'd just used to snap me in half groans and tips and collapses.

Right across the hood of her car.

The alarm shrieks once, twice, then fizzles into silence as

the weight crushes it.

I can't help it. I start laughing, wheezing through the pain, through the blood in my mouth. "Guess not."

"Just get in the car." She doesn't wait for me to answer, just wipes the stray tears streaking down her cheeks with the back of her hand and stalks to the passenger side.

The door slams shut, and I'm left standing there, ribs grinding like broken glass inside my chest. Every breath's a knife. Every step's a reminder that I should've kept my mouth shut back at the manor and let someone else risk their life and limbs to bring her home. Maybe Elodie, she never would have been this vicious to her.

I drag myself toward the driver's side anyway, hand clamped to my ribs. The world tilts every time I bend, and I bite down so hard on my lip I taste copper, just to keep from groaning out loud.

Sliding behind the wheel is its own personal hell. My body folds in slow increments, every joint screaming, until I'm finally in the seat, fingers white-knuckled around the steering wheel.

For a moment, I don't start the car. Just sit there, jaw clenched, listening to her breath shudder unevenly. We're both bleeding, in different ways. And fuck if I know how either of us is supposed to survive the drive home.

The first hour back is a graveyard of silence. She curls into herself, knees pulled tight to her chest, forehead tipped against the window. The blur of highway lights streaks across her skin, but she doesn't speak, doesn't even move.

When she finally looks my way, her eyes land on my hand draped across my chest, fingers spread over my ribs.

"Move your hand."

Yeah. Fuck *that*.

My brow furrows. "Why?"

"Just move it, Marek."

Reluctantly, I lift my palm. She reaches over, tugging the hem of my shirt up, and inhales deep like she's centering herself. Then, her hand presses against my side.

I jolt hard. "Christ, Zaria. Your skin's burning up."

"It'll just take a second."

And then it hits—a low, soothing hum. The ache in my ribs knits together under her touch, the pain evaporating in a sweep of impossible heat. What would have taken hours, maybe all night, with my normal healing time, she mends in seconds.

Her hand slips away, and just like that, she folds back into herself, tucking her knees under her chin and staring out the window again.

I flex my side, roll my shoulders, test the wound that isn't a wound anymore. I shake my head, yet again in awe of what she's become.

"Is the thirst back, Zaria?" I ask, bringing the discussion back to her overheated skin.

"Don't."

"Just answer the fucking question. Is it back? Is that why you're burning up like that?"

Her head snaps toward me, eyes wet, black veins threading faintly at her temples. "It doesn't matter. *None of it* fucking matters. You'll get what you want. I'm severing the bond with Rafe tonight, and I'm leaving New Orleans. There's nothing for me here."

She can't leave.

The thought takes root before I can stop it.

Why the hell would I even want her to stay? This is what I wanted. This is what I've been waiting for. But hearing her say it makes something clench tight in my chest, my pulse kicking like panic.

My jaw locks. "That's impossible." I laughed once, hollow. "You can't sever a mate bond. *Nobody* can."

"I'm High Matron, Marek." Her voice is steel, her hand curling tight around her knees. "Nature bends to my will."

The car hums around us, the weight of her words pressing in from all sides. I can't breathe. My wolf snarls low in my chest.

"You'll break his heart, Zaria." My voice scrapes raw. "You might as well kill him."

Her head tips back against the glass, eyes closed like she's too tired to argue. "I almost killed him tonight. He's better off."

My hands tighten on the wheel. "What happened tonight?"

"Doesn't matter."

"It does matter. He loves you, Zaria. He needs you."

That cracks her open. Her eyes snap to mine, intense and wet with fury, black veins more pronounced now and eyes blown wide with gold. "You didn't care about that when you tried to have me killed. When your assassin turned me into the very monster that you called me out for being tonight at my apartment." Her voice climbs, splintering and shaking. "So, no, it *doesn't* fucking matter, Marek. Drop it."

Her body shifts back in her seat, shoulders curling toward the window. She looks smaller like this, but the reflection in the glass betrays her; gold bleeding into her eyes, veins lacing her throat. Nothing like the girl we knew. Nothing like the woman Rafe bound himself to.

"You can't show up like this, Zaria." My knuckles tighten on the wheel. "You're shifting. Look, the windows are literally fogging."

"I'll be fine." Her voice is empty, drained, like the words cost too much. "Take me by Marigny Place and I'll grab a bag."

I glance at the dash, the glowing red of brake lights stacking up ahead, the nav screen pulsing with a warning. "We're two and a half hours out, and we're about to hit an accident in less than a mile." My jaw grinds. "You're *not* fine."

Her head tips against the glass, a tear streak cutting down her cheek even though she doesn't make a sound. "I don't have much choice here, Marek."

The cabin feels too damn small, walls closing in, the air thick with heat and copper and something wild I can't cage. Every breath tastes metallic, like I've been chewing pennies. My wolf won't sit still, pacing tight circles under my skin, claws dragging along my ribs, restless because she's unraveling right beside me.

I can feel it pouring off her, too much power for one body to hold without splitting. It makes the hair on my arms rise, makes my instincts snarl at me to run.

And I don't know if I'm here to keep her breathing or to keep her from burning the whole goddamn world down around us both.

But at least I know where to start.

"I'm sorry," I rasp out, swallowing my pride for once in my goddamn life. "For what I said to you. For what I *did* to you."

Her eyes don't leave the window. "It's fine, Marek. You win. I'll be gone by morning."

"Fucking hell, Leighton." The curse rips out of me. My

hands twist the wheel, and I wrench us off the highway, tires shrieking. Gravel spits out behind us as I cut quick down an exit, then another turn, and another, until we're buried in back roads and shadows.

I nose the truck into a thicket just off the main drag, slam it into park, and kill the headlights. The dark swallows us whole, silence pressing in heavy.

"Zaria."

Her name comes out too harsh. I drag a hand through my hair, pull air into my lungs, force myself to soften before I break something that can't be mended.

"What happened back there? You nearly killed Rafe from over three hours away. Do you even understand that?" My voice grates, awe and anger knotted together. "You ripped his Lycavor straight out of him like it was nothing."

She flinches but doesn't answer.

"I can't just take you to him. Not like this. Not if you're seconds from breaking. So, you're going to talk. Or feed. Or whatever the fuck it is you need. But we're not moving from this spot until you do." I lean closer, lowering my voice. "Break my ribs again. Heal them. I don't care. Just tell me what the fuck happened."

Her head snaps up, eyes blazing through the shimmer of tears. "Everyone thinks I'm a fucking monster!" she screams, her voice cracking. "A *vulture*. A *bloodsucker*. A pathetic *night crawler*."

Yeah. I'm gonna die.

"Every room I walk into now..." her breath shudders, shoulders shaking, "...there's fear. Fear of something I never asked for."

Her fists clench in her lap, trembling so hard her knuckles

blanch. "I couldn't control what happened with you tonight, Marek. I didn't *do* anything to you. I didn't know that would happen. I didn't even know it was possible." Her voice fractures, softer but no less lethal. "Arousal, sure. We both expected that. But to be pushed over the edge, beyond either of our control? No, I didn't know that."

Her gaze locks onto mine. "And you... fuck, Marek...*you* pulled me onto *your* lap, and then you called me horrible names for something I couldn't control. For something *you* had me turned into. Do you realize how fucked up that makes you? And I'm the vulture?"

Fuck...

"Ask me anything about my witch blood and I'll answer — it's all here." She taps her temple, hard. "It's in my bones. But this vampire thing?" She slams a fist against her chest, veins spidering black beneath her skin. "It's not fucking *mine*! It's an intrusion! An infection in *my* bloodline, and I don't have the goddamn answers!"

She turns her face to the window, but I can see her reflection in the glass, the tears cutting down her cheeks. "I just knew I needed to feed. That's all I had. And now I know what wolf's blood does. And when you called me what you did, when you threw those slurs at me like weapons... I needed my mom. I needed her like I always have. That's always been my default."

Her voice fractures then, turning into soft sobs. "But they shut the door in my face. I couldn't even cross the threshold because of this monster in me. They heard me, Marek. They heard me crying, wailing, and not once did they open that door to scoop me up, to kiss my cheeks, to call me their baby."

Her shoulders hunch, folding inward until she looks breakable in a way that guts me worse than her claws ever could. "I have nothing left. I'm not their daughter anymore. I'm not anyone's. I'm just... this. Whatever this is now." She buries her face in her hands, and it's over. The fury she hides behind collapses. She sobs, raw and ugly, and I can feel her unraveling right there in the seat.

Before my brain even fires, I'm out of the car, rounding to her side. I yank the door open and haul her against me. Her face tucks into the crook of my neck, hot and wet. Her arms lock around me; legs cinch tight at my waist like I'm the last thing keeping her from dropping straight into the dirt.

I don't tell her it's going to be okay. I don't spit out some half-ass comfort that won't mean a damn thing. I just hold her. Stand there in the dark while her sobs rack through me too, heavier than fists, heavier than falling from fifty feet out of the air.

Her words sit on my chest like weight plates, pressing until I swear my ribs might crack all over again.

I palm the back of her head, keep her tucked in while the sobs tear through her. "I told myself you were toxic because it was easier than admitting I was scared shitless. Scared of what you'd do to Rafe. Scared of what you'd do to me. Turns out I was right—you are dangerous. But you're not wrong either. You didn't ask for this. And fuck... your parents—" My voice breaks lower, gravel catching. "That's on them, Leighton. Not you."

I risk a glance down. Tears track over her cheeks, her breath hitching jagged, broken in a way I didn't think Zaria Leighton could ever break.

"You're not nothing," I tell her, rougher than I mean. "You're not 'just this.' You're still you, under all the fire and all the teeth. And yeah, maybe you're a monster now too. But monsters survive. They don't curl up on porches waiting for scraps. They stand. They fight. And you sure as hell don't get to give up when Rafe's out there losing his fucking mind because he can feel you tearing apart at the seams."

My throat tightens as I force the last of it out. I rub my thumb over her cheek, wiping at the tears even as more spill through.

"I've seen nothing, Zaria—and you're not it."

I brace for the backlash. For her to shove me off, snap my ribs again, send me flying into another tree.

But it doesn't come.

Instead, her body pulls tighter, curling into me like I'm the only thing keeping her stitched together. Like if I let go, she'll scatter in pieces neither of us could ever put back.

"Who knew Marek Korolov could be nice..." she mutters against my shoulder, a shaky little chuckle slipping through as I lower her back to her feet.

Smartass. Even now.

She tilts her head up, and I make the mistake of meeting her eyes. Even with the veins still shadowing at her temples, even with the shift in her humming loud enough to rattle the air between us; her beauty slams into me like a fucking freight train.

And for one damn second, I forget every reason I ever hated her.

Fuck...

THIRTEEN

Marek

"Are you going to be okay, or do you need to feed, Zaria?" I force the words out, step back like a few feet of air will keep her out of my head. "No more bullshit. Your veins are threaded black, your eyes ringed in gold. Don't tell me you're fine when you're not."

Her jaw tightens, gaze locking with mine like she'd rather set me on fire than answer. "I'll *have* to be okay, Marek. We can't do that again. I'm not putting myself in that position to be gutted like that again."

Gutted.

Fuck. I hate myself.

My fists ball at my sides, every instinct screaming to close the space between us, to pull her back in, to undo what I said. What I did. But I don't.

"We'll deal with *again* after *now*," I snap. "We've got a couple hundred miles ahead of us, traffic's a nightmare, and I'm not dragging your half-shifted ass through a highway pile-up because you're too stubborn to admit you're slipping."

Her breath hitches like she's about to fire something back, but nothing comes. She just shifts her weight, foot to foot, like she's choosing between poisons and neither one tastes right.

"Zaria," I mutter, softer now, almost against my will. "If you crash on me before we make it back, there's no one out here to save us. So, either tell me if you're about to lose it; or I keep one hand on the wheel and the other ready to pin you down until you do."

I can't overpower her. Not a fucking chance. But I bluff it anyway. Fake it 'til I make it.

Her eyes flick up at me, gold burning through the dark like embers that refuse to die.

I shove her over, drop into the seat, then drag her onto my lap. First thing I have to do is crank the chair all the way back—she's short as hell. When she finally settles, her heat scorches through me. She keeps her chin down, won't meet my eyes, nerves spilling all over the place.

And I shouldn't care. Shouldn't touch her. But I do. Because I'm either clear-headed for once or stupid as fuck. I palm her face, thumb rough against her cheek. "Hey. Look at me."

She fights it for a breath, then finally lifts her gaze.

I lean in, close enough that our foreheads nearly touch. "I will never make you feel the way I did at your place. Not again." My voice grinds low, splintering in my throat. "You have my word."

Her nod is small, hesitant. But it knocks something loose in my chest I didn't know was welded shut. Too close. Too fucking intimate. She's not mine. I keep telling myself that. She's not mine.

She doesn't answer, just breathes, shaky, her exhale brushing my mouth. When I pull back, I push a strand of hair behind her ear. Maybe an excuse to touch her again. Doesn't matter. I try to keep my eyes where they belong, but it's useless.

Her gown's ridden up, high on her hips, nothing underneath. She must've gone straight to her parents' like this, because she sure as hell hadn't changed after I left her in pieces. And now she's straddling me, nipples hard under thin fabric, bare heat pressed against my lap.

"Thank you," she whispers, voice frayed but cutting clean through me. "For saying that. It means a lot."

I nod once, jaw tight. "Do it," I grit, tilting my head back, baring my throat. My hands clamp onto her thighs, holding her down. "Take what you need before you burn us both alive."

And then her mouth is on me.

Her fangs sink deep, tearing past skin and straight into fire.

A sound rips out of her throat the second she bottoms out—low, needy, vibrating against my neck. "Hmmm..."

Fuck. That sound.

Her fangs work in stable pulls at first, almost controlled. My chest heaves, fists digging into the meat of her thighs, and I lie to myself. I can handle this. Transaction. Survival. Just a feed.

But then she moans against my neck, hips grinding harder, dragging across my cock until I'm straining against the thin barrier of fabric. My head tips back against the seat, breath breaking ragged.

"Zaria..."

She doesn't hear it. Or she doesn't give a damn.

Her fangs punch deeper, pain slicing through the pleasure, and the shock rips a gasp out of me.

"Fuck—" My palm slams into the roof of the car.

The sting should snap me out of it, should shove me back into anger, but it doesn't. It only twists the pleasure higher until I'm trembling under her weight.

My body betrays me. My hips buck up, desperate for more. And when she moans again, the sound vibrating against my throat, her fingers threading through my hair like she owns me, something inside me breaks.

I grab her waist, drag her down hard, grinding her flush against me like I'll fucking die if she lets go. She's wet, soaking straight through my shorts, and the heat of it seeps into me, into the hunger, until there's nothing else left.

The bite. The grind. The wet heat. It's all too much, crashing over me faster than I can hold it back.

"Harder..." The word rips out of me before I even know I'm saying it. My head slams back, voice breaking. "Fuck... harder, Zaria."

And she obeys.

Her fangs drive deeper, suction brutal, like she's pulling me apart nerve by nerve until pain and pleasure tangle so tight I can't tell them apart. I come hard, without control, without warning; my roar tearing through the cab as my body convulses under her, cock spilling helplessly while I grind against the slick heat between us.

And then she breaks away.

Her fangs slip free, leaving my throat wet and stinging, the skin humming like it's still open, still hers. Her hips don't stop. They jerk rough, frantic, like she's chasing something just out of reach.

"God, I'm so close. Fuck—"

Her back arches hard, spine bowing backwards away from me; gown riding higher with every desperate grind. Skin bared in strips; first her stomach, taut and trembling, the sexy dip of her waist, the curve of her ribs that look too breakable to cage the power rattling inside her.

My chest caves in. Because fuck... she's unraveling on me, against me, and it's the most terrifying, beautiful thing I've ever seen.

"So close. Oh god, Marek—"

Holy shit. She's saying my name. Like that.

This isn't feeding anymore. This isn't just blood. Her voice is broken, pleading, and my body doesn't know the difference. Hell, I don't think hers does either.

"Please. Oh, fuck, please—"

Please what? Please more? Please faster? Please me? My brain short-circuits on the word, looping it until my chest feels like it's going to cave in.

I should shove her off. Should break this before it breaks me. But I don't. I can't. I'm drowning, and part of me doesn't even want to surface.

My hands move on their own, sliding under the silk, climbing her stomach, greedy and shaking because I need to know if she feels as good as she looks.

Stop. Pull back. End it here before you make it worse.

Yeah. I don't listen. Not for a second. My palms spread wide over her ribs, splayed like I'm staking a claim I have no business staking.

And *fuuuucck*...her skin. Soft as sin, hot enough to scorch. Her stomach hollows under my touch when she grinds down, muscles tight and trembling, and it's the sexiest goddamn thing I've ever seen. Her hips slow, dragging into a brutal rhythm that makes every nerve in me scream. She moans with each thrust, wet enough I can *hear* it, slick against the ridge of my cock straining under my shorts.

I'm gone. Completely fucking gone.

I shove her dress higher, palms spreading over her ribs until her breasts are bared in the dim light.

"Mother. Fucker." The words scrape out of me, strangled, because I know—I'm a dead man. This image is branded into me for life.

Her tits are perfect. Firm, high, her nipples tight little points begging for my mouth, my teeth. I cup one, just under a handful, knead until her body jolts against me, tightens under the pressure of my grip.

"Fuck, yes." Her voice fractures, splinters apart. "Please, Marek. Make me come."

Goddamn. That's it. That's the line. It's gone. Burned to ash. There's no pretending this is about feeding anymore. No walking it back, no going clean after this.

She's mine in this moment, and I'm already too far under to claw my way out.

I roll her nipple between my fingers until she gasps, the sound shooting straight down my spine. My other hand drags lower, slower, like I'm testing myself as much as her. My fingers skim her stomach, dip between her thighs, and then—

Holy fuck.

I find her clit. Swollen, slick, her whole body twitching when I drag over it rough and fast.

"Mother of fuck, Zaria," I choke, hiss tearing out of me before I can stop it. "You're... *fuck*, you're dripping wet."

Her cry answers me, loud and coarse, the kind of sound that rips straight through a man. Her spine arches, her body sparking like I've hit a live nerve.

And I can't stop myself. I press harder, stroke again, then

shove two fingers inside her. The heat nearly undoes me. She clenches around me like she's starving for it, and I swear I almost come again just from that.

Her hips slam down, grinding against me, her gasps breaking apart like she's splintering from the inside out. "Yes...fuck, yes!"

And then she lunges forward, fangs driving back into my neck the exact second her orgasm rips through her.

That timing... it kills me. She *waited* for it, knew what it would do. The second her teeth sink in, I'm gone.

I come hard, violent spurts tearing out of me again and again until I don't know where one ends, and the next begins. My eyes squeeze shut, my hand smacks the roof again with a crack. And the feral sound that rumbles out of me isn't a noise I've ever made before. Not in a fight, not in bed, not in any life I've lived up until this moment.

It vibrates out of my chest like my wolf is dragging its way free.

Each pull of her mouth drags more out of me, crashing through me until I'm shaking under her weight. My cock throbs, pumping helplessly, soaking us both while my body bucks without rhythm.

It doesn't stop. Every nerve lit up, every muscle locked, and I'm pinned between the fire of her bite and the wet heat grinding me raw.

And all I can do is hold on and take it; every spasm, every quake feels like she's wringing the life out of me with her body and her fangs.

The air feels thick, sour in my lungs, and I can't move; I just slump back, muscles twitching, skin buzzing where her fangs were.

I'm a fucking mess. My thighs shake. My pulse is shot to hell. My neck's slick, my chest heaving like I just went ten rounds and barely made it out alive.

For a second, it's nothing but haze. The kind that makes you forget your name, forget why you ever thought you could handle this in the first place.

Then I feel her body trembling, but not with aftershocks. It's smaller. Her breath catches oddly against my throat, not moans anymore; hiccups.

It takes me a beat to realize she's crying.

Her shoulders jerk, her fists curl in my shirt, and then the sobs spill out, quiet but brutal, like she's been holding them back so long they claw their way free now that she can't stop them.

She scrambles, fumbling, trying to get off me, to put space where there can't be space anymore.

But I don't let her. My arm snaps around her waist, locking her tight against me. My other hand fists into her hair, not rough but firm, guiding her cheek back down to my shoulder.

"Shh. No." My voice is wrecked, shredded from what we just did. "It's okay. We're okay. I promise. We're okay."

She fights for a second, her fists pressing weakly at my chest, but she's too shattered. Too fresh. The weight of everything crashes through her, and then she just... collapses.

Her body shakes as the sobs tear out, muffled against me, wetting my skin. I hold her tighter, curling around her like a shield, my jaw resting against her hair as I breathe her in.

"Let it out, Leighton," I murmur, my lips brushing the crown of her head. "I've got you. Just let it out."

And for the second time today, I fucking hate myself. Not for the lies, not for the betrayal, not even for the blood on my hands. But for this; her breaking against me, her tears soaking into my skin, her body shaking because of the monster I set on her path.

Deveraux should've killed her; that was the plan. A clean end, a tragedy that would fade. Instead, I'd unleashed something else, something greater, something unbearable; and now she was paying for it in every sob rattling her chest.

I close my eyes, jaw grinding, holding her tighter as if I could anchor her back to herself. And right there in the quiet wreckage of it, I make a vow I've never made before.

I'll spend the rest of my life making it up to her. Every breath I have left, every step I take will be penance. For Zaria. And for Rafe. Because I'd stolen from them both, and gods help me, I'll bleed every drop I have before I let them feel this alone again.

I tilt her face back, thumbs brushing along damp cheeks, chasing the last of the tears. Her skin is warm but controlled now—the black veins gone, her eyes hazel again, soft and human in a way that feels like a goddamn miracle after what I just saw.

I take my shirt and slowly wipe the blood from her chin. Then her lips. My thumb follows, brushing across her bottom lip as I cradle her jaw. Her eyes lock on mine, and neither of us looks away.

Whatever that feeding lit hasn't burned out; it's still there, brimming between us, humming too loud to ignore. My hands slide her dress back down, settling heavy on her hips. My thumbs trace the crease where her thighs meet, pressing in like I could pin myself to her and not drift into the wreckage I just made.

Neither of us says a word. My cock twitches under her weight, traitor loud enough that I know she feels it. Her breath hitches in her throat, and it guts me because she's not stable yet either.

She leans in, tilts her head, her lips grazing mine. Barely there. Barely a kiss. But it's enough to light every nerve. Our breaths tangle; shallow and uneven.

Then she grinds her hips, dragging her pussy over the ridge of me again. The friction against my already sensitive cock makes me see white, and the moan that slips from her mouth spills into mine like she meant for me to keep it.

Her fists knot in my shirt, hauling me closer, daring me to be the weak one. To cave.

And fuck, I want to. But kissing her? That's worse than everything else we just did. Feeding, the grind, the mess of it...I can *almost* explain that away. Not clean, but close enough. But a kiss? We don't come back from that. A kiss makes it real. Makes it ours. And we're already the worst fucking people alive if we let it go that far.

Somehow, I tear myself back with the scraps of control I've got left, my voice barely functioning. "Let's get home."

She doesn't fight it. Doesn't argue. Just breathes me in like she needs one more hit, then nods. Small. Bone-deep tired, like her whole body's ready to collapse.

I keep my hands on her as she climbs off, steadying her, making sure she doesn't crack the second my hold slips away. Then I circle the car, shove a hand through my hair, shaking my head because I don't even know what the fuck to call what just happened, much less how to walk it back.

The engine turns over, headlights slicing through the trees, dragging us out of the clearing and back onto asphalt.

She folds into herself in the passenger seat, hugging her arms, staring at nothing. Her breath stutters like she's stitching herself together with thread too thin to hold.

And I drive. Shoulders locked, jaw clenched, every mile another nail in the coffin of what I swore I'd never let happen.

But I make the vow anyway.

I'll keep her together. I'll keep her breathing. And I'll bury this deep—so deep no one will ever dig it up.

For Rafe.

For her.

For all of us.

FOURTEEN

Zaria

"You okay?" Marek's voice cut through the low hum of the engine as the tires ground over gravel.

I blinked awake, my neck stiff from the angle I'd been curled in the seat. The manor loomed ahead, shadowed and heavy against the night sky. "Yeah," I rasped, though the word dragged, still thick with sleep.

He didn't look at me; eyes locked on the road. "While you were out, I called in and had one of the guards swing by your place to grab some of your things, clothes, shoes. Everything is already set up in a room for you."

His knuckles flexed on the wheel, too tight, too casual. "And... blood bags. You don't need them, but if you want them..." He cleared his throat, like the words burned on the way out. "They're in a heater by the bed. Room temp."

He hadn't said it, but I heard it anyway. That he hated the thought of me drinking from anyone else. That it scraped him raw. And still, he made sure I wouldn't starve.

Care buried under grit. The Marek special.

And gods help me, it meant more than I wanted it to.

"Why would you do that?" I asked, uncertainty laced through the sleep still clinging to my voice.

His mouth twitched, something between a smirk and a sneer. "Don't flatter yourself, Leighton. If you starve or spiral, it drags all of us down with you. I like breathing. I'm also not a fan of wolf stew. So—" he chuckled, pulling the car into park, "—you're welcome. Or whatever."

Weird. Infuriating. A little sweet, which somehow made it worse.

"Thanks," I said, quieter than I meant to.

"Might as well know—Rafe's out. He's in a wolf coma in the corridor, locked until morning. You can see him if you want, but the doors won't open till tomorrow."

"I'll let him rest," I murmured. "Somebody should."

I climbed out of the car, legs heavy, and followed Marek up the stone steps. His hand landed low at my back, warm in a way that made my stupid spine tingle. The tether was still humming through my thighs, needling me with feelings I didn't want and sure as hell didn't trust.

The front doors opened before we reached them, and he pulled his hand away fast, like he'd been caught sneaking candy from a jar. Maybe he had. Maybe I was the candy.

The second I stepped over the threshold, the air shifted—thick, electric. It slammed into me like a wall and I almost stumbled, masking it quick with a breath through my teeth.

They were waiting. The pack. Faces tight but trying for smiles, arms wrapping around me in those obligatory embraces.

Glad you're okay.

You'll feel better after some rest.

Rafe will be over the moon when he wakes.

Their words touched me. But threaded emotions beneath every single one was fear—thin and taut, like tendrils in the air I could taste. They were afraid of me.

I forced a small smile anyway, murmured, 'Thanks, everyone. I'm sorry for the trouble. I just... I'm going to bed. I'll see you in the morning.'

No one stopped me. No one pushed. That almost hurt worse.

"I'll show you which room is yours. Rafe's was torn apart, so it's getting work done."

Marek's voice cut clean through the quiet, and then he was already moving up the stairs. I followed, quiet, my footsteps echoing in a hall I hadn't walked before.

The place stretched on forever—wings and corridors like veins, a labyrinth it'd take months to map. And all of them lived here together. Not stacked on top of each other, but close. Family layered in stone. Big shared spaces for when they wanted the noise, private suites for when they didn't. A pack pretending at normalcy.

At the end of the hall, Marek pushed open a door. He didn't step inside. Just leaned against the frame, leaving me the choice of crossing first.

The "room" wasn't a room at all—it was a little world. A mini suite dressed in burgundy tones, warm and rich. A curved red couch tucked into the living space, a sleek television mounted above the mantel. A compact fridge hummed quietly in the corner, stocked with bottles of water, sodas, juice—choices. Thoughtful, almost too thoughtful. Like someone had tried to think through every small comfort I might reach for.

The bedroom was simple, but it looked lived-in. The bed was already made, my clothes stacked in neat little piles like somebody had ironed their guilt into every fold. And there, propped against the pillow, was a teddy bear with one button eye; the one my mom bought me. My throat went tight.

The bathroom hit just as hard. Marble counters, a tub with jets, a shower big enough to get lost in. The counters were *curated*. Bath salts, lotions, shampoo in brands I actually used. Too much. Too thoughtful.

I stood in the doorway, pulse loud in my ears. "You did this?"

"It's just a room, Leighton." Expressionless. Like if he didn't put weight on it, it wouldn't matter.

My eyes slid back to the bed. To the bear. My voice cracked. "Mr. Muggles?"

He blinked. "Mr. Who?"

"The teddy bear."

"I told them if it looked sentimental, grab it." He shrugged like it was nothing. "That's all."

"How'd they even get in?"

That earned me a laugh. Again. Twice in ten minutes. Marek fucking Korolov laughing. Must've been the end of the world.

"Thanks," I managed, but it came out paper-thin. Weak. My ribs felt like they were caving in around the word.

He crossed his arms tighter, chin dipping like armor. "It's just a room."

That should've ended it. But it wasn't. My feet were already moving before my brain caught up. I wrapped my arms around his waist, pressed my face into the heat of him.

The bear. The fridge. The bags. The way he'll never admit any of it mattered. And I hated that it mattered to me. I hated him. God, I hated him. He's the reason everything's crashing down, the reason my life is ash.

But something's shifted. He's shifted. Today especially.

He went stiff at first, solid as the stone walls around us. For a second, I thought he'd peel me off like I was nothing more than a bad idea. But then I felt his breath easing, the tension bleeding out slow. His arms came around me, heavy and sure, pulling me in until his chin rested on the top of my head.

Tears pricked. I buried them. "Thank you," I whispered into his chest. Then, softer, shaky, because if I didn't laugh, I'd cry—"I'm sorry I broke you with an oak tree."

I should've stepped back. Should've let go. But I couldn't.

When I finally tilted my face up, his eyes were already waiting for me. Green and bright but not cutting this time. They were burning slowly, like they were memorizing me.

Something in my chest pulled tight.

Cataclysm.

That was the only word for it.

Like the earth tilting off its axis, the air rearranging itself, the universe leaning closer just to watch us fall apart.

His hand lifted slowly, hesitation flickering in the movement, but then his fingers brushed a curl off my cheek, tucking it behind my ear with the kind of gentleness that didn't match the chaos between us.

He did it like it was nothing. Like it didn't set me on fire. Like I didn't still feel the ghost of his hands on my stomach, the bite of his fingers pinching my nipple, the way he'd driven his fingers into me, the sound of him breaking apart beneath me, his fist slamming the roof of the car as though it could ground him when I'd already undone him completely.

My breath caught at the memory.

His did too, the space between us folding in on itself until there was nothing but heat.

"Good night, Zaria," he said finally, his voice threaded with strain, arousal bleeding off him in waves he couldn't hide.

"Good night, Marek." The words tumbled out soft and fragile, like I might shatter if I tried to make them stronger.

But neither of us moved. We just stood there in the thick silence, mouths a breath apart, every inch of air charged, waiting, the kind of waiting that felt like the world itself was daring us to take one more step and watch everything collapse.

His hand curved around the side of my neck, his other sliding down to the small of my back, pulling me closer until there was nothing left between us. His mouth dipped toward mine, open, ready to claim, to end the unbearable distance...

And then footsteps echoed down the hall. A door shut somewhere nearby, the mundane sound splintering the moment clean in half.

We broke apart like guilty teenagers, the thread between us snapping, leaving the air tense and ragged.

"Night," he muttered, rubbing the back of his neck, like the movement could erase the hunger written all over him.

I stood frozen for a beat longer, chest aching, body trembling with the ghost of his touch, before I turned away. Because if I didn't, I wasn't sure either of us would stop next time.

I closed the door, pressed my back against it, lungs strained like I'd run miles. My pulse still throbbed where his fingers had brushed my skin, phantom heat that wouldn't fade.

My eyes squeezed shut, the words slipping out on a splintered whisper meant for no one but me.

"I'm fucked..."

I woke earlier than I needed to. The house still slept around me, but I couldn't—didn't—want to wait for the moment I'd have to make eye contact with anyone.

It's strange, living in this world and still clocking into a nine-to-five like we're nothing but ordinary corporate Americans. Like claws and hunger and curses can be stuffed under blazers and boardroom smiles, hidden in spreadsheets and small talk.

And gods, I miss Rafe. I miss him so fucking much. Everything was perfect before. Before Deveraux's bite, before my bloodline woke up screaming. Now every time the bond stirs, it's not love I feel. It's Rafe's fear. Or Deveraux's rage. A constant tug-of-war, my heart yanked bloody between them.

It's exhausting. Like being the battlefield of someone else's war.

And then there's Marek. And whatever the hell *that* was last night.

He hates me. Or maybe he just *wants* to. Stil, his arousal was overwhelming, bleeding into me long after the moment broke. Bleeding all the way home. If I hadn't slammed my door shut when I did, I don't know what would've happened.

His room's across from mine. Same wing. I don't know if that's intentional or just cruel irony. Probably convenience, to be close enough in case I needed to feed in the middle of the night. Except my vampire heard him less than an hour after he left my room. Heard every ruined sound he made, fisting himself, my name thick in his throat.

I was lying in bed texting Sophie when it hit. The first moan and the unmistakable sound of skin on skin.

I sat up straight, tuned my hearing sharper, focused until

there was no mistaking it.

"Is he?" I muttered to myself.

"Yes," came the whisper. Thin, barely there, but I caught it. "*He* is..." again, softer.

My hand slapped over my mouth. He was responding. To me. While...

"Oh my god," I whispered.

Then his voice, ragged, too low for anyone else in the house to hear. But I think he knew that. "Hmmm. Fuck."

My body betrayed me instantly. My breath caught, my hand already sliding down, fingers finding my clit.

And then...clear as if he was in bed beside me..."Don't stop."

My breath hitched. I slid a finger inside, my back arching off the bed, my other hand clawing at my throat like I needed something to hold me down.

It was so fucking salacious, so wrong. But gods, it was hot. So. Fucking. Hot.

My fingers moved faster, slick sounds obscene in the quiet of my room.

"I can't believe I'm doing this," I whispered, the words tumbling out frayed, already riding the edge.

"Do you want to stop?"

"No."

"How many fingers are inside you right now?"

"One." The word fell out on a shaky breath as I dipped deeper, pulling slickness up to circle my clit until my whole body jumped.

"Add one more. Now."

I obeyed. Slid in two. My head snapped back against the

pillow. "Fuck..."

"Good fucking girl."

Gods help me, that praise ripped through me like lightning.

I couldn't stop. Couldn't stop sliding my fingers inside, chasing the edge like it owned me.

"Just like that," his voice rasped, low and rough in my head. "Keep going. I want you to come with me."

His moans rolled into growls, guttural and primal, and I matched him; fingers pumping to his rhythm. In. Out. In. Out.

"I'm so close," I gasped, legs trembling, hips jerking into my hand.

"Come. *Fuuuuckk*. Now. Come now."

And I shattered. Hard. In sync with him. My body convulsed, walls clenching around my fingers as his growl split the night.

For one brutal second, it felt like the tether itself caught fire. Like we'd crossed a line that could never be uncrossed.

"We're okay," he whispered, like he could already feel guilt clawing its way up my spine. "Good night, Zaria."

"Good night, Marek."

And then I was gone. Knocked out cold. Slept like a fucking rock, deeper than I had in weeks.

Now morning's here, and I don't know what the hell to do with any of it.

Because it's Marek. The same bastard who tried to have me killed. The same bastard who never misses a chance to remind me how much he hates me.

It has to be the blood. The tether. Some twisted, chemical side effect that makes my body mistake him for oxygen.

Because if it's not that... if it's actually him... then I've lost my goddamn mind.

By the time I got to the office, the sky was still black; the building was quiet. No chatter. No phones. Just the hum of the lights and the echo of my own footsteps. I shoved my lunch bag into my desk drawer: a couple juices, some fruit... and blood.

Because that's my life now. That's who I am.

Yay me.

I tried to work. God, I tried; but my mind kept circling yesterday. My parents shutting me out. Marek's voice in the car, soft in a way I didn't expect. The gravel trembling under my sobs. The tree falling. Every moment was fresh enough to sting. Hard enough to keep me from locking down the bond entirely. It tugged at me, and I had to fight tooth and nail to keep it muted.

That's why tonight has to happen. The severing. I won't be responsible for breaking him. I won't be the thing that destroys the one man who made me feel whole. Better he hates me, better he believes I left, than to love me while I bleed him dry.

"You're early, Zaria. How are you?"

Vanessa's voice cut through the silence of my spiral, smooth and professional as ever. I blinked, dragging myself back to fluorescent lights and the faint hum of the office.

I turned in my chair to face her. "I've had better weeks, Vanessa," I said, letting out a small, brittle laugh. "You've heard the whisperings, I'm sure. I'm Blooded now."

Her brow arched, expression unreadable but intense enough to make me sit straighter. "And the High Matron, yes. I've heard. That's exciting news."

"I don't know about that." My voice faltered at the edges.

"Exciting isn't the word I'd use."

She studied me for a long beat, then tilted her head toward the hallway. "You want to come to my office? We can talk about it."

I hesitated. Then, I pushed myself to my feet. "Sure."

Her office was always neat, everything aligned, glass walls shadowed just enough to give the illusion of privacy. I slipped into the chair across from her desk, my legs suddenly heavy.

"You're not the first in this city to be Blooded, Zaria," she said gently, like she was coaxing me to breathe. "But you are the first High Matron we've had in a very long time. People will fear you, yes. But they'll also *look* to you. That's the burden of legacy."

Her words should have comforted me. Instead, they pressed heavier against my chest. Because legacy didn't feel like an honor. It felt like a chain I never asked to wear.

"I haven't been able to really control the hunger on the vampire side, though." I admit, my voice sheepish. "The High Matron part, at least that came with an instruction manual. Everything from my ancestors is right here, running through my veins. I know spells I've never studied; I can sense wards I've never touched. But the vampire side..." My jaw tightens. "It's just always writhing. I don't know anything about being a vampire. I have Deveraux's memories, the man that changed me. I have his emotions, all of them, but not what I need to know about the mix of my High Matron and this."

Vanessa doesn't interrupt my rambling. She just nods once, studying me the way only she can; almost clinical, but not unkind. Like she's assessing a balance sheet, and a fragile soul at the same time.

"I've fed. Three times now. Werewolf."

Vanessa's composure fractures, just slightly, but it's enough. Her brows pinch, her chin tips back like she's making sure she heard right.

"You fed... on *werewolves*?"

"Yes." Shame crawls hot up my cheeks at the look on her face. "This stays confidential, right?"

"It does," Vanessa says evenly, though her tone has shifted; heavier now. "Yes."

I cleared my throat. "There were... side effects."

Her gaze sharpens. "Synchronous orgasm."

The flush hits my cheeks before I can stop it. "...Yes."

"Where are the bodies now? We'll have to spin the deaths; but I'll speak with Rafe."

My head jerks up. "What? No! No, I would *never*...I would never take a life."

Vanessa leans back in her chair, eyes narrowing. "You *didn't* kill them?"

"Him. Just one werewolf. And *no*... That's an odd accusation, Vanessa. I'm not a killer."

"I didn't mean that you were, but Zaria...you are *much* stronger than you give yourself credit for."

She stands and circles her desk to sit in the chair opposite me, taking my hands in hers.

"When a vampire feeds on a werewolf, it isn't civilized — and it isn't just blood. The bite becomes a conduit, a circuit. Energy runs both ways, locking them together in a feedback loop that neither can break.

The vampire doesn't just taste blood; they get the wolf's adrenaline, their heat, their power. And when arousal kicks in, it spikes that surge tenfold. The high is so potent it feels endless, all-consuming.

That's why the feeding doesn't stop. The vampire gorges until the wolf is drained, because the climax itself keeps flooding the circuit. It's ecstasy laced with power, and once a vampire's had that hit... they don't come back from it."

Her voice dips lower as she squeezes my hand. "And yet you *stopped*...more than once. That is impossible."

The words coil around me, tight, and I can't help it—my voice breaks angrier than I mean. "How do you know this?"

Vanessa doesn't flinch at my biting tone. She just keeps my hands in hers, watching me the way someone might study a loaded gun left on a table. Calm. Precise. A little too knowing.

"It's my job," she says simply, "to know the risks. To know the edges. When LeRoux hires Bloodeds, when we put them in rooms with wolves or witches or humans, I need to understand what might snap. Who might bleed. Which hungers we can't control. If one Blooded can't be near another. If a feeding could turn fatal before anyone has a chance to intervene."

Her words are impersonal, but her eyes pin me in place with sincerity.

"You knew this before I told you," I whisper. "Didn't you?"

Vanessa exhales, a slow, measured sound. Then she tips her head, like she's peeling the mask back just enough to show me what's underneath.

"I'm a Seer," she says at last. "An Oracle, if you prefer the older term. My bloodline was built for this—for seeing the cracks before they break the floorboards beneath us. That's my job here, Zaria. Not just the paperwork and hiring. I am Rafe's eyes where he can't see, the warning before any storms hit."

She leans forward then, subtle, her voice softening like

we're whispering secrets instead of talking about something that could set me on fire.

"Tell me, Zaria. Are there feelings for this werewolf? That would explain how you're able to keep the hunger in check."

"No." The word shoots out too fast. I pull my hands from hers, shaking my head. "I don't have feelings for him. That's not..."

I push to my feet, more rattled than I should be, but it doesn't stop me from edging toward the door. "That's not what this is, Vanessa."

Her brow twitches, calm, almost kind. "I didn't mean to offend. I was only going to explain how soul bonds—"

Soul bonds.

"There is no bond. No claiming." My words slice through hers before she can finish. "Thanks for listening."

I grab the door, words tripping over themselves as they tumble out. "I better get back to work—thanks. Thank you, Vanessa."

I close it behind me and exhale hard, chest tight, trying to figure out why a simple question made me feel like I'd been caught in a lie I didn't even mean to tell.

FIFTEEN

Rafe

"How is she?" My voice rasped as the cell door groaned open. Every muscle screamed when I staggered out, sweat cold against my skin.

"I don't know." Marek was there waiting, already holding out a pair of sweats and a shirt like he'd expected me to come out in pieces. "She left early. Before any of us saw her."

"What happened when you found her?"

His mouth worked once, twice, like he didn't want to say it. Finally, he ran a hand through his hair, exhaling rough. "She broke a seventy-foot oak tree in half." His eyes cut to mine unblinking. "With my body."

"*Fuck.*"

"Yeah."

Marek's laugh was short, hollow, but then his voice shifted. Softer. Like the edge had dulled without him realizing.

"But that wasn't even the worst of it, Rafe. She was... she was pretty bad. Laying on their porch, curled up like a toddler. Like she just... folded in on herself."

I froze mid-step.

It wasn't just what he said.

It was *how* he said it.

I'd *never* heard that tone from him before where Zaria was concerned.

No bite. No venom. Just... something damn close to concern. Maybe even guilt.

And that scared me almost as much as the picture he painted of her.

"There's something else, Rafe." Marek stopped halfway up the stairs, his hand curling around the banister like it was the only thing holding him up. His eyes met mine, grim. "She said she's planning to sever the bond."

My chest tightened.

"Well, that's not possible. Why would she even *want* to?"

His jaw worked, a muscle ticking in his cheek before he finally answered. "To protect you. From her. And she says she can."

He exhaled and ran a hand through my braids.

"I talked to the pack last night, and we all think that if it *is* possible, it's best you let her."

The air left my lungs in a rush, leaving me cold.

Sever the bond?

She didn't understand; she *couldn't*.

That bond wasn't just love, wasn't just tether; it was the only thing keeping me whole.

I swallowed hard, my voice breaking. "You *all* think that?"

Marek's silence was enough. His gaze flickered, guilt and steel in equal measure, and then he turned, heading up the rest of the stairs without giving me an answer.

I stood frozen on the landing, the weight of his words pressing down like stone.

She thought she was protecting me.

The pack thought it was mercy.

But all I could feel was the jagged crack forming in my chest, like losing her might just tear me apart for good.

Zaria wasn't at her desk when we arrived at the office. The ride in had been quiet, and that quiet followed us inside like a curse.

The bond hummed in the background with tension strung so tight it could've been sliced with a blade. Everyone felt it, I knew they did. Every heart in sync, every thought running like white noise.

All except Marek.

He'd muted his tether days ago. I haven't called him out on it. Haven't asked, haven't demanded answers, because I knew Marek well enough to know he doesn't do anything without a reason.

But the loss of him in the bond created a void, a hollow space I couldn't ignore.

Like missing a tooth with your tongue; you couldn't help but probe the absence, ache against it.

We dispersed to our respective offices, each wolf shouldering the noise in their own way. The floors were too polished, the glass walls too sterile for what we carried inside us. And yet we sat, booting up computers, shuffling papers, pretending to be nothing but men and women in suits. Pretending we weren't predators, barely holding the seams of control.

For the first time since the corridor, my body felt almost

whole again. My Lycavor had gone quiet in my chest, claws finally sheathed, breath no longer clawing out of my throat. But the echo of it lingered, a low hum beneath my ribs that refused to fade.

The ache was still there, like phantom bruises stamped into my bones. To be forced into a shift like that...it's not something you just walk away from. It rattles the cage from the inside out. My muscles felt wrung out, nerves still buzzing like they hadn't gotten the message it was over.

I knew I'd be carrying it for days. Every step, every breath, a reminder.

My pulse kicked when I heard the knock at my door, then stopped altogether when Zaria stepped in. She looked the same; hair loose around her shoulders, eyes guarded, but everything between us felt different. Like I was staring across a river I wasn't sure I could cross.

I wanted to go to her. To run, to beg, to bury my face in her neck until I couldn't breathe anything but her. But I stayed where I was, gripping the armrests of my chair until the leather creaked.

"Hey, baby," I managed, my voice too soft, too hungry.

"Hi, Rafe." Her reply was quiet, careful, like each word had to be tested before it left her mouth.

"Are you okay?"

Her mouth curved, almost a smile, but her eyes gave her away. "I should be asking you that."

She finally moved, even though hesitantly, walking the rest of the way inside before shutting the door behind her.

Still, it felt like there was a bridge between us. A rickety old thing strung with rope and fraying planks, swaying over a canyon neither of us wanted to fall into.

"I'm so sorry, Rafe," she whispered. "For hurting you last night. If I'd known or realized…"

The words punched a hole clean through me.

I couldn't take the distance anymore.

Couldn't stand one more second of her standing stiff across the room like a stranger.

I crossed the space and wrapped her up, burying my face against her neck, breathing her in, pressing desperate kisses to her skin.

Her arms came up around me, but she was rigid, her shoulders locked tight around her ears. Hugging me back because she thought she should, not because she wanted to. And gods, that sliced deep.

"I miss you, baby," I rasped, my mouth brushing her pulse. "Please… just come back. To whatever we were before all of this. Come back."

The bond between us flickered, faint and muffled, like a radio signal trapped under static. She hadn't shut me out completely, but she was holding me at arm's length even while I had her in my arms.

Her hands slid up my arms, soft at first, then pressing just enough to push me back. Even the gentlest pull-away was a blow to my ribs.

"I need to sever this bond, Rafe."

Her tone was soft, almost tender.

That only made the words hurt worse.

"It's the only way I can keep you unharmed," she continued, eyes shining. "I don't want to risk hurting you more than I already have."

For a second, I couldn't breathe.

Couldn't move.

My wolf clawed at my insides, howling against the very idea, the bond pulling taut like it knew it was about to be cut.

My pulse hammered so hard it felt like it would tear out of my throat.

"Zaria..." My voice cracked, torn between begging and fury. "You *can't*. You don't understand—"

But she did. That was the worst part. She *did* understand. And still, she was ready to burn me alive if it meant I'd survive her fire.

"I do understand, Rafe." Her her hands tremble where they rest against her side. "It's never been done in your pack, so I understand your fears about it. That it will hollow you out, but it won't. I promise."

"Promise? Zaria, you can't promise me that. You can't promise what happens when you tear out a piece of me that was *made* for you. This bond isn't just some spell you can snip like thread; it's *us*. It's every heartbeat, every breath. You rip it out, and you rip me out with it."

"If I stay, I'll rip you apart, anyway. Every time I lose control, every time my rage leaks through that tether; you felt it last night. You *felt* what's inside me. You think I can risk that again?"

I shake my head hard, jaw locked so tight it aches. "I'll take it. I'll take all of it. Every storm, every flame. Just don't...don't cut me off. Don't leave me in the dark."

Her lips part like she might break then, but she doesn't. She braces instead, rolling back, and I realize with a hollow weight that she's already decided.

"I *can* promise you." She steps closer, eyes locked to mine, hazel flashing with certainty. "Do you trust me?"

The question guts me. Because the answer is yes. Always yes. I'd trust her with my life, my soul, every breath I've got left in me. And yet here she is, asking me to trust her with the one thing I can't stand to lose.

"Zaria..." My voice cracks. "You're asking me to trust you while you're tearing me away from you."

Her hand hovers in the space between us, like she wants to close it, soothe me, but doesn't dare. "I'm asking you to trust me to save you. Even if it means losing me."

"Fine." I throw my hands up, the sound of defeat thick in my chest. "Fine. You win. When is this happening?" The question comes out uneven, my voice shaking no matter how hard I try to hold it together.

"Tonight."

The word lands like a hammer, sealing something I can't unseal.

I nod once, blunt, the movement mechanical. "Okay." I shake my head. "I trust you. I need you to hear that. I do trust you."

I drag a hand through my braids, staring down at the desk because looking at her feels like being torn in half. "But don't mistake this for what I want, Zaria. I don't *want* this. Not for a second. And yet..." my laugh comes out rough, bitter, "apparently everyone agrees with you."

Her breath snags, soft enough I almost miss it. When I finally force myself to look up, her eyes are brimming.

"I know," she whispers. "That's what makes it hurt worse."

SIXTEEN

Marek

Zaria shut herself off from all of us the entire day. Not just in the usual way she walls people out, but completely. She abandoned her desk mid-morning and disappeared into one of the reserve offices, laptop bag slung over her shoulder, door shut tight like a barricade.

The only time I saw her was when she slipped into the restroom. The sound of retching carried through the tiles, harsh enough to make the air sting. When she came out, pale and shaking, I opened my mouth—just once—to ask if she was okay.

She cut me off with a raised hand, her voice barely holding together.
"Don't."

And that was it.

She left the office before anyone else, didn't wait for the pack, didn't look back. By the time we made it to the manor, her door was already shut and locked. She didn't come down for dinner. Didn't answer when Simône knocked. Didn't answer when Markus tried.

I couldn't really blame her for avoiding everyone. Hell, I haven't been in the right headspace either. Last night... last night fucked with me.

We nearly kissed. Twice.
She came half-naked in my lap, my fingers inside her, my hand full of her tit like I had every right to it. Then later —Christ— we came together like teenagers on the phone, whispering filthy shit just low enough no one else could hear.

So yeah. Our heads are wrecked today.

She's chosen to hide.
I've chosen to day-drink.

I didn't plan on her hearing me. But the second she asked, *"is he?"* and I answered, it was over. Game fucking over. I lost whatever control I had left.

Well... not *all* control. I didn't end up in her bed with my cock buried inside her. So, I guess that's something.

I don't even know when it happened; when I went from *I hate the bitch* to *I need her to bury my cock inside of her while she calls* **me** *her bitch*. But here we fucking are.

Both of us betraying Rafe in our own ways.

I almost told him this morning. The words were right there, burning the back of my throat, begging to come out.

But I swallowed them.

Because I'm a coward.

I don't want to lose him.

And the worst part? I'm starting to realize I don't want to lose her either.

So that's my day in a nutshell. Running the last twenty-four hours on a loop like some fucked-up highlight reel I never asked for. Every sound she made, every look, every time I should've stopped but didn't.

And while she's been hiding out, I've been drinking cup after cup of whiskey out of my *On my mama. On my pack. I look fly. I bite back.* coffee mug. Classy as hell.

Everyone else has been restless and silent, tension vibrating between us with the weight of what's coming. Waiting for nightfall. Waiting for her.

Rafe's voice was the only solid thing in the noise of it all. "If this goes bad, if she loses control, you keep your distance."

None of us argued when he ordered himself into the corridor cell. It was the only place reinforced enough to hold him if the bond snapped back or if his wolf decided to rip through the house.

He insisted, and though the sight of him locking the door behind himself made Elodie's lip tremble, no one fought him.

The manor feels like a storm shelter before the tornado hits. The air is thick and metallic. The walls are pressing too close. Every tick of the clock slicing thinner the thread between waiting and breaking.

When the corridor doors finally opened, the whole room went dead quiet. Not quiet like respect, quiet like fear. Like someone had dropped a hammer, and all of us froze where it landed. Every voice cut. Every breath held. The pack sat there waiting—waiting for orders, none of us had the balls to give.

And then she came down the steps.

Simple dress. Thin straps. Fabric sliding over her ankles with each step, catching just enough to make you look twice. She was still damp from the shower, hair dragged back into a ponytail, water dripping slowly across her collarbone and disappearing into the fabric.

I wanted to cage her against the wall, put my mouth on her skin, chase every bead down with my tongue.

Goddamn it.

And she didn't even look at me. Not once.

I waved. I actually waved. Hand up, dumb little flick like I was in the bleachers hoping to get noticed by the coach. Nothing. Not even a twitch in my direction.

And fine, yeah, I looked like a fucking idiot. No argument there. But at that moment, I'd have taken even the smallest glance. Half a second of her eyes landing on me. It was the first time I'd laid eyes on her since last night, since everything between us went sideways. No, not sideways...nuclear.

But she kept her eyes straight ahead, calm and measured.

She stopped in front of Rafe's cell, and he was already on his feet, already waiting. Hands flexing at his sides, eyes locked on her face like he was also starving for some kind of sign—anything—that she was breaking as badly as he was.

But she didn't give either of us shit.

Her gaze slid past him to the wall, to the steel cuffs bolted into stone.

"You'll want to use those." Her tone wasn't soft, wasn't cruel either. Just clinical. Practical. A command dressed up as a suggestion.

For a long beat, he just stared at her, jaw clenched, chest tight like he couldn't decide if he wanted to rip the place down or collapse.

Then he let out a rough breath, turned, and pressed his shoulders to the wall.

I didn't wait for anyone else to move.

I stepped inside before doubt could catch me.

The hinges groaned as the door shut; the sound bouncing off the stone. My hands stayed calm even if my chest didn't as I reached for the cuffs.

The clicks rang out loud. One around his wrist. *Snap.* The other. *Snap.* Ankles next, the bite of steel sinking into skin with every lock until Rafe was fixed in place, chained like a beast waiting for slaughter.

When I stepped back, the air itself felt heavier. Dense. Like the room knew what was coming and didn't want to witness it. Nobody spoke. What the fuck could we even say at this point? We were about to witness something that no one thought was possible for eternity.

Then Zaria's voice cut through. "No matter what happens, don't touch Rafe. And don't touch me. Understand?"

We all nodded, automatic. Even me. Instinct knew better than to test her right now.

Her eyes swept over each of us, one by one, holding us there until she was satisfied. Only then did she turn back to him.

"Whatever pain you feel, Rafe, it'll be over soon. Keep your mind centered on me."

She lifted her hands, palms curling as though gripping an invisible rope. The air stilled. Then the lights flickered, shadows bending along the stone walls as the floor beneath us hummed like it was alive.

"Fuck," Rafe rasped, but she didn't cower.

Her arms pulled back slowly. And then, threads of light began to rip free from him.

The sound that tore out of his chest was nothing human nor monster. His head snapped back against the wall, eyes glowing wild, body jerking against the restraints as the bond itself screamed through him.

Zaria's jaw locked, shoulders straining as she dragged the tether out of him strand by glowing strand. The air warped with it, pressing against our lungs.

And the pack—every damn one of us—could feel it too.

The air felt alive, charged, every hair on my body standing on end as Zaria pulled. Rafe's scream rattled the walls; the kind of sound that made my wolf want to claw out of my skin to either fight or flee.

But I couldn't move.

None of us could.

The light-thread ropes kept ripping out of him, one after another, glowing strands thrashing in the air before snapping toward her hands. Each one looked like it cost her more to hold, her arms trembling, black veins now threading against her rich skin.

Rafe's claws strained as if his bones couldn't decide whether to stay human or shift. His head slammed back into the wall again, eyes blazing, and blood seeped where the cuffs dug into his wrists.

The pack was breaking around me. Elodie sobbing into Markus' chest, Simône muttering under her breath, hands shaking like she didn't know whether to jump in or run.

And Zaria... *fuck*, Zaria didn't tremble. She looked carved out of stone, every ounce of her focused on wrenching that bond out strand by strand, like she'd decided she'd burn herself alive before she let it win.

The hum in the air deepened to a roar. My teeth rattled in my skull; my vision swam. Rafe's fangs descended, his bones shifted until finally, the last thread came free.

It didn't just snap. It tore. The sound was like the world splitting open, and the glow that ripped out of him flared so bright, we had to shield our eyes. When I looked again, it was gone. All of it.

Rafe sagged forward, the chains rattling with his weight. His chest rose and fell in shaken jerks, his skin pale, blood streaking down from where the cuffs cut into his wrists. His head lolled against his chest like his neck couldn't remember how to hold it up. Still half shifted.

All I could hear was my own heart pounding, war-drum loud in the hollow of my chest.

My gaze cut to Zaria. Her breath came shallow and ragged. Blood leaked from her nose, from her ears. Her hands shook once, she stumbled back, then she gave out. Her body started to fall.

"Zaria—"

I lunged, but it was too late. Her body hit the stone floor with a sick thud, and the wave came.

Power exploded outward from her in a pulse that wasn't sound, wasn't light, but hit with the same violence as both. It tore through the corridor, flinging us like rag dolls into the walls. My back cracked against the stone, my vision went white, and when I blinked back the haze, the pack was strewn across the ground, groaning, stunned.

I staggered up before I thought better of it and rushed forward.

"Check on Rafe!" I barked, voice rough.

Simône scrambled toward him, Markus right behind. I didn't wait to see what they found. I bent, scooped Zaria into my arms, her body limp and boiling hot as her head lazed against my chest.

"Zaria?" My voice broke on her name. "Zaria, look at me."

Nothing.

Just shallow breaths against my collarbone, the faintest flutter, like she was here and not here all at once.

I bolted for the stairs, clutching her tighter, every step echoing with the same thought tearing me open:

She's not gone. She can't be gone.

I took her to her room and onto the bed, grabbed one of the bags from the heater, and tried coaxing her to drink.

For a moment, it seemed to work.

She stirred, her lashes flickering, and she took one sip. Then another, longer this time, desperate, like it was air she couldn't get enough of.

Relief brushed me, and I took a breath.

But then, she reached for the trashcan and heaved everything back up.

"Fuck." I dropped to my knees beside her, pulling her hair back from her face. Her curls tangled around my fingers, hot with sweat. "What's going on, Zaria?"

Her eyes were dull and frantic when they snapped to mine. "Is he okay? It worked. I can't feel him."

I forced my voice even, even as my chest twisted at her panic. "The pack is with him. They'll let us know if he needs anything. Forget Rafe for one second, Leighton. What's happening with you? Why are you rejecting the blood?"

"I need to check on him." She shoved at the mattress, tried to push herself upright, but her legs buckled immediately.

I lunged, catching her before her head cracked against the nightstand.

Goddamn it. She's not okay.

"Fuck, Zaria." I eased her back down; my arm braced around her shaking frame. "You can't. Look at you; you're damn near shifted. You're burning up, your veins are crawling under your skin. The blood didn't do a thing because you threw it right back up."

She shook her head, trying to push away from me even though she had no strength to spare. "It doesn't stay down anymore. It's like my body rejects it. Every time I try, I get sick. Every time, it comes back up."

"Why the fuck didn't you say something?" My chest was splitting open.

She blinked hard, tears cutting down her cheeks. "I thought...I figured I just needed more time to adjust."

"Fuck."

I scooped her into my arms before she could argue, holding her tight even though her skin scorched mine. She was fire in my arms, live coals searing deeper the longer I carried her. Her fangs had already dropped, and the gold in her eyes was spider webbing darker with black veins.

"Where are we going?" she rasped. Then she inhaled against my throat, running her tongue up the length of it. Her voice broke into a growl. "Mmmm, you smell so *fucking* good, little pup."

My stomach dropped. That was it; the monster rattling its chains, slipping loose. Exactly what I'd been afraid of.

"Zaria..."

Her eyes squeezed shut, jaw trembling as she forced the words out. "Sorry. Dammit. I'm okay. Sorry."

We rounded the corridor, and I shouldered open the far door, shutting it hard behind us.

The eastern wing stretched out empty in front of us. We only kept it for guests or visiting packs when we needed the extra space. Otherwise, it stayed abandoned—quiet, forgotten, tucked far enough from the rest of the house that nobody ever wandered down here.

Which meant if she lost it now, it would just be us.

And when they finally came looking? It'd be weeks before anyone found what was left of me. My desecrated corpse tucked into some corner like a cautionary tale.

Way to be dramatic, Marek. Real productive.

I dropped onto the couch and hauled her into my lap, straddling her across me. She felt weightless in my hands, trembling, her skin hotter than fire against mine. I'd never seen her like this; fading, frail, like she might slip away if I so much as blinked.

"No one's coming here," I said, voice rough, stripped bare. I pulled my shirt over my head, tossed it aside, and forced myself to stay collected when my chest felt like it was caving in. "You need to feed. It's not ideal here at the manor, but it's this or you tear into someone else."

I leaned back against the couch, baring my throat. Her body shifted on my lap, unsteady, her breath ragged against my jaw.

The air vibrated, charged, like it could snap under the weight of the choice sitting between us.

"Come on, baby. You're okay."

SEVENTEEN

Zaria

Baby...

Did he mean to call me that?

Why would he call me that?

To make me more comfortable?

To ground me?

Or was it just... a slip?

Something he didn't mean to let out?

The word burned through me worse than the hunger. I couldn't shake it, couldn't decide if it was tenderness or pity or something else entirely.

And gods help me, a part of me wanted him to say it again.

"Hey." He cupped my jaw, his thumb brushing across my bottom lip. "You're okay."

I didn't answer. My eyes stayed locked on his. And then his gaze dropped to my mouth, lingered there just long enough to make my pulse stutter.

His thumb dragged over the edge of a fang, and fuck— *nothing* could have prepared me for the way that felt. The shock of it lit me up from the inside, my body jerking before I could stop it, heat flaring through me so fast it stole my breath.

His eyes snapped back to mine, wide and burning like he'd been struck too, and for a moment neither of us moved.

Then his thumb pressed again, slower this time, tracing the edge of my fang like he wanted to watch me come apart. My whole body trembled where I straddled him, the shiver running bone-deep.

"Fuuuuck." He groaned. "What are you doing to me?"

I felt his cock twitch hard beneath me, and that was it—I broke. I was starving for him, too far gone to think twice. My fist tangled in his hair, yanking his head to bare the column of his throat, and I sank my fangs in deep.

The rush hit before I even registered it; his arousal lit me up like lightning, igniting every nerve. My hips moved on instinct, grinding against him, like something written into my veins. His response was instant, helpless. I chased friction, needing it like air. We were in the manor, too close to ears, to eyes, to discovery—and still, I couldn't stop.

"Fuck. Fuck." His voice tore ragged, his fist locking at the back of my hair, yanking me tighter, tilting his head, offering more even as his body trembled.

The thread didn't hum this time. It roared. It ripped wide open, a storm of hunger and heat I couldn't shut out. Every pull of his blood slammed his arousal into me, feeding mine back into him until there was no beginning, no end—just one violent circuit sparking hotter, harder.

My fangs sank deeper, and his body arched under me, jerking, fighting.

"Shit. Fuuuuck." The hiss ripped from his teeth. His grip bruised my hips as he hauled me down, grinding forward until every snap of his hips dragged his cock against my clit. The thin barrier of his shorts and my panties was pointless. Every grind burned, every thrust a strike of pressure.

He was trying to stay quiet—I felt it in the shreds of his thoughts, strained and erratic. *Too much. It's too much. She's everywhere—inside me, tearing me apart. Gods, I'm close, I'm so fucking close—*And then darker, louder: *Don't stop. You feel so good. I need to feel my cock inside you.*

I moaned into his throat, hips circling, grinding harder with every pull of blood, every shuddering thrust. The current surged higher, snapping at both of us until he broke with a growl.

He surged to his feet, hauling me with him, my fangs still buried as he slammed me into the mattress. His hips drove down, brutal, piston-hard, his weight crushing me into the sheets. Clothed or not, it didn't matter. My legs locked around his waist, dragging him deeper. The heat, the rhythm, the way his body crashed into mine—it was sex. Hunger and desire fused together, no line left to separate them. I was the monster, and he was the fire that fed it, and together we burned.

His thrusts grew frantic. One hand shoved my dress up to palm my breast, fingers pinching until I gasped. My own hand slid between us, finding his cock inside his shorts, wrapping tight and pulling.

"Goddamn it." His voice cracked, breaking with every ragged thrust. "I can't stop. I can't fucking stop. Fuck, Zaria, I'm gonna—"

I pumped him harder, and his rhythm snapped wild. Then, his fingers shoved inside me, curling rough, and the world detonated. I screamed into his neck as my orgasm ripped through me, my fangs tearing free just as his roar split the room.

His fist grabbed the headboard, wood splintering as he spilled hot into my hand, across my stomach, violent and shuddering. My body convulsed under his, the climax exploding through the bond, dragging me under again with him.

He dropped onto his forearm, shaking, holding himself above me like it was the last thing keeping him from breaking completely. His breath crashed into mine, hot and uneven, his face pressed into my neck like he could hide there, bury himself in the pulse still hammering beneath my skin.

For one fucked-up, impossible heartbeat, it was just us.

The hunger quiet.

The monster caged.

The fire burned out, nothing left but smoke and wreckage.

His weight held me down, pinning me to the mattress, and I didn't push him off.

I couldn't.

My body was still buzzing, twitching, like I'd been struck by lightning and left smoldering.

The bond hummed between us.

And then—

"Since neither of you heard me come in..."

The voice sliced through the haze. Brutal and cold. And furious.

"...you want to tell me what the fuck I just walked in on?"

My entire body went rigid. Marek's head snapped up, eyes blown wide as if he'd been shot. His cock was still pressed against my stomach, twitching from the aftershocks, his breath ragged against my throat.

Simône.

She stood in the doorway, arms crossed, her gaze pinning us both to the bed like we were insects under glass. Her nostrils flared, wolf-sharp, catching every drop of scent that still clung to the air: blood, sweat, sex, hunger.

And I knew—*I knew*—there was no undoing this.

"Fuck." Marek's voice cracked as he scrambled off me, dragging his waistband up over his cock like it might erase what she'd already seen. His chest heaved.

"Simône, let us explain. Please."

"Oh, believe me, Marek." Her tone was ice wrapped in fire. She crossed the room unhurried, like she had all the time in the world to watch us squirm, and dropped into the chair with a precision that made the silence sting.

She steepled her fingers, her eyes never leaving mine. "That's the fucking plan. Explain."

And there I was, standing with him, with his release still sticky on my skin, my dress ruined, my hands trembling because the evidence of what we'd done wasn't going anywhere.

It clung to us.

It lived in the air.

And it stared Simône right in the fucking face.

"Marek's helping me," I blurt out before he could spin it into something worse. "It's not what it looks like. We aren't—" my voice falters on the words, heat crawling up my neck, "—we aren't *sleeping together*."

Her eyes flick. Once. That's all it takes.

To the splintered headboard.

To the tremor still in Marek's body, his chest heaving like he's been wrung dry.

To the waistband he'd only just yanked up, hiding what I'd had my fist around seconds ago.

To my fangs, still not fully retracted.

To the wet patch on my stomach where my dress clings with evidence neither of us can deny.

And then her gaze locks back on me.

"Really?" she says, voice bone-dry, dripping disdain. "Let me tell you what I see. I knocked. No one answered. I hear moaning...and not just any moaning, Zaria. *You.* Moaning." She gestures wide, like the room itself is her exhibit. "I walk in, and low and behold...there you both are. Rafe's brother and his fucking *mate.* From this angle, you were having sex. From the way Marek had to cover his *cock,* you were having sex. From the cum sticking your dress to your stomach, you were having sex. Did I miss anything?"

Marek's jaw flexed hard, but his voice came out pleading, cracked at the edges. "Simône, I swear—"

"No." She cut him off quick, her gaze never leaving mine. She leaned in. "You. Talk. Because if I don't get a straight answer from you right now, I take this to Rafe myself."

"She needs to feed, Simône." Marek's voice cuts through before I can speak. He doesn't back down, doesn't cower. "It was the only way to make sure it was done in a controlled way, so she didn't hurt one of us."

"I almost hurt Rafe," I force out, my throat hoarse. "That first day, before you all came in. If my witch hadn't stopped it, I would've killed him." My chest shakes as I drag in a breath, because saying it out loud feels like confessing to a crime. "Marek is only helping me keep it under control. That's all."

Her eyes narrow with suspicion.

"What you think is having sex..." My voice cracks. I look

away, because, gods, it *did* feel like sex. The memory of his body over mine still pulses hot through my veins. I swallow it back down. "It's a side effect of the werewolf-vampire feeding. Nothing more."

I force my gaze back to her, pleading now. "I love *Rafe*."

When I finally meet her eyes again, mine are pleading. "I love Rafe."

The bond twists hard in my chest as a spike of jealousy bursts from Marek, so thick I nearly gag on it.

"This..." I catch myself, push through. "What you just saw... it's to protect him, not hurt him. And you know as well as I do, he won't see it that way. He'll think it's betrayal. He'll never forgive either of us."

Simône is just...motionless. She studies us like a wolf sizing up prey, weighing whether the kill is worth the mess it'll leave behind. Her stillness is worse than any outburst, worse than any scream. It's judgment, cold and exacting, and it presses down on the room like a vice.

And then Marek breaks it.

"It was me that betrayed Rafe, Simône."

My head whips toward him so fast my neck protests. He doesn't look at me. He holds Simône's gaze like a man daring the executioner to swing the blade.

"I was the one who helped Deveraux. I wanted him to kill Zaria."

The words knock the air from my lungs. Spoken aloud, they're a death sentence. To hear him spit it out, bare and brutal, like confession or absolution... I didn't expect that.

"I hated her," Marek goes on. "You saw it. You heard the fights between me and Rafe. I wanted her gone." His jaw flexes, shoulders rigid, but his eyes never leave Simône's.

"And I couldn't lose him. You, of all people, know what that would do to me. How that would fucking kill me."

Her expression doesn't shift, but I can feel the weight of her scrutiny.

Marek drags in a breath, ragged at the edges. "So, I made her a deal. I asked Zaria if I helped keep her fed, if she'd keep my secret. I begged her. That's all this is."

His fists clench against his thighs, knuckles gone white. "I swear it. That's all it is. I mean, we're fully fucking dressed here, Sims. There's nothing more to it."

The words hang there, thick as blood. I couldn't tell if Marek was trying to protect me or himself.

Simône finally let out a breath, her eyes cutting through us both like only a sister could. "We're opening the corridor in a few hours, once he's awake and fully back to his human form."

Relief surged fast in my chest—then died just as fast when she added, "I suggest you both shower and spritz before you go *anywhere* near him. Because right now, you smell like you just fucked each other, and I guarantee that's what he'll think if it reaches him."

My stomach plummeted. Marek cursed under his breath, dragging a hand down his face.

"I won't tell him what I saw," Simône said, her voice softening, "but you'd better find a more secure way to handle this. Because that—" she gestured at us, at the smashed headboard, the sweat, the mess, "—that wasn't just feeding, no matter how you spin it. It could've been anyone who walked in here. *Anyone.* I just happened to see you walking this direction, and I wanted to make sure you were okay."

Her glare pinned us both, lingering on Marek a beat longer, before she pushed up from the chair and stalked out.

The void she left behind was worse than her words. Because she was right.

The latch clicks, and it's like something inside me breaks open. Marek doesn't hesitate before he crosses the space between us in two strides, and I'm off my feet and wrapped in his arms. The heat of him, the weight of him, is too much. The tears come fast, streaming down my face, burning tracks into my skin.

"I'm sorry," I choke out, my voice muffled against his chest. "I'm so sorry you had to do that."

His arms tighten, fierce, like he's holding me together by sheer will. "It was my choice, Zaria. You don't have anything to apologize for."

I pull back just enough to see his face, the unguarded softness there, and it almost unravels me all over again. "But you covered for me. You..." My throat locks. "You took the blame."

"I did what had to be done," he says simply. "Better me than you. I owe you that much."

EIGHTEEN

Marek

I'd showered quickly and doused myself in enough deodorant spray to choke a horse, and parked my ass on Zaria's sofa like some kind of watchdog. Told myself it was just to keep an eye on her—make sure she wasn't crawling with black veins, no fangs flashing in the dark.

Back to herself. At least, that's the story I fed myself.

The truth was murkier. The feedings blurred everything. It was all too intense. Too close. Too much.

It felt like sex, because how the fuck could it not?

Her straddling me, moaning against my throat, my cock straining. Yeah, you try labeling that "just survival." But that didn't mean I wanted her. I didn't have feelings for her. I just... *owed* her. That's it. That's all it could ever be.

And then the bathroom door opened.

Whatever bullshit I'd been selling myself went straight out the window. Her hair was wet, dark waves hanging heavy over her shoulders. No makeup. Barefoot. Just another flowy, sleeveless dress. Her nipples pressed against the fabric, taut little peaks daring me to stare.

And I did. For half a second too long. Had to drag my eyes away before I gave myself up completely.

She's got to start wearing more fucking clothes.

"Hey." I closed the distance as soon as she stepped out. "I just wanted to make sure you were okay."

What I didn't expect was her arms sliding around my waist, her head pressing against my chest like it belonged there. For a second, I just froze, every instinct telling me to push her back before I did something stupid. But I didn't move.

"I don't know," she admitted, voice muffled against me. "But I'm trying to be. Things are so confusing right now. I feel overwhelmed."

And I had no idea what the fuck to do with that, except stand there and hold her.

"It'll be a few hours before he's up," I said finally, my chin brushing her hair. "You want to talk about it?"

"No." Her voice was small, frayed at the edges. "I'm just exhausted. I'm going to lay down."

"Good idea." I gave her one last squeeze, forcing myself to let go, and turned toward the door.

"Will you stay?" she asked softly. "For a little bit?"

The words stopped me cold. My hand hovered on the knob, the rest of me already betraying the answer I hadn't even spoken yet.

No. I can't stay. I'll do something stupid. I'll say something stupid. I absolutely can not stay.

***

I stayed...

I know what you're thinking. Fucking idiot.

And yeah—*guilty*. But I couldn't say no.

So now here I am, flat on my back with Zaria sprawled across me. Her head on my chest, her leg hooked over mine like we've been doing this forever. She's out cold, breathing easy, and I'm the idiot lying here cataloguing every bad life choice that landed me in this purgatory.

She smells so fucking good. And when she's asleep, her body hums, like a vibration I can feel in my bones. I can't stop staring at her.

We've been laying here for two hours. Which means Rafe should be waking up any moment now. And I can't stop wondering if she will tell him things have shifted with us? That she's conflicted, maybe even about me? Maybe I'm reading into it, but she asked me to stay. She laid her head on my chest. Draped her leg over me. Every turn we've taken has been her pulling first.

What the hell am I supposed to do with that?

My phone buzzing cuts me off. I shift slowly, careful not to jostle her, and check the screen.

Simône: Where are you? I was just knocking at your door.

I've been keeping close to Zaria's room in case she needed anything, so I haven't been in my normal quarters.

Me: I'm with Zaria.

And fuck, the second I hit send, I know I've stepped in it.

Simône: In her quarters?

Me: Yes.

Simône: Okay, I'll be there in a sec.

Shit. Shit, shit.

I don't want to wake Zaria, but goddamn it.

Me: *Now isn't a good time, Sims. She's sleeping. Is Rafe awake?*

Simône: *Why are you in her quarters if she's asleep? Just come to mine, then. I need to talk to you.*

Me: *Sims...is it urgent? Is someone dying? Can it fucking wait?*

Simône: *Too late. I'm at the door.*

Fucking hell.

Me: *Fine. Come in. Keep your voice down. And it's not what it fucking looks like.*

I see it the second she rounds the corner. Her brows damn near climb into her hairline, arms folding tight as she props herself against the doorframe like she's settling in for a show.

"Cozy..." She whispers, lips twitching like she's chewing back a grin.

Fuck.

I roll my eyes and snap the bond tether open to her. *Like I said, it's not what it looks like.*

Her mouth curves wider, but her voice stays silent; her answer firing straight back down the tether. *Marek, it looks exactly like what it looks like. Don't insult me.*

I grit my teeth, careful not to shift under Zaria's weight. *She asked me to stay. She was breaking down. That's all this is.*

And because the universe fucking hates me, Zaria lets out the softest moan and slides her hand under my shirt, palm flattening against my bare stomach as she shifts in her sleep.

I squeeze my eyes shut. *Don't you fucking say a word, Simône. Whatever this is, it cannot be worth this level of awkwardness.*

You're rocking a pretty solid erection for it "not" to be what it looks like.

Fuck.

I nearly choked, biting back the urge to bark out loud. *I hate you. I actually hate you.*

Her answer slid back quick, colder this time. *I hope you know what you're doing, Marek. From here, you look like you're in way too deep for this to end pretty.*

Nothing is going on, I shot back, jaw clenched so tight it ached. *I'm the reason she's so fucked up. I owe it to her to be here when she falls apart.*

Simône's gaze didn't waver, pinning me to the mattress like she could see every lie in my chest. *Be careful,* she warned, her voice barely more than a whisper across the tether. *Debts have a way of turning into shackles before you notice the weight.*

And then she was gone, leaving me under Zaria's hand, under her scent, under the kind of pressure that made it impossible to tell if Simône was wrong—or if I was just too far under to admit she was right.

Another hour crawls by and Zaria's still out cold. Not a stir beyond the small shifts—rolling, tugging, dragging me with her like I'm part of the furniture. And every damn time, she's stayed connected. Fingers laced in mine. Pulling me in closer when she turned over. At one point she used my stomach as a pillow, head nestled dangerously close to my cock like the universe was daring me to break.

Now she's two inches from my face, her arm looped lazily over my neck.

Yeah, it's torture. Pure, merciless torture. But gods help me, I love that she's comfortable enough to sleep this way. Like she trusts me, even after everything. Sleeps peaceful, like the weight of the world finally let her go.

The last thing I want is for Rafe to walk in and see her draped all over me like this. Wouldn't be easy to explain away. And knowing that makes me feel like shit, because it means

I'm hiding things from him.

I start to move her arm, careful, ready to slip out before I make this worse. But her fingers fist in my hair.

"I need you. Please don't go."

Her voice is barely there, and her eyes are still shut, but it shatters me anyway. She tugs me down, closer, until I can feel her breath on my mouth.

"Zaria..." I whisper, but she doesn't answer. Just tilts the tiniest bit, and then her lips brush mine.

And, fuck me, it's over.

That first touch of her lips feels like getting hit by a truck. Every nerve lights up, my chest caves in, and I grab her before I can stop myself, hand buried in her hair, holding her there. Her mouth is soft, warm, everything I swore I'd never let happen, and now it is happening, and I can't pull back.

She sighs into me, lips parting, and the sound tears through me like a goddamn bullet. I kiss her harder, desperate, starving, like this is the thing I've been waiting for without even knowing it.

Then her lashes flicker, eyes cracking open mid-kiss. And I feel the shift. The instant she realizes what's happening and who she's kissing.

I brace for her to shove me off. To snap back to herself and burn me alive for letting it get this far.

But she doesn't.

And I sure as hell don't stop either.

Her mouth stays on mine, hungry, shaky, like she's just as caught in it as I am. And that tiny flicker of realization doesn't snuff it out, it throws gasoline on it.

Her leg slides higher over my hip, pressing in, and now she's flush against my cock. I groan into her mouth because, *fuck*...she *has* to feel how hard I am. And instead of pulling away, she grinds closer. I tilt her head, tongue sliding against hers, and she moans into me like she's starving for it.

I know this is a mistake. Biggest one I've ever fucking made.

"You didn't turn your bond tether off, Marek. Your thoughts are pretty fucking loud."

Fuck.

The haze snapped like we were hypnotized. I tear my mouth from hers, chest heaving, my wolf rattling hard against its cage. Her eyes stay locked on mine, pupils blown wide, her breath just as ravaged as mine.

"And Rafe's awake," Simône adds, her voice shot through the tether just before I slam it closed.

I squeeze my eyes shut, drag in a breath that does nothing, and ease Zaria off me. She's dazed, still half in it, still soft against my hands in a way that guts me.

"Rafe's awake," I say out loud, my voice as defeated as I feel.

She gasps. Her hand flies to her mouth, panic flashing fast across her face. "Oh, God. Oh—oh *God*. Marek, what..."

"We're okay." I say quick, because I can see her spiraling already. "You were asleep. Confused. I should've stopped you." I shake my head, swallowing down the ache. "I'm sorry."

And the truth I don't say hangs between us, burning me alive. I didn't want to stop her.

I push to my feet, composing myself, because every part of me is screaming to finish what we started. Instead, I force out, "We can go down to see him together if you want."

She nods, small, cautious. "That's fine."

I can see the nerves working through her as clear as day. The way her steps come small, measured. The way her hands wring in front of her like she doesn't know what the hell to do with them.

The severing's still raw. The silence of it hums in the walls, pressing on all of us, but I know she feels it worst. And for once, I don't have a single thing intelligent or clever to throw at her. Just the weight of everything we're about to face and everything we've done.

But when we stepped into the living room, there he was. Like nothing had happened. He looked stronger, healthier, as if whatever had been draining him all this time had finally released its hold.

She froze in the doorway when their eyes locked. And for a moment it wasn't just her who stopped breathing — it was the whole fucking house.

"Hey, baby." His voice cracked through the room like thunder.

And that was it. That was all she needed. Whatever restraint she'd walked in here with shattered in an instant. She ran to him, feet barely touching the floor, and he stood just in time to catch her as she leaped into his arms.

Her body folded into his like it had never been anywhere else, her arms knotted around his neck, her sobs muffled against his mouth as she kissed him. And he kissed her back with the kind of devotion that made the rest of us vanish.

Fuck.

Fuck.

Fuck...

"Hi, baby," she choked out between kisses, her hands cupping his face, trembling so hard she looked like she was afraid he might vanish if she let go.

And I swear to god, it split me in half.

It slammed into me like a truck, the sight of her in his arms. I don't even know what the hell I expected — regret, hesitation, anything to show she still felt the wreckage of what went down between us.

But there was nothing.

Things had gotten so goddamn intense. Less than twenty-four hours ago, her pussy clenched tight around my fingers while I spilled into her fist. Less than ten minutes ago, she had her tongue in my mouth after napping and fucking cuddling with me for hours. And now she's wrapped around him like none of it ever happened.

Should we talk about it? Call it what it was? Try to untangle how the fuck we went from feeding to practically fucking to making out to this? Because right now, I feel like I'm the only one drowning in the aftermath. Like she can just use me, bleed me, get herself off in my lap and then walk straight back to him like I'm nothing more than a vein on tap.

It should've felt like relief. Like victory. She severed a mate bond and still had this — him, *them*.

She'd done the impossible, and I should've been grateful just to still be breathing in her orbit.

But all it felt like was loss.

Because I'm fucking falling in love with her.

And there's not a goddamn thing I can do about it.

"Can we talk to everyone later?" She asked, her gaze flicking over the room, then back to him. "I need to be with you."

Rafe nodded, setting her on her feet. He gave us a glance — brief, unreadable — and then they were walking out, his hand settling at the small of her back, thumb brushing just above her ass as he guided her toward the stairs.

The same ass I'd had in my hands less than an hour ago.

I shoved the thought down hard, clearing my throat, forcing my jaw to stay locked.

But when I turned, Simône was already staring at me. Markus and Elodie were busy giggling with each other in the corner like fucking teenagers.

But Simône's eyes were equal parts indignant and worried, weighing me in silence. She didn't have to say a word. I could feel her questions. Her doubts. Her judgment.

And me? I stood there stone-faced, pretending I wasn't burning alive. Pretending I hadn't just crossed a line I swore I'd never touch. Pretending I wasn't already in too deep.

"It's been a long fucking night." I dragged a hand through my hair and dropped into the chair across from Markus and Elodie. My body felt like lead, my bones still humming from the corridor, from her, from all of it. "You guys okay after everything that went down?"

Markus doesn't answer right away. His arm is around Elodie, holding her close, practically on his lap. Finally, he sighs.

"We're alive, not sure *okay* is the word."

"I'm going for a swim." Simône's voice cracked through the air. She stalked out before anyone could answer, her fury trailing behind her. Even with my tether muted, I felt the burn at the edges of my chest, restless and cold.

I leaned back, motioning with a tilt of my chin between Markus and Elodie. "Is this thing official?"

Elodie's hand tightened around his, a small squeeze that gave her away before she even opened her mouth. When she finally did, her smile was sheepish, almost shy.

"Official."

And that was it. Just like that, another line drawn, another bond cemented.

Then there were two.

I pushed to my feet, the chair legs scraping against stone, loud enough to make them both flinch.

I needed space.

Air.

Anything that didn't feel like it was pressing down on my chest, squeezing until I couldn't breathe.

"It's about time," I muttered, leaning down to press a quick kiss to Elodie's cheek before she could pull back. My hand clapped Markus' shoulder, solid, grounding. "I'm happy for you two." And I meant it, even if the words tasted foreign on my tongue.

I turned, heading for the hall, but I barely made it three steps.

The air shifted—thick, electric, like a storm had crept into the manor. My skin prickled, the hairs on my arms rising before I even registered why.

The first wave hit like an open nerve through my spine, snapping my knees forward until my palm slammed to the wall. My breath hissed out between my teeth.

"What the fuck..." I rasped, jaw locked.

The next wave buckled me. My vision blurred, my cock straining hard against my shorts. I swallowed a moan, but it clawed up anyway; animal and shameless.

Panic hit just as hard.

What the fuck is happening to me?

I spun, staggered down the hall, and slammed into my room. I shut the door and made my way to the bathroom. I slapped my hand on the doorframe, gripping it, shattering it in my fist as another wave crashed over me.

My head tipped back with a snarl, my balls tightening, my body coiled to break.

I turned the shower on; the water roared. Another surge hit before I could even brace against something, dragging me to the floor next to the tub. My knees cracked against the rug, my fists clenched until the threads cut into my palms.

My back bowed like it was going to snap clean in two, every nerve flaring white-hot, every vein sparking like someone had jammed electricity straight into my spine. My chest heaved, desperate for air that didn't feel like fire.

And then it clicked. The pulse, the drag, the unbearable hunger curling low in my gut. My brain slammed into the only answer it could give me. The one I didn't want.

"Are you fucking him?" The words rasped out, broken. "Is *that* what I feel right now?"

The room gave me nothing but the sound of my own ragged breathing. And then...her voice. Not a memory. Not a dream. Her. Inside me.

"Marek? Oh god, no...You can't be here, How—? Oh fuck."

My head jerked back, teeth bared though I was alone. "I don't know. But *fucking make it stop.*"

"I'm trying—" her voice cracked, ragged, undone, tearing through me like barbwire dragged under my skin. *"I'm so sorry. We're still tethered somehow. Oh... fuck... oh god..."*

Her gasps bled through me, her moans catching like hooks in my chest, dragging me under with her. My cock strained hard, painfully throbbing against my shorts, every thrust that wasn't mine ripping through me, anyway. I slammed a fist against the floor, another wave breaking me in half.

Her climax built inside me like it belonged to me, like I was the one inside her, and I couldn't hold it back.

"Please, I didn't—oh god!—I didn't know. Marek, please... don't be angry with me. I can't stop it. I can't close it."

Another brutal surge hit, ripping the air from my lungs. My hips bucked forward like they weren't mine anymore. My hand was on my cock before I even knew it, fist locking tight, dragging hard, fast and desperate. The hunger wasn't just mine—it was hers, pouring through my veins, coiling around every nerve, every muscle, until I couldn't tell if the pleasure was me jerking off in the dark or her riding him into the mattress.

"God—Marek—I can feel you." Her cry cracked in my skull, frantic and breathless. *"You're gonna come. I can't close it—I tried. Oh—right there, FUCK—oh GOD!"*

My free hand clawed the rug, tearing fibers loose, my whole body bowing like it wanted to break in half. Every stroke I dragged was hers. Every gasp in my throat braided with her moans. Every shudder in my spine felt like it came from her body, not mine.

"Fuuuuck." The sound ripped out of me, ragged, helpless. My fist pumped faster, tighter, slick with precum, my cock straining like it was going to tear through my skin.

"I'll be fine," I choked, my voice breaking on a moan. "Stop fighting it. Just—*fuck*—just come. Maybe the connection will snap if we both—" My words splintered into another groan. "Come, baby. Just fucking *come.*"

Her voice climbed, higher, wilder, desperate enough to gut me. *"Marek—fuck—it's too much—yes—oh god—oh god! Yes, Marek! Fuck, Rafe!"*

Her climax blew through my head like a goddamn thunderclap, ripping me apart with no mercy. My body locked, strung too tight, and then I was gone—spilling into my fist, fire ripping through me, a growl tearing up my throat until it felt like I'd coughed up glass.

When it finally let me go, I dropped. Rolled onto my back on the tile, shaking so hard I could barely breathe. Sweat poured off me. Felt like I'd run for miles but couldn't get a single full lung of air.

And through all of it—her scream. Still echoing in my skull. Still clawing at me.

Proof it wasn't mine. Never was.

I don't know how long I laid there before I forced myself up. Splashed cold water on my face just to calm the tremors, then stumbled to the bed. Sat there hunched over, head in my hands, body still humming like I'd been rewired.

The bond finally snapped after the climax, but it left me wrecked. Every vein buzzing like I was still tied to her, still inside her, even while she was in another room, wrapped up with him.

A knock shattered the haze, loud enough to make me flinch.

"Yeah," I rasped, voice shredded to gravel.

The door swung open, and Zaria rushed in, slamming it behind her. Two strides and she was on me—arms locked around my neck, trembling. I sat frozen, every muscle coiled, because if I touched her now—if I even let myself breathe her in—I'd come apart all over again.

Didn't matter. Her scent wrapped me anyway. Clinging to my skin until the burn underneath threatened to split me wide open.

"Where's Rafe?" The words cracked out, the only shield I had left.

"He's in the shower." Her voice was frantic, ragged at the edges. She pressed closer, chest flush to mine, and my traitor heart hammered against her like it didn't care what lines we'd already crossed. "Please. Marek, I'm so sorry. Are you okay? Are you hurt?"

A sound tore out of me. My fists dug into the mattress on either side of me, fabric tearing under my grip, holding myself there instead of doing what every part of me wanted, shoving her off or dragging her down.

"You tore through my head like a fucking storm, Leighton." My eyes locked on hers, fury and want twisting until I couldn't tell one from the other. "Do I *look* okay to you?"

Her face crumpled. Tears brimmed, streaking fast before she could stop them. She cupped my jaw with shaking hands. "I didn't know, Marek. I didn't know there'd still be a tether after the feeding. It's been hours."

"Well, maybe you've never fucked him hours after feeding either. So, I guess we're both still learning how this bullshit works."

Fuck, that came out too harsh. I need to step away.

I peeled her arms from me, one finger at a time, until her hands fell useless at her sides. Then I stood, forcing space between us before the weight of her broke me in half.

Her breath hitched. Her lips parted like she wanted to argue, to reach for me, to promise me something that wouldn't make this worse—but she didn't. She just stared, eyes locked on mine, searching for something I didn't have. Something I couldn't even find for myself.

"You better get back. I need to grab a shower."

I didn't wait for her to move. Didn't give her another second to try and bridge the space I was already drowning in. I turned, walked into the bathroom, and shut the inner door hard enough to rattle the frame.

Then, because I'm such a mature fucking adult, I put my fist through the wall.

Knuckles split. Pain flared. Didn't fix a damn thing.

Fuck...

NINETEEN

Rafe

That was the hardest we've ever gone. The most intense. But something was off.

She was there, beneath me, around me, nails dragging trenches down my back—and yet she *wasn't* there.

Not fully.

Not with me.

And without the hum of our bond anymore, I couldn't feel her out. Couldn't read her the way I used to.

The scratches she left are already gone, healed before the water could rinse them away, but I can still feel the echo of them. She's never come that hard in my arms, not once. Not like that. And gods help me, I don't know if it was because of me—or in spite of me.

It was the first time we'd been together since the day she woke and I fucked her shifted. I can't stop replaying it. How far I went. How feral. My hand around her throat until bruises bloomed, just to watch them vanish. My claws carving into her back, and her body convulsing, milking me like she wanted the pain as much as the pleasure.

But something shifted halfway through. Her eyes slammed shut, her lips parting like she was somewhere else.

With someone else.

And suddenly it didn't feel like I was fucking my mate—it felt like I was fucking a ghost of her, and she was doing the same to me.

Two strangers wearing each other's skin, clawing our way to release like it would save us.

And it worked.

We both shattered harder than we ever had.

But the aftermath? It broke me wide open.

I showered, scrubbing until my skin stung, and when I came out, she was just stepping back into the room.

"I went to check on everyone," she said quickly, climbing under the covers without looking at me. She turned her back, pulled the blanket up like armor. I could smell the tears still fresh on her skin, even if she didn't let me see them.

I should've pressed.

Should've demanded the truth.

But instead, I slid in behind her, draped my hand over her hip, and breathed her in like that alone might tether her back to me.

"You're so fucking powerful, baby. I can't believe how powerful you are." The words slipped out against her skin as my mouth moved—shoulder, back, the warm curve of her neck. Little claims. Quiet confessions.

I kept my voice low, almost a whisper, like if I said it any louder I might spook her, might break whatever fragile thread was keeping her here with me. "I know you worry," I murmured into her hair, "that it's just fear. That maybe we don't see you anymore—just what you've turned into."

Her back twitched under me, the smallest flinch. My arm tightened across her waist, locking her against my chest so she couldn't pull away. My heart beat so hard it felt like I was trying to pound the truth into her ribs.

"Yeah, there's fear," I admitted, words rough, rushed out before she could twist away. "I won't bullshit you. But it's not *just* fear. It's fucking awe. When I look at you—when I feel you—it's like standing in front of a storm. Scares the shit out of me, yeah. But it's beautiful too. It's bigger than me. And I wouldn't walk away. Not even if I could."

I pressed my forehead to her shoulder, breathing her in like it might center me. "Don't hide from me, Zaria. Not your strength. Not the ugly parts. Not the parts you think are gonna break me. I'm not afraid of you. I'm fucking in awe of you."

She shifted, her chin ducking, her lips parting on something that cut straight through me: "I was worried it was just the bond that tied you to me. And I wouldn't have been able to handle watching you turn away from me too. Not wanting me. Not loving me. That's why I pushed you away. I'm sorry."

The words undid me.

"Zaria." My voice came out rough, scraping low, as I caught her hand and pressed it flat to my chest. The constant, wrecked beat hammered against her palm. "Listen to me. The bond is gone. You cut it clean. I felt it snap. And yet—" I pressed harder, desperate for her to feel it. "I'm still here. Wanting you. Loving you. Nothing dragged me here. Nothing bound me here. This is just me."

Her lips trembled. Her eyes flicked up, storm breaking open in them—fear, doubt, grief she shouldn't have to carry.

The words gut me. The ache that slices through my chest is almost worse than the severing itself. She doesn't see it. She doesn't see me.

I lean in, kiss her forehead, then her temple, lingering like maybe my mouth could brand truth into her skin. "You didn't force me into this. You never could. Sever the bond a thousand times and I'd still find my way back to you. Not because I have to. Because I choose to. Every fucking time."

Her breath caught; her voice splintered. "I missed you so much. I'm sorry I hurt you. I'm sorry I ran. I didn't know what else to do."

"You were in your head. I could tell. You were here—" I pressed my forehead to hers, voice rough, "—you were coming with me, shaking apart with me...but your mind was someplace else. Is that what's been eating at you?"

Her eyes locked onto mine, shining, brimming until the first tear slipped free.

"Hey..." I kissed her lips, soft, a whisper of a kiss meant to anchor her, to bring her back. "Whatever it is, just talk to me, baby."

Her chest heaved against mine, the words breaking out like they'd been trapped too long. "Everything is different now. I'm different now, Rafe." She buried her face in my chest, her sobs tearing through both of us. "My hunger—it's made me do things. And I don't..." Another sob cracked her voice, this time, like she hated herself just for speaking.

I rubbed slow circles on her back, holding her tighter, refusing to let her slip away again.

"I've made some really bad choices," she whispered. "And I can't walk them back. I can't undo them. And I don't know how to live with that."

"Zaria," I breathed, cupping the back of her head, pressing my forehead to hers. "You've been Blooded for days. Days.

You're newborn in this, stumbling in the dark. Of course, you're going to make mistakes. Of course you're going to fuck up. And yeah—some of those choices are gonna scar. They'll live with you forever." My thumb brushed a tear off her cheek. "But no one—*no one*—expects you to know how to navigate this yet."

I let my nails graze her scalp, soothing, then dragged them down the length of her spine until her trembling softened against me. Anchoring her, the only way I knew how.

"You don't owe anyone an explanation for your choices," I murmured into her hair. "Not the pack. Not me. Not a goddamn soul. You'll find your rhythm in this life, baby. You'll learn what your hunger demands, what balances you, what doesn't. No one can decide that for you. No one can carry it for you." I tipped her chin until her eyes met mine again, fierce through the tears. "You hear me? This is yours. And you don't have to apologize for surviving it."

"The bags are making me sick. And I...well...*before* the bags..."

"Baby." My hand slid to the back of her head, pulling her closer until her breath warmed my throat. "You don't owe me anything."

"You don't understand, Rafe. Just let me finish so I can get this out, please?"

I huffed a laugh, kissed her temple, trying to play it light even as my chest ached like hell. "I kindly decline your request, baby."

Her brows pinched, confusion flickering through her tears, but I caught her face in both hands before she could argue. "I called Elowen. Our pack threadseer. She can help you. Maybe even bind some of the power, help you get a handle on it."

Her whole body jolted, and she sat up, twisting to face me

fully. "What?"

"She can help, Zaria." I reached for her hands, but she pulled back, retreating an inch that felt like a mile. The space between us felt colder immediately. "It's not permanent. Just to dim some of it, take the edge off before it eats you alive."

Her head snapped, eyes wild through the shimmer of her tears. "You *know* that's not how binding works, Rafe. It's not some dimmer switch. It's binding all of it. All or nothing." Her voice broke, disbelief cracking into it. "You called her here? To strip the power from me?"

"No." My chest clenched, words tumbling out dry. "Not like that, Zaria. That's not what I meant. I wasn't trying to take anything from you, I was trying to help. You're struggling, baby. I can see it. We can all see it."

Her laugh was short and bitter. "Then why not ask me before reaching out to her? Why not trust me with the choice, Rafe? You decided for me. Again."

My hands were aching to touch her, to pull her back in, but every inch of her body screamed that I'd pushed her further away.

"I'm going to make some tea." Her voice was steady, but the way she pulled from me felt anything but. She slipped her dress back on, quick, like she couldn't get covered fast enough.

"Are you okay? Are *we* okay?"

She froze in the doorway, her hand gripping the frame. She didn't look back. "I don't know, Rafe."

Fuck...

And then she walked out, leaving me in the aftermath she didn't want to carry.

TWENTY

Marek

"Do you have feelings for her, Marek?"

Of course, that's the first thing out of her mouth. Not a hello, not a knock, just barging in here like four in the goddamn morning is the perfect time for a heart-to-heart. Apparently, Simône has decided that breaking into my room uninvited counts as sibling bonding now.

Not that she woke me. Sleep hasn't touched me since last night. Since the tether. Since Zaria. I've been flat on my back for hours, staring holes into the ceiling like maybe it'll cough up some kind of answer. Hands locked behind my head, chest tight, body humming with too much I can't name. Not hunger. Not lust. Not grief. Some fucked-up tangle of all of it that doesn't fit into words.

So when Simône slides in, shuts the door like she's sealing us in for interrogation, it doesn't even surprise me that's her opener. Just pisses me off that it hits as hard as it does.

"No," I fire back.

"You're lying."

"You're projecting."

"You're being a dick."

"And you walked into my quarters," I snap, finally dragging my eyes from the ceiling to hers.

She's posted against the wall, arms folded, chin tipped down, gaze breaking me open. Simône's wolf doesn't miss much—not the crack in a voice, not the stink of guilt, not the rot of someone trying to bury feelings alive. And she's looking at me like she already knows the answer, like she just wants to hear me choke on it.

My chest is pulling so tight, it feels like something might snap. I can already feel her winding up for the next strike, and, fuck me, I don't have the strength left to block it.

"How long have you had feelings for her?" Her voice drops softer than I expect, and somehow that cuts deeper than if she'd just screamed at me. She pushes off the wall, moves closer, perches on the edge of the bed. Her scent fills the room; familiar, grounding, strangling all at once.

"I don't know."

That's the truth. I don't fucking know when this started.

"So, you do." Simône's head tilts, eyes narrowing like she's peeling me apart piece by piece. "You have feelings for her."

My hand drags down my face. I tip my head back against the headboard, staring straight ahead. "I don't know."

"Marek." Her hand lands warm on my calf, grounding in a way that makes me want to shake her off and cling tighter all at once. "You despise vampires. Always have. Your entire life you've hated what they are, what they do. You've hunted them for sport, killed them for breathing wrong. And now?" Her grip tightens, nails just shy of digging in. "You let her feed from you. You *enjoy* it. She curled up next to you for hours. You kissed her. And your thoughts—fuck, Marek—they were something else."

I shut my eyes, jaw locked tight enough to crack. I don't want to think about this, let alone speak it into air. Goddamn her for making me.

"I know." It's all I've got.

But she doesn't let me off. "Does she know?"

I force a breath. "No. She thinks I hate her." I run a head through my hair. "Why would she think otherwise? I tried to have her killed."

"Are you going to tell her?"

"Nope."

"Why?"

I closed my eyes, wishing the ceiling would just cave in and put me out of this conversation. "Because I've loved two people in the past few hundred years, Simône. Two. And those two people..." My throat works, but I force it out. "...they love each other. Not me. So, what's the point?"

Her silence hangs heavy, like she wants to argue but doesn't know where to start.

"Marek..."

"What, Simône?" My voice snaps hard.

"You just said you love her."

My chest locks up, every instinct screaming at me to deny it, to throw the words back in her face. But what's the point? Lying now would be a joke.

"I know."

Before I can brace, she dives on top of me, arms looping my neck, dragging me into an involuntary hug. Pretty sure this qualifies as assault in at least three countries.

"I know you're hurting," she murmurs into my shoulder,

stubborn as hell, "and I'll let you get some sleep as soon as you hug me back."

I glare at the ceiling, arms pinned, dignity bleeding out by the second. "Are you blackmailing me for physical affection?"

"Yes." She doesn't budge an inch. "Yes, I am."

I stare at the ceiling another long beat, jaw tight enough to crack. Her arms don't loosen. She's not going anywhere.

"Goddamn it," I mutter, finally lifting an arm and looping it stiffly around her. The world's most reluctant hug.

"There it is." She squeezes tighter, smug as hell.

"Don't get comfortable," I warn, though my hand settles at her back, anyway. "This expires in thirty seconds."

"Uh-huh. Sure it does." She tucks her chin on my shoulder.

I keep my arm around her longer than I should. Too long for a brother–sister hug. Too long for someone who's been trying all goddamn night to forget everything.

She's warm, solid, the only thing in this house that doesn't feel like it's sliding out from under me. When she leans back, it isn't far—her breath still ghosts over my cheek.

And for a second, fuck it. A woman's on top of me. One I've already crossed that line with once before. Maybe I can bury all this shit under her mouth, under something that isn't Zaria.

I grip her chin, tilt her face, and take her mouth. She lets me—for a heartbeat. Her lips crash into mine, familiar, hungry, and I almost believe this is what I need. My hand slides up her back, under her shirt, gripping the nape of her neck as my tongue dips deeper.

Then she pulls away. Breathless. Her hand firm on my chest.

"Marek..." Her voice is quiet, but it slices me clean. "Don't do that. Don't use me to forget her."

I freeze. Every excuse, every denial dies in my throat.

Her eyes lock on mine. "I won't be a stand-in for something that doesn't belong to me."

And that's it. She climbs off the bed.

"Fuck." The word rips out of me. I shoot up, chasing her before she can hit the door.

"Hey... Sims." My hand catches her wrist, pulling her back just enough to wrap her up in my arms. "Fuck, I'm sorry. You're right. My head's messed up and I shouldn't have done that. I'm so sorry."

"I get it." Her arms press into my back before she lets go. "I just can't let myself go there. Even if it would feel good in the moment."

I arch a brow. "So, you're saying it felt good?"

"I hate you."

Her fist drives into my gut; playful, but enough to knock a grunt out of me, and then she's walking away. Not before tossing me a smirk over her shoulder that feels like salt in the wound.

"What is that smirk?" I growl, pushing off the wall and following her down the hall. "There is nothing to smirk about. I am confident in my abilities, Simône."

She quickens her pace, ignoring me like I'm background noise.

"Goddamn it, woman. Did it or didn't it?"

Now she's practically sprinting, her laugh bouncing off the walls, and I'm on her heels like a lunatic, chasing an answer I know she'll never give me.

As soon as I gain on her, she whirls, plants a hand on the

wall, and does some kind of parkour bullshit that gets her past me. I stumble forward, straight into the table at the end of the hall.

"Mother. Fucker."

By the time I push back to my feet, she's gone. Vanished like smoke. I shake my head, laughter breaking out of me anyway. Damn it, I fucking needed that.

I head toward the kitchen, still grinning, ready for water to wash down the ache in my ribs. But the second I step in, the grin dies.

Zaria's there.

She's at the far end of the island, knees pulled up under her like a kid too small for the chair. A cup of tea steams at her elbow, a book balanced open across her lap.

I stop dead, just watching. For a moment she looks... ordinary. Human, even. Like nothing about her could possibly hold the kind of power that ripped me apart last night. Like she isn't the reason my chest still feels raw.

"You know we have a library for that," I say finally, aiming for light, casual. Teasing, even.

Her head lifts, eyes catching mine. A small smile ghosts across her mouth, but it never makes it to her eyes. "Sorry," she murmurs, slipping a ribbon between the pages and closing the book. She reaches for her cup, her phone, already pulling herself together like she can't get out of here fast enough.

"I wasn't saying to leave, Zaria." The words come out too fast. I rake a hand through my hair, cursing myself, then force the edge down. "I was... I was just..."

Her eyes flick up, guarded.

"Stay," I say finally. One word I didn't mean to give. My throat works once before I add, quieter, "Please."

She hesitates, mug caught in her hands, body half-turned like she's ready to bolt. The clock ticks on the wall, loud enough to count every second she doesn't move. Then she eases back into the chair, fingers brushing the rim of the cup like she's testing how long it'll hold her.

I drop into the chair across from her, careful not to lean in, not to show that every nerve in me is lit with shit I'll never say.

She's the one who breaks it. "Sorry again about what happened last night. We didn't see you at dinner. Are you okay?"

"Yeah." The word lands empty, so I clear my throat. "Fine."

Her eyes flick up to mine, unflinching. "You don't seem fine."

A laugh slips out, short, empty. "And you don't look like someone who just ripped a centuries-old bond out of an Alpha's chest and walked away standing." My gaze stays on hers. "Guess we're both liars."

She swallows, her gaze dropping back to her tea. "I didn't mean to drag you into it. Any of it. I keep pulling people into the fire with me and...I'm sorry, Marek. For all of it."

I lean back in the chair, folding my arms. "You didn't drag me anywhere. I walked. Eyes open. Maybe that makes me the idiot."

She looks up at me then, and there's something raw in her face, something unguarded. "Why?"

It's my turn to swallow hard. The truth claws at my throat, but I choke it back down. "Doesn't matter."

Her lips part, like she wants to press, but she doesn't. She just nods, quiet, and for a moment all I can hear is the tick of the clock and the faint clink of her spoon against the cup.

"I think I better try to get some sleep before we have to be at the office," she says finally, pushing her chair back with a soft scrape. "It's a big day with the Montgomery family coming in to meet with you all." Small talk, exit strategies, her way of easing out before this conversation can dig its claws any deeper.

"Do you need to feed before work?" I close the distance before I can talk myself out of it, close enough to breathe her in. "Or is Rafe going to take that over now that you two are... you two again?"

Her spine stiffens, her fingers tightening on the edge of her book like she's strangling the truth out of it. She doesn't look up right away, and when she finally does, her eyes are careful and measured. Like she's debating whether to hand me honesty or just another deflection.

We're standing too close. I know it. I should back off. But I don't.

"I can't feed from a Lycavor. I'd kill him." Her voice is clipped, controlled. "I have my bags."

"They don't work, Zaria."

"They will." Her chin tips up, defiant, as if sheer stubbornness can make it true. "It's fine."

"In the meantime?"

Her jaw flexes. "It's fine, Marek. I'm going to bed."

"Goddamn it, Zaria."

I grab her hand before she can slip away again and pull her with me, my stride longer than I mean it to be.

"Where are we going?" She asks, stumbling once to keep up.

"Somewhere we can talk this shit out. Privately." My voice is a growl now, low enough not to rattle the whole fucking manor, but intense enough to slice through any protest.

"If you want to stop me, then you're gonna have to throw me against another goddamn oak tree."

That makes her falter. Her eyes flash wild for half a heartbeat before she reins it in. But she doesn't stop me. She doesn't let go.

I snatch the keys off the hanger, and we slip out into the night, both of us barefoot, both of us in pajamas like fugitives running from the same crime. The SUV's parked on the side of the manor, and neither of us says a word as I gun it down the back road. The suffocating quiet in the car thrums hot, almost unbearable, the air thick with everything we're not saying.

"I don't have my keys," she mutters finally as make it to her apartment door.

"Zaria..." My voice drags with warning.

Her shoulders sag. "*Fine.*" She presses her palm to the lock. The tumblers click, the deadbolt snaps back, and the door eases open like the apartment itself is obeying her.

I push it wider and step aside. "After you."

She slips inside, quiet as a shadow, and I follow. The air's thick with her—jasmine, storm rain, and that copper thread I can't shake. The space feels smaller with her in it, the charge between us climbing higher instead of burning out.

She doesn't flip on a light. Just stands there in the middle of the room, arms crossed tight, eyes on me like she's already done with whatever this is.

"Well?" Her voice is brittle, almost breaking. "You dragged me out here in the middle of the night. What is it you think we need to talk about so badly?"

I stand there longer than I should, jaw clenched, every excuse I thought I had falling apart.

I shut the door behind us. "Everything you're refusing to say out loud. About the tether. About why you can't keep the blood down. About why the hell I could feel you when you were fucking him."

Her breath hitches, shoulders tightening, but she doesn't deny it. Doesn't even look away.

TWENTY ONE

Zaria

"Then we came here for nothing, Marek."

The words are bitter the second they leave me. I fold my arms tighter across my chest, nails biting into my palms just to keep control. "I don't have any answers. None. And you don't have to keep giving yourself to me; I get it. I fucking get it. You made everything clear last night."

His head snaps up, green eyes locking on me. "What the hell are you even on about, Leighton? Clear?" He lets out a rough laugh. "I was head fucked into a *threesome* at your mate reunion with Rafe after we got each other off in the east wing and made out in your bed. Tell me, Zaria, what exactly did I make clear?"

I flinch, heat rising in my face, but the words are already clawing their way up, pressing against my. "You made it clear that I'm just… an obligation. A fucking problem to manage. A tether you never asked for, feeding you things you don't even want to feel. That's what last night showed me."

His chest heaves, his voice grits low. "And how exactly did I make that so clear to you, Leighton?"

"You were… angry. You pushed me away."

His laugh is jagged, ugly, nothing like humor. "You fucked him after you had your tongue in my mouth and my cum all over you. What exactly would've been the better reaction, Zaria? You want me to clap for you?"

"Exactly…I have my bags, Marek." My voice is thinner than I want, frayed, already breaking.

His eyes narrow, suspicion darkening them, but I don't give him the chance to cut me down. I push through.

"I won't say anything to him. I'll keep my promise." My throat burns, the weight of it catching fire on the way out. I can't look at him—not when his face might undo me. "Just… just take me back to the manor. This was a mistake. Coming here. Thinking there was anything left to talk about."

"You don't even realize what last night did to me, do you?" His voice is ragged, confused, furious all at once. His chest rises hard, like every word is being ripped out of him. "I could feel you fucking him, Zaria. Do you understand that? I felt it like it was my cock inside of you. I was dragged along for every thrust, every moan, every clench—and none of it was mine."

He takes a step closer, eyes blazing. "You. Aren't. Mine."

Another step. The heat of him bleeding into me. "But you feel like you are when your hand is wrapped around my cock."

Closer still, his timber dropping so low, it sent sparks straight through my legs. "When I'm coming on your stomach."

His eyes pin me as he closes the last bit of space between us. "When your pussy clenches around my fingers."

Fuck.

My whole traitorous body jolts, heat coiling deep even as

shame lances through me.

Fuck. Fuck, fuck.

His voice is lower now. "So why, Zaria? Why the fuck did you let me bring you here?"

"*You* said you wanted to talk." I could barely get the damn words out.

"We could've talked at the manor. The pool house. My room. South wing. Anywhere." His body crowds mine until my back hits the wall. "But you let me drag you here."

"So what? This is some kind of test now?"

"No. I think you did it on purpose. Last night. You could rip a mate bond out of Rafe's chest and survive it, but you couldn't shut down that tether? Couldn't block me out while you were riding his cock?"

"I didn't!" My palms press weakly into his chest. It's pathetic; he doesn't even budge, because I don't want him to. He could be flung into the wall with a flick of my wrist. But, my body's moving without my mind's permission, shoving just to prove I can, not because I actually want distance.

"I don't believe you, Zaria. Either you did it on purpose, or you were thinking about me while you were fucking him. That's why it tethered."

My breath stutters. "You're an arrogant, self-centered bastard."

His eyebrows raise, almost daring me to keep going. So, I do.

"You think I'd *choose* that? You think I'd tether myself to you while I'm in Rafe's arms? Do you have any idea how fucked that sounds?" My voice cracks again. "I don't even want this, Marek. Any of it. You think I want your wolf's blood clawing through me like flames every time I feed? You think I want *you* bleeding into me when I'm trying to hold on to the only man I've ever loved?"

My hands tremble. "You were supposed to be a secret. A solution. Nothing more. And now you're standing here accusing me of *wanting* this? Fuck you. You don't know what I want."

"Then tell me you weren't thinking about me."

My mouth opens, but nothing comes out.

He doesn't give me space to dodge. His hand tips my chin up, rough but not cruel, forcing me to meet him. He's so close I can feel the scrape of his breath, the ghost of his bottom lip brushing mine.

"Because when you came, Zaria..." his jaw ticks. "You moaned *my* name. You caught yourself and *then* called out for Rafe. I heard it. I *felt* it. And I've replayed it since. Over and over. The sound of you coming. You. Screamed. *My*. Name."

The air between us snaps, charged so thick it's choking. My stomach lurches; my pulse riots. His chest heaves like dragging the words out split him open, like he's bleeding in front of me just to get the truth out.

"Say the words, Zaria." His hand clamps around my throat firm enough to steal the breath from my protest. And the fact that he's still standing here, not pinned to the wall by my power, tells him everything he needs to know.

His eyes bore through me, molten, dangerous. "Say it. You wanted my cock to be the one inside you while you were fucking him. The truth. Now."

Fuck. The denial burns on my tongue, but my fangs ache, my power hums; and nothing comes. I can't force the lie. I can't make it stick.

"Yes."

Hi grip on my throat tightens as his growl deepens. "Good. Fucking. Girl."

The words are barely free when his mouth slams into mine. It's not even a kiss; it's fury and hunger and need tearing at each other. Teeth clash. Breath steals.

Hi lifts me against the wall, anchoring me there, pinning me to the truth I just confessed. The truth I can't take back.

I don't want to.

My hands clawed into his shirt, yanking him closer, his body pressing into mine, every line of him taut.

"You think I haven't thought about this?" he growls into my mouth. "Every fucking time you fed, Zaria. Every sound you made. Every goddamn taste of you."

My answer is a whimper into his kiss, my hips grinding against the hard line of him, needing friction like breath.

The kiss turns hungrier and filthier by the second. His hand fists in my hair, dragging my head back so his mouth can devour the line of my throat.

Clothes become weapons, barriers we tear at. His shirt goes first, ripped over his head and flung aside. My dress is shoved up, bunched around my hips, his hands gripping bare skin like he's trying to hold on while losing control.

He carries me to my bedroom, and we crash onto the bed, the world narrowing to breath and sweat and the violent drag of mouths. He thrusts against me through his shorts, brutal and needy, and it's already too much. My teeth clamped down on his shoulder as I bit back a scream.

"Say it again," he rasps, "Say you thought of me."

"I thought of you," I breathe, voice shattering. "I thought of you, Marek. I wanted you."

And then his control breaks. His hips slam into mine, his

mouth claims me again, and it stops being about hunger or feeding or survival. This is sex. Brutal, consuming and inevitable.

He tears at the thin fabric of my dress, dragging it down until my breasts are bared to the cold air and his heat, until his mouth is on one, teeth grazing, tongue dragging, while his hand grips the other like he'll never let me go.

There's no hiding after this. No pretending it didn't happen. No taking it back.

"Marek—" My protest shatters and dies in my throat when his hips slam again, grinding me against the blunt, hard press of him through his shorts, the pressure sparking fire straight through me. The sound that tears from my chest isn't words— it's a helpless, my body betraying me as much as the truth already has.

"We're done lying," he growls, his forehead pressed to mine like he's anchoring himself there. "Done pretending this isn't what it is."

His hand drags low, pushing his shorts down just far enough—and then he's inside me.

Everything crashes down at once.

I gasp, choking on the stretch, the impossible fullness of him.

Massive.

Ruining.

Nothing else I've ever known could compare, not even close. My nails rake down his back, aching for something to hold on to as my body splits wide open around him.

He doesn't move. Not yet. Just buries himself deep, forehead pressed hard into my neck, his breath ragged and breaking against my skin like it costs him everything to hold still.

"I knew you'd feel like fucking heaven, Leighton," he grits out, every syllable vibrating through me. His hand fists in the sheets beside my head, shaking. "But goddamn... I'll never recover from you."

He pulls nearly all the way out, leaving me empty, aching—and then slams back in, deep and brutal.

And again.

And again.

Each thrust is savage, cracking something wider inside me until there's nothing left to hold together. My back arches, a ragged moan tearing out of me as the monster and the woman inside me blur together, writhing beneath him.

He pulls out suddenly, my protest barely forming before he's flipping me with barely any effort, hauling me up and straddling me over his face. My knees nearly buckle, but his grip on my hips is iron, dragging me down until his mouth seals on me. His tongue pushes deep, his mouth French-kisses my cunt like he's starving, like he's been waiting a lifetime for this.

I jolt, a cry tearing out before I can stop it, one hand clawing at the headboard for balance. My whole body trembles.

"Oh god, Marek!" Everything feels on fire. "Fuck—oh fuck, that's so good!" The scream rips out of me, my body already tensing, the coil snapping tighter and tighter with every flick of his tongue. He must feel it, because he doubles down, mouth burying deeper, tongue locked on my clit, relentless. Flicking and sucking.

My body lights up, every nerve blazing, tension winding quick at the base of my spine. The air itself stills around us, suspended in the pull of what he's doing to me, until my toes curl and my body bows forward, straining for release.

"Marek... I... I... oh, fuuuuck," I drag out, every word splintering, and then I break. My orgasm tears through me like fire in dry grass, violent, consuming, and so strong he has to press his palm flat against my back just to keep me upright.

And still—he doesn't stop. His mouth works me ruthlessly through it, licking, sucking, devouring, until I'm shaking so hard, I can barely breathe.

"No... no more," I gasp, my hands gripping his thighs, nails biting into his skin as I lean back, wrecked.

He finally pulls away, lips wet, chin glistening, his smile is feral and satisfied. His tongue drags slow across his mouth, savoring every last drop before he murmurs. "Fucking delicious, Leighton."

And then suddenly I'm on my back again.

God, I love the way he tosses me, commanding my body like it was always his to wield.

The bed catches me hard, his body crashing down over mine, pinning me beneath the full weight of him. His mouth crashes into mine again, while his thigh wedges between mine until I'm grinding down helplessly, chasing the friction.

He drags his cock along my soaked slit, slow at first, taunting, making me shudder with the motion until I'm begging without a word. And then—he sinks into me in one hard thrust.

"Fuck, Marek," I gasp, back arching, body clenching tight around him.

His hips piston into me, punishing, every drive brutal, each one punching the breath right out of my lungs. The bedframe slams against the wall in time with him. My nails rake bloody lines down his back, dragging fire through his skin, but it only makes him go harder. Faster. Like every thrust is a curse he's been holding back for months, and now he's finally letting them all spill into me.

"I need you. Fuck, I need you, baby." His voice is jagged, breaking against my ear.

"I'm right here," I pant. "You feel so good, Marek. So perfect."

My hands knot in his hair, fisting it, dragging him closer as he slams into me. His forehead presses to mine, sweat dripping between us, his eyes blazing with something that looks like hate and devotion and hunger all tangled in one.

The climax builds, and I'm straining, trembling, wrecked beneath him, and he's right there with me, breath sawing hard as his thrusts turn erratic, brutal.

"Zaria—fuck—I'm—"

He snarls, shoving harder, his rhythm savage now, the sound of our bodies colliding louder than my cries. I claw at his shoulders, desperate for air, for mercy, for more.

And then I snap. Just a flick of my finger against his chest, a whisper of power, and his whole body topples back. The world flips. Suddenly I'm straddling him, slamming down in time with the brutal beat of my own pulse.

"Fuck!" His head jerks back, his fists buried in my hips, his chest heaving as I take over. My thighs clamp around him, and I ride him like every word I bite out through my teeth. "You. Wanted. The. Truth? This. Is. It."

Every thrust wrings another sound from him—groans, curses, my name torn from his chest.

"Zaria. I'm so fucking close—"

"Do it," I growl, grinding harder, claiming every inch of him. "Come with me."

And then it cracks. His roar splits the air, gravelly and feral, as his back bows and his fists shred the sheets. His release tears through him, every thrust breaking into wild, sloppy pulses. And then I feel it...his knot swelling, locking deep, his wolf claiming what his mind swore it never would.

"Oh, *fuck*—" My head whips back, mouth open on a scream. "Marek!"

His growl erupts beneath me, so deep it rattles my spine, shakes the air, makes the whole bed frame quake like it might splinter apart.

Centuries of restraint tear loose, a primal claim no living soul has heard from him until now.

His knot swells brutally inside me, locking us together, forcing me down onto every inch of him until there's no space left, no escape. The stretch is unbearable and perfect, and my scream tangles with his roar as my body convulses around him, climax detonating again.

He's nearly shifted, claws carving crimson into my thighs, eyes burning molten gold, fangs flashing as his chest ripples with the threat of fur.

He thrashes beneath me, lost to it, his wolf rutting hard, determined to bury every last drop, and the sound ripping from his throat isn't human anymore.

"Marek—oh god, yes—Marek!" I scream out as the knot throbs again, each pulse tearing through me until I'm trembling, shattered, clawing at his chest just to stay tethered to something real.

The animalistic huffs tearing from his chest slowly ebb— feral growls collapsing into snarling moans, then ragged breaths—until at last the storm burns itself out and he's human again beneath me.

By the time the final wave lets go, I'm shattered, my chest heaving, skin slick with sweat, my body still locked tight around him, his knot thick and throbbing in aftershocks.

His heartbeat slams against mine, frantic, like we share the same body now. His arms cinch tight around my waist, pulling me down into him, holding me like he'll never let go.

And all I can think, as I press my face to his shoulder, his scent, his heat, his everything wrapped around me, is one single word that drowns out the world.

Mine.

TWENTY TWO

Zaria

"You look drunk."

Marek's voice carries a chuckle as he steps out of the bathroom, with a towel dragging over his hands.

I blink at him, disoriented. Did he just laugh? I don't think I've ever heard Marek laugh. Not really. A couple of rough sounds he kept to himself, sure—but never this. He's always been carved from stone: stoic, severe, untouchable. This version feels dangerous. This version is new.

"I guess I am a little," I murmur, head tipped back against the headboard. I'm too wrung out to care. "That made me... heady."

After his knot, everything in me went slack, drained, like I'd poured myself out. Before I knew it, my body started to shift, veins blooming. And, this time when feeding, he fucked me at the same time. It was different. Stronger. The blood hit harder, so thick and wild, and the rush came fast. It burned and bloomed at the same time, filling every vein until my skin sang.

It's more intense than any feeding we've ever had. Potent. Euphoric. Like his body is still inside me, even now.

I feel high.

"What does it feel like?" he asks, climbing into bed beside me. We're both still naked, the air dense with what we haven't said. Neither of us is ready to touch it yet. Maybe we're afraid to.

I glance at him, acutely aware of how undone I must look — hair damp against my shoulders, skin buzzing like it hasn't caught up with itself. "Which part?"

"When I let go," he says. "When you're feeding. Does it... do something different to you?"

"Yeah." I pull in a breath. "It's like taking a hit of something dangerous. The first taste slams into me pretty hard, and it just keeps rolling through. I can't stop it. Makes me... well, you get it."

His eyes flicker, a storm behind them. "I do."

His hand drifts, drawing slow circles over my stomach, sliding higher, just under the curve of my breasts. My body answers before my mind can.

"So, you need it daily?" His tone is even, but the weight of it presses down. "To feed?"

"I guess so. I wasn't expecting that." My throat tightens around the admission. "Rafe said he can hold off for weeks."

"Yeah, but that's because of his wolf," Marek mutters, jaw tightening. "You're different."

"That makes sense."

He exhales and lets out a snort. "None of this makes sense."

I turn to him, searching his face like it might hold the map I'm missing. "Why do you hate me, Marek?"

He looks at me surprised, like I've struck him and he's figuring out how to take the blow. For a second he looks ready to pull the walls back up, to sneer and vanish behind them.

Then his shoulders loosen, the taut line in his jaw softens, and the truth slides out of him as if it's been rusting in his chest.

"I don't hate you, Zaria. Well... not anymore."

"But why *did* you? Did I do something to you?"

He folds me toward him and pulls me into his chest, as if the motion could rearrange what's inside both of us. His palm presses into the small of my back.

"I was in love with Rafe. For a long time."

He waits for my reaction, but I'd already suspected. So I let him continue.

"I've always liked both—men, women," he says, fingers rough as they rub his face and then bury in his hair, dragging down like he's trying to tear the memory loose. "But Rafe never reciprocated. And then you came around, and he was so..." He falters, voice wavering. "Infatuated. I hadn't seen him like that with anyone."

He lays his hand in my hair like it's the simplest thing in the world to do—that familiarity bruises me more than it should. His thumb ghosts along my temple. The sound of him, the raw edge in his throat, makes the room smaller.

"So, I convinced myself you were toxic. That you'd destroy him. That you'd take him from us. From me." His throat works, and for the first time the sentence he gives me is stripped down, vulnerable and ugly all at once. "But I was wrong. And I know nothing I do will make you forgive me for what you are now. That's on me. My fault. Which is why I'll do this for you, even if you decide to tell Rafe one day. This is my penance."

Penance.

"What does it feel like for you?" I ask, voice small and cautious, still pressed into his chest. "Does it hurt?"

"No. It doesn't hurt." He takes a breath, like he's searching for the words. "It's... strange. It feels like arousal, but not the kind you're thinking. It's not something pulled out of me. It's like something is being poured into me. Like I'm filling up with it. When you drink, it's like every nerve inside me lights up at once. But it's not pain, and it's not just pleasure. It's... giving. That's the closest I can get to it. Like giving life."

His mouth tightens, a flicker of embarrassment shadowing his face. "The only way I can describe it... it's what I'd imagine breastfeeding feels like. Being pulled from but knowing you're pouring something vital into someone else at the same time."

He lifts his gaze finally. "So, no. It doesn't hurt. It feels... human, in a way I don't know how to explain."

I study him for a moment, watching the way his shoulders stay tight even as his voice softens.

"Have you ever fed anyone else?" The question slips out before I can second-guess it.

"No. Never." He says quickly. "I honestly used to think it was vile. Because of how we were hunted." He exhales, eyes dark. "It was always the thing they wanted most from us—our blood. They killed us for it, chained us for it, built legends around it. So, the idea of giving it freely..." He shakes his head, a muscle ticking in his jaw. "It felt like surrender. Like betraying every wolf that had ever died because someone wanted to taste what we are."

His eyes lift to mine, calm, resolute. "And yet here I am, letting you drink. Because Rafe... because I—" He cuts himself short, jaw snapping tight, words swallowed back before they can surface.

His voice still echoes in my head—wolves chained, hunted, butchered because of what ran in their veins. And here I am, drinking it. Drinking *him.* My chest tightens like it can't contain the truth.

"We can stop, Marek." I run my hand along his jaw. "I don't want you to feel that way," I rush on, searching his eyes, needing him to understand. "Like you're betraying them. Like you're betraying yourself. If it costs you that much, we need to stop."

For a long moment, he just looks at me. And I realize he isn't weighing whether he *should* stop. He's weighing whether he'll admit he doesn't *want* to.

When he finally speaks, his tone is gentle, but firm. "No. You take it from me. Only me."

I can't stop the whisper of guilt. "But look what it just made us do. We just spent the night cheating on Rafe."

"You're not his mate anymore."

He says it with a shrug, like that means any of this is okay.

"That doesn't change anything."

Marek sits up, the confusion plain across his face, pained in a way he can't hide. "You're *staying* with him? After this...after what we did? Even without the mate bond?"

Heat rushes through me, shame and want flickering together. For a second I can't tell which one's louder. My chest tightens because I know I have to course-correct to get us out of this spiral before it wrecks us both. He's in my head, and it's just a side effect of the blood. That's what I tell myself. He can't see it. I was lost in it too.

"Marek..." I reach for him as the tether between us flickers thin, fading, but enough that I can feel the brutal edges of his agony cutting into me. "I'm sorry. I didn't mean—"

"It's fine." He spat. "I misunderstood, and I was the one who brought you here. I wasn't thinking. You're right, it was a mistake. I'm sorry."

He's moving before I can stop him. Too quick, too controlled, his body wound tight as a bowstring. Shirt pulled over his head, shorts shoved on, hands working like if he just moves fast enough, he won't have to feel.

I sit frozen, every word I want to say dissolving before it leaves me.

He doesn't look at me, not once. His voice is so businesslike, already halfway out the door. "We'd better get back to the manor. We've been gone too long."

"Marek... stop. Please."

He keeps moving, feet thudding against the floor, shoulders rigid, refusing me the grace of his eyes.

"It's the feeding," I say quickly, the words tumbling out, sad. "That's all this is. We don't have feelings for each other, not like that. It's like an addiction for us, because of the blood. Because of the conduit."

That makes him pause. Slowly, he turns. His gaze finds mine. For one heartbeat, I think he might argue, might break, might tell me what I already feel clawing under my skin.

Instead, his voice comes across guarded. "If that's what you have to tell yourself, Leighton."

Then he turns away, the finality of it heavier than any slammed door. "I'll meet you at the car."

TWENTY THREE

Rafe

"Hello, Alpha."

"Elowen." I dipped my head, voice even, and the word was both welcome and command. "Thank you for coming."

She swept past me with those eyes already searching the room, measuring—never idle, never soft. "Of course. It's an honor to stand in the presence of the High Matron of this generation."

We held each other for a breath, a formalness that carried heat beneath it. My hand stayed at the small of her back longer than necessary, a private insistence before I stepped aside and let her cross the threshold into the manor.

Elowen is not ordinary. She is a Threadseer—blood braided between Binder and Seer—and everyone in this room knows the difference between legend and truth when she walks in.

Threadseers don't only read futures; they see the cords that bind people to one another, the threads of loyalty and hunger that run through a pack.

Her counsel is surgical. Her sight cuts through bullshit

with a kind of callous clarity. A Threadseer never comes without a price, and she never comes for small things.

Still, with what Zaria carries, that storm of power bleeding through her, leaving that power unchecked would is a gamble I can't afford. Calling Elowen was necessary.

"You must understand," Elowen said as she entered the main room and lowered herself into the armchair near the fireplace, folding her hands with the grace of someone who knew exactly how much she unnerved the rest of us. "There may be nothing I can do with such power. I may not be able to truly bind it."

Her gaze lifted, catching mine. "She severed a mate bond, Alpha. Do you understand what that means? In all my years, I have never witnessed such a thing. Not in witches. Not in any Blooded that walks this world.

The force that erupted from this manor that night..." Elowen's voice dipped lower, solemn, almost nervous. "It did not go unnoticed. The Council felt it. They are already whispering, already circling. They will come for her, and likely soon."

"Marek took her to pick up a few things from her apartment," I said, my anxiety spiking not knowing what to expect when Zaria returns. "She'll return soon. Can you at least speak with her? Touch her? You may be able to do more than you think."

"Leave me, Alpha. I'll confer with the ancestors."

Simône, Markus, and Elodie shared a glance, silent agreement rippling between them, before we shifted our eyes away and filed out of the main room into the study. The door shut softly behind us, sealing Elowen into her communion.

Markus leaned against the mantel, his arms crossed tight, his brow furrowed. "What are you going to do if she can't help,

Rafe?" His tone wasn't accusatory, but the weight of the question pressed against the air.

"What are we even worried about exactly? Simône cut in before I could respond. "This started because she hurt Rafe when the bond was still tethered. But she cut it. Severed it clean." She glanced between us, her dark eyes intense, resolute. "So *why* are we trying to bind her?"

Simône's gaze didn't waver. "What's the difference between what we're trying to do to her and what they've always done to us? The Council hunts us because we're powerful, because they fear us. They put chains on us, collars on the witches, blades to any other Blooded they feared more powerful. And now here we are, talking about doing the same damn thing to Zaria."

She yanked her ponytail loose, ran her fingers through her hair with an edge that was more agitation than vanity, then tied it back again, tighter this time.

"I think we've lost the plot. We've lost focus on what our intentions are supposed to be."

Elodie shifted uncomfortably, her voice quiet. "She hurt Rafe, Simône. And she wasn't even here when it happened. It's not just about power for power's sake; it's naïve not to protect the pack. Protect all of us."

Simône's head jerked toward her, sparking fury. "Yeah, she hurt him. *Once*. And then she came here, and she fucking *sacrificed herself,* not even knowing what it would do to her, to make sure it *never* happened again. Her only thought that night was Rafe's safety. She's not waving her power around; she's not threatening us. She's only ever protected us." Simône's voice broke on the edge of her anger. "She wanted to *leave* that night to protect us. And now you want to bind her? You're all being fucking hypocrites, and I'm ashamed to be part of this conversation."

Her eyes burned into mine. "And you, Rafe. *Fucking hell.* I expected better of you."

That hit like a blow to the chest, leaving the air gone from my lungs.

Simône turned, fury in every line of her body as she swung toward the door.

But the door was already open.

Zaria stood there, Marek just behind her, the look on her face enough to hollow me out. Betrayal. Deep, searing, and unflinching. It was etched into every line.

She'd heard *everything*.

Her eyes swept over us—each of us in turn—then shifted to the closed door where Elowen sat beyond, as if she could feel the Threadseer's presence humming through the wood.

"You brought her anyway? Knowing how I felt about it?"

"Zaria..." My voice cracked, useless, because I didn't know what to say that wouldn't sound like a lie.

"It's fine." Her voice came out hollow, a brittle thing that could shatter. Her head shook once, slowly, and she closed her eyes as if shutting out the weight of the room. "I'll do it. If it can be done, I'll do it."

Her tears slipped free before she could catch them, striking the floor. She turned away, shoulders curving inward as if the weight of all of us had settled there, pressing her down.

"Just, uh..." She cleared her throat, forcing the break in her voice into something steadier, straighter. Her spine lifted, the armor sliding back into place. "Just let me know when she's ready for me."

Then she walked out, her footsteps echoing hard and lonely against the floor, the weight she left behind heavier than anything she'd said.

The moment the air closed over her absence, Marek's furious voice tore through it. "What the fuck is happening?" His gaze darted from face to face, searching, demanding answers.

Simône's jaw clenched, her glare cutting toward me and the others. "Rafe, Markus, and Elodie want to bind Zaria's power. Strip her. Put her in chains, just like the Council always wanted."

"The fuck?" Marek's voice was a growl, raw fury rolling off him. "That would fucking destroy her. Hell, hearing it just *did* destroy her. What the fuck are you all thinking?"

"She's too powerful, Marek. Too dangerous. It's not your call. It's not *any* of your call. This is what needs to be done." My voice lowered to the authoritative tone of an Alpha, crackling through every word.

Marek stalked closer, unphased; his steps measured, his body coiled like he was barely holding himself back. And that's when it hit me...her scent. Sweet, bright, threaded through him, clinging to his skin like a goddamn confession.

My chest seized.

"And where was this logic," he bit out, eyes blazing, "the last two hundred years while you've been walking around with a Lycavor at your side? More powerful than anything we've ever run across...and you never once thought to bind him. But Zaria? Suddenly you're scared because she's stronger than *you*? She hasn't ripped anyone apart, if anything, she's fought her power to keep us fucking safe!"

The words barely registered past the storm building in my head. The scent was unmistakable, scorching through me until my vision blurred.

"Why is her *scent*...all *over* you?"

Marek froze. His jaw tightened. He stepped back just enough to make the truth plain.

The snarl ripped out of me on instinct. "Why is her goddamn scent all over you, Marek?"

Heat tore through my skin, my wolf clawing to the surface, rage and possession tangling in a single brutal truth.

He fucked her.

"Did you mate with her, Marek?" Markus' voice split the noise in equal parts shock and accusation. His eyes darted between us, like he couldn't quite believe what he was hearing.

"She feeds from him," Simône cut in, her tone biting, unapologetic. "That's the only reason any of us still have our fucking throats. Because he's the one keeping her in check. Because she's been keeping *us* safe."

Her words hung heavy, acidic, but she didn't stop.

"She shifts and we're dead. She takes a human, and she's gone. Gone to the Council before we can even breathe. Feeding on Marek was the only way to control it, to keep her anchored."

I felt the room tilt, fury and confusion spinning out of me, but Simône was already moving—stepping between us, her body a barrier, her eyes locked on mine like she dared me to argue.

"And it's been *killing* them, Rafe," she roared. "But go ahead. Bind the woman who's done nothing but bleed herself dry to make sure this pack is safe. Strip her down, cage her, treat her like the fucking enemy—while she's the only reason we're not ash in the Council's fire right now."

My wolf snarled in my chest, restless, clawing, demanding I act. Behind her, Marek's eyes burned into mine, unblinking, immovable.

"She could've fed from me," I hiss, "I'd have let her."

"She would have *killed* you. A vampire can't feed from a Lycavor, Rafe. Not without draining you dry. And you know it." Marek's jaw tightened, his hands fisting at his sides. "She fought it that day. She fought off the vampire inside her, and she did it in agony, just to save you. To save all of us."

The truth slammed into me, but it didn't wash out the scent. It still wrapped around him, threading the air between us until it clawed at the inside of my skull.

My eyes narrowed, the possessive burn of my wolf boiling over. "Her feeding on you doesn't explain why you smell like you fucked her." My voice dropped to a snarl. "You don't smell like *blood*, Marek. You smell like her *pussy*. And in case you've forgotten...I fucking know what she smells like."

The words shredded the last thread of restraint between us.

And then the door opened.

"I'm ready for her. We can try." Elowen's voice cut into the room like cold water on a fire ready to burn out of control.

Marek and Simône exchanged a look, then shook their heads almost in unison before walking out together — silently making their stance known without saying a word, leaving me standing there, every nerve vibrating, torn raw between rage and the hollow truth.

And I couldn't shake it.

Was I only afraid because she was more powerful than me?

TWENTY FOUR

Marek

I was so fucking close to telling him. To spitting it in his face. That I laid with her. That I claimed her with my knot. That I wanted to sink my teeth into her and make it permanent, make it unbreakable. The bond is gone. She's not his anymore. But she thinks she is, and that's what matters.

And fuck, maybe that's the cruelest part.

Because what's the point in blowing up her life if she doesn't want me? If she thinks the fire in our veins, the way she trembled under me, the way I damn near lost my mind inside her...that it was nothing more than a side effect? Just blood and hunger. Just circumstance.

I swallow the truth down until it burns.

I went straight to my quarters after that, pacing like a caged animal, Simône shadowing me step for step, both of us burning with what just went down. Binding her. Stripping her. Like she's a weapon they need to neutralize instead of the woman who's bled for every one of us.

Every muscle in me twitched with the urge to tear the walls apart, to get to her, to pull her out of this house and never look back.

"I can't believe he would do this." Simône's voice splintered as she stopped pacing, dropping onto the sofa like her legs gave out.

I shook my head. "She'll never fucking recover from this. Her parents did this to her over and over again; collars, wards, fear. They broke her every time she showed who she was. If we do it too, it'll destroy her. We're all she has left. They didn't fucking see her that night, how fractured she was."

Simône just buried her face in her hands, shoulders shaking. But I couldn't stop moving. My feet wore grooves into the rug; my chest was a furnace.

"I slept with her, Sims." I couldn't hold it in anymore. "It wasn't the feeding; it wasn't the tether; it was just us. And he was right. Rafe was fucking right. I slept with her."

The words hung there, ugly and heavy, but Simône didn't balk. She just dropped her hands from her face, blinking up at me like she'd been waiting for me to spit it out.

Finally, she sighed. "Marek... it was only a matter of time."

My chest snapped tight. "Don't—"

"No," she cut in, firm but not cruel. "Don't twist that statement into judgment. It's not, I swear it, Marek. You've been circling each other for months. The fighting, the feeding, the way you watch her when you think no one's paying attention." She shook her head, pulling her hair loose from its tie just to twist it back again, restlessly. "Something was always going to happen. The only surprise is that it took this long."

I stopped pacing, every nerve sparking. "You're not... mad?"

Her mouth quirked, not quite a smile, not quite pity.

"Mad? Marek, I've been your friend long enough to know better. You've only ever let two people close enough to cut you. The other's her."

I dropped into the chair across from her, elbows braced on my knees, head buried in my hands. It felt like she'd ripped the truth out of the dark and shoved it in my face, daring me to finally fucking look at it.

"She was crying when she walked away." The memory clawed at me. I could still smell the salt on her skin, hear the hitch in her breath. And now she's alone. The thought slammed into me.

"I know."

"This is going to split the pack wide open. It's already us versus them. Fuck. I need to talk to her. She needs to fight this. It's not fair to her."

I pushed out of the chair and went after her, but by the time we made it near, Elodie and Rafe were already there flanking her, steering her straight toward Elowen like a lamb to the slaughter.

I followed; Simône's was quick behind me, my chest pulled so tight each footfall landed like a drumbeat against my ribs. By the time we entered the main room, my heart was thundering, a storm with nowhere to break.

Zaria was folded into herself the same way she'd been on the drive back from her parents' house. Small in a way she should never be. Her light dimmed; her strength hollowed out.

Alone. Hollow.

And all I could feel was the fucking weight of it, pressing me down, begging to be carried.

"High Matron," Elowen said, her voice calm. She bowed her head low. "It is an honor."

Zaria's chin lifted slightly, though her eyes were still red from crying. "Nice to meet you, Elowen."

"You know who I am, then? My truth?"

"Yes. I do."

Elowen's gaze softened, though her words carried weight. "Then I am blessed to stand in your presence. You understand why I am here."

"Yes." Zaria's reply was thin, a brittle shell of composure.

"And your mate?"

"Well, he's the one who called you here," Zaria said with a ghost of a shrug, her tone sharp around the edges. "So, I'm guessing we're A-okay."

Elowen's head tilted, her expression cooling into something unreadable. "No, High Matron. Alpha Rafe summoned me."

"Yes, I know." Zaria glanced back over her shoulder at him, confusion flickering across her face. "My mate."

Rafe stepped closer then, his hand sliding around her waist to stake his claim, but Zaria stiffened under his touch. She recoiled, just enough to make the air split open between them.

Elowen stiffened. "Are you not the High Matron's mate?"

The words cracked through the room like a fucking whip. For a second, I thought maybe she meant Rafe. Had to mean Rafe. But no—her eyes were locked on me.

I actually turned my head, glanced behind me, like there might be some poor bastard standing there she'd mistaken me for. But there wasn't. Just me.

"What the fuck?" It slipped out under my breath, because surely this wasn't real life.

But she didn't look away. Didn't blink. Just kept pinning

me like she'd nailed the truth to my chest.

"No…" I muttered. My throat was dry, my head buzzing. "No, I'm not."

Across the room, Rafe looked like he was about to tear the walls down, jaw tight enough to crack bone, eyes sparking with fury.

Simône's stare flicked between us, confusion plain on her face. Everyone else mirrored it, the whole room caught in the same what-the-fuck freeze-frame.

"Rafe is my mate," Zaria said quickly, her voice shaking but firm. "I'm bonded to him. I mean —I *was*. But I'm…still his mate."

Elowen's gaze never wavered. "High Matron… if I may?"

She lifted her hand, holding it hovered in front of Zaria's chest, waiting for her permission to do…*something*.

Zaria blinked down at the hand, then back at Elowen. Finally, she gave the smallest shrug.

Elowen curled her fingers, and my whole world lit up.

Pain slammed me, lightning through bone, ripping me forward like I'd been yanked by the fucking spine. My feet barely touched ground, body dragged toward her, toward Zaria.

Elowen raised her other hand to her lips, exhaled slow. The air shimmered, silver and alive, and then I saw it —thread spilling out from her touch, glowing, unspooling from the center of me; stretching taut from deep inside my chest… straight into Zaria's.

Elowen lowered her hand, her eyes burning with quiet certainty. "This is your mate, High Matron." Her voice carried the weight of judgment, of prophecy. She turned her gaze back to Zaria, unblinking. "How are you not aware of this? Have you not been claimed?"

"No... no." Zaria's voice cracked, her hands trembling as she stumbled back a step. "He hasn't. No." Her brimming eyes darted toward me, wide and frantic. "I haven't been claimed. We're not mated."

The thread was still shimmering between us, unquestionable. My heart slammed so hard it hurt.

And it's true.

I haven't.

I never put my mark on her.

I never sealed it the way it's supposed to be sealed.

But my mind betrays me, anyway. I *knotted*.

The thought crashes through me like a blow.

My stomach twists.

Fuck.

What the hell is happening?

That's not possible, even with the knot.

Rafe snarled, breaking the silence that had fallen; his wolf clawing so close I swore I could feel the air ripple around him.

"The fuck you're not!" His arm jerked away from Zaria's waist, his whole body vibrating with rage. "Explain this. Now."

"It's not—" I started, but Simône's voice cut through the storm.

"It *is*. You saw it. Elowen showed you. The bond's right there, Marek. Zaria is *your* mate." Simône said gently.

"Bullshit!" Rafe's roar rattled the walls. "She's *mine*." His eyes burned gold, his fangs flashing. "She chose *me*."

"She severed you!" Simône snapped, stepping forward, eyes blazing. "She cut the bond herself. What the hell do you think that means? That she has to live chained to a ghost while the truth's standing right in front of her?"

Zaria's breaths came fast, shallow, her hands clawing at her chest like she could rip the glowing thread out with her bare nails. "Stop. Just stop."

But Elowen's calm voice slid over the chaos, soft and cutting, like she'd been waiting for this exact moment. And, gods help me, part of me wanted to thank her for it, because somebody needed to, holy shit.

"There is no denying it. The thread does not lie. He *is* tethered to her. Whether either of you accepts it is irrelevant."

"Stay the fuck out of this, Elowen!" Rafe barked, his wolf snapping so close to the surface the room itself vibrated. The sound was enough to rattle the hinges, deep enough to scrape your bones from the inside. Markus and Elodie reacted on instinct, stepping in, shoulders squared, like their bodies alone could barricade her from the storm rolling off him.

"Mind yourself, Alpha." Elowen's voice turned cold.

"Rafe," I growled, stepping forward, my own wolf snapping at my bones, "Don't."

His eyes snapped to mine, blazing, unhinged. "Don't what? Don't rip your throat out for touching what's mine?"

And that's it. The line I can't walk back from. My teeth bare before I even think, my chest tight with fury. "She's not your mate anymore."

The words hit like a death sentence.

The room erupted.

Zaria gasped like she'd been struck, the sound tearing up her throat. Simône's shouting something I can't hear, my pulse drowning everything out. Markus shifts, ready, like he's preparing to drag bodies out of the wreckage. Elowen took one step back, getting the hell out of dodge. She might act like she's untouchable, but even she knew better than to stand in the middle of this powder keg.

And then Rafe lunged.

But he never reached me.

Zaria was there in the next breath—fangs down, claws lit, her body angled in front of mine like a shield. None of us even saw her hand move until the air cracked. Rafe hit the wall hard enough to make the stone sing, and the sound after… that was a break. Clean. You could hear the bone give.

He staggered, clutching his side, eyes blazing murder.

Zaria didn't move. One arm barred across me, the other curled, ready to carve anyone dumb enough to test her. When she spoke, it wasn't loud. Didn't need to be. It was a knife laid across a throat.

"Do not. Touch him."

The room froze.

Confusion hit Rafe first, quick and brutal. Then disbelief, like he couldn't reconcile what he was looking at. And then the wound. You could see it hollow him out where he stood.

She didn't drop her stance. Didn't retract her fangs.

And in that silence, in that razor-thin breath where no one knew what the fuck to do next, the truth hit me square.

The pack had split. Just like I told Simône.

One side: Simône, Zaria, and me.

The other: Rafe, Elodie, Markus.

Fractured.

Not pack.

Not family.

Not anymore.

Then, as she realized what she'd done, Zaria stilled. Her fangs retracted with a slick sound, vanishing as if they'd never been there. Her shoulders shook, her chest rose and fell in ragged gasps, like the air itself was cutting her open.

"Rafe..." Her voice cracked on his name, fragile where moments ago it had been carved from steel.

His eyes were glassed, grief screaming louder than the rage. He looked at her like she'd just ripped out his fucking soul. When she reached for him with her hand out, he flinched. Flinched from her.

"You're hurt." Her voice broke again as her hand hovered near the jagged bone pushing through his skin. The blood had already started to spill from the wound. "Let me."

That's when Elowen's mask slipped. For the first time since she walked in, calm wasn't cutting it. Her eyes narrowed, started to glow, like she was trying to strip Zaria down to the marrow.

"You're fanged?" Her words slipped out like a question she hadn't meant to ask. "How..." Elowen's voice faltered, a crack down her composure. "How can I not see you?

The words landed heavy. Like even the universe was refusing to pin down what Zaria was.

"I keep her caged." Zaria says softly, as if that answers every question burning in Elowen's gaze.

Then she turned, and the air fucking shifted. "I'm sorry I hurt you." Her words aimed at Rafe, soft enough they could've snapped bone on their own. Her hands shook as she hovered close, already working, already pulling him back together. Bone knitting, flesh sealing, the mess gone in seconds.

Yeah, she healed him. His body anyway. But that hollow in his eyes? That was untouched. She couldn't stitch that up.

That kind of wound bleeds long after skin closes.

And then—like a switch—the softness burned out of her voice. Gone. What was left was steel. "Can we go talk, please?"

Not a request. Not a suggestion. Command.

Rafe's throat worked once, like the words got stuck there. Nothing came out. Couldn't have if he'd tried. He just gave a short nod, eyes locked on her like he couldn't look anywhere else.

And then they walked out together. No more talking. Just the sound of their footsteps echoing down the stone hall, hollow as a goddamn grave.

I can't explain the kind of silence that hit once they walked out. Not just quiet—hollow. The kind that seeps under your skin, makes every breath sound too loud. The kind that presses down until you're not sure if you're even breathing at all.

And it didn't ease when they left. No, it thickened. Folded around us like fog, choking. Every one of us sitting in it, replaying the last ten minutes, trying to stitch sense into something that was never gonna make sense.

Elowen hadn't moved. Still standing there stiff, eyes wide, like she'd just peered into a crack in the world and was waiting for it to split clean open. Simône had her arms locked around her middle, trembling in a way I almost never saw—like her wolf was the only thread holding her together. Markus and Elodie shared a look across the room, taut, loaded, saying all the shit they didn't dare out loud.

And me?

I stood in the ruins of it. In the chair. In my own skin. In the wreckage we'd just made. The echo of her weight still burning into me, the ghost of her arm still barring me off like I needed protecting, even as she walked out with him. Her scent still clung to me—blood, skin, storm—like it belonged here. Like she belonged to me. And I knew goddamn well she didn't.

It split the ground beneath me. Ripped something out of me clean. Because after everything—after Elowen yanked that bond into the open, after I nearly tore Rafe's throat out, after Zaria put herself between us like I was worth shielding—she still gave him the chance. Still gave him the words, the door back to her.

And he followed. Of course he fucking followed.

I stayed rooted where I was, my wolf pacing, snarling, shredding me from the inside out. Every instinct screamed at me to go after her, drag her back, shove the truth in her face— that the thread tied to my chest wasn't a lie, wasn't some accident of hunger and blood. But I couldn't. Not when she hadn't chosen it. Not when she still thought he was hers.

"Elowen," I ground out, voice rough with the effort it took not to shift, not to tear this house down beam by beam. "Please join me in the study? I need to speak with you as well."

Her gaze slid to me then, cool and unreadable. "Of course, Alpha."

My jaw locked so tight I thought it might crack. "No. I'm not the Alpha. Rafe is. I'm his beta."

She crossed the room like she'd already decided the verdict, her hand catching my arm. My skin prickled, wolf stirring under her stare. "Let's talk in your study, Marek."

The war started in my head before we even hit the hall. She called me Alpha. Why? I'm no one's Alpha. Never have been. Never will be.

I held the door, shut it behind us with a thud that felt final. We dragged the chairs around to face each other.

"Marek, the pack is split." Her tone was even, but it landed heavy. "Simône has already chosen. She stood with you against Rafe. And you—" her head tipped, just enough to cut, "—you've claimed a mate. What you all choose to do with that truth is yours. But know this: fractures like these draw predators. They bring enemies already watching for weakness. And from what I just witnessed, Alpha... none of you are ready."

Her words slammed through me hot and cold. My wolf surged at the sound of it—Alpha, mine, claimed. The man in me shoved it back, because claiming her was one thing. Owning it? Owning her? That was fire I didn't deserve.

Elowen's gaze cut sharper, like she was reading every war I couldn't hide. "I assume the High Matron has been drinking from you?"

My throat went dry. No use lying with Zaria's scent still clinging to my skin. "Yes," I rasped.

Elowen's lips pressed into a thin line. "Then the bond is not new; it is already woven. Whether she accepts it or not, the feeding only sealed it. You need to understand what that means."

My heart thudded painfully against my ribs. "So, this bond... it's a side effect then? Nothing more than that." My stomach dropped at the words...just like Zaria had said.

She tilted her head. "Quite the opposite, Alpha."

The title makes my wolf stir, restless, but I couldn't look away from her eyes.

"She would've had to show excruciating restraint not to kill you." Elowen's tone didn't waver. "A feeding between a vampire and a wolf isn't gentle. Your blood is addictive—yes. That much is known. But addiction doesn't weave threads."

She caught my hands in hers before I could pull back, firm, like she knew I'd fight every word out of her mouth. "This bond was a choice. A choice made by both of you. A choice that didn't need a bite to claim. To create a thread binding this strong…" her eyes didn't blink, "…there had to be an extreme emotional connection during the feeding."

Her voice dropped lower, like she was laying down a fact I couldn't wriggle free from. "And that, Alpha, is no ordinary bond. It is one of the rarest. One of the strongest known to Blooded."

Before I could tell her to cut the dramatics, her hand pressed against my chest, and then the fucking air moved.

Threads ripped out of me, visible, stretching out in different directions like my insides had been yanked out and set on display.

They pulsed, faint gold, weaving away into the room, and I didn't need her to tell me who they belonged to. I felt it.

Simône. Markus. Elodie. Rafe.

Every one of them tethered in me, in ways I'd never seen like this.

Then she pulled one apart from the rest. Not gold. Not faint. White-hot. Blinding. It burned like it knew it didn't belong with the others, like it was carved out of something else entirely.

Her gaze locked to mine. "Can you see the difference?"

My breath went tight, pulse hammering up my throat. Every nerve in me screamed to look away, to tear the thing loose with my bare hands. But I couldn't. It dragged at me, pulled until my skin felt too small to hold me.

"A Soul Bond."

The bottom dropped out of me. My jaw locked, breath catching.

Soul Bond. With her.

Not *chance.*

Not *accident.*

Not *side effect.*

Choice.

My wolf in me howled at the word, clawing my ribs raw, demanding I claim what was already mine.

But my head…

My fucked-up, spinning head.

That part of me was still replaying Zaria's voice.

It's nothing.

Hunger.

Addiction.

Don't mistake it for more.

Except addiction didn't weave glowing goddamn threads out of my chest. Addiction didn't tie me to her like a leash.

She chose me. And fuck, I chose her.

The weight of it pressed down so heavy I thought I might split clean in half; my wolf pumped his fist in the air like he just won the Super Bowl.

The man sitting in the wreckage whispered, *oh, we're the no lube kind of fucked.*

Because if Elowen was right, there was no undoing this.

No "oops, my bad, let's call it off."

No annulment papers for a soul bond.

This was permanent. Forever.

Stamped into my marrow like a bad tattoo I couldn't laser off. And my wolf was grinning ear to ear about it, while I was still wondering if drinking bleach counted as a loophole.

TWENTY FIVE

Zaria

"Did you sleep with him? Just tell me the truth, Zaria."

The accusation split through the air before the bedroom door even clicked shut behind us.

My stomach dropped. My lungs seized.

"Rafe—"

"Yes or no." His voice was a snarl, his wolf prowling in every syllable.

I closed my eyes, hating the sound of the truth even as it tore its way free. "Yes. Twice. Yes."

His hands tore through his braids, like he could rip the answer out of existence.

"Fuck. *Fuck*, Zaria. Is that why you wanted to sever our bond?" His growl shook through me. "So you could be with him?"

It wasn't that simple. It had never been that simple.

My lips parted, but no sound came at first. Only the quake of breath, only the pounding in my chest so loud I swore he could hear it.

"No, Rafe. I did that to protect you. To protect *all of you*. I nearly killed you from hours away; you don't understand. Severing the bond was the only way I knew to keep you safe."

"I don't believe you." His voice cracked. His eyes were wet, burning, fixed on me like he could pull the truth out with sheer force. "Are you in love with him? Are you..." His chest heaved, a shudder breaking through the growl. "Are you *choosing* him?"

"That's not what this is, Rafe." My voice shook, but I forced the words through anyway. "It's not you or him for me. You're both—" My throat locked. Gods, this was breaking me. "You're both important to me. And I am so fucking sorry. Sorry I hurt you downstairs. Sorry for all of this."

His face twisted, the bitter ache inside him curdling into something uglier.

"You hurt me while you were protecting him. Choosing him." The words spat like venom, every syllable designed to scar. "He—and by *he*, I mean the man you're fucking—was right all along." His chest heaved, his eyes burning holes through me. "You are a goddamn cancer to this pack."

The floor dropped out from under me. His words didn't just hurt; they hollowed me out. Left me standing there with nothing to hold but the wreckage of what we'd been.

"Look at us now... Simône and him choosing you. Markus and Elodie choosing me. We're split down the middle because of you. Collapsed. Because of you."

My mouth fell open, heat flooding through me, disbelief heavier than anger.

"That's not fucking fair." The words tumbled rough, but I kept going. "I left, Rafe. I tried to leave—more than once. And you—" I shook my head hard, forcing him to hear it, " —you're the one who brought me back. You're the one who begged me to stay."

His jaw clenched so tight I thought it might snap clean off. "Well, if you can fling me across the goddamn room, you sure as hell could've fought a little harder if you really wanted to be gone."

Each word landed like a lash across my skin.

He turned on his heel, stalking for the door, shoulders stiff as stone. "Let's get this binding over with. Then you can get out of our fucking lives."

The bottom dropped out of my chest. My voice came out scraped hollow. "You know this could kill me, right?"

He froze in the doorway, but didn't turn.

"You knew that when you brought her here," I pushed, trembling but unrelenting, "and you're still willing to have me go through with it? Just to secure your place in power?"

That he's said nothing was worse than if he'd roared. Because it meant he'd already chosen.

"Are you really that fucking afraid of me?" My voice split, jagged with desperation.

"I'm not afraid of you," he snapped. "Your power just needs to be fucking contained."

"And you're a liar. You call me a cancer, while hiding your own. You never told them you were a Lycavor. You spent weeks killing for sport, knowing the rage could come back at any time—and you said nothing. Two hundred years you kept that secret. And the second something threatens your power? You want it bound and buried. Tell the truth, Rafe."

I closed the distance between us, my pulse hammering, the air vibrating with the power pushing at my skin. "If you can't tell the truth about this—after lying to your pack for centuries—maybe it's *you* that doesn't deserve to be with them."

Rafe's face twisted, raw with hurt and fury, eyes burning. "You don't know the first fucking thing about *my* pack, Zaria."

This wasn't about Marek. Not really. This was about us. About the cracks that had split us wide open long before a Threadseer dragged them into the light.

"Be honest with yourself. You're afraid."

When he still said nothing, the last thread of my restraint snapped.

"Fine," I hissed. "Let's do this the fucking hard way."

I straightened, every inch of me thrumming with that ancient, terrible pull. My voice was no longer mine when it ripped through the air.

"Speak truth. *Now*, Alpha."

The air buckled under the weight of my command. Threads curled invisible and endless through the room, binding him in ways no hand ever could. Rafe's chest heaved, his breath fighting me even as the truth tore free.

Then, words started to spill.

"I am afraid of you. You aren't yourself anymore. You don't even smell the same. Your body hums, and it makes the hair on my arms stand up. I'm afraid you'll look at me one day and I won't be enough for you. I don't know what I can offer you anymore."

The words yanked out of him unwilling, dragged into the light like exposed nerves.

"You were weak before, and I liked you weak."

I staggered back as if he'd struck me. My heart plummeted, my hands shaking, but the threads held and the truth kept coming.

"It's not that I want you to still be weak, but you make me feel less of an Alpha. Even now, with you pulling my words out of my mouth, I hate you for it. You slept with Marek and now nothing will

ever be the same. You broke my rib with a flick of your wrist, yes, I'm fucking afraid of you. I fucking hate what you've become. You're not the woman I fell in love with. I just want my Zaria back and you're not her anymore."

I froze.

My stomach dropped, my vision blurred at the edges, the threads trembling at my fingertips like they weren't sure whether to lash or to unravel.

I'd wanted the truth. I'd begged for it.

But gods, I wasn't ready for this.

The weight of it pressed into my bones, and for a breath, I couldn't move.

Then I straightened, dropping my hand, snapping the thread between us.

"Finally," I said. "Some fucking truth."

And I turned to walk out, leaving him choking in the impact of his own confession.

The moment the door closed behind me, the storm bled out like a vein torn open, leaving nothing but the ache. My chest hollowed; my bones felt splintered. I could feel myself breaking again; splintering like glass, the way I had at my parents' house. Another door slammed in my face. Another voice telling me I wasn't the same. That this version of me — the one I never asked for, the one I couldn't undo — was unworthy. Unworthy of love. Unworthy of belonging.

"Zaria!"

I turned just as Simône rushed toward me, arms outstretched, eyes swollen red. She collided with me, clinging tight, sobs spilling hot against my shoulder.

"I'm so sorry. I'm so sorry this is happening to you." Her chest was heaving like she wanted to carry the weight for both of us.

I stood stiff, unfocused, for a beat too long. Then gently —carefully—I eased her arms from around me. Her touch only made the ache worse, because she meant it. And I couldn't let myself believe it. Not now.

"I'm sorry, too," I whispered. My eyes burned, but no tears came. I'd shed too many already. "I don't belong here. I never did. I need to go get bound, and then..." My throat clenched, but I forced it out. "Then I'm being asked to leave."

"Asked to leave?" Her breath hitched, disbelief shattering through her voice.

"Yes." I swallowed hard, shaking my head against the sting rising behind my eyes. "Rafe doesn't want me here.

Excuse me, please, Simône." My voice split on the edges of politeness. "I need to go get this done."

I pushed forward before I could unravel, my steps carrying me down the hall to where Elowen and Marek sat waiting.

They both looked up when I entered.

"Are you ready for me, Elowen?"

She nodded. Marek's jaw tightened, unreadable, but he didn't look away.

Behind me, I felt Simône's presence hover like a shadow —and then, heavier, Rafe's as he walked in. His scent coiled into the room before he even crossed the threshold.

The binding had become a funeral march.

And I was the one walking myself to the pyre.

Elowen rose slowly, her hands already trembling with light. Silver-blue threads shimmered between her fingers, delicate and terrible all at once, like spun glass woven straight from the marrow of the world.

"This *will* hurt, High Matron" she said softly, her calm breaking for the first time. Her eyes flicked over me, over Rafe, over Marek, as if searching for someone —*anyone*—to stop this. No one did.

I stepped forward anyway.

Marek's jaw ticked, his fists curling at his sides, but he didn't move. Simône's breath came fast and shallow behind me, a silent plea she didn't dare speak aloud. And Rafe stood like stone. His silence was louder than every scream I'd ever heard.

I lowered myself onto the chair Elowen had placed at the center of the rug, the old wards etched deep into its wood catching the light. My hands shook as I gripped the arms, forcing my body still, even as my heart threatened to rip itself out of my chest.

"Are you certain?" Elowen whispered.

"No." My voice cracked. "But that doesn't seem to matter."

Her lips pressed tight, but she lifted her hands. The threads unfurled like living things, slithering through the air, wrapping around my arms, my shoulders, my chest. Cold fire sank into my skin, and I bit back a cry, nails digging into the wood beneath my palms.

The pack watched. Silent. Fractured.

I told myself I was doing this for them. For my parents. For whatever was left of the family I'd been born into. Maybe if I carved enough of myself away, if I let them bind me down into something smaller, quieter…maybe then they'd want me. Maybe then they'd love me.

The threads sank deeper, burrowing beneath my flesh, searching for the wild magic thrumming in my veins. It fought back instantly, coiling, raging against the intrusion. My breath caught, my body jerking against the chair as the two forces clashed inside me.

"Elowen—" Simône's voice wavered, frantic. "She's—"

"I know," Elowen cut her off, sweat breaking across her brow. "If her body rejects the binding, it will kill her."

The words landed heavy, a death sentence laid bare in the middle of the room.

My vision blurred, spots of white bursting behind my eyes as the threads tightened. My own power roared up to meet them, furious, violent, unwilling to be caged.

My head jerked back as I screamed.

The sound ripped out of me, wild and unearthly, shaking the walls until picture frames clattered to the floor and glass shattered in their panes. The threads bit deeper, searing through me like molten wire, and then—suddenly—I was weightless.

Arms caught me. An arm wrapped around my waist, pulling me upright against a chest that burned hot and solid. A hand cupped my face, grounding me as the last of the threads snapped loose with a hiss.

"We're not fucking doing this." Marek's voice tore through the room, a growl so thick it rattled the air.

I sagged against him, body gone slack, nerves screaming one second and dead the next. Couldn't feel the floor under my feet. Couldn't feel my fingers. Just the pounding in my chest, savage and desperate, like my own heart was trying to claw its way out.

"Just let me die," I whispered, the words tumbling beaten out of me. My head lolled against his shoulder, lips barely shaping the argument. "Please. It's better."

Simône sobbed, her knees buckling as Elodie caught her.

Elowen's face had gone pale, her threads still sparking uselessly between her fingers before guttering out completely. Rafe stood rigid, his fists clenched, eyes blazing—but he didn't move.

Not a single fucking step toward me.

And right there, whatever fragile tether my heart had been clinging to snapped clean through.

Marek's hold tightened, his jaw grinding hard against the top of my head. "Don't you dare," he muttered, so low only I could hear it. "You don't get to quit. Not like this."

And gods, I wanted to believe him. But all I could taste was blood. All I could feel was the hollow ache where the binding had tried to cage me and nearly succeeded in killing me.

The pack had fractured. And I was the fault line tearing them apart.

Marek lowered me onto the couch, but he didn't let go. His arms stayed braced around me, solid, unyielding, his hand dragging slow circles over my back like maybe he could sew me back into one piece. My head sagged against his chest, every breath jagged and too loud in the quiet.

Then the doorbell chimed.

The sound was so absurdly normal, so domestic, it almost didn't register through the ringing in my ears. A noise that belonged in another life—one where monsters didn't bleed through the walls and I wasn't cracking apart in front of everyone.

And then I heard it. Her voice.

"Mama?" The word left me before I even realized, small and hoarse, like it had been waiting in my throat for years. Like a kid calling out at the end of a long day.

I twisted, my heart slamming hard enough to hurt.

And there she was.

My mama.

Oh god. She's here.

She stood framed in the doorway, the sight of her like a lifeline thrown into a tornado.

"Hi, bébé."

The sob tore out of me, shuddering, breaking. I stumbled to my feet, Marek's hands trying to hold me balanced, but I wrenched free, crashing into her arms. Relief split me wide open.

"What are you doing here? Gods, I'm so happy to see you. I needed you." I clutched her like I could crawl inside the memory of home. "Is Daddy with you?"

Her hand smoothed down my hair, gentle, familiar. Her voice was soft as a lullaby.

"I'm sorry; this is for the best, bébé."

Confusion speared through me.

"What—?"

Then the fierce, burning shock.

The knife slid straight into my sternum, hot and precise.

I stumbled back, choking, my hands flying to the hilt sticking out of my chest. The warmth of her embrace vanished, replaced by searing agony. The betrayal hollowed me faster than the blade.

The room erupted.

Simône's scream burst through the air, high and panicked. Elodie's cry followed, marked with horror. Marek's roar shook the walls; savage, unhinged. And over it all, Rafe's voice thundered like a commandment, his fury filling every shadow in the manor.

And all I could do was choke on my own blood, staring at the face of the woman who'd raised me; her eyes calm and cold, unreadable—as if she hadn't just shattered me in front of them all.

Is that a smirk?

Mama?

I hit the floor hard, pain blooming like flames through my chest, the knife a burning brand with every shallow breath. My vision swam, sound crashing in and out, too loud, too far away.

Through the haze I caught glimpses—Marek's body slamming into hers, Mama dragged down beneath snarling hands, wrists yanked back and bound.

Subdued.

Still fighting.

Still my mother.

But then, closer. Heat at my side. A weight pressing against my wound.

"Stay with me, baby." The voice was laced with desperation. "Don't you fucking die."

Marek.

The world tilted, black spots swimming, but I could feel him there, hovering above me, his scent wrapping around me like a shield. Hands steadying me, trying to stem the flow of blood, trying to hold me together while everything else broke apart.

I blinked up at him, my throat thick with blood and betrayal.

She tried to...

Mama...

Why…

His face blurred above me, jaw tight, eyes wild. "Look at me. Just look at me."

And I tried. God, I tried. But the dark kept pulling.

It's better this way. Safer. For all of them.

I had to tell him. Before the dark won. Before it was too late.

With everything I had left, I lifted a trembling hand, my fingers finding his face, smearing him with my blood.

"I love you, Marek."

And then the dark swallowed me whole.

TWENTY SIX

Marek

"I love you, Marek."

The admission broke me wide open.

"Baby…"

My jaw went slack, my chest seized, and for the first time in over a century, my eyes burned wet.

Then her hand slipped from my face. Her arm dropped like dead weight. From here…*fuck,* it looked like she just fucking died in my arms.

Simône screamed, a sound that carved through my bones.

Rafe moved towards us.

"Don't you fucking come near her." The words ripped out of me before I even thought them, my body already curved around Zaria like she was the only thing keeping me alive. If he so much as brushed her right now, I'd put him through the floor.

Her blood was everywhere—soaking hot through my shirt, down my arms—and I bolted. Legs moving before my head caught up. Out the front doors, down the steps, past the guards who scattered out of the way.

"Jones!" I roared, spotting him by the line of SUVs, hand already on the comm. Loyal bastard, always where he needed to be. "Let's fucking move!"

He didn't ask questions. Just yanked the back door open as I barreled toward him, Zaria dead weight in my arms, and slid into the driver's seat like his life depended on it.

I climbed into the back, pulling her tight against me, trying to hold in what kept spilling out.

The SUV roared alive under us, engine growling like it knew it had one goddamn job tonight: don't stop, don't break down, get her there or she dies.

Simône piled in beside me, shaking, her hands still slick with Zaria's blood. She didn't waste a word. Just pressed both palms hard against the wound, whispering prayers fast and fierce, like if she said them enough times, the gods would have no choice but to listen.

Rafe slammed the passenger door shut up front, his voice quick with orders I didn't care to register. I had one focus. One heartbeat slipping too fast under my hands.

Elodie and Markus stayed back with grounds security. Their job: contain Claudine.

The thought of that woman's name nearly snapped my wolf free. I wanted her goddamn throat. I wanted her heart in my teeth. Wanted her gone so Zaria would never have to see her face again.

My claws were already sliding out when Simône's hand clamped around my arm, yanking me back from the edge.

Not for mercy.

Not for pity.

For Zaria.

Because if—when—she made it through this, she'd want to

face Claudine herself. Tear her down with her own hands.

If the bitch survived long enough for that.

It felt like someone had reached into my ribcage and ripped my soul straight out.

Rafe twisted in his seat to check on Zaria. His eyes lingered on her for a second too long before flicking up to meet mine.

My growl tore out low, fangs still bared, every inch of me strung tight. I've never felt more feral, more possessive, than I did right then. I didn't want him even breathing her air, let alone looking at her.

She's mine.

Fuck anyone who thinks otherwise.

He must've read it in my face, because after that one last glance at her, he turned back around, stiff as a board.

Simône's hand slipped over my forearm, a squeeze, trying to keep my wolf from exploding all over the backseat.

I tried not to look at Zaria. Just held her, rocking like an idiot, like motion could fix what was broken. But the second I gave in, and looked down at her face—I lost it. A sob ripped out of me, and the tears came nonstop.

She didn't even look *alive*. Pale. Limp. Soaked in blood. Nothing but dead weight in my arms except for that thin, impossible hope we were all hanging on: her vampire might keep her alive long enough for the witch in her to kick in and heal shit. Was that even how it worked? Fuck if I knew. None of us did.

Simône sat stiff beside me, wringing her hands until the skin went white. I'd never seen her like that—stripped bare, fragile. And it hit me right in the chest, this need I didn't ask for, didn't understand. To shield her. To hold her up when I couldn't even hold myself together.

Without thinking, I reached over, grabbed her hand, and squeezed. Hard. She squeezed back, like we were both drowning and clinging to the same plank of wood.

The hospital rose up ahead, familiar and yet more foreboding than I'd ever seen it. Ravenridge Memorial. To human eyes, just another small-town hospital—brick façade, glass doors, too ordinary to matter. But to Bloodeds, it was sanctuary. A place where secrets were stitched, bones were set, and lives too fragile for daylight were mended in silence. Every member of the pack had passed through these doors at some point. It was our rite of passage.

But never like this. Never this desperate.

I flung the door open before the SUV had even fully stopped, gathering Zaria's broken form in my arms.

The hospital's double doors burst open for us, staff already moving into formation, quick and silent, recognizing Rafe instantly. Faces I knew. Healers who'd patched me together more times than I could count.

"Rafe." A familiar voice cut through the panic.

Dr. Evelyn Hart.

She swept forward, boots heavy against the tile, her eyes raking Zaria like a surgeon's scalpel. But then—she froze. Pupils blew wide, lips parting as recognition snapped through her.

"The High Matron?" Her gasp wasn't small. It cracked the room open.

"Yes." My voice was a snarl I couldn't leash.

Her gaze snapped back to Zaria, lingering on the blood soaking her, the too-pale skin, the stillness that wrecked me. One beat. Two. Felt like a noose cinching tighter with every second she didn't move.

Then her command came, loud, clean. "Trauma One. Now!"

Staff surged forward, a blur of white coats and sterile hands. A stretcher clattered into place between us, wheels squealing against tile.

I bared my teeth, tightening my grip around Zaria, fangs flashing as the sound ripped out of me. "No one touches her. You tell me where to go, and I'll fucking take her."

"Come with me," Evelyn snapped, already spinning on her heel.

I followed, every step a pounding vow, Zaria's limp body burning against my chest. Rafe's footsteps shadowed mine, too close, but I didn't waste breath on him. Not now. Not when her blood was still warm on my hands.

The doors swung open ahead of us, sterile light flooding out. I carried her through, straight to the bed Evelyn motioned toward, laying her down with a care I didn't even know I had in me.

My hand shook as I reached into my back pocket, pulling free the blade still slick with her blood. Her blood. The sight of it nearly made my wolf snap its leash all over again. My vision tunneled, breath gone jagged, but I forced my grip solid as I held it out to Evelyn.

"She was stabbed with this."

Her eyes flicked down, then back up, cool as ever. She took the blade without hesitation. "Thank you, Alpha."

There it was again. That fucking title. Burning a hole in my chest.

And it wasn't lost on me that Rafe's eyes blew wide at the word. His head snapped toward me, wolf bristling, hackles all the way up.

"Please step out. We'll come get you as soon as we can."

And just like that, the doors slammed in our faces. Staff surged in behind them, a wall of white coats and gloves, shoving us out into the hallway like we were nothing but furniture in the way.

So now it's just him and me. Pacing outside a whitewashed room that smells too much like bleach and blood. My ribs feel splintered from the inside out, my wolf howling every second she's out of reach.

Whatever storm's waiting between Rafe and me can wait its turn. She can choose whoever the hell she wants. She can spit in my face and never look at me again. I don't care.

As long as she lives.

My heart thudded restlessly as I watched through the window, glimpsing Evelyn's gentle yet precise movements as she assessed Zaria's wound. A fairy by birth, Evelyn's presence radiated an aura of gentle strength, her silvery hair catching the faint glow of hospital lights, casting an ethereal shimmer around her. Though small in stature, she was bound by oath to safeguard all supernatural beings, no matter the cost.

My jaw ached from tension. Zaria lay motionless, skin pale. Machines beeped rhythmically beside her, their soft chimes the only indication she was still holding on.

"She told you she loved you. Her last words were to you."

"They weren't her last fucking words." My voice came out harsher than I meant, ripped straight from the gut. I turned on him, eyes blazing. "Don't *say* shit like that. She's not done. She's not—" I cut myself off, jaw locking, chest heaving.

I dragged a hand over my face, the burn still in my throat. "And don't think for a second it didn't rattle me the same as it did you."

"I doubt that. She's never once uttered those words to me."

The words hit like a blow to the ribs, but I didn't flinch. Couldn't. My fists curled so tight my nails bit into skin.

"Don't make this a fucking contest, Rafe. You think I wanted to hear it like that? With her blood all over me, barely breathing? You're her mate. You always have been. I've spent the last twenty-four hours trying to forget the way she looked at me, because it doesn't fucking belong to me."

I stepped closer, close enough he could feel my breath when I spat the next words. "So don't stand there and act like I stole something from you. The truth is, if she makes it out of that room alive, we both already lost her in different ways."

"Are you not even going to recognize that you're betraying centuries of our brotherhood, Marek? What the fuck happened that you were willing to take it this far?"

The words hit me square in the chest, but I couldn't back down. My jaw locked, and I forced myself to meet his eyes.

"I fucking love her, Rafe." The confession ripped out raw, ugly, the kind of truth you can't dress up. "I didn't ask for it. Didn't go looking for it. It slapped me in the goddamn face, and I knew it was wrong the second it hit." My voice shook, not from weakness, but from the weight of saying it out loud. "But I can't apologize for loving her. I won't. The only thing I can apologize for is hurting us in the process. For tearing apart what we built. That's on me."

His chest heaved, his eyes gleamed wet, and for a second, I thought he'd swing. Part of me wanted him to. Maybe I deserved it.

So, I pushed instead.

"You say she's never told you she loves you." I stepped

closer, voice steadier now. "But have you ever told her?"

His jaw ticked, teeth grinding like the words were fighting him on the way out. "No," he admitted, low. His hands fisted at his sides, knuckles white. "Because I thought she knew. She was my mate. I didn't think I had to spell it out." His voice cracked, fury and grief twisting tight in his chest.

"If you loved her, Rafe, you'd have shouted it from the rooftops. Whispered it in her ear every night before she closed her eyes. We've seen you in love before—you weren't quiet then. But with her? You've been silent. Maybe it's time to face that what you called love was just fondness. Lust. Comfort. But not love."

That did it. His fist connected with my jaw so hard I saw white—full Alpha strength, like he'd gone fucking Super Saiyan. My head snapped sideways, ears ringing, the copper taste of blood already on my tongue.

I wiped my mouth with the back of my hand and laughed, bitter and breathless. "Yep. I deserved that. But before you wind up for round two, ask yourself if it's true."

We stood there locked in it, two idiots trying to out-glare each other like maybe we could settle centuries of blood and loyalty with nothing but mean faces. Every muscle in my body coiled for the next swing.

Then the door cracked open. Evelyn stepped out, calm as ever, gave us both a look like she'd walked in on a schoolyard brawl, and tipped her chin toward the room. "You can come in."

We moved instantly, the door softly clicking shut behind me as we stepped into the quiet room.

"How is she?"

Evelyn exhaled slowly, her composure calm even as her

eyes betrayed the gravity of what she was about to say.

"Honestly, I don't know what to make of it."

My gaze dragged back to the bed. Zaria lay there like a ghost of herself, skin leached gray under the sterile light, chest barely lifting, barely falling. Too still. Too fucking quiet.

"Explain," I bit out.

Evelyn's focus stayed on her, something almost reverent in her stare, like she was looking at a miracle—or a curse. "That wound should've been fatal. The blade—" her hand twitched toward the cloth-wrapped steel I'd handed over "—it's a god killer. I couldn't tell you which hands forged it, but I know what it is when I see it. There are only three I've ever heard of. Their sole purpose is to kill the unkillable. To strike down what should never fall."

Even the hum of the machines felt too loud in the room.

"It poisons. Starts in the sternum, spreads out until the whole body seizes, then collapses. Nothing survives it. That's the design. That's the point." Her gaze shifted back to Zaria, narrowing like she couldn't reconcile what she was seeing. "And yet...she's already healing. Faster than I've ever seen. Faster than should be possible."

Rafe's hand dragged down his face, his shoulders sagging.

My fingers curled hard into my hair, tugging until my scalp burned, because I needed pain to keep from losing it. A weapon built to end gods should've ended her. It didn't.

Which left one question burning a hole in my chest: *what the fuck is she?*

Disbelief chewed at me, biting down hard, but under it, there was finally a thread of hope. Fragile, reckless, something I had no right to hold on to but couldn't fucking let go of either.

Then the air shifted.

A rustle of sheets.

A stutter of breath.

Her lashes flickered, lids dragging open like they weighed a ton. Barely there, unfocused and hazy, but open.

"Zaria," I breathed, the word breaking out of me before I knew I'd said it. I stepped closer, slowly, carefully, like the floor might split open and drop me straight through if I moved too fast. My heart was pounding so hard it hurt.

Her gaze dragged toward me, glassy, searching, like she wasn't sure yet if I was real. Her lips parted, pale and trembling, and the sound of her voice was so weak.

"Marek…what…happened?"

The truth clawed its way up my throat—*your mother tried to kill you*—but I shoved it back down where it belonged. She was too fragile to carry that weight. Not like this. Not now.

Rafe's eyes caught mine across the bed. We didn't need words; the look was enough. "That's not important right now."

I couldn't stand another second of distance. I reached for her hand, wrapping my fingers around hers. Her skin was cold, too cold, but when her fingers twitched weakly against mine, it was like the world tilted back onto its axis. Proof she was still here. Still tethered.

"Are you in pain?" My voice cracked low, useless at masking the panic ripping me apart. I didn't care if she heard it.

Her lips moved, dry and barely shaping the sound. "Tired…" she whispered. Then her lips curved the smallest fraction. "And maybe still a little pissed."

Relief cracked through me so hard, bowed over.

Evelyn leaned closer, fingers pressed to Zaria's pulse, her

brows furrowing as she counted. "Remarkable," she murmured, almost to herself. "Her ancestors are clearly protecting her. There's no other explanation."

Zaria groaned faintly, rolling her eyes even as they fluttered shut again. "Great. Ghost babysitters. Just what I needed."

That smart-ass spark, even half-conscious—it undid me. I couldn't fight it anymore. Couldn't care that Rafe was standing right there, bleeding heartbreak all over the floor. My hand shook as I brushed damp curls off her face, fingertips trembling against her skin, and I bent down.

For a heartbeat, I braced.

Braced for her to shove me away, for the inevitable rejection.

But she didn't.

Her lips met mine; weak and soft, but willing.

The kiss was brief, barely more than a breath, yet it shattered the fragile balance of the room.

Rafe staggered back like the air had been punched out of him.

Nothing would be the same after this.

Not for me.

Not for her.

And sure as hell not for him.

Evelyn's hand cut through the noise, motioning us out. Firm, practiced—the way someone clears wreckage off a battlefield.

"You rest. We'll be right outside." I bent down, kissed her temple, and met her eyes. A silent thank you to Luna herself for giving her back.

Then Evelyn was at the door, hand on the frame, easing us into the hall. The latch caught with a muted click, shutting Zaria in that too-quiet room, and leaving the rest of us on the wrong side of it.

The fluorescent lights overhead hummed, stark and unflattering, casting every shadow into relief. They made Evelyn look older somehow—the worry etched deeper across her face.

She let out a slow breath, eyes moving between me and Rafe, like she was sizing us up. "What we're seeing is… unprecedented." Her voice dipped lower, like she didn't want the walls carrying it back. Then her gaze locked on me, waiting, like I had the missing piece she needed.

"What exactly is she?"

The question hit and stuck. My throat tightened. My throat went tight. I glanced at Rafe—saw the same storm in his eyes, the same silence that said he didn't have the answer either.

Finally, I forced it out, voice rough. "We're not entirely sure." My hand raked through my hair, useless. "She's High Matron," I said, quieter this time, like the words weren't big enough to hold her. "And vampire. But it's not that simple. Just like Rafe gets slapped with Lycavor, like that's supposed to explain a damn thing—" I shook my head, frustration snapping loose. "We don't know what to call her. We don't know what the hell she is. What I do know—" I jabbed a finger toward the closed door, toward her—"is she's powerful. Scary powerful. And she was still weak when the blade hit. Rafe had a threadseer try to bind her right before everything happened."

Her eyes snapped to Rafe so fast I almost missed it. "You tried to bind a matured High Matron, Alpha? Do you know how deadly that is?"

"He knew…" I threw in, because apparently I don't know how to shut the fuck up.

"Give it a fucking rest, Marek." His voice snapped, but his eyes—yeah, those went soft. Almost pleading. He turned back to Evelyn. "Yes. But the circumstances—"

She stepped in close, and if it weren't for the fact Zaria was lying half-dead behind that door, the whole picture would've been comical. Evelyn barely came up to his chest, and yet she was staring him down like she'd climb the man with a ladder if she had to.

"There is no circumstance," she hissed, "not one, Alpha, that warrants binding a mature High Matron. That was nearly a death sentence. The only reason she's still breathing is likely because her vampire carried her while her witch healed. You've abused your position, Rafe. The only reason a threadseer would take that risk is if you commanded it as Alpha. How dare you?"

Listen. Outwardly, I was stoic. Hand on my jaw, nodding like I was the picture of calm.

Inside? Different fucking story.

Fucking tell him, Evelyn.

Drag. His. Ass.

Call it for what it was.

Binding a matured High Matron?

Bullshit.

What does matured mean?

Doesn't matter.

That the kind of bullshit only Rafe could cook up and actually convince himself was noble.

Yeah, exactly! How dare he.

*How fucking **dare** you, Rafe.*

Fucking idiot.

Rafe's jaw ticked, and for a second, I thought he might actually snap back at her. But instead, his voice dropped low, forced through his teeth.

"I didn't order it lightly, Evelyn." he said, each word ground out like it hurt to speak them. "She was unraveling. She nearly killed me from hours away. I was trying to protect the pack."

Evelyn's eyes narrowed, not budging an inch. "You were trying to protect yourself and your station. Do not confuse the two."

Rafe's chest heaved once, a flicker of guilt flashing behind the rage in his eyes before he looked away.

She finally tore her eyes off Rafe and turned to me.

"I'm sorry for the outburst, Alpha. Let's get back to discussing your mate."

There it was again. Alpha.

My hand rubbed my jaw; I nodded slowly as she spoke.

Yeah, let's get back to that.

*Let's talk about **my** mate.*

*Let's talk about the part where you called her **mine**.*

And while we're at it, let's talk about how you keep throwing that goddamn title at me like it belongs.

"Then you're going to need our help. When it's time to deliver the babies, you ask for me. No one else. Do not trust anyone else with this; do you understand?"

…Wait. The *fuck* did she just say? I wasn't listening!

I blinked.

I froze.

Rafe froze.

The whole goddamn hallway tilted, the floor pitching under us.

"Babies?" Rafe croaked, like he'd swallowed glass.

So, she *did* say it. She said babies. Plural babies. Bunches of babies…

"What babies?" I rasped.

Was that out loud? Did that even come out?

"WHAT BABIES?"

Yeah, that's better. Now I'm screaming.

But before Evelyn could answer, the hospital door behind us slammed open, ricocheting off the wall with a violent clang.

All three of us spun toward the sound.

Zaria.

She stood in the doorway, pale and furious, her hospital gown hanging loose around her shoulders, hair a wild tangle framing her face. Her eyes blazed wide, exhaustion burned clean away by fury. Black veins already spidered beneath her skin, pulsing like dark lightning, and her fangs gleamed in the sterile light.

"Deliver the *WHAT?*"

TWENTY SEVEN

Rafe

"Deliver the *WHAT?*"

Zaria's voice cracked like thunder through the hall, and I froze where I stood. She was braced in the doorway mid-shift. Fangs glinting, black veins threading her skin like ink spilled too deep. I hadn't seen her shift since that morning, and now — now it was for me. For *this.*

Evelyn looked startled, then fascinated, but I barely saw her. My whole focus was Zaria.

And the stunned silence from Marek and me... it was enough. Confirmation.

"I'm sorry; did you just say *babies?*" she demanded again, voice pitching high, panic bleeding through the edges.

Babies. Ours? Hers? Theirs? My mouth opened, but nothing came out.

"As in a tiny, screaming humans?" Her hand pressed flat to her stomach, her eyes were wide and frantic. "No—no, *not* human."

I stepped forward without thinking, instinct clawing through me, even though she looked at me like I'd betrayed her twice over. The distance between us was only a handful of feet, but it felt like a chasm.

"Wait.. Baby witches? Vampires?" Her voice spiraled, faster now, panic tangled with that biting sarcasm that always cut deeper than she meant it to.

"Oh god—*baby vampires*. Fuck. You might as well call them Count Snakula, because no one would be safe!"

The words were absurd, ridiculous—but they cracked through me all the same. Because all I could see was her: wild-eyed, breaking, clutching herself like this revelation had carved deeper than the god-killer blade ever could.

"Evelyn was just explaining—" I started, desperate to ground her, to give her something solid.

"Oh, *was she*?" Zaria's snarl cut me off. She spun on Evelyn, and though the oversized gown and her tangled hair made her look more like a feral kitten than a predator, we all knew better. The power simmered just under her skin, veins still dark, fangs still bared.

"Care to share with the *actual pregnant person* in the hallway?"

Evelyn's composure cracked only slightly, but she recovered quickly. She offered Zaria a sheepish, reassuring smile and stepped forward, her hands raised in calm surrender. Gently, she guided Zaria back into the room, murmuring something soft, before easing the door shut behind us with a quiet click.

I turned to Marek. He looked shell-shocked; eyes glazed, mouth ajar, like someone had sucker-punched the air from his lungs.

And God help me; I knew the feeling.

"You've healed rapidly, Zaria," Evelyn said softly, her

voice pitched low and soothing. It threaded through the tension in the room like balm, though I could see the flicker of nerves in her eyes. She drew in a breath. "But during your examination..." She hesitated, then spoke the words that split the air in two. "I detected *three* heartbeats."

Zaria sank heavily onto the edge of the bed, her hospital gown gaping at one shoulder. She stared at the floor, her face pale, blank, emptied of everything but shock. "Oh my God," she whispered.

Marek was on the floor in front of her in an instant, crouched low, his movements slow and measured—like he was approaching a wounded animal. His expression was cautious, but there was warmth there too, a kind of grounding that made my chest twist. "Baby," he murmured. "We'll figure this out together. All of us."

I forced my voice into the space, thick and tight though it was. "He's right. You're not alone in this."

She scoffed, the sound bitter. Rolling her eyes, she turned her face to the wall, her body curling inward. And I couldn't even blame her. After everything—after bringing Elowen, the binding, the things I said in truth and in anger—it was no wonder she turned away from me.

"Are you okay, Zaria?" Evelyn's tone softened to a whisper as she edged closer. Each movement was careful as her hand extended in quiet offering. She sank to one knee in front of her, laying a gentle palm against her knee. "Can I get you anything? Any questions I can help you answer? Do you need blood? I can have an attendee bring a bag for you?"

It was brave—foolish maybe—but brave. Every step Evelyn took had been taut with tension, and now, with Zaria fully shifted, the air was tight with waiting. Waiting for her to snap, to lash out.

I was waiting.

But Marek…sitting close enough to feel her breath, his knees nearly brushing hers, he looked calm. Utterly unshaken. Like he *knew* she wouldn't break.

A trust I hadn't let myself feel. Not once.

Maybe that was the problem.

"I'll feed her," Marek said, voice low and gentle.

Zaria's head turned, her eyes finding his. And in that look; a softness flickered. A gentleness she hadn't given anyone else in this room. My chest ached at the sight of it.

Zaria's eyes stayed on him, calm despite the panic shadowing her face. Then she nodded once.

"I'll wait," she said softly. Her voice carried that quiet steel that always managed to undo me. "I'm okay. Thank you… for trusting me."

The words hit heavy. Not because she spoke them—but because of *who* she spoke them to.

I stood there, silent, watching the faintest curve of relief soften Marek's mouth. Watching her meet his gaze and hold it, like he was the anchor she'd chosen.

And God help me, maybe he was.

"You're more powerful than anything I've ever witnessed, Zaria," Evelyn said at last, rising slowly to her feet. Her back straightened, but her eyes stayed on Zaria, wide with awe. "But when it's time for the birth…" Her voice faltered just slightly, then steadied. "You'll be extremely vulnerable."

The word seemed to crack the air.

"There's only one recorded birth in the High Matron lineage. Centuries ago." Evelyn's gaze flicked to me, then back to Zaria. "She and her child were both slaughtered in that moment of weakness. A single vulnerability; and it was exploited."

Silence fell heavy again, thicker than before, pressing down on all of us. My wolf clawed against my skin at the thought—Zaria laid bare, unprotected, her strength dimmed. The image was enough to make my hands shake.

And I knew without question, history was waiting to repeat itself. Unless we stopped it.

"We'll surround the building with magic wielders," Evelyn said firmly, her voice carrying a conviction that made the air itself feel tighter. "And only the most trusted will be allowed inside. Even then; it is no guarantee. There are factions who believe the High Matron should not exist. That power like yours shifts the balance too far. That it must be snuffed out before it grows."

She stepped closer, her presence radiating authority, her eyes locking on Zaria's with unflinching certainty. "But I will give my life to protect you. And your children. That I swear to you."

Zaria's eyes shimmered, tears spilling over and carving wet tracks down skin marbled with black veins. The sight hollowed me out; terrifying and breathtaking all at once. A High Matron, radiant and monstrous, undone by an oath she hadn't asked for but needed like air.

And I couldn't look away.

Evelyn's gaze lingered, marked with fascination. "May I ask," she said carefully, "how you're holding such restraint? You're fully shifted, and I've never witnessed a vampire maintain this kind of control; especially surrounded by wolves." Her eyes flicked briefly to me, then back to Zaria. "Rafe being Lycavor... that should have provoked something. And yet, here you are. You've fed from Marek, and he's still breathing. That alone is unheard of."

Zaria's throat worked, her breath unsteady, but her answer came sure and low, vibrating with pain and defiance. "It's excruciating," she admitted, her fangs flashing as her voice cracked. "Every second of it burns through me. But I'd never hurt them." She lifted her chin, her gaze sweeping from Evelyn to me, then to Marek. "None of them."

Her words thudded through me like a pulse. *Excruciating, but she endured it. For us. For me. For him.*

And in that moment, I didn't see the monster the Council feared. The one I feared.

I saw Zaria—the woman bleeding herself dry to keep us safe. The woman I'd promised to protect... and betrayed.

"Amazing," Evelyn whispered, reverence curling around every syllable.

"Yes, she is," Marek said softly, his gaze fixed on her like she was the only thing that existed. His voice carried none of Evelyn's awe, none of my fractured guilt. It was unshaken, filled with a quiet warmth I'd only ever heard from him a handful of times in my life.

And it wasn't for me. It was for her.

Evelyn cleared her throat, her tone shifting back to professional, though the reverence still clung to her edges. "You're free to go, Zaria. Come back and see me next week, and we'll check how the babies are progressing."

The word still rang in my head like a tolling bell—*babies.*

"I'll bring in one of my colleagues, Dr. Edison. I trust her completely. She'll assist me throughout your pregnancy. My assumption—" Evelyn hesitated, as if weighing how much truth Zaria could take in this moment, "—is that you'll progress quickly. But we'll run those tests next week. For now, get home. Rest. Let your body catch up."

Her words hung heavy in the sterile room, and for the first time since the knife struck, there was something like direction. A path forward, even if it was paved in shadows.

TWENTY EIGHT

Zaria

It was too quiet as I dressed to leave the hospital. The kind of silence that crawled under your skin, made you second-guess every breath. Everything felt hazy — why I was even here, what they weren't telling me. Because they *were* hiding something. I could feel it pressing against me like static, clinging to every inch of me. Someone stabbed me. There was a knife. And I knew, bone-deep, I wasn't going to like the truth when it came.

My anger with Rafe still simmered, a constant burn just beneath the surface. With all of them, really — except Simône and Marek. They were the only ones who hadn't tried to shove me into a box, the only ones who still looked at me like I was something other than a weapon waiting to blow. But now... pregnant. Plural fucking babies.

How the hell was I supposed to be a mother? I had no one. Not really.

I could feel them watching me as I moved. Rafe waiting for me to combust, because I was still fully shifted. Marek wondering — hoping — if I'd choose him now that we knew we were mated. Which, what the actual fuck. Like I needed that complication stacked on top of everything else.

The walk to the lobby felt endless. Marek seemed so far away, even though he was only a couple of steps behind me. Close enough to catch me if I fell, but not close enough to touch. Just watching and waiting.

I gave him a look over my shoulder, then reached my hand back for his. His palm swallowed mine, rough and certain, and something in me stilled.

One thing I hadn't expected; how much I needed his touch to feel anchored. I'd realized it the night I slept next to him, but I'd been fighting it ever since. Fighting him. Fighting myself. Yet even now, just the weight of his hand in mine made me feel like I wasn't drifting off the edge of the world.

When the doors opened, the air left my lungs.

There were at least thirty people waiting. Maybe more. A sea of faces that turned toward me the second I appeared.

And then—they stood. Every single one.

"High Matron."

"High Matron."

"We're here to protect you, High Matron."

"We're glad you're healing, High Matron."

One voice after another, a rising tide of reverence. Heads bowing, bodies bending low, devotion etched into every gesture.

None of them—not a single one—batted an eye at my shifted features. The black veins crawling my skin. The fangs. The monster.

It nearly broke me.

I wanted to scream at them. To tell them I wasn't their Empress, that I couldn't even save myself. But all I could do was stand there, hollow and filled at once, with their devotion pressing down like a crown I hadn't asked for and couldn't set aside.

And then—a small voice.

A girl, no more than seven, stepped forward. Her hand was curled in her mother's, but her wide eyes never wavered as she looked up at me.

I knelt, lowering myself to meet her gaze. "Hi."

She lifted her chin, bold for someone so small. "Hi, Matron. I'm Leighla."

Something inside me cracked. "Hi, Leighla. I'm Zaria."

Before I could say more, she wrenched her hand free from her mother's grasp and threw her arms around my neck. The hug was fierce, pure—love unfiltered. A bolt of warmth shot through me so suddenly it stole my breath.

Love. From a child I'd never met.

"We all felt you dying," she whispered. "I'm glad you're okay."

I looked up, expecting her mother to pull her away from me, from the fangs, the veins, the monster.

But the woman didn't move. She only watched me with the same reverence as the others. Eyes soft. Trusting. Loving.

"Thank you," I managed, my voice breaking at the edges. "All of you. So much." I bit down on the tears clawing at my throat. "I can't explain how much this means to me. You should go home now. I'm okay now. Thank you for being here."

Marek squeezed my hand. Pride radiated from him, so bright it nearly stole my breath. He had only ever respected my power, never feared it. I'd broken his body against a tree over and over, and every time, he'd stood and come back to me. I hadn't seen it until now.

As the crowd parted, Simône cut through, all warmth and laughter, wrapping her arms tight around me. "I know my neck is kind of close to you right now," she teased, a laugh bubbling from her chest, "don't bite." She squeezed me tighter.

Over her shoulder, Markus and Elodie lingered back, unreadable, their bodies tense. The fear pouring off them was thick, almost choking. Still. Even fucking now.

"We brought extra security with us, just in case," Markus said, his tone clipped. "And Claudine is in a cell in the corridor."

My heart seized. "Claudine?" I looked at Rafe, then at Marek, the words scraping up my throat raw. "My mom? What do you mean—in a cell?"

The sterile lights burned too bright. The voices swelled too loud. My head spun.

Marek caught me before my knees could give, his arms wrapping around me, solid, grounding. "Your mom is the reason you're here, Zaria," he said gently, though I could hear the restraint coiled in his voice. "She stabbed you. With a blade—something we don't fully understand yet. She's not hurt, just locked away until we know more."

The memory slammed into me like a wave. The knife. Her face. The betrayal.

It was mercy that Marek was holding me when the sob tore out of me, a wail powerful enough to shake the walls.

And then the bleed hit.

It poured out of me wild and unchecked, surging through the tether until it wasn't just mine. The coven staggered beneath it, their voices cracking open, their own sobs spilling into the waiting room. One voice became ten, became thirty, all crying, all breaking with me.

The sound rose like a storm—grief multiplied, grief magnified, filling every inch of the hospital lobby. A choir of anguish, unstoppable, unbearable.

"I got you. I got you," Marek whispered into my hair, his arms tightening, his chest a barricade against the tide. His wolf vibrated under his skin, straining to hold me, to shield everyone else from what I was unleashing.

And then Simône's hand slid against my back, her touch warm. A tether inside the tether. She pressed her forehead to my shoulder, whispering soft words I couldn't catch, grounding me deeper.

But the bleedover didn't stop. Not yet.

"What's happening?" I heard Rafe demand, his voice jagged with panic.

"I don't know!" Markus shouted back over the rising cries, his hands pressed to his ears like he could shut out thirty voices breaking all at once.

Marek's mouth pressed to cheek, then my neck, my temple. Words rumbling against my skin. "Breathe, baby. Just breathe. Let it go slow. You don't have to carry all of it at once."

I clung to him, shaking, his voice threading through the storm. Simône's circles on my back grew firmer.

And slowly, the cries around us began to thin. One by one, voices dropped. First a lull, then a hush, until the storm drained back down into me.

My chest still hitched, but the weight pressing on the room eased enough for breath to return.

Marek tipped my chin up, intense but gentle, his thumb brushing the edge of my jaw until I had no choice but to meet his eyes.

"That's a good girl."

The words sank deep, anchoring me, pulling me out of the echo still rattling in my bones. My breath hitched, but it evened under the cadence of his, his gaze holding me there, steadying me like I was the only thing in the room that mattered.

"Take me to her." My voice split, but I forced my spine straight, wiping the wet from my cheeks with the back of my hand. "I need to see her."

Marek just nodded, no hesitation, and guided me toward the exit doors. The fractured pack moved behind us in step, shadows of loyalty and resentment thick in the air.

Before walking out, I turned and glanced at the sea of strangers who had just walked through my grief with me as if it were their own.
"Thank you, everyone. For being here."

As one, they bowed their heads. Then their hands lifted — palm pressed flat against their sternum, fingers spread wide, before curling in and tapping twice over their hearts. A gesture of reverence, a vow of loyalty, the silent mark of respect for a High Matron.

The weight of it nearly buckled me.

Outside, engines idled—two SUVs waiting, armored cars positioned front and rear like we were heading into a warzone instead of a family reunion.

Marek opened the back door, his safe hand ushering me inside first. Simône, Markus, and Elodie climbed into the SUV behind us, their silhouettes caught in the flashing reflection of headlights.

I glanced back as Rafe stepped forward, jaw tight, reaching for the door handle.

"Maybe ride with them, Rafe." Marek's hand shot up,

stopping him cold. His voice was calm, but the edge underneath was steel. "She needs to feed before she sees her mother."

Rafe's eyes burned into him. "I'm riding with her."

Marek's lips pressed into a thin line, his wolf thrumming so close to the surface I could feel it crackle in the air. He leaned closer, low enough that his words vibrated like a growl.

"Suit yourself, Rafe." He said, pulling his shirt over his head, leaving only a black tank top underneath. "But don't fucking interfere. She needs to feed."

Goddamn it. That was hot.

I really need to unpack these new Marek emotions.

And there I was, getting ready to be stuck between them, with the truth pounding through my veins. Because whatever waited on the other side of this ride, it wasn't just my mother locked in a cell. It was every choice I'd made, every fracture we'd carved into this pack—and there was no unmaking it.

It was every fracture splitting us wider, waiting to shatter.

Marek slid in beside me, strong hands guiding me over until I was settled squarely on his lap. He reached up, slid the partition closed with a quiet click, sealing us off from the driver.

Rafe climbed in last, his confusion etched across every line of his face as he took in how I was positioned. He hadn't even shut the door before Marek rapped his knuckles against the glass, signaling the driver to move.

"This isn't awkward," I muttered with a laugh, covering my face with my hand.

"Not at all." Marek's chuckle was low, warm, as his fingers brushed a rogue curl away from my cheek. He tilted his head toward Rafe, almost smug. "He made his decision. He's gotta deal with it."

I looked at Rafe then, letting my gaze hold his. And gods help me, part of me *wanted* him to see. Wanted him to watch. To know the difference between them.

Marek trusted me. Every time. He put his life in my hands, again and again, and believed I wouldn't push too far. Wouldn't drain him. Wouldn't kill him. That I was in control of my power.

He feared me. And after today, after what spilled out of him when I pulled the truth from his lips... maybe he was right to. Because the anger still hummed in my blood.

I threaded my hand through Marek's hair, tugged his head gently to the side, and sank my fangs into the heat of his throat.

The first taste hit like fire.

I had been starving, hollow to the bone, and the second his blood touched my tongue, my hips jerked forward on instinct, grinding down against him as need tore through me, wild and unstoppable.

Memories flashed; his body inside mine, the way we had come undone together, and the flush of it lit me up from the inside, stoking the hunger hotter. He felt it too; I knew he did. His fists clamped around my hips, holding me down with a strength that only made me move harder.

"Fuck..." he hissed, voice torn between pain and pleasure.

I was trying, gods, I was trying to keep the edges from blurring. To feed without letting the arousal swallow me whole. But the truth came fast and brutal: there was no separating it. Not with him. Not with this bond threading fire through our veins.

Other than Simône stumbling in once, no one had ever seen us like this. Tangled together. Feeding. Consumed.

And then his cock swelled hard beneath me, pressing against me through thin layers, undeniable. My fangs sank deeper with a groan as I bucked again, harder this time, grinding against him until sparks danced low in my belly. The friction was exquisite, unbearable, exactly what we both craved.

Rafe's breath hitched. I didn't need to look to know because the scent hit me next, lust braided with rage, thick enough I could taste it on my tongue.

My pulls on Marek's blood grew harder and deeper, each draw flooding me with more of him—strength, fire, desire pounding through his veins until it bled into mine. The arousal heightened, coursing between us like lightning.

The gentleness unraveled into need, until our bodies were crashing together, hips grinding, breaths tangled in the same desperate rhythm.

Marek's breathing hitched into soft, quivering moans, the sound vibrating against my skin. I could feel it in his blood; he was close. So close.

Rafe had pushed himself flat against the door, every muscle taut, his whole body twisted toward us despite the fury tightening his jaw. Watching. Breathing us in.

I couldn't care. I couldn't stop.

It was coiling too tight, too deep. Tremors wracked me, every nerve snapping like frayed wire. And then it hit—violent and shattering. My orgasm tore through me, ripping a cry from my throat as I tore my fangs free, blood painting my lips, my head thrown back in abandon.

Marek tumbled after me, burying his face in the curve of my neck, his body shaking as release ripped him apart. "Fuck..." he hissed, breath hot and jagged against my skin, his voice breaking as the last waves tore through him.

The SUV was thick with the scent of blood, sex, and the unbearable truth of what we'd just done.

Our breathing slowed in uneven tandem, the air still trembling with the echoes of it. Marek shifted beneath me, his chest still rising fast, and reached up with calm hands. He brushed the damp strands of hair from my face, his touch so careful it nearly undid me again. Then he tugged his shirt free from his waistband and used it to gently wipe the blood from my mouth.

"You okay?" he asked.

I nodded, my throat tight, and leaned in, wrapping my arms around him, clinging to him like he was the only solid thing in a world that kept tilting beneath me. "Thank you," I whispered.

The warmth of Marek's embrace still clung to me as I shifted, climbing off his lap to sit between them. The space felt too small now, the air too tight, as if the walls themselves had shrunk to keep us pressed against the unbearable truth.

Rafe leaned forward, elbows braced on his knees, fists clenched tight. He hadn't said a word—not one—but his body told the story, anyway. His jaw locked, his chest heaving slow, and the straining hardness tenting his pants, plain as day. Fury and desire knotted together, burning off him in waves.

But still, he stayed silent.

Marek let his head fall back against the seat, eyes slipping closed, his posture loose in a way that only made the contrast more evident. He looked spent, sated, unbothered. A man at peace with what had just happened—while Rafe was a storm waiting to break.

Not awkward at all.

Not at all.

TWENTY NINE

Zaria

The car hadn't even rolled to a full stop before Rafe shoved the door open and stepped out, his silence still ironclad after the entire ride from the hospital. His back was rigid, shoulders coiled tight, and the slam of the door echoed like a thunderclap.

"Do you want one of us to go with you to the corridor?" Marek asked softly, his voice soft as we approached the manor doors, his hand brushing close but not quite touching.

"No. I'll be fine." My steps slowed, dragging until I stopped completely, turning to face him. "But..." I swallowed, the words tasting heavier than I meant them to. "Can we talk? Later?"

He nodded, though there was something guarded in the set of his jaw, a quiet reserve pulling him back. "Yeah. Of course."

I reached up anyway, my fingers brushing his stubbled cheek, holding him still, forcing him to meet my eyes. And for the first time, I let him see me stripped bare. No walls. No shields. My heart wide open.

"I meant it, Marek." My voice softened, letting the tension in his shoulders finally give. "Before, when you were holding me. I told you I loved you."

It hit him clean. His brows shot up, eyes widening like the words had just punched the air out of his chest.

"I meant it," I repeated.

His chest rose fast, his eyes brimming before he could blink it back.

"I love you." His voice broke on it, unguarded. "Fuck, I don't know when it happened or how, but I do."

I rose on my toes, cupped his face, pulled him down. My lips brushed his first—just a whisper of contact, tasting the restraint still holding him taut. Then I pressed harder, deepening the kiss, and his exhale tore out of him —relief, awe, love, all spilling into me in that single breath.

When I pulled back, I lingered close, foreheads almost touching, eyes locking like I needed him to see every part of me.

"Thank you," I whispered, voice trembling but true. "For seeing me."

My heart grew heavier with every step down into the corridor. The stone walls felt colder, tighter, closing in around me. The last time I'd been here, I was ripping the bond out of Rafe, tearing myself in half just to set him free. Now it felt like something else was being torn out of me, piece by jagged piece.

And then, I saw her.

Mama.

The sight nearly dropped me to my knees. Shackled, smaller somehow in the dim light, but still her. My chest caved inward as my mind screamed the truth: she had tried to kill me. With her own hands.

Her gaze lifted when she sensed me, and instead of defiance, she raised her hands in surrender.

"The Council sent me, bébé," she said, her voice breaking on the words. "They took Bernard."

For a moment my knees threatened to give, but, something was off.

The scent. It was like acid on my tongue.

Deceit.

"Where is he?" I stepped closer, closing the distance inch by inch.

"They're holding him," she rushed, words tumbling out too fast. "They made me come to you. Kill you, bébé, or they'd hurt him." Her shackles rattled as she leaned forward, trembling hands outstretched. "I'll take you to him, just... just let me go."

This wasn't my mother.

Her voice.

The cadence.

The accent.

It was off. Everything about her was off, by a hair.

Like a song played in the wrong key.

Even her scent, layered beneath the acrid deceit—it was damn close, but not *hers*.

Not the woman who raised me.

Ice poured through my veins.

"Who are you?" I whispered, stepping back.

My gut twisted hard, screaming at me to move.

I staggered back, turned, and bolted up the stairs just as the air cracked. Windows shattered inward, glass raining across the floor. The doors blew open under brute force, and they poured in—wolves, shifting mid-stride, snarls splitting the air.

The manor erupted in chaos.

"Get downstairs, NOW!" I screamed, my voice cutting through the panic.

One of them lunged at Simône, claws flashing. Instinct took me—my wrist snapped in a sharp flick, and his body slammed into the wall so hard the plaster cracked.

Rafe was already shifting, bones snapping, his growl splitting the hall as he barreled toward the fight.

"No!" My voice was desperate, ringing with command. "Rafe! No! Get downstairs—in the corridor!"

I could feel the storm building in my veins, power threatening to pour out of me in a wave I couldn't control. I didn't want them near me when it broke. I didn't want to hurt them.

"Marek, get them downstairs!"

He caught Rafe's arm, yanking hard. "Fucking listen to her!" he roared.

I twisted back just in time to make sure they were clearing the doors, when claws clamped around my throat. The snarl ripped from me before I flung him off, my wrist snapping in a brutal twist. His neck broke clean, his body hitting the floor before the echo of the crack had even died.

The pack disappeared behind the corridor's heavy bolts, safe. Only then did I stop holding back.

I let the power take me.

It ripped through my chest in a surge, flooding every vein, every nerve. Energy radiated outward, a shimmering field snapping into place. They hurled themselves at it, claws, teeth, rage—but none could breach it. None could reach me.

Twenty. At least. Blooded, circling like vultures, their hunger clinging to the air.

And then—

"High Matron."

The voice slid from behind me, smooth and dark, curling over my spine like fog in my brain.

"We meet at last."

I turned, and the sight jolted something deeper than my own memory. Recognition not mine, but layered—ancient echoes unfurling in my marrow, carried in the bloodline that bound me. Faces I'd never seen, voices I'd never heard, all whispering the same name in one chorus.

Lucien.

The name burned on my tongue like fire, my voice cutting through the charged silence.

"Hello, Lucien."

His smile tilted.

"Too bad dear old mama didn't make it here before we did. You're supposed to be dead already, Matron."

I laughed.

Boy, did he pick the right day to fuck with me.

"Still trying to take out the High Matron. Fail after fail, century after century. Tell me, does the sting of failure ever dull for you?"

Because I knew him. Not from my own life—but through the memories that poured into me when the doors of my bloodline split open.

Lucien A. St. Cyr.

A witch of staggering power. A traitor to his own coven. The man who had once stood beside the High Matron of his age, sworn loyalty in her name, then bartered it away to the Council for the promise of bloodline immortality. He'd lived long enough to watch that power return in generation after generation—and each time, he tried to choke it before it could take its first breath.

It was his hand that guided Claudine's blade into Mary-Ange, his whisper that hollowed my mother's ear, his shadow behind every strike against us.

And still he stood.
Still he hunted me.

"You should be on your knees, Matron. Bound. Delivered. The Council gave me one task—bring you in. Drag those puppies you keep behind you with a leash if I have to. Dead, if it comes to that."

The air shifted when he drew the pouch from his coat. My gut twisted before he even touched it, because the memory wasn't mine alone.

Elden Ash.

Lucien tipped the pouch, pressed it to his lips, and blew.

The dust scattered in a glittering arc, a haze colliding with the shield that pulsed around me. It struck like rain on fire, violet streaks licking across the barrier, eating at its edge.

But it held.

No collapse. No unraveling. The field only swelled brighter, humming, swallowing the ash until nothing remained but silence and light.

His eyes narrowed, the first flicker of doubt breaking across his face.

I let a smile edge across my mouth. "Did you really think

the same trick that killed Mary-Ange would work on me? On us?"

The memories pressed hard against my skin—every Matron he'd betrayed, every time he'd struck to keep us buried. Their fury moved through me like a tide, reminding him that he wasn't facing one Matron. He was facing all of us.

And for the first time, I understood why he feared me.

Because I wasn't just their descendant. I was their weapon, sharpened to its final edge.

But if he wanted to test me—so be it.
I drew in a breath, heart thrumming against my ribs, and let the shield unravel. The energy cracked and hissed as it dissolved, leaving me bare before them.

Gasps rippled through the wolves ringing Lucien, but I only smiled.
"Go ahead then, Lucien," I said, my voice laced with steel and venom. I tilted my chin, daring him closer. "Blow me."

For a moment, his mask held—the calm, the arrogance. But I saw it. The tiniest crack. His fingers tightened on the pouch, his stance widening just enough to betray doubt.
He thought I was bluffing. He thought wrong.

"Thanks, Matron," he sneered, lifting the pouch. "You just made this easy for us."

The purple powder burst into my face in a glittering cloud. I let my body jerk, feigning pain, lips curling into a grimace. But behind it—behind the charade—I was smiling.

Lucien didn't notice. His smirk deepened as he snapped his fingers and turned for the door. "Take her."

The pack of Blooded surged forward, snarls tearing from their throats, claws flashing.
I lifted my hand, mimicking his gesture. And snapped my

fingers.

One by one, bodies hit the floor. Thuds cracked through the chamber in brutal rhythm, a drumbeat of their failure. Not one reached me.

I never broke my gaze from Lucien.
He froze mid-step. Slowly, he turned, eyes widening as he took in the carnage.

The room was silent save for the groans of his fallen, my power humming through the air like a storm daring anyone to breathe wrong.

"Claudine…or whoever that was you sent here. She did arrive before you, Lucien."

I stepped forward, flicking my wrist twice to toss two of his downed wolves aside as if they were nothing more than debris in my path.

"They opened the door for her," I continued, my tone deceptively soft, "thinking my mother—my *mama*—was here to hold me. To tell me everything would be okay."

Another step. The echo of it carried, and his eyes widened.

"Instead, she drove a blade into my chest." My smile got colder. "But here I am. Still alive. Still standing. Well…"

I lifted my hand and snapped.

The sound split the air. Lucien's body slammed into the wall, bricks groaning as they fractured, dirt raining down. Blood burst from his mouth and nose on impact.

I didn't slow.

Another step. His shoulders strained against an invisible vise, breath rasping through clenched teeth.

"Do you have a mother, Lucien?" My voice dropped low, intimate. "Can you imagine that pain?"

Another step. His gaze darted, desperate, searching for an escape that wasn't there.

I tilted my head. "Where can I find the Council, Lucien?"

Silence.

His jaw locked. Arrogance still clung to him like brittle armor, but the crack was widening—the twitch near his eye, the vein hammering in his throat.

"You can tell me, Lucien. It'll be our little secret."

I let myself drift closer, toes grazing the floor as if gravity had relaxed its grip on me.

He drew a deep breath as I closed the distance to a whisper of space between us.

"Fuck." His voice broke. "What are you?"

I released the restraint I'd been holding. My fangs slid down with a hiss, black veins threading across my skin like fractures in porcelain. The storm inside me spilled outward, saturating the space between us until even the air trembled.

"What do you think?" I smiled, baring the points for him to see. "I've been debating a little cosmetic work—maybe shave these down; they're not quite as elegant as I'd like. But the veins?" I tilted my head, letting the black mar the pale canvas of my skin. "They're growing on me. Adds the perfect pop of color. And they match my eyes."

"You're a fucking lunatic."

I glanced around the room, lifting a brow.
"Can you believe how rude he's being?"

Only silence answered—just the groans of his Bloodeds, sprawled across the floor.

I sighed, turning back with a mock frown.

"Tough crowd."

"Abomination."

"Believe me, I've been called worse." I laughed. "Alright—enough foreplay. As much fun as this has been... what's it going to be?"

His sneer wavered, just for an instant, before he spat at the floor, blood flecking his lip. "You think you can threaten me into betraying them? The Council does not fear you."

I snapped my fingers, and the pressure around him tightened. His breath caught, spine bowing, as the wall groaned beneath the force holding him there.

"I don't need *them* to fear me," I whispered, stepping closer, fangs bared. "I need *you* to."

A shudder ran through him. His jaw worked, stubborn, but the storm pressing against his ribs was relentless, squeezing, crushing. Finally, the words broke out of him in a ragged rasp.

"Svalbard."

The name was foreign on my tongue, but my ancestors' memories stirred, threads unspooling through me—endless ice, a barren place where the world itself felt godless.

"The Council hides where no one dares to tread," Lucien choked, his eyes burning with hate. "Buried in the permafrost, locked in vaults of stone and ice. They believe themselves untouchable."

I leaned in, close enough he could see the black webbing crawling beneath my skin, close enough he could feel the weight of what I was becoming. His breath stuttered, caught between terror and rage.

"Now," I murmured, my voice low, silken, lethal, "wasn't that easy?"

I lifted my hands, cradling his head almost tenderly, my fingers threading through his hair. For a heartbeat, it could've been mistaken for mercy.

But Lucien knew better.

His eyes went wide, panic spilling raw. "Wait—wait—I can—"

The plea cut off in a sudden crack as I twisted.

His body went limp, dead weight in my grip, the sound of his neck snapping echoing like a gunshot in the silence.

I let him fall, his corpse crumpling at my feet among the rest of the Council's mangled dogs.

And I stood over him, power humming through me, my ancestors silent but present; watching and approving.

THIRTY

Marek

I can't explain the sickness crawling under my skin—the helplessness of sitting in wait while someone else bleeds in your place. While someone else fights your battle.

But when Zaria told us to get out... I knew. She wasn't saving us from them. She was saving us from her.

We heard nothing from the corridor. No growl. No crash. Just stillness. Until one bone-rattling thud shook the ceiling like the wall itself had been struck.

Then nothing again.

"This doesn't feel right." Simône's voice cracked, thin and trembling. Her eyes were wide, wet, shining with the kind of fear we never admitted out loud. "We should be up there."

"She sent us down here for a reason." The words tasted like ash. I hated them. Hated the truth in them. Because all I wanted was to tear through those doors, stand at her side. But my gut wouldn't shut up. She wasn't afraid of being overrun. She was afraid of us seeing what she'd have to unleash.

Claudine hadn't said a word.

She just sat there, shackled, calm as still water. Not pale, not shaking like a mother with her daughter upstairs facing slaughter. No. She just…watched.

Her gaze was controlled. Calm in a way that curdled my stomach. Something about her—the way she held herself—itched at the back of my mind.

Wrong.

Eerie.

Like she already knew the ending before the story had even started.

Markus and Elodie kept to themselves, shadows in the corner.

Rafe paced like a caged animal, braids slipping through his fingers as he raked them over and over. He hadn't said a word to me since the ride from the hospital, but I could feel it radiating off him—rage, shame, frustration. A storm looking for somewhere to land.

For an Alpha, law was law: you fight. To the death, if you have to. Being sidelined was eating him alive.

We all shot to our feet at once when the doors finally opened.

Zaria walked in without a scratch on her. No blood. No limp. Just her power thrumming under her skin, a hum that made the air taste like lightning. Not even a nod to the dozens she'd just put down.

"Is everyone okay? Anyone hurt?" Her eyes swept the room like she was taking roll.

"We're okay. Are you?" Simône's voice overlapped mine because I asked the same damn thing at the same time.

"I'm fine." Clipped. Confident. But then her gaze cut to Claudine—hard enough to pin her to the chair.

"Back to you," Zaria said, voice like iron. "Easy way or

hard way. Your choice. Now."

"Oh, chère..."

But the voice wasn't hers.

It crawled out of her throat wrong, warping, deepening into a man's cadence. Claudine's shape rippled, shimmered, and then broke apart like smoke burning off in the wind.

Broad shoulders. A cruel smile. Eyes I knew too well. Devereaux.

Can we catch a fucking break, universe?
Why does this bastard get a season two?
Goddamn it.

"Finally, back to my own skin," he drawled, spreading his hands like a man stepping onto his stage. "Thanks to my good—assuming dead?—friend Lucien upstairs."

"Did you hurt my mother?"

She didn't wait for his answer. With a flick of her wrist, power surged, and Devereaux's body slammed into the wall.

He laughed—choked and breathless, but still laughing—as he peeled himself off the crack in the stone he'd left behind.

"Ahh, there she is. The Matron with a temper." He brushed invisible dust from his shoulder, his grin widening. "To answer your question, chère... no. Your dear mama's alive and well. For now. Though I can't promise the Council hasn't developed a taste for her tears."

Simône growled low in her throat, feral and uncontained. Elodie stiffened like a bow pulled taut. Even Rafe's pacing stopped dead, his whole body coiled.

Zaria stepped forward, every inch of her radiating power. Her fangs glinted, the black veins lacing her skin spreading wider, pulsing.

"There it is again," she said. "That scent. Lies." She flicked her wrist and the cell unlocked and the door opened. "It's the one thing that gave you up."

We all braced, ready for the inevitable.

His grin faltered, just barely.

"The Council doesn't have my mother," she went on, her voice sharp, ringing like steel in the chamber. "Because I've seen them. I went myself. And while you were busy slithering your way into my house, I put a ward of protection on hers. On *them*. So no, Devereaux. They don't have her. They never did."

She warded them that night. The circles.

She tilted her head, a ghost of a smile flickering across her lips, humorless, cruel.

"So tell me. What *was* the plan? Lure me? Cage me? Bind me like some cornered beast?"

She lifted her hand, fingers curling into the air as though plucking at a string. And there it was—the shimmer of something unseen, an invisible thread thrumming between them. She wrapped it around her fist and began to pull.

"Truth," she commanded, "Speak."

Devereaux's body jerked, his lips parting against his will. His eyes went wide with panic, but the words spilled out anyway, dragged from his throat in a strangled torrent.

"Lucien...found me after you cursed me." He said. *"He tried to lift it, but he couldn't. He turned me into a shifter instead. Sent me to take your parents, but we failed. So he sent me here—as her. As Claudine."*

The words poured faster, tumbling over themselves, ripped clean from him as her grip on the threads tightened.

"The Council—" he gagged on the word, but it still came — *"they fear you're too strong to walk this earth. Too strong to let live.*

Lucien works for them. He always has. He's a Council son. He's their blade. Their shadow." His breath hitched, eyes bulging. *"They're building an army. Witches. Wolves. Bloodeds. Anything. Anyone. By any measure they can, to take you down."*

The only sound filling the corridor was his ragged panting as though she'd torn the truth from his lungs one rib at a time.

And Zaria? She didn't even flinch. She just stood there, holding the thread like it was nothing, like unraveling him had cost her no more effort than breathing.

Holy fuck.

That's my girl. My mate.

Just look at her.

Goddamn.

I'm going to marry that woman.

"I showed you a mercy once. That won't happen again."

Her grip on the thread didn't loosen—it changed, tightening into something heavier. And then her voice… Christ, it wasn't hers anymore.

It dropped low, deeper than it should've gone, carrying an edge that made the air itself vibrate. Every word scraped like it was too old for a human mouth, but it came out of her all the same.

"Ou nax rès valen. Korr ven'keth, naem makor'neth. Exal draem hall, andh fènwa va harrekh dèyè sen'th vos."

The words landed like thunder. The floor shook under us.

Devereaux's eyes went wide, then rolled back white. His body snapped and bucked, a scream tearing loose that didn't sound human. It ripped through the chamber raw, endless, clawing at the walls, at the marrow in my bones.

"Every death you caused," Zaria hissed, stepping closer,

her black-veined hand lifted, "you will relive them all. Every cut. Every fire. Every breath stolen."

His screams cracked higher, breaking. He clawed at his face like he could tear the visions out, but there was nowhere to run.

The wall behind him groaned, mortar splitting, bricks shoving outward until the stone itself yawned open.

With a sweep of her arm, his body flung backward into the hollow. His nails screeched across stone, desperate, but the pull didn't let up. It dragged him under.

Zaria's hand curled into a fist. The wall sealed, brick by brick, stone by stone, swallowing him whole. The chamber went still. Silent. His screams cut off like a string snapped.

And then she spoke—soft, almost gentle, like she was setting flowers on a grave.
"May the earth remember what you were, and may no one else."

She pulled in a breath, shoulders rising, then falling. Her head bowed, hair curtaining her face. She kept her back to us, rigid, unreadable.

"I'm sorry you all had to see that," she murmured, the words soft but carrying, a knife of shame hidden under steel. "See me...like this."

None of us moved. None of us spoke.

She stepped toward the door, her voice flattening into something almost casual, almost cruel in its dismissal. "Be careful upstairs. There's bodies everywhere."

And without another glance, without letting us see her face, she walked out.

Her absence pressed harder than her presence. The air felt wrong without her storm filling it, and all I could do was stare at the sealed wall where she'd buried a monster alive and wonder if any of us really knew what kind of power we were standing beside anymore.

We climbed in silence, boots crunching on shattered glass, the scent of blood and ash thick in the air. The corridor gave way to the main floor, and the sight stopped us cold.

Bodies everywhere. Wolves, witches, Blooded—strewn across the marble like discarded puppets. The walls bore scorch marks, long gouges clawed into the stone. Windows were blown inward, jagged teeth of glass glittering under the low light.

Elodie pressed her hand over her mouth, eyes wide, voice trembling as she took it all in.

"She did all of this?" Her gaze swept the carnage, landing on one corpse with its neck twisted the wrong way, another pinned to the wall by nothing but invisible force. "To save us?"

Simône's throat bobbed, and for once, she had no clever retort. No anger. Just a whisper, reverent and ruined.

"No. Not just to save us." She shook her head slowly, her eyes shining. "She did this to keep from hurting us."

The truth of it settled heavy between us, heavier than the blood soaking the floor.

I followed her scent upstairs. It led straight to my quarters. When I pushed open the door, her clothes lay in a crumpled heap on the floor, and steam curled from the bathroom.

I knocked softly, then eased the door open. "Are you okay?"

No answer, just the muffled sound of crying over the hiss of the shower.

I stepped inside, and the sight carved something out of me.

Zaria was curled in the corner of the shower, knees pulled

tight to her chest, her body shaking as sobs tore through her. Water cascaded down her hair, plastering it to her cheeks, but it couldn't hide the truth — the High Matron, breaker of curses, the woman who had just entombed a monster alive, was shattering in silence on the tile floor.

I didn't hesitate. I climbed in with her and pulled her into my arms, dragging her against me as I sat down on the wet tile. I didn't care about the water, didn't care about anything but the feel of her trembling against me.

I didn't speak. I just held her, letting her cry into my chest, my arms a shield, a promise. The fact that she was here, in my space. That she needed *me* and no one else. And I'd hold her until her breath evened out, until she remembered she wasn't alone.

Finally, her voice broke through, sobbing against my skin.

"They're going to think I'm a monster. All of them. I killed all those people."

"You were protecting your family, Zaria. That's not monstrosity. That's love. Survival."

She pulled back just enough to look up at me, her eyes burning, wet. "Why don't I scare *you*?"

I brushed her soaked hair from her face, thumb stroking her cheek, and met her gaze without flinching. "Because you're still you. High Matron. Blooded. Whatever name you want to carry; it doesn't change the fact that you're Zaria. And nothing about that scares me."

Her eyes searched mine. For a heartbeat she hovered there, trembling between belief and despair.

Then she kissed me.

There was nothing hesitant about it. It was a crash, a need, her lips finding mine with a hunger that had nothing to do with blood. This was what she'd been craving, *recognition*. Someone to see beyond the veins blackened with power, beyond the title, beyond the terror. Someone to just... *see her.*

Her fingers fisted in my shirt, pulling me closer, deeper, her mouth opening under mine. The kiss turned into an intimate heat spilling into something biting, wetter, the kind of kiss that leaves no air between two people. I groaned into it, tasting salt, water, her; everything tangled together.

Steam wrapped around us, heat rising off her body and mine. Her legs shifted, sliding across my lap, her thighs gripping my hips as the kiss spiraled, becoming erotic, hunger becoming demand.

And I gave her everything she asked for, every ounce of restraint and devotion, even as the shower poured over us like rain on fire.

With my hands on her waist, I guided her up to her feet. Water cascaded down her body in rivulets, tracing every line, every curve. She braced against the tile, chest rising and falling in jagged breaths, her eyes dark, burning, locked on mine.

I bent low, hooked her thigh over my shoulder, and pressed her back against the slick wall. She gasped, the sound breaking into a shiver as I leaned in, tasting her.

Her heat flooded my tongue; her flavor was intoxicating. I started slow, letting my tongue tease the length of her folds, circling, savoring, until she was trembling in my hands. Her fingers tangled in my hair, tugging hard, her hips jerking against me, chasing what she wanted.

I gave it to her.

I drew her clit into my mouth, sucking, flicking, stroking with the flat of my tongue until her moans grew louder, bouncing off the shower walls.

My grip on her tightened, one hand braced beneath her ass to keep her steady as the other slid between us, pressing two fingers inside her, filling her in time with my mouth.

"Fuck—" she gasped, her head hitting the tile, her voice breaking as her body bowed.

I curled my fingers, hitting that spot again and again, relentless, my mouth never leaving her, dragging her higher, tighter, until she was shuddering in my arms.

She came undone with a desperate cry that tore through me like fire. Her thighs clenched around my shoulders, her whole body convulsing as I dragged her through it, tongue and fingers coaxing every last wave of release from her until she collapsed back against the wall, trembling and breathless.

I eased her leg from my shoulder, kissed the inside of her thigh, then her hip, tasting the water, the salt of her skin. When I stood, her eyes met mine—wild, wet, luminous. She grabbed my face, pulling me into a kiss that was all tongue and teeth, tasting herself on me, her hunger sparking against mine.

"Take me," she whispered against my lips, the words hoarse, commanding.

And fuck if I wasn't already halfway gone, ready to give her everything.

Her back pressed to the cool tile, water streaming down her face, her chest rising fast and uneven. She looked at me like she was still breaking—still bleeding from the inside out—and something inside me snapped.

"Let me set the pace," I whispered, my hands cradling her hips, my mouth brushing reverent kisses across her stomach, her ribs, the curve of her breast. Her fingers tangled in my hair.

I took my clothes off and tossed them aside, pulling her down on my lap. When I slid into her, it was tender and grounding, every inch of me sinking into her like an anchor finding its home. Her lips parted, a soft gasp spilling free, and I kissed it away, my mouth gentle on hers, our foreheads pressed together.

"Breathe," I murmured, rocking into her with a rhythm made for us alone. Her arms wrapped around my neck, pulling me closer, and I kissed my way along the line of her jaw, down the column of her throat.

Every movement was worship—slow thrusts, deep and careful, my lips never leaving hers for long. "You're not alone," I breathed between kisses. "Not in this. Not ever."

Her body clung to me, each roll of my hips drawing soft moans that melted into whimpers, then into cries. Her nails dragged down my back.

"That's it," I whispered, kissing her jaw, her temple, her lips again. "Just let go. Don't fight it. I've got you."

Her climax came like a tide, rolling and building until it crested and crashed through her. She arched into me, trembling; her cry muffled against my mouth. I slowed, let her ride it, coaxed her through it with soft murmurs and deep thrusts, until the quake of it left her limp against me.

I followed her over the edge with a quiet groan, spilling into her with shuddering restraint, my forehead pressed to hers, our breaths ragged and shared.

When it was over, I didn't let her go. I kept her on my lap, still joined, kissing her slow and deep while her tears slid between our mouths, salt lingering on my tongue.

"You're everything," I whispered against her lips. "And I'll remind you every damn day, for as long as you let me."

THIRTY ONE

Rafe

I feel like the world's biggest fucking idiot. Like I fumbled the bag so hard I might never get it back.

She's powerful. So fucking powerful. And I—like a coward, like a fool—wanted to bind her. To strip her down, cage her, clip her wings. If we'd succeeded? If Elowen had succeeded? We'd all be corpses right now. Every one of us. Because those bastards dismantled my grounds security, infiltrated the manor, cut through everything I thought made us safe; and she was the single force that held them off.

Zaria. My mate. The woman I claimed. The woman I betrayed.

Watching her feed from Marek in the SUV on the way home from the hospital—*fuck,* it ruined me. It was the most infuriating, erotic goddamn thing I've ever seen. My wolf wanted to rip his hands off her, shred him for touching what's mine. My vampire? He wanted to sink fangs into his throat while she was coming apart, wanted to taste what she tasted. It split me in half, burned me alive, left me silent when I should've fought for her.

I couldn't even speak. Barely had the restraint to keep from lunging at them both.

So instead, I did the only thing left to me. I called my team in, ordered them to clean up the carnage—secure the grounds, patch the breaches, clear the bodies before word spread. The Alpha in me handled the logistics, barked the orders. But it felt hollow, mechanical.

Because none of it mattered. None of it fixed the truth staring me down.

She was the one who saved us. She was the one who stood between life and annihilation. Not me. Not the pack. *Her.*

And while I buried myself in cleanup, in control, I could feel her slipping further from me. Further into his arms.

The things I said to her today, standing by willing to let her die if the binding didn't work. I'll never be able to walk that shit back. I made her hate me today, and I'll have to live with that forever.

I made my way upstairs, thinking maybe—foolishly—that I'd find her in my room. *Our* room. That some part of her would still come back to me.

But her scent pulled me elsewhere. His door. His space.

I should've turned around. Should've gone back downstairs and swallowed the ache, the rage, the truth of it. But instead I drifted closer. Close enough to hear her.

Coming apart for him.

The sounds wrecked me. Tore me apart. Each moan, each gasp, each shuddering cry—every one of them used to be mine. Used to be *for* me. And now...now they were his.

I pressed my head against the wall, fists clenching until my claws threatened to break skin. My wolf snarled to claim her back. My vampire ached to taste her again, to feed where she fed from him. And the man in me—the fool—could only stand there, listening, imagining him inside her, her body writhing beneath him, taking what I once believed only I could give.

Rage burned hot, arousal burned hotter, both flooding me until I thought I'd break.

I cracked the door, keeping as quiet as possible, even knowing I didn't want to see. But I needed to.

And it fucked me up, just like I knew it would.

I eased the door open another inch, and the sight hit me like a blow.

They weren't just tangled together; they were *woven*.

Marek's body curved over hers, their movements we so fucking intimate. His hand cradled the back of her head, fingers stroking through her hair like she was something fragile even as he drove into her with unrelenting rhythm. And her eyes—gods, her eyes—never left his face.

I'd seen Zaria undone before. I'd seen her scream my name, clutch at me like I was oxygen. But this was different. This was quiet. Sacred. Her body moved with his like they were carrying out some ancient oath, like they'd signed the contract of each other's souls and were sealing it now, breath by breath, thrust by thrust.

I wanted to look away. I couldn't.

What she and I had shared; it was heat, blaze, two storms colliding and burning everything in our path. It was fucking, feeding, clawing. But this?

This was lovemaking in its rawest damn form.

Marek whispered something against her mouth, and she laughed; soft, breathless, joy spilling out of her even as tears streaked her face. She kissed him back like he was the last man left in the world. Like he was the one she'd been waiting for.

My wolf snarled to take her back. My vampire begged to taste the bond they were forging between them. And the man in me — the man who claimed her — was forced to stand there and watch her *choose*.

Every gasp, every arch of her spine, every moan that belonged to him and not me carved me down to bone.

And gods help me, it was beautiful.

That's what ruined me most.

I should've turned away. Should've spared myself the ruin of it.

But I stayed.

I stayed as Marek's pace deepened, as Zaria's body arched beneath him, her nails clawing down his back. Her cries grew higher, each one pulled from a place I'd never touched.

Her eyes stayed locked on his, wet and luminous, even as her mouth fell open on a ragged moan. "Marek —" she gasped, breaking on his name.

And that was it.

Her climax tore through her, her whole body bowing against his. He whispered something against her lips, and then he came with her, burying his face in her neck, groaning her name.

It wasn't the sound of fucking. It wasn't the edge of hunger or power or proving. It was the sound of a man giving himself away.

And she took it. Every drop, every word, every breath — she took him into her like he'd been hers all along.

I was torn between my wolf howling to rip them apart and the man breaking under the truth of what he was seeing.

I didn't even hear her approach until a hand tapped my shoulder.

I spun, fury ready to strike, but it was Simône.

Her eyes were wet, her face pale, and she just shook her head. No words. No judgment. Just a silent plea.

No. Don't.

The fight drained out of me in a rush, leaving only defeat. I let her tug me from the doorway, my body heavy, my head bowed, my heart splitting open with every sound that still carried down the hall.

I followed her away.

Because if I stayed, I'd either kill him...or fall to my knees at their door.

"Why were you watching them? You have no right!"

Her eyes blazed, wet and furious. "You were the reason she was weak, the reason she almost died!" Her chest heaved, every syllable carved with betrayal. "You wanted to have her bound, Rafe. *Bound*." Her voice broke on the word. "You don't get to hover outside that door while he—" she jabbed a trembling finger back toward the hall, "—repairs what you broke inside of her."

Her fury hollowed me. Because it wasn't just Zaria anymore.

It was Simône. My blood. My sister. And the way she looked at me—like she didn't recognize me, like I was just another monster she had to protect Zaria from—shredded me worse than the sight I'd just walked away from.

My mouth opened, but nothing came out. No defense. No excuse. Because every word she threw at me was truth. And truth was heavier than claws, heavier than hate.

"She's pregnant, Simône."

The words ripped out of me before I could stop them. Low. Harsh. Shaking with everything I couldn't hold back anymore.

Her face went still. Anger froze mid-swing, her mouth half open like she'd been about to flay me again.

"Pregnant?" she echoed, breathless, the word breaking apart in her throat.

"Yes." The weight almost buckling me. "With twins. And I don't even know if they're mine. Or his. Or both. But gods — she's carrying them. Carrying them after everything I did to her, after everything I tried to take from her. And you think I don't know I ruined it? You think I don't know she'll never look at me the same again?"

I dragged a hand over my face, claws raking through my scalp, a sound tearing out of me halfway between a laugh and a sob. "I tried to bind the mother of my children. I almost destroyed her — and them — before they ever had a chance to exist."

Simône's eyes shone, her fury crumbling, but the sorrow behind it was worse.

"You destroyed her. You've lost her, Rafe." Simône's voice had gone soft, trembling, the fury stripped away until only grief remained. "And if you don't stop clawing at what's left, you'll lose them too."

She sagged back into her chair, wiping her face, her eyes red. "She loves Marek, Rafe. She loves you too, even though she hates you right now. If she can forgive Marek for working with Deveraux to have her killed, she can forgive you."

The words barely landed at first. My brain refused to take them in, like she'd just spoken in a language I didn't fucking know.

Then the meaning clicked. And the floor dropped out.

"The fuck did you just say?" The growl ripped from my throat. My body went rigid, claws snapping free as I lurched forward, my chair skidding back with the force.

Simône flinched but didn't look away, didn't take it back.

"You heard me."

My pulse pounded in my skull. "Marek. Worked with Deveraux?" My disbelief curdled into fury. "You're telling me he—he's the reason she almost died? And she—" My breath tore out of me in a ragged sound I couldn't cage. "She *forgave him*?"

The betrayal burned through me hotter than any wound, scorching until I swore it would hollow me.

And for the first time, I wasn't sure who I wanted to kill more—him for touching her...or myself for letting it get this far.

Simône's voice broke through, softer now but sharper for it. "I wasn't going to tell you, but you need to know this: her heart is capable of supreme forgiveness. But only if you're forgivable. So, work on being forgivable, Rafe. Or you'll lose everything by waving your anger and fury and Alphahood around like weapons."

And with that, she stood.

She didn't flinch at my claws being out, didn't linger to see if I'd snap. She just turned and walked out, like she hadn't just detonated a goddamn bomb and left me choking in the smoke.

My fists shook. Every instinct screamed to storm down the hall, tear through doors, demand answers from Marek, from Zaria, from anyone who could explain how the hell I was supposed to come back from this.

But all I could do was sit there with my wolf pacing, my vampire ravenous, and the man in me...

The man in me just broke.

THIRTY TWO

Zaria

Where...what? Where am I?

It looks like the manor, but wrong. Tilted, warped—like someone rebuilt it from memory and missed the details. The wallpaper curls in cracked strips down the walls. Chandeliers sway though there's no wind. The air hums metallic, sharp in my lungs, every breath like biting foil.

And the floors—fuck. The floors are streaked with blood. Not fresh, not wet. Old stains, blackened into the grain like the house itself is rotting from the inside. Footprints overlay each other in chaotic layers—small, large, human, wolf—all swallowed into shadow at the edges.

"Hello?" My voice echoes.

I keep moving, door after door opening into rooms that are shells of themselves. Rafe's study: shelves toppled; Marek's office: desk overturned, paper scattered like ash. Simône's laugh should echo through these halls, but the house is emptied of sound.

"Rafe? Marek? Anyone?"

My footsteps echo too loud. My own breath is louder still,

a ragged thing bouncing back at me from walls that feel closer than they should.

I shove open the courtyard doors.

And stop breathing.

Two figures sit on the stone bench in the center. Teenagers. A boy and a girl. Their shoulders squared, their spines too straight for their age. Familiar in a way that yanks the ground out from under me, so familiar it terrifies me. I want to run to them even though I don't know their names.

"She's here."

The words come in unison, their voices braided together. They glance at each other, then rise to their feet.

The boy turns first—dark hair falling into his eyes. One green, one brown. My stomach twists at the sight.

Then the girl shifts, curls catching the strange, sourceless light. Her eyes: one gold, one green. And when she smiles, dimples flash, so achingly familiar I can't breathe.

"Mama."

The boy's voice is warm, sure, threaded with something that feels like home and heartbreak all at once.

The sound breaks me. My knees nearly buckle. It's not just the word—it's the way he says it. Like he's been waiting centuries. Like I should've come sooner, and he's still forgiving me for the delay.

The girl's voice follows, softer but just as certain. "Hi, Mama."

The world tilts sideways. My vision fractures. The manor groans around us, walls bowing inward, the blood on the floor pulsing in thick veins like the house itself is alive and listening.

"Are you my...?" The words claw raw from my throat.

"Yes." The boy answers without hesitation, stepping closer. "My name is Isaick. This—" he reaches back, taking her hand, grounding her as much as himself, "—this is Ilyssa."

Her hand slides into his like it's always belonged there. She nods once; her mismatched eyes on mine.

My breath shudders hard in my chest. My lips tremble, useless against the flood inside me. "How old are you?"

"In this realm, we're sixteen," Isaick says, as calm as if he's naming the weather.

"May I... can I hug you?"

Ilyssa's smile blooms soft, radiant, too much like mine and not at all, dimples carving deep. "Of course."

I don't remember crossing the space. One breath I'm trembling by the doorway, the next my arms are reaching—aching—to close the distance.

They step into me at the same time. No hesitation or fear.

When I pull them against me, when my arms lock around their shoulders, it's like the universe itself exhales. Clicks into place.

Isaick's chest is solid against mine, heartbeat grounding. He's tall. Ilyssa tucks under my chin, her curls brushing my throat, her arms clutching me with the strength of someone who's already had to lose too much.

The love flows into my veins. Irrefutable. Every ounce of what a mother should feel floods through me in a single, annihilating wave—protective, fierce, endless.

No mistaking who they are.

My knees buckle, but they hold me up.

My children—*my children*—grounding me when it should be the other way around. Two teenagers with shoulders too strong for their years, arms wrapped tight around me, keeping me upright as if I'm the fragile one. Tears stream hot and relentless down my face. Still, they don't let go. Still, they don't falter.

"Mama," Isaick whispers again. Softer this time.

I press my lips to his temple, to Ilyssa's hair, greedy for them—for their weight, their warmth, the impossible certainty of them. No spell, no dream could counterfeit this love. It's pure. My heart knows them, even if my mind can't keep up.

"What is this place? What are you doing here?"

They hesitate, and the pause is enough to make the world quiver beneath my feet. Isaick's hand finds Ilyssa's, steadying her before he answers.

"We needed to warn you."

"Warn me?" My gaze darting between their faces.

The manor shudders, then splits apart like paper burning. Walls peel back, colors run like paint in rain. The courtyard bleeds into a room I know and don't know—my body wracked with agony, the air thick with iron and smoke. I'm screaming, body splitting open as I bring them into the world.

Shadows crowd the windows—wolves, shifters, witches— a storm of bodies descending.

Rafe is slammed against the wall, a witch's blade pressed to his throat before it carves deep, crimson spraying in a savage arc. Simône falls. Markus. Marek. My family cut down one by one until the house is nothing but screams and silence.

I clutch two slick, frantic newborns to my chest—my babies—and sob as hands wrench them from me. I fight, claw, thrash until my nails tear, but I'm too weak. Gods, I'm so weak.

The blade plunges into my sternum.

White-hot pain explodes through me, deafening, blinding.

Through the haze, I see them shoved into a car, tiny fists

waving, their voices screaming for me though they've barely drawn breath. The doors slam. Tires screech. And they're gone.

My body crumples with the others, blood pooling fast and endless, soaking into the floor until I'm drowning in it. My chest rises once. Twice. Then stills.

And all I can do is watch the world burn from inside the ruin of myself.

The manor shatters like glass around me. The vision cracks, reforms, and when I blink, I see them again—my children. Not infants now. Older. Hardened.

They're locked away in stone rooms with no windows, no sunlight. Shackles gnaw at wrists too delicate, skin rubbed raw from chains. Their eyes—those mismatched eyes that still carry pieces of me—are dulled, emptied, trained into submission. Ilyssa's curls hang, Isaick's jaw set like forged steel.

Time bleeds past me in a breath. I watch them dragged from those cells into arenas stinking of blood and rot. Soldiers. Killers. Weapons carved from children. Their hands drip crimson again and again, and each time they return, there is less of them left. A little more hollow. A little less human.

No laughter. No smiles. No childhood. Only orders barked until they obey. Until the sound of crying is replaced by the sound of blades cutting through flesh.

My heart claws against my ribs, frantic, breaking. "No," I whisper, shaking my head so violently my vision fractures. "No, no, gods, please, no."

Isaick lifts his eyes to me then. His voice cracks for the first time, soft but certain. "This is our future."

Beside him, Ilyssa threads her trembling fingers through

his. Her mismatched gaze glimmers with something far too ancient, too heavy, for a girl her age to carry. Fear flickers, yes—but beneath it a spine of iron, unbending even as her voice shakes.

"We've been trying to get you here for sixteen years, Mama." Each word strikes like a hammer to iron, fragile and unyielding at once.

She steps forward, lifting her free hand, palm open, offering. "I'm a dream weaver. But I needed something of yours to connect us here."

Her bare feet whisper across the stone as she moves to the bench. She bends and retrieves a ragged stuffed bear, cradling it like it's holy. Mr. Muggles. His seams split, his fur stained and worn, but I know him instantly. The sight tears through me.

"Grandpa gave me this," she whispers, returning to me, holding the bear out like a relic. "He told me it was yours."

The air quivers. The scene rips apart, bleeding into something darker.

"Kill him, Number two. Now."

The command shatters through the room. A man looms over my daughter, his black eyes devoid of mercy. Grey streaks his hair, but it does nothing to soften him.

My scream claws free as the nightmare unfurls—Mama's body sprawled lifeless on the floor beside Daddy. Isaick stands tall above her like she is his trophy.

"This... this was your mama's, bebé." Daddy's voice is hoarse, wrecked. From beneath his bed, he drags Mr. Muggles into the light. The bear is stiff, darkened with dried blood. His hands tremble as he presses it into Ilyssa's palms.

"Number two. Now. Don't make me repeat myself."

Tears blur my sight. My knees buckle, my palms press to my mouth as if I could hold the sound in.

Daddy's gaze lifts to hers. "Go on now, bebé. Do what you need."

Her hand twists, fingers slicing the air like a thread being cut.

Daddy's head drops instantly. His neck snaps with a sound too final, too clean. Peaceful and painless.

I crash to my knees, the world tilting, collapsing in on itself. My palms slap the ground, searching for something solid, but all I find is smoke.

"Good job. My perfect soldiers."

The words slither through the air, oily and proud.

Isaick doesn't even blink. His voice is toneless, hollowed of anything human. "Thanks, Father."

Ilyssa's reply splinters, her sob cutting jagged as she forces the words out. "Thanks, Father."

The sound rips something inside me wide open.

"Why?" My voice claws into the void, cracking under the weight. "Why would they do this?"

"Eradicate the bloodline," Isaick answers coldly. "The High Matron lineage."

The words curdle in my veins. Rage unspools inside me, eating through every vein, every nerve. I stagger to my feet, shaking so hard I can barely hold myself up.

"You both called him Father. Who is he?"

Isaick's eyes flicker, just once. "Head of the Council. William Allard. He's our Father. He raised us."

"That is not your father!" The words tear out of me, raw, ragged. My whole body feels like it's splitting apart. "That...

that is a *monster*."

Ilyssa's eyes brim, trembling, but her chin holds firm. "We know, Mama. We know who our real dad is. Father is just the man who raised us. The man who tried to make us into weapons." Her voice hardens, the child gone, replaced by something honed brilliant and practiced. "We had no choice. Not until we were strong enough to find you. Not until we had what we needed to stand here and warn you."

A sudden pain lances through my arm, lightning bursting under my skin, causing me to flinch.

Isaick lifts his hand, touching the fractured gleam in his eyes. "My father is Marek. But I'm soul-bound to Rafe." His tone is low, solemn; like the truth itself weighs him down.

Ilyssa mirrors him, fingertip brushing her mirrored fracture. "My father is Rafe. But I'm soul-bound to Marek."

The symmetry of it chills me, like fate carved it with a cruel hand.

"You'll give birth to us in six months, Mama." Her voice wavers, but she pushes on. "It happens suddenly. You weren't prepared. You were vulnerable. The Council waited for that moment. When it came, they took us. They slaughtered the family. Then they hunted every blood relative. One by one."

My breath stumbles. The world tilts and heaves.

"Grandpa knew who we were," Isaick says, his jaw taut, grief flaring in his eyes. "When he gave us the bear, it tethered us. Gave us the thread we needed to find you."

Ilyssa clutches Mr. Muggles to her chest, knuckles white against the worn fabric. "You'll need help, Mama. More than you've ever known. Magic. Protection. Allies. Because what's coming..." Her throat bobs as she swallows, mismatched gaze locking onto mine, heavy with prophecy. "You can't face it alone."

Isaick stiffens suddenly. His head jerks toward the shadows, every muscle tight. "They've found us." The words drop like stones. His hand shoots out, finding Ilyssa's, their grip desperate, unshakable.

The twins turn to each other. That mirrored bond sparks between them like a flare in the dark. Isaick's voice softens, stripped bare. "I love you, Sister."

Her lips tremble, but her reply is calm. "I love you, Brother."

Then they face me together, shoulders squared, already wearing the acceptance of soldiers who know their fate.

Isaick's grip tightens on her hand as his eyes—so achingly familiar, so marked by fate—burn into mine.

"Please, Mama. Fight. Do what we couldn't. This world..." His voice breaks, grief tearing raw through the cracks. "This world is an ugly place now that the Council has full control of us."

Ilyssa leans into him, tears streaking her face, but her voice doesn't falter. "We love you, Mama."

And the words crush me. Because they are saying goodbye.

They faded. My children, my soldiers, my blood—turning to sand before my eyes, scattering into nothing.

I collapsed, knees slamming into the ground. My chest felt caved in, my ribs splitting with the weight of it. The pain was unbearable—not just what I felt, but what they'd been forced to endure in the timeline I hadn't stopped. What they had to do because I failed them.

I failed them.

"I got you, baby."

The whisper brushed against my ear, like a lifeline tossed

into a storm. "Come back to me. I got you. We're right here."

I latched onto it, gasping for breath, dragging air into my lungs like it was fire. My fingers trembled, clawing at the sound, the presence, the tether.

Marek.

His voice pulled me from the nightmare's grip, thread by thread. Until suddenly I could feel him—arms wrapping around me, anchoring me. My forehead pressed to his chest, his scent grounding me. His hands moved slow, circles against my back.

And just like that, the world shifted back into place.

My mate. My chosen.

He brought me back.

THIRTY THREE

Marek

They say it's called falling in love for a reason. Nobody stands at the edge and dives in clean.

You trip.

You stumble.

You go down hard.

That's what this feels like clawing at my chest.

And I hate it. Because I'm not the type. Never have been.

Live long enough, you stop believing in forever. 'Happily ever after' is just a nice story people tell themselves before the world proves them wrong.

I loved Rafe—still do—but that's loyalty built out of fire and blood, not some fairy tale ending.

Now? Now I've got Zaria asleep on my arm. Her breath warm against my chest, her fingers curled over me like she owns the spot. We wrecked the shower, then my bed, and I left her shaking in both. That wasn't the bond. Wasn't compulsion. Wasn't hunger.

It was the best fucking night of sex I've ever had.

And that's the problem.

The guilt's been eating me alive. One night she was Rafe's. Now she's wrapped in my sheets, smelling like me. I don't know how to walk that back, how to explain it, how to apologize for something that felt impossible to stop once it started.

We even tried to keep quiet. That's the part that sticks. Her biting into my shoulder to smother the sounds, me grinding my teeth to keep from groaning too loud—like Rafe wouldn't hear. Like he didn't already *know*. Wolves don't need walls to tell them when something's shifted.

And we weren't trying to rub it in his face. Doesn't matter. It's still a betrayal.

Truth is, I don't have answers. It feels like she's chosen me—she's told me she loves me, she's in my bed, she's reached for me at every turn. But if I let myself believe she's mine, I'll walk out of this ruined if I'm wrong. My soul in pieces, and each one jagged enough for them both to finish me with.

That's where my head was when the knock came. I dragged on a pair of shorts and crossed the room, already bracing for Simône with her endless questions.

But when I pulled the door open, it wasn't Simône.

It was Rafe.

And fuck, the sight of him standing there hit harder than any punch I'd ever taken. He didn't need words—his eyes carried them all. They skimmed over me, bare-chested, skin still flushed from the night, the air thick with the scent of sex. Then they moved past me. Straight to the bed.

To her.

Zaria, asleep under my sheets, her body curled toward the spot I'd just left. My pillow under her head. My mark all over her.

I didn't move. Didn't bother trying to block his view. What good would that have done?

His jaw flexed, his fists curled, and for a second I thought he might finally let it break. Part of me almost wanted him to — because at least that would've been simple.

Instead, he swallowed it back. "We need to talk."

"Yeah."

His gaze flicked to her again. This time he looked away fast, eyes dropping to the floor like it was the only thing in the room worth looking at. His words clipped. "I'll be in the study."

Then he turned and walked off, storm wound tight under his skin, not a single crack showing.

And that quiet, that restraint—it was worse than a fight.

I checked on Zaria before I followed. Made damn sure there were no signs of her shifting, no twitch under her skin that said she was close to breaking. Only when I was sure she was balanced, still, did I pull on a shirt and leave her sleeping.

She hadn't fed yet.

The manor halls felt longer than usual on the way to the study. Heavy. Like every step dragged me closer to a verdict I already knew I wasn't going to like.

Rafe was waiting, of course. He'd already poured us both a couple fingers of whiskey, amber catching firelight. He doesn't do small talk. Doesn't do dramatics. He just sets the stage and waits.

I shut the door behind me and crossed the room, dropping into the chair opposite him. The study was exactly what you'd expect from him—order and weight. A stone fireplace big enough to heat the whole manor. A Persian rug that probably cost more than my first apartment. Two black chairs that swallow you whole if you let them. And between them, a table that might as well have been a battlefield.

I lifted the glass. The whiskey burned on my tongue, but it didn't soften the air. If anything, it sat heavier with every second, pressing down like the fire itself was waiting to see which one of us burned first.

"Do you want to claim her?" Rafe asked finally. No preamble. No hesitation. He didn't even look at me—just stared into the flames and took a slow sip.

"Yes."

"Yeah. Okay." Another sip.

What the fuck does that mean?

"I do, Rafe. I fucking do."

His eyes finally cut to me. "Do you? Or is this about punishing me, about getting back at me?"

My grip tightened around the glass, heat spiking in my chest. "What the fuck are you on about?"

"You know what I'm talking about." He didn't raise his voice, but the weight of it hit harder than a shout. "You fucking hated her, Marek. Don't pretend you didn't. You couldn't stand the sight of her. You *seethed* every time she was close. You threw a goddamn tantrum like a child because I invited her to the corporate games. And now you want her?" He shook his head, a bitter laugh slipping through. "Sounds like bullshit to me."

I set the glass down hard, the crack of it against the table cutting through the fire's low roar. "Yeah, I fucking hated her. Because she was a walking complication, Rafe. Because she was dangerous for you from the second she stepped into our world, and I was the only one who wasn't pretending otherwise."

His eyes narrowed, firelight cutting harsh angles across his face. "Dangerous? That's your excuse? You wanted her gone because she threatened your control over me. Because she pulled my focus off you for once in your goddamn life."

"Fuck you." I leaned forward. "I wanted her gone because I could see what you wouldn't. She wasn't some fragile little thing we could shelter. She was a liability waiting to come cashed in. And you—" I jabbed a finger across the table at him, "—you were blind to it because you were already infatuated with the new fucking toy in the office."

His jaw clenched, glass trembling in his grip before he slammed it down beside mine. Whiskey sloshed over the edge, dripping onto the rug neither of us cared about. "Don't you fucking turn this around on me. You had every chance to walk away. Every chance to let it go. But no—you had to have her. So, tell me—was it about her, or was it about me?"

That hit deeper than I wanted to admit. Yes, I know I should have walked away. I forced the words out, anyway. "It's about her."

"Bullshit." His voice finally rose, the snap of it echoing off the stone. "You wanted to hurt me. You wanted to prove something. You think I don't see that? You think I don't know you?"

I stood then, chair scraping back, the air between us charged. "I didn't touch her to get at you. I touched her because I couldn't fucking stop myself. Because she's under my skin, in my head, and there's nothing—*nothing*—I can do about it."

His lip curled, half-snarl, half-smirk. "So now you're the victim? Poor Marek, couldn't help himself? That's your play here?"

"No," I stood, stepping closer, every word a growl. "My excuse is I fucking love her. You wanted the truth? There it is. I love her. And she's already told me the same. You heard her!"

The room went still. The fire popped, the whiskey burned, and the air between us thickened until it felt like we were breathing smoke.

"She's pregnant with my children, Marek."

My grip tightened at my sides, nails biting into my palms. "We don't know that they're yours."

His eyes cut into me, smug. "Don't we?"

I sank back into the chair. "What I think is that you're so goddamn sure of yourself, you can't even admit the truth—that you don't know any more than I do. And it's killing you."

The muscle in his jaw ticked, just once, before he buried it again. But I saw it.

He lifted his glass, took another sip, then set it down and finally turned toward me. His eyes locked on mine, unblinking.

"You tried to have her killed. You want to know how I'm so sure of myself? You were the one who put Deveraux on her path. You were the one who opened this house to him—with my fucking pack inside it. You put us all at risk. That's how I know."

Fuck.

I wasn't expecting that one.

My chest locked tight, lungs seizing. I couldn't move. Couldn't breathe. My eyes stayed fixed on his face, like if I looked away it would all be real.

"Yeah. Exactly." His voice cut clean. "Tell me again how much you *love* her. Tell me this has nothing to do with me." He turned back to the fire, picked up his drink, and took another slow sip like he'd already won.

I dragged air in, forced it out, praying words came with it.

"It was only supposed to be her." My voice sounded hollow, pathetic, even to my own ears. "She was the target. Not the pack. He was supposed to kill her, not change her."

Rafe's head tilted, eyes still on the flames. "Do you really think that matters, Marek?"

"No." I raked both hands through my hair, the guilt clawing its way up my throat. "Fuck. I know it doesn't. I'm just trying to explain where my head was at."

He leaned back in his chair, his expression carved from stone. "You're lucky your head isn't on a goddamn spike beside my bed."

And the way he said it—calm, measured—was somehow worse than if he'd shouted it in my face.

"Rafe..." My chest cracked open as I pushed to my feet, legs unsteady. Then I sank down in front of him, on my knees like the weight of it all had finally leveled me. "Rafe, look at me."

When his eyes lifted to mine, all I saw was hatred.

"I would never intentionally put you or this pack in danger." My voice shook. "I just... I needed her gone. That's the ugly part of it. I thought she was the threat, and I convinced myself that cutting her out would keep us safe."

I dragged in a breath, let it out rough. "But something changed. I don't even know when it happened. I didn't want it. I didn't look for it. But I'm in love with her, Rafe. And this with her, it's only about me. Not you. Not the bond. Not the politics. Me."

His stare didn't soften. If anything, it hardens. But I kept going, because stopping now would be the real betrayal.

"I wasn't trying to hurt you. Gods, I wanted the opposite. I wanted her away from you before. I told myself it was to protect you, to protect the pack. But I know the truth now." My throat tightened, words scraping raw. "I was hurting because *you* wanted her. Because you claimed her. Not me."

The fire cracked behind us, spitting embers into the silence, but neither of us moved. Just his hatred staring me down and me, finally stripped of excuses, kneeling in it.

"She knows, Rafe." My voice came out low, raw. "Zaria knows. And she's in my bed, anyway."

His eyes narrowed, but I pressed on. "She loves me anyway. That doesn't mean she doesn't love you or want you. I'm not stupid enough to think this is simple, and I'm not arrogant enough to think she's already chosen. I don't know where her head's at." I shook mine, breath coming hard. "But I need you to know where mine is."

I leaned forward, fists braced against my knees. "I'll spend the rest of my fucking life making sure I repair what I've damaged. With you. With her. With the pack. I can't erase it, but I'll bleed every day to fix it if I have to."

His eyes stayed locked on mine. "But I won't pretend she's only yours anymore. I won't lie to either of us like that. The question is—can you be with her, all of her? Because she feels it, Rafe. She feels how she scares you. Every time you flinch, every time you look at her like she might break—or like she might break you—she folds herself smaller. Boxes herself up to make you comfortable.

Can you give her all of you knowing she's stronger? Knowing she can crush you if she wanted? Honestly?"

Rafe's lips parted, the first crack in his armor. "I...I don't—"

The door slammed open, hard enough to rattle the glass on the table. Simône burst in, breathless, eyes wide.

"Something's wrong with Zaria."

Her panic ripped through the study.

I was on my feet before I even registered moving; the chair toppling back behind Rafe as he bolted. My chest seized, everything I'd been holding back shoved aside in one violent rush.

The fire, the whiskey, the fight—it all vanished. There was only her.

THIRTY FOUR

Marek

We followed Simône out into the courtyard, boots hitting stone before giving way to grass. The night air was damp, cold enough to bite, but that wasn't what put the hair up on my neck.

Zaria stood in front of the alcove, rigid. Locked like invisible hands had nailed her in place. Elodie and Markus flanked her, squared up and protective, but uncertain—like they couldn't tell if moving closer would save her or kill them both.

Rafe's gaze snapped to mine. He felt it too. The charge in the air. Heavy. Wrong.

"Her eyes are white," Simône hissed, panic cutting through the quiet as we closed the distance. "She's talking to someone that's not here."

We stepped into the grassy circle, shadows from the alcove dragging long under the moonlight. And then I heard her voice. Not exactly hers, but ripped out of her body all the same.

"Varrekh suul naxèn draem?"

Wait...

I froze.

"What is she saying, what language is that?" I heard someone ask, but I was too locked in to place who.

"Why would they do this…" I whispered under my breath, my gaze locked on her as the translation crawled down my spine.

Rafe's head snapped toward me, Simône's too, but I kept my eyes on Zaria; on the body that looked like hers, but the voice that wasn't.

"I can understand her," I said, my voice rough. "She said, *'why would they do this.'*"

The fire in the torches guttered all at once, flames choking down until only shadows danced; long, jagged things that climbed the courtyard walls like they were alive.

Rafe's voice cut through the dark with a panic I've never heard from him. "What's happening?"

Her lips parted to speak, but her eyes stayed fixed on something none of us could see.

"Tuul ven'ar naxèn voskar. Veyr talekh su?"

I tilted my head, every muscle drawn tight. "She said… 'You both called him Father. Who is he?'"

Simône's brow furrowed. "How are you understanding her?"

"No fucking clue. I've *never* heard this language before."

Zaria's voice cut through again, uneven and otherworldly.

"Draem voskar naem'talekh! Varrekh… varrekh naxèn morvak."

"Fuck," I muttered, "She said... *'That man is not your father. That is a monster.'*"

"Goddamn it." Rafe groaned as he pushed past me,

crossing the courtyard fast. "Zaria, baby. Snap out of it."

He reached for her arm—gentle, *too gentle* for what we were standing in—and the second his hand touched her, the air around her split. A violent burst of energy exploded outward, invisible but fucking brutal.

Rafe was flung backwards like he'd been hit by a siege ram, his body slamming into the side wall of the manor hard enough to rattle the stone foundation. The echo of impact rolling through the courtyard like thunder.

"Fuck!" he roared, staggering to one knee, then pushing himself up with a snarl. His shoulders shook with fury, but behind the rage there was confusion he couldn't mask.

Zaria's eyes still burned white, lips moving in that ancient language.

"Rafe, are you okay?" Markus darted to his side, bracing him under the arm, hauling him upright. His eyes kept cutting back to Zaria, wide and unsettled. "What the hell is going on?"

"Nobody touches her. Something's wrong," Rafe barked, his voice all command, no compromise.

Simône and Elodie faltered where they stood, feet shifting back instinctively, concern etched across their faces. They obeyed.

But I couldn't stand there.

Not when her fists tightened hard against her chest, knuckles white like she was trying to hold herself together from the inside out. Not when her body seized, every muscle locking, then buckled; dropping her to her knees in the grass as if the earth had yanked her down.

And then came the sound. Christ. It wasn't just a cry—it was a wail that cracked the night wide open, a sound that felt like it had been birthed out of the marrow of pain itself. It shredded something in me clean through.

So, I moved on instinct alone. My legs carried me before my head could catch up, before I even knew if I could help. I just knew I had to get to her.

It didn't matter if I ended up thrown like him, or if the courtyard spat me against the wall and left me shattered. It wouldn't be the first time.

I dropped hard to my knees, closing the distance in one breath, and wrapped her up before my brain could warn me off.

Nothing happened.

No explosion of power. No violent throw.

Just her.

Shaking, trembling, breaking apart in my arms.

I crushed her tighter against me, caging her there. "I got you, baby," I whispered against her hair. My palm dragged slow circles over her back, the only rhythm I could give her to hold onto. My hand cradled her head, tucking her face to my chest. I pressed my lips to her temple, grounding us both. "Come back to me. I got you. We're right here."

Her body heaved with each breath, shallow and frantic at first, then tugging softer, easier, like she was tethering herself to the sound of me.

I looked up, meeting their eyes one by one.

Simône and Elodie stared with wide, tearful eyes. Markus had a steadying hand on Rafe's shoulder, but even he couldn't tear his gaze from me, stunned, like he couldn't piece together what the hell he was seeing.

And Rafe...

Rafe's face cut me deepest.

It wasn't even rage or confusion this time, it was like resignation. The kind that lives in your bones, like he'd already known this was coming. Like he'd seen it carved into stone long before tonight.

Because whatever force had thrown him across the courtyard, whatever wall of power wouldn't let him lay a hand on her... it let me through without hesitation or resistance. No violence. Just me, pulled in, anchored in her arms as much as she was in mine.

And that was the truth neither of us could run from.

She didn't have to say a word.

By letting me hold her when she was lost to everyone else, she'd already made a choice.

"Marek?"

I pulled away to meet her eyes. "I'm right here. You're okay." I brushed the hair away from her damp forehead. "Right here."

Her eyes shifted, the white haze bleeding away until hazel bled back in, glassy and wet. Her lips trembled once, then she broke; diving at me, clinging so tight it nearly knocked me backwards.

She straddled my thighs where I crouched, arms locked around my neck, tears burning hot where they buried into the crook of it. Her whole body shook against me.

"I saw them." The words hit in ragged sobs. "The babies." Her breath caught, breaking. "They weren't babies. They were teens. They took them. The Council took them!"

For a beat no one breathed. We all exchanged looks—confusion, fear, disbelief—rippling through the group like shockwaves.

I tightened my hold on her, one hand cradling her head,

the other rubbing circles against her back. "Let's get you inside."

I shifted my weight and stood, not breaking my grip on her for a second. She clung tighter, trembling, every tear soaking into me.

Rafe was there, watching, his expression a sadness so intense it cut even from across the courtyard. But I couldn't focus on him. Not now.

Everyone fell in behind us, steps muted as we crossed back into the manor. The quiet was thick, every face turned toward her, but no one daring to speak.

Inside the living room, I lowered myself onto the couch, settling her onto my lap, keeping her caged against me. My palm smoothed over her hair, down the line of her spine, while she struggled to even her breath.

They gathered close, a half-circle of eyes and nerves, some sitting, some standing. All waiting. Waiting for Zaria to lift her head, to give voice to what she had just lived in that vision.

"I'm sorry."

Her breath trembled with it. She slid from my lap to sit at my side, and though I let her move, her hand stayed locked with mine, small and shaking in my palm. Holding tight like it was the only thing keeping her tethered.

Rafe's gaze flicked down, straight to where her fingers tangled with mine. His jaw flexed once before he forced his eyes away, the muscle jumping like the restraint cost him.

"I realize," she said softly, voice rough, "we haven't even sat together since I came home from the hospital yesterday." Her throat bobbed. "But... I'm pregnant."

The words dropped into the room like a stone into still water, and the hush they left behind rippled out, touching every face.

Her grip on me tightened, but her eyes—her eyes went to Rafe.

Simône shifted on her feet, Elodie's lips parted like she wanted to speak but couldn't, Markus glanced between them all with wide eyes. Uneasy, restless, bracing.

"One baby," she continued, fighting the wobble in her voice. "A girl. Her name is Ilyssa. She belongs to you, Rafe."

His head snapped up, eyes wide, every bit of him going rigid. His gaze tore from her face to mine, sharp and accusing, then back to her again like he was trying to make sense of a riddle that shouldn't exist.

"And the other..." Her eyes lifted to me. "The other is a boy. His name is Isaick. He belongs to you, Marek."

The sound that left me was half breath, half disbelief. "Holy shit..." My hand dragged over my jaw, rough with the rasp of stubble, like I could ground myself with the scrape of it.

Her fingers squeezed mine again, harder this time. "In six months, I'll give birth to them," she said, words tumbling quicker now. "Sooner than we expect. And when it happens, I'll be vulnerable. My powers will be tied up in the birth, channeled and drained. I won't be able to fight."

Her eyes pinched shut, lashes wet, body trembling with the effort of holding herself together.

"The Council either triggers my labor or waits for it, but their timing—" her voice cracked, "—their timing is perfect. That night... they slaughter us. Every last one of us. And they take the twins."

Her chest heaved, sobbing air in between words she could barely force out. "They take our children and twist them. Turn them into killers. Murderers. Their private magical soldiers.

And then they erase me completely. My entire bloodline. My parents included."

The room recoiled as if her words had claws.

Tears streaked down her face as she choked out the last of it, broken and burning. "They make my babies kill their own grandparents."

I didn't let go of her hand. Not for a second. My thumb dragged over her knuckles, settling both of us, even as her body trembled with the last of her sobs.

"They've been trying to reach me for sixteen years," she whispered, her voice frayed but clear enough to cut through the quiet. "Trying, failing, over and over. Until now."

Her eyes lifted to mine, glassy but shining, her lips curving into a fragile smile. She squeezed my hand, tight, grounding herself in the contact.

"And they finally could... because Daddy somehow got ahold of Mr. Muggles."

The smile faltered, bitter and small, but it stayed.

"They needed something that belonged to me, something that was mine, tied to me. And when they had it—when Daddy gave it to them—that's when they made the connection. That's how they reached me in this…realm is what they called it."

No one moved, no one breathed, but I felt the shift. The way understanding crept over all of them, unease sharpening like claws.

But I didn't look at them. I kept my eyes on her. My hand in hers, my grip solid, because even though her whole body shook, she wasn't letting go of me either.

Her free hand slid down, resting against her stomach.

"At first, I wanted to fight, to go after them all. Hunt every

Council location, every loyal faction. Burn them to the ground. But we don't have time. We don't have enough help. And we don't have the strength to take on all of them alone."

She drew in a breath, shaky but firm. "We need help. Real help. Protection. And they told me—we'll need a shit ton of it."

Her eyes swept across the room, fierce despite the tears still drying on her face. "I don't care about dying. I need that clear right here and now—I'll put my life down without hesitation. But they won't touch my children."

Simône's hand flew to her mouth, tears brimming, her whole frame trembling with the weight of Zaria's words. Elodie's lips parted, whispering a prayer in a tongue I didn't recognize, eyes wet and glassy. Markus straightened where he stood, his jaw set, fists flexing like he was already preparing for war.

And Rafe—

Rafe stared at her, chest rising and falling too fast, his knuckles white around the back of the chair he stood behind. There was no fury this time, no denial, no sharp snap of command. Just a hollow look, carved deep into him, like every word had cut him open and left nothing but resignation behind.

"Then we don't let them touch them," I said, breaking the stillness Rafe wasn't willing to. "We bring in whoever we have to. We do whatever it takes."

Her eyes flicked up to me—just a second, but I saw it. A thank you in the middle of the storm.

"Alpha? What's our move?" Markus asked.

Every head turned toward Rafe.

He just stood there. Shoulders stiff. Eyes locked on Zaria like he was staring at something he couldn't hold onto anymore.

Fuck. Just do something. Say something.

Simône's voice cracked through next, thin but urgent. "Rafe, say something. Please."

Elodie leaned forward on her knees, eyes wide, desperation in her tone. "We need direction. We can't just sit in this."

And still, he didn't answer.

Zaria's hand found mine, squeezing tight, grounding herself in me. My chest tightened. The dead air dragged too long, the pack restless, watching him like their whole future was about to fall out of his mouth.

When it didn't, I cleared my throat and let my voice cut through the air.

"We don't wait. We don't freeze. We reach out—pull in every ally we've got and then some. Elowen can bring magic wielders. Dr. Hart too. And Zaria's got hundreds, maybe thousands behind her, like we saw at the hospital. Knowing what happens gives us an edge we wouldn't have otherwise."

I looked down at her, lifting her knuckles to my lips. "We don't fucking cower."

Rafe's eyes finally snapped to me. Hard. Cold. But still silent.

The pack was looking between us now—between their Alpha, stone-quiet, and me, the one cutting through his silence.

And I felt it. The shift. Heavy. Irrevocable.

Alpha.

THIRTY FIVE

Rafe

All their eyes were on me.

Markus' questions still hung in the air, *Alpha, what's our move?* Simône's voice had trembled, Elodie's carried desperation. And Marek... fucking Marek had stepped into the void I left, filling it with his voice, like the room had already started tilting toward him.

I should've spoken first. I knew that. But the words wouldn't come. Not with Zaria still clinging to him. Not with her hand wrapped tight in his like it belonged there.

I couldn't stop staring at it—their joined hands. Every second it burned hotter in my chest, but I kept my face carved from stone. I couldn't let them see it.

The fire cracked, spitting embers, and I forced my jaw to unclench.

Say something. That's what Simône had begged. But what could I say? That the woman I'd claimed, the one I'd sworn to protect, had turned in her fear to another man? That the power that had thrown me across the courtyard had let him in instead? That she'd already chosen without saying a word?

Marek's voice echoed in my head—*Then we don't let them touch them. We bring in whoever we have to. We do whatever it takes.*

And the worst part was... he wasn't wrong.

But gods, it felt like losing.

My chest ached.

I lifted my gaze to Markus. "Our move is survival. We fortify the manor. We call in allies. And we prepare for war."

The pack straightened at once, shoulders easing, relief bleeding into their faces. They had what they needed from me.

Direction.

Orders.

Purpose.

But Zaria didn't look at me.

Her fingers only tightened around his.

I forced my jaw to stay still, to keep the muscle from jumping. "Get some sleep if you can," I said, the command coming out rougher than I intended. I dropped into the chair I'd been gripping for the past fifteen minutes, letting the weight of it hold me. "We'll secure plans first thing."

Markus nodded, Simône gave a shaky smile, Elodie brushed a kiss to Zaria's hair. One by one, they filed out, soft words, quick hugs, a glance back at me like they weren't sure what to read on my face.

And then it was just us.

Zaria. Marek. Me.

Part of me wanted to walk out too, leaving the room before the truth suffocated me. But I didn't. Couldn't. This conversation needed to happen, and running from it would only prove what I already feared—that I'd lost ground I might never reclaim.

Zaria finally loosened her grip on him, sliding her hand free, setting distance between them like it meant something. But it didn't. Not really. The mark had already been made. The choice already carved.

The elephant wasn't in the room.

It *was* the room.

Zaria's voice broke the quiet, soft but stable enough to carry. "I'm sorry, Rafe. It wasn't intentional to make you feel like I'd chosen Marek over you. That's not what this has been, even if it seems like it at face value."

Her words landed heavy, right in the raw place I'd been trying to bury under stone.

She leaned forward, hands knotting in her lap before she forced them still. "You were the first person I saw when I woke up after all of this. You were the one who kept me breathing when everything inside me was telling me to give up. I don't forget that. I can't. My care for you, it's not gone. It's just different now with all the hurt we've caused each other." She swallowed, eyes flicking to Marek and back to me, guilt sharp in the movement. "And complicated. More complicated than I ever wanted it to be."

Every word carved me open. She didn't even have to touch me to do it.

"I didn't ask for this pull toward him," she said, her voice trembling now. "I didn't look for it. It just… happened. And I don't know what to do with that. I don't want you thinking I've abandoned you or that I'll ever stop caring for you. That's not what this is."

Twice. Twice, she said care for. Not love.

My fists curled against my thighs, the words lodging somewhere between my chest and my throat.

Marek stayed silent beside her, stone-faced, letting her take the floor, but his silence only made it worse. Because if she hadn't chosen, why did it feel like she already had?

The words clawed up my throat. "It's a hard statement to believe when you were fucking him under this roof not hours ago." My voice came out cold. "So, forgive me if I'm having a hard time following your logic here, Zaria."

Her shoulders flinched, but she didn't look away. Hazel eyes locked on mine, like she knew she deserved the blow but wasn't going to back down from it either.

Marek shifted just enough to catch my attention, jaw flexing, but he still didn't speak. He didn't need to. His silence was a weapon all its own—letting her defend him, defend them, while I sat there bleeding under the weight of it.

And gods help me, that was the part I hated most.

Zaria's eyes flashed, her spine stiffening as she snapped, "You're right and that wasn't done to hurt you. I was spiraling in a pretty bad way, and Marek anchored me. I'm sorry we hurt you in that way."

She pushed to her feet, sudden enough to slice the air, and turned for the door like this was done. Finished. Nothing left to say.

The heat in my chest burst. Even with her apology, the anger boiled over. "He tried to have you fucking killed!"

The room shook with it—my growl, my rage, the truth I couldn't bury.

She froze mid-step, shoulders locked, the weight of it crashing down on all of us.

Marek's head dipped for half a second before his eyes lifted back to me.

And Zaria... gods, Zaria turned slow, her tears streaking

down her cheeks, but it wasn't grief that burned in her gaze. It was fury—scalding, unrelenting, aimed straight at me.

"And you tried to have me bound." Her voice cracked, then hardened. "You called me a cancer to your pack. You told me you wanted me out of your life. You watched me almost *die* when Elowen tried to bind me, and Marek was the only one that stopped it. You, Rafe—" her chest heaved, her hand shaking as she pointed at me, "—you were willing to let me die, just so you could stand as the most powerful being in the room."

A sob tore through her, but she shook it off, standing taller, steel in her spine.

"You told me…you hated me."

Marek dragged a hand through his hair, disappointment rolling off him in waves.

"Which do you think is more unforgivable?" she asked.

The question hung in the air like a noose.

And gods help me, I didn't have an answer.

Because she was right. Every word. And it cut deeper than any wound I'd ever taken.

Her breath hitched, but she didn't stop.

"In six months, we will have the fight of our fucking lives—and I don't even know if we'll walk away from it. If we fail, if we lose again, we hand a life sentence to our children."

Her hand moved to her stomach, protective. "They are soul bound to both of you. They are beautiful. And they hold a piece of all three of us. That is not a coincidence. It's fate. And you don't get to pretend otherwise because we hurt each other."

She stepped closer, the fire in her eyes refusing to dim. "But if you can't get your head around this—around any of it—long enough to have an adult fucking discussion about what we do next, then you don't deserve to lead this pack. It's late, and I'm exhausted, but you can guarantee that I'll be out of your house and your life by morning. As fucking requested."

Her words hit harder than the wall had when she'd thrown me across the courtyard.

And then she turned and walked out.

Gone, just like that. Leaving me hollowed and stripped to bone and truth.

If you can't get your head around this... then you don't deserve to lead a pack.

The quiet aftermath rang louder than a war drum, pounding in my ears. Her eyes—wet, burning, unflinching—still seared into me like an afterimage, daring me to break.

Marek hadn't moved. He sat stone-still, watching. Waiting. Judging. And the weight of it pressed in until I couldn't breathe.

THIRTY SIX

Zaria

Allard. William Allard.

I hadn't made it ten paces before the thought slammed into me. I spun on my heel and strode back inside.

"William Allard," I blurted, no context, just the name burning on my tongue. Then I caught myself and steadied. "He's head of the Council. Or at least he will be, in sixteen years. And I think I know how to find him."

Marek was already rising to his feet, his gaze locked on mine. He knew. I could see it in the set of his jaw, the flicker of recognition sparking in his eyes.

"Deveraux," he said flatly.

"Yes." My pulse kicked harder. "*Exactly.*"

"You're going to... untomb him?" Rafe asked.

"Yes," I answered without hesitation. "That's exactly what I'm going to do."

I turned toward the corridor, my steps sharp, decisive. I'd left him there, buried in shadow and silence. Now I was going back.

"I'm calling the pack," Rafe said, following behind.

"What do you need, baby?" Marek asked.

"Nothing yet." My hand brushed the wall as we walked, tracing the pulse of old stone. My chest burned with the weight of it, with the inevitability. "But when I do, you'll know."

The corridor was always colder than the rest of the manor, the air damp and humming with a pulse that didn't belong. Every step drew me closer to the sealed wall, the stone veined with black, like blood clotted into its very marrow.

I stopped, pressed my palm against the chill, and the world seemed to hush. The pack waited behind me, silent, their breaths held like they knew the house itself was listening.

My throat burned, the words clawing their way up before I even understood them.

"Naem'th korren draem. Veyr sael'ven. Exal voskar dén'rahn."

(*Break the dream's stone. Call the buried. Release what is bound.*)

The walls and floors shuddered.

I spread my fingers wider, forcing the pulse of power outward. My veins thrummed black, threading through my skin, and the stones groaned as though something inside them stirred.

"Ou ven'thall, korr veyr'nax. Harrekh draem'thal, suul makor'neth."

(*Come forth, shadowed one. Tear open the dream, unbind the silence.*)

The stone wall split, glowing faint with sickly light, widening with each syllable that tore from my mouth.

The sound built—a low moan at first, then a scream of stone giving way.

And then the wall collapsed inward with a thunderous crash, choking the corridor in dust.

When it cleared, I saw Deveraux.

His body slumped in the hollow, bound by chains so corroded they looked grown into his skin, his eyes still closed, his lips parted like he'd been waiting to take his first breath in centuries.

The air reeked of him—rot and iron.

I'd sent him to a realm where hundreds of years passed in moments, a torture chamber to relive every horror he'd ever caused on repeat.

His eyes were still white, his face frozen in a scream that never made it to sound. A grotesque, silent cry.

"Ou ven'thall, korr veyr'nax. Harrekh draem'thal, suul makor'neth."
(*Come forth, shadowed one. Tear open the dream, unbind the silence.*)

I repeated the words, pushing them harder, each syllable burning my tongue.

Deveraux convulsed, body jerking like a puppet on strings. His chest heaved once, twice; then he gagged, clawing at his throat.

The sound came next. Skittering.

Spiders.

Hundreds of them.

Pouring from his open mouth in a writhing, endless tide. They cascaded over his chest, down his arms, scuttling back into the tomb that had held him. Their legs clicked like a thousand knives on stone.

"Holy fuck..." Rafe whispered, voice ragged, the sound of a man staring at something he could never unsee.

I tilted my head, letting a smug smile curl my lips. "Maybe you were right to be afraid of me."

The spiders vanished into the shadows, leaving only silence and the echo of their breath. Deveraux sagged forward, gasping, wheezing, his eyes rolling before they flicked back to human, dark and wet with tears.

He looked at me, his body trembling, and then he covered his face with shaking hands.

"I'm sorry," he sobbed, the words unguarded. "I'm sorry. Please! Please don't send me back!"

The sound ricocheted through the corridor, thin and pathetic, not the monster they'd braced for but something fractured and desperate.

"William Allard."

I stepped closer, shadows peeling away underfoot. Marek moved in beside me, his presence a wall of iron, but I raised a hand without looking at him. *Stand down.* This was mine.

"Deveraux." I called, pulling his gaze up. "Focus. William Allard. Do you know who he is?"

His breathing hitched, and for a moment his eyes rolled white again, his body twitching like the tomb still held part of him. His fingers dug into his scalp, nails dragging lines down his face as though the name itself scalded him.

Behind me, I heard Simône's sharp inhale. Rafe's growl simmered low, feral, ready to spill over. Marek stayed stone-still, waiting, trusting me to hold the line.

Deveraux's lips trembled, words spilling like blood through clenched his teeth. "Yes. I know him. I served him." He sobbed and he rocked forward, forehead nearly touching the floor. "Head of the Council. Lucien's father. The one who — " His body convulsed, shuddering like the words themselves seared him. "The one who will end you all."

Lucien's father.

Fuck.

Vengeance given a name.

"Why can't I see him in your memories?"

"He has witches. Powerful ones. He's cloaked." His eyes darted wildly, rolling white again. "They've sealed him from the Thread, buried him from sight."

"Where can I find him?"

He shook his head violently, over and over, like the motion itself was all he had left to fight me.

I turned. Met Marek's eyes. He gave the smallest nod—permission, solidarity, whatever it was, it anchored me.

I stepped forward until Deveraux was trembling under my shadow. He tried to crawl back, but chains of fear held him rooted.

"No," he whispered, voice splintering. "No, no—you can't. You *can't*."

I placed my fingers against his temples. His skin was cold, clammy, pulsing with something foul beneath it. His breath stuttered in terror.

"I don't need your permission," I said.

Then I pushed.

The world ripped. His memories crashed into me like a flood of broken glass—images, screams, fire and stone. Wards snapping shut like jaws, witches chanting in circles of salt, shadows crawling where men should be.

And somewhere beneath it all, buried deep in the rot of him—William Allard. A silhouette cloaked in darkness, his face obscured, his presence smothering like ash poured down my throat.

I gasped, forcing myself deeper, clawing past the wards, past the screams Deveraux let out as he tried to fight me off. My nails dug into his skin, but I didn't let go.

I *would* see him.

The wards slammed into me like iron doors, runes glowing and snapping shut across Deveraux's mind. They clawed at me, pushed back with teeth of shadow and fire, shrieking in a hundred voices not his own.

He screamed with them, thrashing beneath my hands. "You can't—you can't break it! He's sealed! He's—"

But he didn't know me.

He didn't remember what I was.

What I *am*.

I bared my teeth, dragging breath deep into my lungs until the words rose.

"Feyr'hal draem, naxèn korrahl. Ou ven'dral, sael morvak. Harrekh suul veyrahn!"
(*By dream and blood, I sever the false bindings. Come forth, shadowed truth. Show yourself to me!*)

The air convulsed. The runes split, sizzling like oil in flame. I pressed harder, my fingers burning against his temples as black light veined across his skin.

Deveraux shrieked, his head snapping back, but the wards cracked under me, peeling away like old bark.

I pushed again, voice louder, thrumming with the High Matron's power.

"Exal draem hall! Korr voskar, suul makor'neth!"
(*Break the dream's veil! Tear the stone, unbind the silence!*)

The wards shattered—exploding outward in a storm of sparks and ash. For a heartbeat, the corridor itself flickered like it couldn't hold what I'd just unleashed.

And through the breach, I saw him.

Cloaked in shadow, standing at the heart of a circle carved with blood, witches kneeling around him. His eyes were black pits, his smile thin, sharp as the knives at his belt. He looked straight at me—as if he'd been waiting.

The floor under my knees lurched. Deveraux screamed louder, smoke pouring from his mouth.

And I whispered, voice cutting straight through the distance, through the wards I'd just broken:

"Found you."

The circle of witches faltered; shadows snapping, wards quaking as the echo of my voice bled through their spell work. His smile twitched, just once. The smallest fracture.

The circle trembled, witches chanting, their shadows weaving tighter around him. They thought they could shield him, thought they could wall me out.

I bared my teeth, ancient syllables clawing their way out of my chest, my tongue burning with power older than their covens.

"Sael'nax draem! Korr ven'thall voskar! Stand down. If you protect him, you stand against the High Matron—and you will suffer fates worse than death."

The words didn't just echo—they *burrowed*. My voice threaded through the wards, through their skulls, bleeding into the marrow of every witch in that circle. I felt them seize under me, heard their gasps fracture into screams.

I pressed harder, my will flaring through the tether like fire through dry grass.

And they broke. One by one, their knees hit the ground. Their hands clutched at their heads, blood dripping from their noses, their mouths, as the weight of me crushed them down. My voice was in their minds, in their bones, filling them with the certainty of their own ruin.

Allard's shadow cloak writhed as the circle wavered.

I stood taller, my grip on Deveraux's temples tightening,

the surge of power vibrating through every thread of me.

"Suul makor'neth. Kneel... or burn."

The chamber on his end erupted in chaos—witches crying out, folding, some clawing at their own skin as if to tear me free. But there was no escape. I was already inside them.

And I smiled, because for the first time, they understood.

The High Matron was not their prey.

I was their collapse.

The chamber quaked under the weight of my words, the circle already broken, the witches writhing on their knees.

I leaned in, power threading out of me in jagged arcs, ancient enough to rattle the stones.

"Ou veyr'nath draem. Korr voskar sael. Harrekh suul ven'dral."

The command didn't travel as sound. It *rooted* itself in their bones, thrumming in their marrow like an oath they couldn't break.

The witches convulsed, their hands twitching, their eyes rolling back as if strings had been yanked from above. One by one, they turned to him; still cloaked, still sneering, as their broken voices overlapped.

"High... Matron... calls."

Their hands seized his cloak, clutching, dragging him forward against his will. His shadows recoiled, snapping at them like teeth, but they were bound to my words, my law. Even as they screamed, their knees split and bleeding against the circle, they *dragged him*.

Through the tether, the distance shrank. His presence lurched closer, closer—until I could taste his breath in the air of the manor corridor.

For a breath, it was as though two worlds collided. His outline bled into mine, shadows stretching, his form flickering at the edge of my vision as though he was *here.*

"Feyr'hal morvak voskar. Sael draem'neth, suul veyr'thall cen ash. Harrekh ven'dral makor'thas, (*Burn the monster to ash. Break the circle and scatter him. Send your most powerful to carry his remains to my home. Do this, and your defiance will be forgiven under the High Matron's law.*)

The words struck like a hammer through the tether. The fire leapt, wild and consuming, and William went up like dry kindling.

And so did Deveraux.

His scream ripped free in hundreds of voices at once, a chorus of agony spilling from his mouth as fire devoured him. I tore my hands from his temples, but the connection was already seared into me. The flames curled over his skin, peeling it away in sheets.

I flicked my wrist. His burning body shot back into the tomb, chains clanging, the stone groaning shut around him with a final, echoing crack.

And then I fell.

The corridor tilted sideways, the air a blur of smoke and dust. My knees hit stone, my hands shaking violently as my breath tore ragged from my chest.

Fangs snapped down, claws curling into the floor, my vampire surging forward to compensate for the cavern of power I'd just emptied.

I could feel myself unraveling, light and dark ripping at my insides until there was nothing left but depletion.

Marek was there in an instant, pulling me to him.

"Drink, baby," he murmured, voice gentle and calm even

as I shook against him. "Drink. Take what you need."

The thrum of his pulse beat against my lips, rich and maddening. The scent of him filled me, and the hunger roared.

"It's not safe." My voice cracked, torn between need and terror. "I'm too weak to fight it. I'll take too much. Get me a bag."

"I'll grab them," Simône said, already sprinting out of the corridor.

"Please." I scrambled back from him, shaking my head. "You need to leave. All of you."

Pain ripped through me, as I curled against it, claws raking stone, my body trembling as the hunger tore me apart from the inside out. Every breath was fire in my throat, every heartbeat a drum of blood I couldn't have.

"Baby—" Marek reached for me.

"No!" The word snapped out of me, half-scream, half-snarled command. My body recoiled, my back bowing as if invisible hands were trying to break me in half. "Don't touch me. I'll tear you open—I can't stop it."

They froze. All of them. The air was thick with their helplessness, their fear of me and Marek's fear *for* me.

I pressed my forehead to the stone, fangs cutting into my own lip, shaking so hard I thought my bones might splinter. I was starving, every instinct clawing toward Marek, toward Rafe, toward anyone close enough to sink into.

And then—Simône.

She skidded back into the corridor, a bag in her hands. Her face pale, her breath ragged, but she didn't hesitate. She dropped to her knees, ripped the seal, and shoved it toward me.

"Here. Take it."

My body moved before my mind could, claws puncturing the plastic, blood spilling hot across my tongue.

Relief. Agony. Both at once.

I sucked it down, every drop, until the bag was nothing but torn plastic in my hands.

And still—no. My stomach heaved. My body rebelled.

Please, no.

I lurched forward on shaking arms, crawling to the corner, and the blood came back up just as fast. It burned my throat as it hit the stone, leaving me retching, hollow, the hunger clawing worse than before.

Marek was there instantly, strong arms closing around me, holding me upright as I shook. His voice was pleading. "We don't have any choice here, baby. You *have* to. Please."

"No, Marek!" My snarl cracked into something closer to a sob as I thrashed weakly against him. My limbs had nothing left, but rage still lived in me. "I'll take too much!"

And then Simône's voice cut through the chaos. "Then take it from all of us."

The words froze me.

I turned, trembling, wide-eyed, but she didn't flinch. She stepped closer to us, her gaze flicking across the others, daring them to contradict her. Markus gave a single nod. Elodie's chin dipped in quiet agreement.

"No," I whispered, shaking my head violently. "Fuck, no. *Never.* I can't do that. I'll drain you all—I can't—"

My back buckled, the world tilting sideways as the hunger tore through me, ripping past my last thread of control. I hit the stone hard, clutching my stomach, my chest, anywhere I could hold myself together. "Please," I sobbed, half growl, half plea. "Please just leave me. Lock the door. Don't let me near you."

But they didn't move. Marek sat and pulled me so my back rested against his chest and his against the wall.

Simône crouched in front of me, unafraid. "You don't get to decide this, Zaria. Not when you've bled yourself dry for all of us. Not when you've carried this pack on your back since the second you walked into our lives." Her voice trembled, but her eyes didn't. "This is your family. This is your pack."

My tears burned down my cheeks. My pack.

And then Simône's arms slid around me. She tilted her head without hesitation, baring her throat.

I didn't have the strength to fight anymore.

The hunger roared, and I sank.

My fangs pierced her skin, and the taste of her—salt and heat and life—hit me like fire, flooding every broken vein inside me.

THIRTY SEVEN

Marek

As soon as Zaria's fangs slid in, Simône's fists twisted in my shirt, clutching like she was hanging on for her life. Her whole body bowed, strung tight, her back arching until every line of her was pulled taut with need. She tried to bite it back, tried to keep it quiet, but there's no hiding what it feels like. The rush hit her hard, shuddering through her in waves, and the whisper still slipped free.

"Oh god."

Zaria dragged her closer, pulled her down until they were flush, straddling Simône's over her hips and pinning her there. Her moan vibrated against Simône's throat, guttural, ravaged—like the taste itself was salvation. Watching them wasn't spectacle. It wasn't cheap. It was terrifying. It was beautiful.

Rafe, Elodie, Markus… none of them moved. None of them even breathed. The awe in the air was heavy, thick enough to choke on.

Simône broke first. The little sounds she'd been holding back unraveled into helpless whimpers, her body quaking under Zaria's hold. Her hips rolled instinctively, searching for friction that wasn't there, her chest rising fast, trembling with surrender. Her nails dug into me, biting through fabric, like I could ground her when Zaria was already pulling her under.

And gods, I almost let myself believe it. That they'd go all the way. That Zaria would take her over the edge right there in front of us, strip her bare and leave her ruined on the stone.

But before the edge could snap, Zaria tore her mouth free. The sound of it was wet, brutal. She shoved Simône back with sudden strength, fangs bared, lips slick, chest heaving like she'd ripped herself out of the spiral by sheer force of will.

Simône gasped, head tipping back, the loss written all over her body. Her hips trembled with the ache of something unfinished, her breath hitching high in her throat. The sound that escaped her wasn't relief—it was anguish. Half cry, half frustrated sob. She braced on her hands, shaking, denied.

Zaria's voice came torn, as she forced the words out.

"Fuck, Simône. I'm sorry."

The sight of her—feral and merciful all at once—made the room tilt around me. Sloane climbed from Zaria's lap and sat across the room, breath breaking, her face hidden in her hands. But her body still shook, still hummed with what Zaria had left burning in her veins.

Zaria lifted her head, eyes wild and unfocused, hazel but rimmed with a hunger that hollowed her out. She scanned the room, fangs glinting, chest rising and falling in frantic rhythm.

And then Markus moved.

Zaria's head snapped toward him, her eyes hazel but ringed with feral hunger, her fangs gleaming in the firelight. He didn't flinch. Didn't hesitate. He stepped closer, unbuttoning the collar of his shirt with calm, deliberate hands, baring his throat.

"Take from me next," he said, voice quiet, but carrying enough weight to cut through the charged silence. "I can handle it."

She rose in a fluid motion, one moment trembling on the floor, the next seizing his shirtfront in her fists. She yanked him down to his knees before her, her claws curling into his shoulders, holding him in place. The sound she made—half moan, half growl—vibrated through the room.

And then she sank her fangs into his neck.

Markus's head snapped back, a primal sound tearing out of him. His hands grabbed at her waist, gripping hard as if to anchor himself while his whole body shuddered. He tried to swallow it down, tried to keep it quiet, but the arousal coursing through him just the same. His chest rose in sharp, staccato breaths, his lips parting on words he couldn't form.

Zaria moaned into the bite, drinking deep, her body pressed flush against his, claws dragging at his shirt until it tore beneath her hands. She wasn't careful. She wasn't gentle. Every pull of her mouth was desperate, hungry, taking what she needed without apology.

Markus trembled, jaw clenched tight, but he didn't fight her. He tilted his head back farther, throat bared like a man begging to be undone. Sweat broke across his temple, his chest rising fast, but still he held on. Still he gave himself to her.

The sight burned through me. Through all of us. Rafe's jaw locked so hard it looked painful. Elodie's lips parted, pale and transfixed, her eyes wide and unblinking. Even Simône, still sprawled and trembling from before, stared like she couldn't decide whether to sob or beg to take his place.

Zaria drank him down until his whole body shook beneath her, his hands clutching her hips like he'd die if he let go. His throat worked around broken sounds until finally —finally—he couldn't hold it.

"Fuck—no, I can't… I can't hold it. I'm gonna—"

Zaria tore her mouth free. The sound was wet, brutal, fangs ripping away from his throat.

Markus doubled over with a guttural cry, one long "fuuuuuckkk" spilling out of him as his body bowed, trembling, ruined by the denial.

Zaria staggered back, lips wet, chest heaving, claws still flexed like she was fighting herself every second not to lunge for him again.

Elodie was on him in an instant. She dropped to her knees at his side, hands skimming his shoulders, his face, searching for wounds that would already be healing. "Markus—are you—"

He waved her off, breathless, laughing under it all. "Fine. Gods, I'm fine." His voice was shaky, but his grin flickered sharp. "Fuck, I've never felt anything like that."

Elodie glared at him, lips tight, but the flush across her cheeks gave her away.

And still Zaria's hunger wasn't gone.

Her gaze locked on Elodie where she knelt—close and vulnerable.

And Elodie… gods help her… she didn't hesitate. Didn't waver. She shifted from Markus' side, her hand lingering just long enough to be sure he was grounded, then rose gracefully to her knees in front of Zaria.

Her face was pale, but her eyes were clear. She brushed her hair back from her neck, baring the delicate line of her throat, and tilted her chin without a trace of fear.

"Me next," she said softly. Almost tender.

Zaria's whole body shuddered, her breath catching ragged in her chest, but the feral edge dulled. She reached for Elodie with trembling hands, cupping her jaw like she was afraid to break her. For the first time tonight, she wasn't savage. She was reverent.

She cupped Elodie's jaw with a tenderness I hadn't expected, kissed it soft, brushed a strand of hair back from her face. Her voice was low, coaxing. "So beautiful. Such a good girl."

And look—*fuck*. I *know* that wasn't what this was about. I know. But goddamn. I am not only a man, but an Alpha wolf, and that… *that* was pure sex.

Zaria's fangs slid in then with deliberate care.

Elodie gasped, sharp and sudden, but not from pain. Her lips parted, her spine arched, and instead of pulling back, she pressed closer, offering more.

And then the sound started. Moans, soft and unguarded, spilling from her before she could stop them. They rolled out of her like truth, each one sharper, needier, until she wasn't even trying to hold them in anymore.

Each one cut through the hollow stillness. Not frantic like Simône's. Not ragged like Markus'. Just pure, unrestrained surrender.

Zaria drank slower this time, savoring, each pull measured but deep, her hands holding Elodie gently, anchoring her without restraint. She pressed her forehead against Elodie's temple, her moans muffled against her skin, until their sounds tangled together—two women caught in something neither could disguise.

Elodie's hands lifted. Her fingers trembled against Zaria's skin, her nails grazing up the fabric of her shirt as though even in this moment of surrender she wanted to give back.

My throat went dry watching it. The whole room felt it—the intimacy, the difference between how she fed from each of us. Markus was still on the floor catching his breath, but even he stared, wide-eyed. Rafe's jaw tightened, but the rage had drained from his face, replaced with something far more dangerous. Ache.

And then Zaria pulled back, slowly this time, her fangs slipping free with a soft sound. She cradled Elodie's face in both hands as though she couldn't bear to let go just yet.

Elodie's lips parted on a shuddering breath, her moans quieting into silence. Her cheeks were flushed, her eyes glassy, but there was no shame there. Only awe.

"Thank you," Zaria whispered against her skin. "You did so good."

And Elodie smiled. Small and dazed.

Before the air even settled, Rafe stepped forward. Alpha Rafe. Kneeling in front of her.

And gods, what a fucking sight. Our Alpha, the wolf we'd all followed without question, dropping to his knees before her. Submitting. To *our queen*.

Zaria's eyes went wide, horror and hunger colliding across her face. She shook her head so hard curls spilled around her shoulders. "No."

But he didn't flinch. Didn't waver. His voice was measured, soft in a way I hadn't heard from him in years. "I trust you, Zaria. Let me prove that to you. I'm not afraid."

He moved closer, a hand sliding to her waist.

She backed away, eyes flashing.

"No. You don't. I can smell it on you; the fear, the doubt, the hatred. Even now. This isn't trust. It's appearance. You're trying to play Alpha in the room, and I don't want your performance."

"Zaria. I...," he whispered, but he just shook his head. "I'm trying to prove it to you, not them."

She sighs and closes the distance. She takes his face in her hands and softly kisses his lips. It's not romantic, it's like she's closing a chapter. He wraps his arms around her waist and lays his head on her stomach.

"I forgive everything we done to each other, Rafe. I've made some mistakes here too, pretty fucking big ones."

She tilts his face up to meet hers as she looks down at him. "But you don't need to prove anything to me. I'm not yours anymore."

Wait.

Does that mean—?

Yeah. It means something.

Don't panic.

Don't fucking panic.

"I know you aren't," Rafe said, voice strong but stretched thin, like every word scraped its way out. "I've accepted that. But I'll still do the work to earn your trust and your friendship again, Zaria. I promise you. Not just for us but for our children. They deserve the best of us."

He rose to his feet, slow, deliberate, and folded her into his arms. His cheek rested against the crown of her head, his body closing around her like this was still his to protect.

My chest tightened. Instinct moved before thought—I reached for the tether to him. But there was nothing. It's empty. Severed.

I'm not his beta anymore. I'm Alpha to my own pack.

The truth of it furrowed my brow, sat heavy in my chest,

like a door that had been shut without warning. And then Elodie, damn empath that she is, drifted over and wrapped her arms around me. Tight. Close. Her lips brushed my ear, her whisper softer than breath.

"He said to tell you he forgives you. That he loves you. That he knows she'll be safe with you and that he's never seen you so happy as you are when she's in your arms. He says he's proud of you, Alpha. Well done."

Her words cracked something I didn't want broken. And for the first time in years, I didn't know whether to stand taller under the weight of it—or fall to my knees.

And then his eyes found mine.

A nod. Small. Measured. But I caught it for what it was.

Approval.

Permission.

Brotherhood.

EPILOGUE

Marek – 6 Months Later

"Oh, god, Marek..." Her moan broke into a gasp as I slid deeper, pushing slow at first, then snapping my hips harder just to feel her clamp around me.

Her body was so tight, so goddamn perfect, even with her belly full and round beneath my palm. Especially with it. My hand stayed splayed there, possessive, feeling the faint ripple of life inside her even as I slid inside of her from behind.

"You're so fucking wet for me, baby," I groaned into her neck, biting down just hard enough to make her gasp. "Gods, I love how you take me; every inch. Fuck, you're made for me."

Her hand scrambled back, clawing at my hip, urging me deeper, harder. And I gave it to her—thrust after thrust, slow enough to make her beg, hard enough to remind her who was inside her.

"I love waking up to this pussy," I growled, grinding in to the hilt, rolling my hips until her moan turned into a desperate cry. "I could spend every morning like this, you stretched tight around my cock, swollen with my children. My perfect fucking queen."

Her nails dug into me, her head falling back onto my shoulder, and the sound she made when I shifted my hand lower—cupping her belly with one palm, circling her clit with the other—was pure euphoria.

Her body quaked against me, every breath coming out ragged, every moan higher, sharper, like she couldn't hold the sound in anymore. I kept the rhythm, dragging myself out of her slick heat and pushing back in until I was flush, grinding deep until she trembled.

"Gods, listen to you," I rasped against her ear, my lips brushing her skin. "Fucking shaking for me. You love it, don't you, baby? Being full of me. Full of us."

Her nails clawed at my thigh, desperate, frantic. "Marek—"

Her thighs clenched, her whole body trembling now, her hips trying to buck back harder against me, trying to chase it. "Please—please, I can't—"

"You can," I growled, thrusting harder, until the sound of my cock driving into her was slick and obscene in the quiet. "You'll take it, baby. You'll come for me when I tell you."

She sobbed my name, voice breaking, my hand pressed harder against her clit, my hips pistoning deep, until the dam broke.

She shattered with a scream, her body clamping down around me in violent, convulsing waves. Every muscle locked, her thighs shaking uncontrollably, her whole frame trembling in my arms as her climax tore through her.

I held her there, grinding her through it, whispering ragged against her skin. "That's it. Fuck, that's it, baby. My perfect queen. Good girl."

She came undone, writhing, sobbing, trembling so hard it shook me with her.

And gods, I couldn't hold back anymore.

"Fuck, baby—" I drove into her harder, faster, chasing the edge that had been burning me alive since the moment I slid inside her. Her body squeezed me so tight, every thrust like fire up my spine, every whimper she made pushing me closer to ruin.

Her climax hadn't even finished when mine hit. My hips jerked, my whole body locking as I spilled into her, pulse after pulse until I was growling against her skin, teeth scraping her neck like I couldn't decide if I wanted to bite or just hold on.

"Gods, Zaria," I gasped, my chest heaving. "You're mine. Always mine."

She moaned weakly, still shaking, and I held her through

it—both of us trembling, both of us undone, wrapped so tight it felt like the world had narrowed to just this bed, this body, this bond.

The pause after was heavy, broken only by the ragged sound of our breathing. My chest was pressed to her back, sweat cooling between us, her body still fluttering around me in the faint aftershocks of release.

I kissed her shoulder, soft, lingering, tasting the salt of her skin. My hand, still splayed over the swell of her belly, rubbed gentle circles there, grounding both of us.

"You alright, baby?"

She hummed, tired but content, her head lolling back against my chest. "Mmm. More than alright. I feel... calm."

After everything we'd done, everything we'd taken from her, she could still say that. Still give me that piece of herself.

I tightened my arm around her, kissing along her neck, softer this time, reverent. "Good. That's all I want for you. Calm, safe. Taken care of."

Her fingers drifted down to rest over mine where it curved protectively over her belly. "They kicked when you said that," she whispered, and I swear my fucking heart stopped.

I chuckled, quiet, kissing her hair. "Smart kids. Already know their old man means business."

She laughed too, soft and breathless, and I held onto that sound like it was the only thing keeping me alive.

"You ready to get downstairs?" I murmured against her shoulder.

"Do we have to?"

"We can wait here. No rush. They'll wait for their queen."

Her head tipped against mine, her voice a hush. "I love you, Marek."

"I love you too, baby. You still worried?"

Her hand smoothed over the curve of her stomach. "No... with the covens and everyone here, I know we're protected, but nothing is foolproof. I don't like not being in control of it. But I'm sure everything will be okay."

"It will be." My voice came out steadier than I felt. "After what you did to Allard, we haven't heard a peep. Things are quiet. You're safe. They're safe. And we've got his ashes here to prove it."

It's been four months since she burned him—since she used Deveraux's mind as a conduit and dragged Allard into the flames with nothing but her will. Power went out for miles. She drained herself so completely we had to hold her up, feed her from all of us just to bring her back from the brink. The night she claimed her as hers.

And even though Allard's gone, even though the earth itself felt it when he went up in smoke, we know better than to think the Council went with him. One monster doesn't topple an empire. With her pregnancy rounding six months this week, I can see the nerves in her even if she tries to hide them. She knows the birth won't just test her—it'll test all of us.

The covens started arriving weeks ago. The grounds look like a goddamn hippy convention—tents, fires, incense, people everywhere. The manor's overflowing with Blooded, witches, shifters—all ready to lay their lives down for their High Matron. For our children.

Elowen's even moved in, brought her son Kestrel, and Simône latched onto him like they've known each other their whole lives. Inseparable.

Elodie and Markus are expecting, too. Just a couple months along, but she's glowing already—like carrying life lit her up from the inside out.

And Rafe… Christ, Rafe. That first month was brutal. After Zaria saved us all—after she proved what she was, and he had to face how wrong he'd been, what he'd said, what he almost let happen—he couldn't look at us. Couldn't look at her. He disappeared for three weeks. We knew he was alive, but he didn't want to be found. He was drowning in guilt, punishing himself in ways none of us could reach.

He broke something in her that night, and the hardest part has been him realizing she can't just lay a hand on it and heal it away. Some wounds don't close like that.

When he came back, he was lighter. Humbled. He made his rounds apologizing, and he and Zaria found their way back to friendship. It's still tender in places, but it holds.

My relationship with him took longer, but we've managed to meet eye to eye. Strange thing, being an Alpha now. My pack has tripled. I've got two teen pups who joined us—lost, no family—and they've been training on the grounds, finally learning what it feels like to belong. So I've gone from just Simône to three, and it's been one of the greatest fucking feelings I've ever had.

Last month, I took Zaria to visit her parents, to try and bridge that gap again. I fought her on it at first, didn't want to see her gutted if they turned her away. But she pushed, and thank gods she did.

Claudine opened the door, saw Zaria's stomach, and burst into tears. Bernard tried to keep his face straight, but it didn't last.

What Zaria doesn't know is that I went to them a week before. They didn't invite me in, but they listened. I told them I was the one who broke their oak tree. I told them Zaria needed them now more than ever. I told them about her vision.

She doesn't need to know that part. All she needs is what

came after—the warmth of their embrace, the way they invited her over the threshold, the glow in their eyes when they felt the babies kick.

They've been here the past three weeks, calling her baby, cupping her face, hovering like only parents can. Fierce protectors, filling the cracks with love she didn't even realize she was starving for.

She finally told her friend Sophie the truth, though Joey had already convinced her before Zaria ever found the courage to say it. They were just waiting on her to feel strong enough to step out into the open.

It feels like we've spent these last months laying the foundation, smoothing every fracture so these little ones come into a life without fault lines. No breaks. No questions about where they belong.

I thought I'd be terrified. Having a child had never even touched my radar. But here it is anyway, staring me in the face. And instead of fear, I feel ready. I get to do it with her—with the woman I love. And gods, that makes all the difference.

"Where are you? Your head's all foggy."

Zaria's hand smoothed through my hair, her touch dragging me back to her.

"Just thinking." I leaned in, kissed her lips, anchored myself in her warmth.

"And what is it that you're thi—" Her words cut off quick. Her hand shot to her stomach, her body bowing into me.

"Oh God."

I shot upright, heart slamming into my throat. "Zaria?"

Her eyes locked on mine; wide and brimming, already glassed with tears. Her voice cracked when it came.

"My water just broke. It's time…"

What was bound, unraveled.
What was betrayed, will not be forgotten.
Now, what is begotten will rise.

The final chapter begins with *Blood of the Begotten*.

Anaiis D. Roet

www.ingramcontent.com/pod-product-compliance
Lightning Source LLC
Chambersburg PA
CBHW071754310726
48976CB00001BA/205